A CROWN BROKEN

FAE OF TÍRIA, BOOK TWO

K. A. RILEY

SUMMARY

Taken captive by a Fae whose cruelty is legendary throughout the realms of Kalemnar, Lyrinn must find a way to escape and get back to the High Lord she loves.

But when she finds herself a prisoner in a distant realm, she quickly discovers that not all is as it seems. Torn between two lands and two lives, she learns of the Elar—an Immortal imbued with lethal powers whose shadow casts an ominous threat on all the realms of the world.

For Lyrinn, the only Immortal of any importance is the one she left behind.

She must find her way back to him—but she knows the cost should she escape. And ultimately, she is faced with a choice that may break her.

PREFACE

A brief caution for my readers—more particularly, my readers' *parents:*

I have written quite a few books by now, most of which are suitable for younger readers. I try to keep my language light, though there are occasional acts of violence on the pages—and occasionally, a beloved character meets their untimely end.

I've had messages asking if certain books are "spicy," and in this case, the answer is yes. *A Crown Broken* is a novel that is not suitable for younger readers.

So I leave it to you, the parents, to determine what level of "reader discretion" you wish to exercise when it comes to this book and series.

The next book in the series is:

Of Flame and Fury (available for pre-order until release day)

For those of you delving into this world, thank you for coming on this journey, and I hope you enjoy!

KARiley

To J.K.
(no, not THAT J.K.)—
thanks for your eagle eyes.

PROLOGUE AND MAP

"*WELL? WHAT IS IT?*" *Kazimir asked.*

"*Your Grace...*"

"*Spit it out, you jackass! What did you see?*"

My heart threatened to leap from my chest as I awaited the reply. And when at last it came, I fell to my knees, a torrent of tears blurring my vision.

"*It's a silver eagle, your Grace,*" *the lookout said, his voice trembling.* "*The sigil of Fairholme.*"

Map of Aetherion

CHAPTER ONE

A POWERFUL, unseen force propelled the Tírian ship over the cresting waves. The vessel moved with unnatural speed, quickly gaining on the Lightblood galleon where I was being held captive.

I stared out at the sea, my breath trapped somewhere deep inside my chest. Even from this distance, I could now see the silver eagle emblazoned on its sails. The sigil of Fairholme.

Mithraan's sigil.

My heart pounded so violently that I was certain it could be heard from clear across the expanse that lay between us. A signaling drumbeat to my allies to hurry to my side—and to bring me what I desired most in the world.

Faster, I pleaded silently. *Faster.*

Triumphant to witness their failure, I turned to watch the Lightblood crew scramble in vain, attempting every conceivable maneuver in hopes of evading our determined pursuers. I pulled my eyes up to see the sails above me slackening, unable to catch the wind. The High King's ship languished inexplicably even as the Tírians gained on us.

Nature itself, it seemed, was laughing at my captors.

High King Kazimir—my father by blood—shouted a string of angry commands at his underlings, but to no avail. Nothing they did increased our chances of evasion.

If anything, we seemed to be slowing to a crawl.

I was beginning to wonder why Kazimir didn't simply cast one of his arsenal of powerful spells and blow the Tírian ship out of the water—or whatever it was that High Kings did in situations like this. He was supposed to be one of the most powerful Fae in existence, after all.

Intimidating and cold as ice, he had a reputation that made others cower at the mere mention of his name. Yet for some reason, he now looked as bewildered and helpless as a lost child seeking its mother. Something was holding him back and confounding him all at once...

And I reveled to watch him squirm.

"You should have known that Mithraan would come for me," I shouted over the sound of desperate Lightblood voices as Kazimir wilted before my eyes.

"I wouldn't get too excited, Daughter," he growled back, his expression quickly shifting to rage as he twisted around to take a long stride toward me. "Your precious lover is..." But there was little conviction in his voice as he tried to bring himself to utter the final word.

Still, his effort was enough. The word worked its way into my mind like a cruel, creeping virus.

Dead.

For all I knew, it was the truth. The last time I laid my eyes on Mithraan, he was gravely wounded...and Prince Corym, the mortal heir of Kalemnar's throne, had a blade pressed to his throat. The Fae lord I had grown to love more than I'd ever loved anyone in this world had been mere seconds from his end.

Yet I never saw Corym draw his weapon across that beautiful neck.

I never saw Mithraan die.

The simple truth is, I couldn't fathom it. I *needed* him to be alive. I couldn't imagine a world devoid of his presence, his strength—not after everything we had both endured since the fateful night when we first met.

With sudden fear driving the blood through my veins, my fingers were so tightly wrapped around the ship's railing that my knuckles had gone bone-white. The distant ship was growing ever closer, but now it was moving all too slowly for my taste. I gasped for breath, asking myself the intolerable question...and unable to answer it.

At long last, I forced the words to my mind.

Is.

He.

Dead.

A breath.

No.

He is on that ship. Otherwise, why would it pursue us so relentlessly? Why...

*He **has** to be alive.*

I had only recently come to accept how much I cared for Mithraan. How much I craved him, how desperately I wanted—and yes, *needed*—him by my side. I wished more than anything in the world to rebuild Tíria alongside him, to renew the beauty that had once existed in the Fae's lands high atop the Onyx Rise. I wanted us both to witness the birth of a new world, a new realm. To put an end to the rise of King Caedmon and Prince Corym, and their rule of deceit and corruption.

Tíria was my mother's birthplace, after all. I had discovered during the Blood Trials that she was the daughter of High King Rynfael, the Fae seated on the Tírian throne.

Which meant I was a rare hybrid of Lightblood and Tírian. The forbidden result of a forbidden bond—a tale that might have had a romantic conclusion, were it not for Kazimir's abject cruelty.

My tale, on the other hand...had still not come to its end.

All I want is to see Mithraan again. To feel his touch, his lips, his body against mine. I would give a thousand years of my Immortal lifetime for five more minutes with him, if that's all I'm to have.

As the tenuous fantasy began to weave its way through my mind, a rough hand grabbed my wrist and twisted me around to face away from the sea. I looked up to see Kazimir's piercing hazel eyes glinting with amusement and anger combined. As always, he looked simultaneously beautiful and terrifying, his skin like burnished bronze in the sunlight.

Exquisite on the outside, I thought, *but festering with internal ugliness.*

He may have been my father by blood, but I despised him with every particle in my body and mind.

"Do you understand what is happening, girl?" he spat, then added hoarsely, "You left your lover with a blade at his throat. His end most likely came seconds later. And had I not extracted you from the Trials, you would have been next. It was not a Tírian who saved your life. It was *me.*"

"You said most likely," I half-muttered, my mind toying with the words. "So, you admit you don't *know* if he's dead." I felt myself fill with a renewed conviction. "You assumed Corym killed him—but you forget Mithraan is a High Lord. He's strong —powerful. He *is* alive, and he will never stop hunting me so long as he can draw breath." I spoke through gritted teeth, convincing myself with each syllable that my words were the absolute, irrevocable truth.

Kazimir laughed, and I was certain I detected nervousness in the sound. "If he is alive—and if his Fae weaklings want to follow us to the ends of the seas—I welcome the pursuit."

I smiled when I asked, "Then why do you look so terrified, *High King*?"

"Terrified?" To my surprise and irritation, Kazimir's smile only spread wider. "Terror is an emotion I am incapable of feeling, and the farthest thing from my heart at this moment. But I will admit that I do feel for you, Daughter. It will hurt when you realize the truth about your High Fae."

Silently, I cursed the cruel glint in his eye. "Oh? What truth is that?"

"That if indeed your Tírian High Lord is alive and hunting you, it is only for sport, and not for love. You are a trinket to his mind, a mere plaything. An amusement, nothing more. He does not love you. The emotion is alien to him—impossible, even. Trust me when I tell you Tírians are not creatures capable of true affection. I had the privilege of centuries spent with your dear mother, remember, and a more cold-hearted bitch there never was."

The words hit me like a mallet to the chest.

I'd seen my mother's memories—I was certain I had *felt* the brutality of her life under Kazimir's oppressive thumb.

But I forced myself to meet Kazimir's derision with a laugh and a shake of my head.

"You're wrong," I said, my chest filling with a consuming rage. "Mithraan loves me. And even now, I can feel his presence...just as he feels mine. He will follow me to the farthest reaches of this world, if that's what it takes to find me—not because I'm anyone's plaything, but because he and I are meant to be together. And you are powerless to stop him."

I could feel my words tearing into Kazimir's mind like daggers. I could feel his growing rage mirroring my own like wildfire on the air, his eyes searing with flame.

"Lies," he spat. "Even if your Tírian lives, you have not the power to feel his presence from this distance."

"You have no idea what I can and cannot feel," I replied, a smug grin stretching my lips.

And with each word that escaped my mouth, the truth grew clearer in my mind. Mithraan *was* out there. His eyes were locked on this ship even as I spoke. I could feel them searching the deck for me. I could feel the ache in his heart, the rage at Kazimir for what he had done to us both.

"Perhaps," I added, "I am simply more Gifted than you think, your *Grace*."

A look of pure, volatile ire overtook Kazimir's features. But after a moment, his face softened again, and he let out a quiet chuckle that almost sounded like a surrender. "You're trying to toy with my mind," he scoffed. "To prey on my weaknesses. But I am far from weak—and you are no powerful High Fae, Daughter. Not yet—and not without my guidance. Right now, you're little more than one of those foolish, bright-eyed mortals who flit about Kalemnar with too much arrogance for their own good. Do not delude yourself into thinking otherwise. You are *nothing*."

I leveled him with a hate-filled glare. "My mother was the daughter of a Tírian High King. Her blood was powerful, as is yours. I am no mere mortal, and you know it."

Impulsively, I raised my hands to him to cast a spell— something punishing and painful—to prove to him that I wasn't so weak as he thought.

But no magical explosion erupted from my fingertips. No blast of light came; no conjured weapons of war.

Whether it was Kazimir who had hobbled me or my own mind filling with doubt in the moment, I couldn't say. All I knew was that I had failed.

I lowered my hands, my cheeks scorching with shame at my weakness.

Kazimir let out a vicious snicker. "Your powers are pathetic, because your mind is consumed by your obsession with your Tírian. But don't worry, Daughter. When we get to Aetherion, you will learn to see your true potential."

"I will *never* set foot in Aetherion," I growled, stomping my foot like a petulant child.

"Your Grace!" a sudden voice cried from the crow's nest.

"What?" Kazimir snapped, his hand taking renewed hold of my arm, tightly enough that I could perfectly imagine the bruises that would soon form on my flesh.

"The Tírian vessel is moving impossibly fast—it will catch up to us within the hour. We need something more powerful than wind if we're to evade them."

Kazimir shot me a look—one full of a strange, distant understanding, then let me go.

"Let them come!" the High King shouted. "Let them do their worst."

"But, your Grace..."

I could hear a quaking fear in the lookout's voice.

Lightbloods were known to be powerful warriors—and I found myself shocked at how fearful they seemed of the Tírians' arrival.

Perhaps I'd overestimated the Fae from Aetherion, after all.

"You heard me," Kazimir snarled. "Let them come. Let them have their fun. This farce will end soon enough."

"Yes, your Grace!"

You're giving up, I thought, hardly daring to allow myself a faint sense of victory.

"You will have children one day, Lyrinn," Kazimir said, turning back to me. His voice was little more than a low rasp now. "And when you do, you will summon every bit of your strength and power to protect them and to help them fulfill their destiny. Even if it means stealing them away from a land they have grown to love. If you want to call it cruelty or selfishness, so be it. I don't care. I will do what I can to see that you live up to your full potential—and even to keep you *happy*. You may not believe it, but it is the truth."

The words were a shock, coming from a Fae who seemed to have no concept of happiness. I stared at him numbly for a moment before anger began to boil inside me once again.

"Shall I give you a medal for that speech?" I snapped. "Father of the century, perhaps?"

When he replied with a sneer, I spun away and strode to the stern, fingers gripping the railing once again. I breathed in the sea air, my eyes locked on Mithraan's ship.

"Faster," I said. Out loud, this time. "I need you to take me away from this monster."

CHAPTER TWO

I COULDN'T SAY how long I watched the pursuing ship advance on us, how long my eyes remained fixed on the eagle sigil emblazoned on its sail.

All I knew was that at some point, most of the Lightblood crew moved into combat formation to await the enemy's arrival. Some had longbows at the ready; others held gleaming swords in hand.

Nausea assaulted me as I witnessed the scene from a distance, reality sinking in like a lead weight on my soul. A bloody battle was coming, and I had no way of knowing which side would win. I could only hope there wouldn't be too many casualties.

"You know what you need to do, Lightbloods!" Kazimir cried out, and when I turned to look at him, I was certain I saw sadness—*sadness,* of all emotions—in his eyes. He was the most gifted Fae I had encountered, not to mention a being of utter cruelty, of malice and greed. He had stolen me from Kalemnar, from Mithraan, from my sister Leta. He had proven himself heartless.

What could possibly stir up sorrow in his frozen heart?

I could feel the nearby Lightblood guards tensing as Kazimir grabbed me by the shoulder and yanked me backwards, dragging me across the deck and pressing me up against a wall of thick wood far from his fighters.

"Stay out of the fray," he growled. "Keep well back, or—"

His light eyes stared into mine, yet he seemed suddenly a thousand miles away, as though his mind were occupied with visions of something happening in another world.

"Or what?" I sneered. "You'll *kill* me?"

He grabbed the front of my tunic and pulled me close. "Do not start with me, Daughter," he said with a feral grimace, his white teeth bared and glinting in the sunlight. "By the Elar's wings! You're as stubborn as that damned..."

That damned mother of yours.

I could feel the unspoken words hanging in the air between us. The mother I should have known. The mother I never bonded with—because of you. The mother who is long gone...*because of you.*

Without thinking, I slapped him hard across the face so sharply that my palm stung with the fierce bite of it. He yanked a hand back, eager to return the favor.

But he stopped himself, the veins in his neck pulsing with quiet rage.

"You do not yet understand," he breathed, his chest heaving. "But you will learn soon enough that my interests and yours are in alignment. Now, stop being such a stubborn creature and make yourself scarce, or you'll die before you so much as lay eyes on a single Tírian."

With that, he turned away and darted over to shout more commands at his small army.

Most of them were dressed in some form of armor—silver mail or thick, embossed leather—and though each seemed well enough trained, they looked surprisingly afraid, just as their

leader did. It was almost like they had seen their fates coming...
and they knew the future did not bode well for them.

When the Tírian ship had drawn close enough, Kazimir
called out for the archers to ready themselves. They prepared
their arrows, aiming high, their bowstrings tight with deadly
potential.

"Nock!" Kazimir called out.

I pulled my eyes to the other ship, searching its deck for
Mithraan. But all I could see was a line of Tírian Fae eager to
begin a deadly assault. Unlike the Lightbloods, they didn't have
arrows ready. Instead, some of them held daggers or short
swords of gleaming Fae silver.

Don't be fools, I thought. *Unless your blades can stop razor-
sharp arrows, you will die.*

Helpless, I watched in horror as the High King opened his
mouth and called out to his archers. "Draw!"

I tried to shout to him—to stop him.

"Please..."

But the word came out in a whisper, useless and weak. A
mere shadow of a sound disappearing on the wind.

Please...

The archers tightened their grips, their bodies as taut as
their bowstrings.

The killing was about to begin.

I slammed my eyes shut, trying in vain to force away
thoughts of what was about to happen. Too many arrows
would loose. Too many Tírians would fall—and Mithraan
might well be among them.

Kazimir would win, and I would lose everything.

Again.

But my prediction was torn to pieces when a sharp, shrill
cry pierced the air, echoing among the clouds high above
Kazimir's ship.

I opened my eyes to see that several of the Lightbloods, startled out of their focus, pulled their chins up to look toward the sky.

With a loud curse, Kazimir did the same.

As I followed their eyes, I understood what had set them into a panic.

I knew what it was that had inspired the deep fear in their hearts—and yet it filled my heart with pure joy.

An enormous silver eagle soared and banked above us, moving faster than any gust of wind. Its feathers, delicate and exquisite, looked as though they were crafted of the finest metal woven with silk.

I was right...

Mithraan is very much alive.

Before another command had made it across Kazimir's lips, the silver eagle swooped down, his wings spread wide. One or two archers got startled shots off, but they were uncontrolled and reactionary, and no serious threat to their attacker.

As the eagle collided with the line of Fae archers, a set of dagger-sharp talons raked chests, arms, faces. Lightbloods fell with cries of agony to the ground. A few were even tossed overboard, shouting for aid as they thrashed in the waters below.

As the eagle turned and came in for a second attack, Kazimir threw himself down, pressing his chest to the deck. I watched him, stunned that he hadn't shot a glowing hand out and sent a spell soaring through the air to collide with his assailant.

Why aren't you fighting back? What's stopping you?

Not that I'm disappointed.

I told myself to push the questions from my mind and revel in Kazimir's defeat, in his fear, his weakness. Whatever the reason for his cowardice, it meant Mithraan might survive to see another day—and so might I.

Nothing else mattered.

The eagle banked sharply and swept downward to land several feet away from the High King, shifting instantly into the Fae I knew—and loved—so well. My heart soared as Mithraan strode forward, slashing any threatening Lightbloods with fierce silver talons—the only weapons he needed.

Blood seeped from Lightblood chests, necks, and arms as the guards crashed to the ground, and once again, I wondered why they seemed so helpless, so weak. Why they didn't fight back with everything in their bodies and minds.

During the Blood Trials when I had seen them from afar, I had feared their kind with everything inside me...and now, they seemed like little more than children playing out a battle scenario in their garden—and failing miserably.

There's something more at work here, I thought. *Something that has instilled a grim terror in the Lightbloods. Some deep magic has broken them—it's the only possible explanation.*

Even as Mithraan advanced toward Kazimir, a group of Tírian Fae leapt with wild cries onto the Lightblood ship and attacked, their cries fierce and determined.

I froze, watching the one-on-one battle erupt, struck by a sudden, awful realization that every drop of blood being shed was my fault. The Lightbloods lying lifeless on the deck had fallen because of me. Any injured Tírian would suffer...*because of me.*

I had never asked for this.

I'd never wanted it.

Or had I?

I had willed them to me. I had begged them in my mind to come. And now, my selfishness was resulting in dying Fae.

I cursed Kazimir for putting his people in this position. For risking their lives just so he could steal me and hold me captive.

It's your fault, your Grace, I muttered. *Not mine. You caused this.*

Weapons glinted in the sunlight as blinding bursts flashed bright and violently around me. The Fae had begun resorting to spell-casting. The opposing factions began to take one another down with fire, ice, explosions of pure light.

Part of me hoped it would mean a less bloody battle...but instead as I watched, it became more brutal still. More ferocious.

As a series of agonized screams cut through the air, it was all I could do not to slam my hands over my ears in terror. The stench of seared flesh met my nose, accompanied by the metallic smell of copper, of acrid blood shed by far too many who did not deserve to suffer.

Desperate to put an end to the conflict before more lives were lost, I looked around for Mithraan. But it seemed he had disappeared into the fray—there was no sign of him anywhere.

As I searched the jostling bodies on the deck, I spotted Kazimir, who was now on his feet, narrowing his eyes into the colliding crowd slowly turning crimson with blood.

He, too, appeared to be hunting for his nemesis. But as he twisted around in his quest to uncover Mithraan's where-abouts, Khiral—one of Mithraan's closest friends—leapt toward the High King and thrust a hand out, casting a spell that prompted a series of green, twisting vines to spring up from the deck and wrap around the High King's legs and waist, holding him in place. I watched as the snaking greenery moved up, up, until it had pinned his arms to his sides and coiled tightly around his neck, threatening to squeeze the life out of him.

Another Tírian—one I had never seen, with dark brown hair and eyes the color of the clear sky above us—strode forward, grabbed hold of Kazimir's jaw, and spoke a few quiet, vicious words to him. As the Tírian's lips moved, the entire Lightblood crew froze in place, each and every one of them now standing motionless and helpless, the whites of their eyes expressing their silent terror.

"Who *is* that?" I murmured, stunned by the Fae's apparent strength.

Even as I tried to decipher what the Tírian was saying, a set of powerful hands grabbed hold of me from behind and pulled me farther away from the fighting, pinning my arms tight behind me.

"Let me go, you bastard!" I shouted. I tried and failed to fight off my abductor, flailing and kicking backwards in a desperate attempt to yank myself free. But the arms only tightened, wrapping around my waist and pulling me hard against my assailant.

Whoever had taken me was far too strong for me to fight off, but still I squirmed and struggled against him. Prickly tears of rage stung my eyes as I cried out, "Set me free, or I'll have your head!"

A deep voice whispered, "My head—and the rest of me—already belong to you...Lyrinn Martel."

In the blink of an eye, my rage turned to pure bliss. A sudden, intoxicating warmth filled my chest, my stomach, as a set of lips met my neck.

My eyes slammed closed, and my head fell back as I savored the touch of the most extraordinary mouth I had ever known.

CHAPTER THREE

"You're really here," I breathed, twisting around the moment Mithraan's grip loosened so that I could take it in and confirm the truth with my eyes. "You're alive."

"As are you, thank all the gods living and dead," he replied. He cupped my jaw in his hands, his eyes darting wildly from one feature to another as if to ensure I was still in one piece.

"I'm fine," I promised.

"When we were separated, I reached out with my mind but couldn't...I couldn't find you. I was terrified that..." Mithraan's voice faltered, and he slipped his hand over my cheek, pressing his forehead to my own.

"It was awful," I told him. "One second, I was in the fighting ring at the Blood Trials, the next, I was here with Kazimir. All I wanted was to get back to you—I was so scared—I thought Corym had..."

My voice, too, wavered and cracked, warning me against saying anything more.

"The prince's blade was sharp," Mithraan said. "But the High King's Light spell separated us before he had a chance to do me any harm. My mind went blank, and when I came to, I was with Khiral and Alaric, standing some distance from the fighting ring. I don't know how—or *why*—Kazimir didn't simply wait for the prince to open my throat."

I let out a bitter snicker. "Kazimir said he was protecting me—keeping me from killing you both. But I can't imagine Kazimir wanting to protect you, if that's what he was doing. Still, I'm glad he did—even if it was purely accidental." I turned to look over my shoulder, only to see that the small Lightblood army was still frozen in place, some with their weapons held high in the air. Even Kazimir still stood motionless, a look of rage engraved deep into his features. "So, how do we get out of here before he manages to free himself?"

"I could fly us," Mithraan replied, gesturing toward his ship. "But it's not so far. I say we jump."

"Jump?" I asked, but instead of replying, Mithraan shouted a quick command to his crew members still assembled on the ship. Moving like a flock of birds in perfect harmony, the Tírians abandoned the Lightblood vessel, easily leaping the impossible distance onto their own craft.

"Come," Mithraan said, taking me by the hand. He led me to the ship's rail—which was more rounded than I had noticed when I was gripping it earlier. He leapt up onto it with ease, balancing as effortlessly on its tenuous curved edge as if he were standing on a broad platform. "Do as I do," he said, turning to look down at me.

"Are you serious? I'll fall into the sea if I try jumping up there!" I protested.

"You're more agile than you think, Fae." He leaned down, balancing on one leg, when he asked, "Do you trust me, Lyrinn Martel?"

"Maybe you should ask if I trust my*self*."

"All I ask is that you have a little faith. I would never do you harm—and I would hate to see you chilled by a tumble into the sea."

With that, he leapt onto his own ship as the others had done—despite the fact that it was at least fifteen feet from where he had stood a moment earlier. He turned and gestured for me to follow, an enticing grin on his lips.

I had little choice. I could do as he said, or stand on this deck, ticking down the moments until Kazimir would free himself and take hold of me once again.

"Here I go," I muttered under my breath.

Utterly lacking in confidence, I climbed cautiously up onto the railing. I was surprised at how secure I felt as I balanced there, my leather-soled boots gripping as strongly as a bird's talons.

But as I glanced down at the raging sea below, fear began to claw its way up my spine. My instincts and self-doubt told me I was a fool for thinking I could accomplish what the other Fae had. I may have their blood in my veins, but I was not yet fully one of them—at least, not mentally.

Kazimir had said it himself—I was practically a mortal still. Useless, weak. An embarrassment to our kind.

"Jump to me," Mithraan called out. "You'll find it easier than you imagine—I promise. Don't think about it. Just leap into my arms."

Into my arms.

The choice was the easiest one I'd ever made. There was nowhere in the world I would rather be.

Forcing cruel doubts from my mind, I hurled myself through the air, my eyes shut against my growing terror.

Mithraan caught me as promised, and I laughed with relief and amusement combined as I opened my eyes. "I didn't know I could do that," I said.

"There is a new world at your disposal, my Lady," he replied. "You have only to access it."

He kissed me hard, then turned to his crew and shouted, "Take us home to Tíria!"

His command was met with cheers and yelps, and as swiftly as the wind itself, the ship turned back toward Kalemnar and home. We moved fast on the waves, the silver eagle on the vessel's sails displayed proudly for all the world to see.

Spinning back to face the Lightblood vessel, Mithraan lifted one hand into the air. I watched as an oppressive fog began to form on the sea behind us, rising and thickening until I could not see a single trace of the Lightblood vessel in our wake. It was as though a wall of solid stone were now floating in mid-air between us and them, protecting our ship like an impenetrable fortification.

"Impressive," I said. "Tell me—the wind that brought you to us so easily—was that a spell of yours, too?"

Mithraan shook his head. "I wish I could say it was, but my talents don't generally lie in spells that call on the power of Nature. I relied upon a Fae more talented in that department."

"What Fae is more gifted than you?" I asked, puzzled. Mithraan was a High Lord of Tíria, after all. I'd seen his skill firsthand. I knew his power—and I *was* certain I had seen fear in Kazimir's eyes as he realized what he was up against.

Mithraan turned and pointed to the remarkable Fae I'd seen earlier—the one with dark brown hair and light eyes who had frozen the Lightbloods in place. "Thalanir, come here," he said, gesturing to him to join us.

For the first time, I got a proper look at the stranger. He was tall, broad-shouldered, and, not surprisingly, exquisitely handsome. His smile was crooked and somewhat mischievous, and in his eyes I saw the same ageless quality so many Fae possessed. A profound, daunting wisdom without the appearance of years.

He wore armor that was a mix of leather and silver, and at his side, an impressive short sword was sheathed—though something told me he seldom had need of it.

"It was you, then?" I asked as he approached. "You were the one who brought the wind?"

"Not exactly," he said with a bow of his head. "Consider me a mere conduit of Nature spells—an ambassador of sorts, for a Fae far from here."

My brow wrinkled with confusion. "Far from here," I repeated. "What do you mean?"

"Your grandfather," Thalanir said. "Rynfael, High King of Tíria."

"My...*grand*—" I choked. So, this stranger knew of my lineage. I wondered as I looked into his eyes just how *much* he knew. "You've met him, then?"

"I have known him for several hundred years," he laughed. "And to say he is delighted to learn of your existence is something of an understatement."

I looked at Mithraan, a nervous flutter making its way through my mind. How did this Fae know so much about me? How had my grandfather—whom I had never met—heard about my existence?

Then I remembered that there were ways of watching the Blood Trials—bird-sight, they called it, where each faction had a flyer witnessing the events and channeling the goings-on to spectators in their home territories.

Still, it wasn't as though anyone had announced during the Trials that I was Rynfael's kin. That had come out in secret, in the Taker's Lair.

I nodded, grateful for Thalanir's part in my rescue, but disconcerted by his depth of knowledge of my life, my ancestry.

"Are you able to communicate with my grandfather?" I asked. "With...others?"

I was desperate to find a way to get word to Leta—to find her and make sure she was safe...and to explain why I'd disappeared as I had. Now that we were headed home, I would find my way to her. And when I did, I could finally tell her everything that had happened since we'd been separated.

"How long will the enemy stay frozen?" I asked Thalanir, but my question was answered when I heard a loud cry of rage boom across the water from the direction of their now distant ship.

"*That* long, apparently," Mithraan said with a grimace. "Kazimir is not pleased—but don't worry. It will be impossible for him to locate us for some time. We're masked by more than mere mist; I threw in a few spells to keep us temporarily safe. The High King's crew is disoriented, and they will be for some hours. At best, they'll sail in circles for a day or two before the spell breaks and they regain their ability to navigate. By then, we'll be far ahead of them."

As he finished speaking, Khiral and Alaric raced up to us. One after the other, they each gave me a quick, almost violent embrace.

"I'm so glad to see you alive, Lyrinn," Alaric said. "When I heard about your abduction—Well, I wasn't entirely hopeful. Kazimir is not reputed to be the kindest Fae in the world."

"For this bastard's sake, I'm grateful as well," Khiral added, slapping Mithraan on the back. I knew it was as much of a compliment as I could hope to receive from him. He'd always been a bit of a jackass, and I didn't suppose that would change anytime soon.

"Well, I'm very glad to be alive," I replied. "I only wish it hadn't taken a bloody battle to bring me back to you."

"Those Lightblood bastards will be fine," Khiral said gruffly.

"No Fae ship ever casts off without at least a few skilled healers on board. That was a mere play fight, nothing more."

"Now," Mithraan said, clapping his hands together to halt the talk of fighting. "I'm sure we could all use some sustenance, after that. What say we have a bite to eat?"

"I don't suppose there's a change of clothes on board that I could slip into first?" I asked, looking down at the garments I'd been wearing since I awoke on Kazimir's ship. "The Lightblood's offerings are making my eye twitch. Now that I'm here with you, I'd rather put on something more...I don't know, *Tírian*."

"Come with me," Mithraan said, taking me by the hand and guiding me toward a nearby door. Over his shoulder, he called out, "Lay the table for us, you dolts!"

"We'll consider it!" Khiral shouted back.

Mithraan pulled the door open to reveal a small cabin containing trunks and crates of various sizes. At its center was a large, solid wood table that looked like it must weigh more than some houses I'd seen.

"Help yourself to whatever you need," Mithraan said, gesturing to a black leather trunk on the other side of the room. "There are some clothes in that one that should fit you nicely, I think."

He stood back, watching as I opened the trunk and rifled through until I found a white silk blouse and a pair of black leather trousers that looked to be the right size. I pulled them out, glancing sideways at him, my cheeks flushing as I tried to determine if he was intending to keep his eyes fixed on me as I changed out of my clothing.

Not that it should bother me. We *had* bonded, after all—we had been intimate in every way imaginable. It wouldn't be the first time he'd seen me naked.

Still, my self-consciousness—the timidity of someone who

had been raised mortal, feeling the eyes of a High Lord upon her —had returned to me with a vengeance. I felt like an inexperienced, naive human under his watchful gaze, though I tried to remind myself I was, in fact, a powerful Fae who had been through more in the last few weeks than most endured in a lifetime.

"Would you like me to leave, my Lady?" he asked with a sly grin that told me he had no intention of doing so. As if to prove my point, he closed the door tight and leaned back against it.

My Lady.

I smiled, thinking back to a time when I didn't like him calling me by that title. A time when I resented his teasing, his mischievous eyes.

How things have changed.

"Of course I don't want you to go," I said. "It's just..."

It feels like centuries have passed since you last saw all of me.

Mithraan crossed his arms over his chest, his eyes burning into my own. As I stumbled to find my words, his gaze moved down my body then up again, inspiring a deep, insidious hunger to work its way inside me.

"You're feeling bashful," he said, taking a step closer. Chin down, lips twitching. "You're hesitant to reveal yourself— worried that I will find you wanting. But I can tell you that if the others weren't waiting for us out there, I would tear those damned clothes from you and slip my tongue over every part of you until you begged me to claim you all over again."

Tightening, I succumbed to the smile that was forcing its way onto my lips. "If the others weren't waiting for us," I said, "I would insist on it."

"Then take off your clothes. Torment me with visions of what is to come. And when we've dined, I will bring you to my chamber and show you pleasures you've only ever dreamed of."

I stared at him, paralyzed by desire and trepidation, but he raised his brows and gestured toward the garments I'd picked out. "Please," he said. "Put them on. I promise I'll control myself...for now."

I hesitated, then, inhaling a sharp breath, yanked off my tunic, revealing my bare breasts to his watchful eyes.

But instead of giving in to instinct and crossing my arms over my chest, I fought the urge to cower and stood tall, lifting my chin to watch him as his gaze slipped over me again, his lips parting slightly.

"More," he half-whispered.

I loosened my trousers and let them drop to the floor.

That, it seemed, was the last straw.

Mithraan stepped over to me and, slipping the tips of his fingers down my stomach, let them continue their trajectory until they had worked their way into the waistband of my undergarments. His lips were mere inches from mine, his breath heating my skin and filling me with quiet desperation.

I let out a hard breath as his hand delved lower. He sighed, then closed his eyes as I tightened under his touch.

"You said you were going to control yourself," I whispered.

"This *is* me controlling myself."

It was a struggle to forbid the moan escaping my lips as he teased the sensitive place between my legs, slipping two fingers briefly inside me as if to offer the merest taste of what was to come.

"You do not disappoint, my Lady," he said softly, extracting his hand and licking his fingers clean, one by one.

Backing away, I pressed myself against the large desk at the cabin's center, desperate to lie back, spread my legs wide and plead with him to take me there and then...

But my desire was stifled by a sharp knock at the cabin door.

CHAPTER FOUR

"Mith!"

It was Khiral's voice, calling through the closed door as I quickly snatched up the white blouse and pulled it on, then, grappling with my shaking fingers, slipped into the trousers.

"What is it, man?" Mithraan called, a feral snarl erupting with the pain of being denied my naked form.

The door creaked open and Khiral issued me a crooked, mischievous grin before saying, "Only to let you know dinner is served. But I humbly beg your pardon—it looks to me like you were about to eat a meal of your own."

Before either of us could respond he left, closing the door behind him. Mithraan let out a half-growled sigh, turning back to me. "Soon."

Evening was falling as we made our way below deck to the dining room. The mist that Mithraan had summoned over the water seemed to have dissipated a little, but as far as I could tell, there was still no sign of Kazimir's ship—not even in the far distance.

Propelled once again by an unnaturally powerful wind, our ship was leaving a violent wake behind us, and all I could think was that we would soon be back home, safe from Kazimir's grasp.

When we entered the dining chamber, Khiral shot us both another raised-eyebrowed look of "I know exactly what you were about to do in there, you insatiable lust-filled beasts." But all he said was, "You two look...*famished.*"

"You might say that," Mithraan replied. "Or you could simply keep your lewd thoughts to yourself."

"Help yourselves to food," Alaric said by means of distraction, gesturing toward the table, which was already laid out with chicken, bread, every vegetable I could imagine, roast potatoes, and more.

Until the moment when I laid my eyes on the spread of delectable dishes before us, hunger hadn't ravaged my insides. But now, I felt as though I hadn't eaten a thing in weeks.

"You haven't touched a meal since the Trials were interrupted, have you?" Alaric asked with a look of concern, as if reading my mind.

"No," I said. "But that was only a few hours ago, so I really shouldn't be quite so..."

"A few *hours*?" Khiral asked, his eyes narrowing in confusion. "What the hell did High King Bastard do to you?"

"What does that mean?"

Khiral looked over at Mithraan, who was standing next to Thalanir. "Do you want to tell her?"

"It's been six days since the battle," Mithraan said softly. "Six days since our separation. Kazimir's ship was nearly to Aetherion when we caught up."

"Six...days..." I gasped. "But it can't have been."

"I'm afraid it's true. Six days spent unsure whether you were alive or dead—unsure what Kazimir might do to you. Our departure was delayed, as I only had the luxury of leaving

Kalemnar after these two convinced King Caedmon to call the Trials *incomplete*."

"Incomplete," I repeated, blowing out a breath. "Well, I'm honestly surprised he didn't claim his prick of a son as victor."

"His prick of a son was too badly injured to be victor of anything, and Caedmon knew it," Khiral shot. "If you recall, the prince's face was torn to shreds. Mithraan would've ended him in a matter of seconds, if Kazimir hadn't stopped the battle cold."

"That's a little over-confident of you," Mithraan protested with a snicker as he reached for a cup of wine. "The last time Lyrinn saw me, I had a blade to my throat, remember."

Khiral snorted. "That sniveling little weasel could never have ended you. And if by some miracle he had, I would have flayed him and served up his skinless corpse to his parents for their next meal."

"Appetizing image, Khir," Alaric said with a roll of his eyes. "Come, you two. Eat."

I seated myself at the table, taking Mithraan's hand when he took the chair next to mine. "I must say, I'm grateful this ship was harbored at Domignon. I'd forgotten the Tírian party brought it from the North."

"Yes—for the duration of the Trials," Khiral said. "We never expected to have to pursue Kazimir, though. Hell, I was hoping for a nice cruise up the coast."

"I'm sorry you ended up engaged in less pleasurable pursuits," I replied. "But to say I'm grateful for what you've done is a massive understatement."

"Why does that white-haired skin-sack want you, anyhow?" Khiral asked, taking a sip of wine. "What business does Kazimir have with you?"

"I..." I began, confused. "Didn't you see the Trials? I thought you watched via bird-sight. I thought you would know..."

"We *saw* everything," Alaric replied. "But it was from a pretty vast distance, and we didn't hear much of what was said. Perhaps the birds were too high in the air to hear your voices as you spoke."

"And you didn't tell them..." I began, looking at Mithraan.

"It wasn't my place to tell," he said. "And to be honest, I wasn't entirely certain you would want me to."

With a sigh, I glanced at the other three, trying to decide if I wanted to divulge the truth. Khiral and Alaric, I trusted with my life. But Thalanir was a virtual stranger.

Still, Mithraan seemed to trust him...

"Kazimir," I said slowly, "is my father by blood."

Khiral, who had made the mistake of drinking, spat a mouthful of red wine over the table. Alaric looked no less shocked.

Thalanir, on the other hand, looked unsurprised, as though he had known the truth of it all his life.

When Khiral finished a brief coughing fit, he said, "Your father is...*that* Fae? Good gods, you have my sympathy. What a shock to find out you were sired by the world's biggest arse."

"Maybe you would have been less eager to rescue me if you'd known the truth," I said, laughing bitterly. "My ties to him make me instantly repulsive, I'm sure."

Khiral almost looked as if he was about to say, "You're damned right about that," but instead, he shook his head. "We still owe you a debt for saving Mithraan's life. Tyrannical Lightblood despot of a father or not, you're clearly more one of us than one of them."

"I am not one of them in the least," I replied, almost offended. "Whatever blood may course through my veins, I have little in common with Lightbloods. I like to think I favor my mother's Tírian side."

"I'm not so sure," Khiral laughed. "You can be quite cold-hearted when you wish to. In hindsight, I can definitely see the Lightblood in you, my Lady. Or—wait—should I call you *Princess*?"

"Oh, gods help me," I laughed. "Don't call me either. Honestly, I'd rather you just called me a bitch and left it at that."

"Bitch it is, then."

"Now that you two have that settled," Mithraan said with a hard glare at his friend, "Could we discuss plans?"

"Please," Alaric said with a roll of his eyes and an elbow to Khiral's side.

"Yes," Khiral said woefully. "Enlighten us. What does the future hold?"

"We'll head back toward Domignon and anchor in the harbor. From there..." Mithraan glanced at me. "One or more of us will head to the palace."

"Why would we want to do that?" I asked, my pulse instantly accelerating. "I want to be as far away from that godawful place as from Aetherion."

Khiral leaned his head back and let out a loud moan. "So, she doesn't know," he lamented. "You haven't told her, Mith?"

"Know what?"

Mithraan laid his hand on mine and squeezed gently. "Leta is still in the palace," he said. "In Domignon. The prince and king are keeping her there."

"What?" I nearly screamed, yanking my hand away. "Why?"

"You can guess why," Khiral said, an undercurrent of rage coiling its way around his voice. "The Trials never reached their conclusion, which means the prince failed to acquire your bloodline's Gifts—which he wanted for reasons that have just become all the more obvious, now that I know you're half-Lightblood. You're a veritable font of potential—and so, then, is your sister. Leta is his chance at acquiring magic more powerful than anything our realms have seen in many centuries."

With a sickening flash of memory, I recalled what Corym had said to Mithraan on the Trials' last day. *My taste runs more along the lines of, say, redheads. Like her younger sister...*

"Are you telling me Corym is going to demand that the Taker extract Leta's Gifts?" I shuddered at the thought of the strange being I had encountered under the Eternity Tree sapping Leta of her blood-right—Gifts she didn't even know she had. As far as I knew, Leta wasn't yet aware of our complicated family history. She didn't know the truth about the man who had raised us, or about our mother.

The Taker was not cruel. But it *was* submissive and fearful, and if King Caedmon made demands of it—threatened it with punishment—I had no doubt it would give in to his orders without question.

Mithraan spoke gently. "He won't use the taker. He'll find another way. Leta has not yet come of age, but given that your mortal father lied to you both about your birth-dates all these years, it's hard to know when she will come of age. The prince will be watching her closely—though I have no doubt he's currently doing his best to charm her into marrying him. It would be the wisest strategic move he could make."

"It won't work," I retorted. "She saw what he did to us during the Trials...didn't she?"

"There's no way of knowing," Mithraan replied. "If the prince and King Caedmon were intelligent, they would have prevented her from witnessing the Trials—at *least* the final battle. It wouldn't do to let her know how cruel Corym can be."

The thought sent a vicious shudder through my every nerve. "Leta's no fool," I said. "But we need to get to her—we need to let her know whose company she's in. The second she knows what they have planned and why, I'm sure she will leave his side."

"Let's hope so." With that, Mithraan took his cup in hand

and raised it. "In the meantime, let's drink to freedom. To Tíria's rebirth. And to a future filled with promise for us all."

We each raised a cup, clinked them together, then proceeded to drink the night away, our cares melting temporarily from our minds.

After all, there was still no sign of Kazimir's ship. The sea was calm, and the winds blew in our favor. The night was a happy one, filled with laughter—even from the mysterious Thalanir.

But even as we laughed and joked, never did the thought of Leta stray too far from my mind.

What must she think happened to me? What has Corym told her?

No matter, I assured myself. *I'll explain everything when I see her again in a few days. I'll get her away from the bastard of a prince and his father, and together, we will make our way to Tíria.*

CHAPTER FIVE

THOUGH HE DRANK the night away with the rest of us, Thalanir barely uttered a word.

Instead, I caught him on occasion studying my face as if trying to piece together a puzzle. A disconcerting instinct had begun to tell me he knew far more about me than he was letting on—yet I had no idea how, or why.

"Were you raised in the North of Tíria?" I asked him after a time, remembering his mention of my grandfather and their surprising connection.

"I was," he replied. "Though I left when I came of age long ago. I don't remain in any one place for long. I tend to venture where I am needed."

It was the most he'd spoken all evening, and I smiled in response.

"Yes—Thal goes where he's needed," Khiral said with a chuckle. "*And* where the money lies."

"Money?"

But both Fae fell silent, and I found myself looking from one face to the other in search of an answer.

"Thalanir is a sell-blade," Mithraan finally said. "He's one of those known as *Valdfae*. They serve Tíria or Aetherion—or both, and have no particular allegiance. He's a mercenary skilled in the art of battle—and in the arts of stealth and shadow." He glanced at me and added, "You two have that last bit in common."

"Stealth and shadow," I repeated with a smile. I could imagine it now, looking at Thalanir. He moved like a prowling cat, never speaking unless it was absolutely necessary. He assessed those around him as an animal studies its prey before attacking.

I'd never seen anyone who was so beautiful and so inconspicuous at once.

"Are you a spy, then?" I asked him bluntly.

"Sometimes," he replied, and I was surprised at his honesty. "When I am called upon to spy, I do it. I am a master of deceit—which I realize makes me sound incredibly untrustworthy."

"Um...yes," I replied. "What exactly do you mean by 'deceit?'"

He issued me a sly smile, but didn't say a thing. Instead, he rose to his feet and gestured to his face.

As we watched, his brown hair turned silver and grew long and straight, his blue eyes changing to hazel.

All of a sudden, I found myself face to face with a Lightblood Fae who looked enough like Kazimir to inspire a jolt of nausea in my belly.

"Is that...glamour?" I asked, my voice tight as I forced myself to look at him.

"It's a little more intricate than mere glamour," he replied, his voice smooth, deep, and eerily familiar. "Glamour is a tool of the mind—one that twists perception and convinces others of what they see. *My* change is real. Like Mithraan, I am a shapeshifter. I am able to move about in any room, whether it be filled with High Fae or mortals, and never be noticed—or I can demand reverence from thousands, depending on my wishes. For me to take on the guise of a king is not unheard of—though it's a risk I hope I never have to take."

"But Thal is far more than that," Mithraan replied. "I don't dare recount some of his extraordinary exploits over the centuries. He has infiltrated some of the highest Houses in Fae lands. There was a time when my ancestors wanted him dead for his abilities—they considered him far too dangerous. I, on the other hand, see his value."

"I see," I replied, though the truth was, I didn't. At least, not entirely. Thalanir felt like a liability—an unnecessary danger that Mithraan had brought almost to Aetherion's shores with him.

I made a mental note to ask him later how much he trusted the Valdfae. How could we be certain he was on our side? What if he was actually a Lightblood, posing as a Tírian? What if he was working as an agent of Kazimir?

He had admitted himself that he was guided by money—not integrity, loyalty, or pride.

"You fear that my motives are corrupt, Highness," Thalanir said, reading my thoughts once again, as though they were scrawled in tidy script across my face. "You are afraid I will betray Lord Mithraan and yourself."

I considered denying it, but instead, I raised my chin and said, "I have no way of knowing where your loyalties lie—if indeed you have any. Forgive me, but I was just stolen from my life in Kalemnar and transported over the sea to who knows what fate? I need to know I'm in the presence of Fae I can trust."

"Thal wouldn't be here if I didn't trust him," Mithraan said, a hard edge to his tone. "If anything happens to any of us, it won't be his doing."

"But he is to receive payment for his service to you, I

assume," I said. "In my limited experience, those who can be bought for one price can easily be swayed for a higher one."

"You have not experienced *me*, Highness," Thalanir said with a bow of his head. "But perhaps it will take time to prove my worth to you, after all you have been through. I can't say I blame you for lacking faith in your fellow Fae."

I narrowed my eyes at him. I wanted to read him as he read me—to know what he had ascertained about me. Something told me every bit of information he had gleaned of my life and history was his own doing—that he had delved into my mind and stolen pieces of me without my consent.

It was a skill that could prove useful, to be sure. But one that frightened me, too. I wished I could stop it—put up a blockade of some sort and prevent him from learning a single thing more. Information, after all, was currency. And learning my weaknesses could prove a powerful blade to wield against me.

"Come," Alaric said, slamming a palm down on the table. "Let's talk about something more pleasant. Mithraan, have you ever told Lyrinn about the days when all High Fae could fly?"

I glanced at Mithraan, curious, but he shook his head. "Later," he said, laying a hand on my thigh and squeezing gently. "For now, Lyrinn must be tired—and I know I am. I believe it's time we all called it a night."

"Lies," Khiral said through a playful smile. "You just want an excuse to get her into bed."

"Can you blame me?" Mithraan replied, pushing back from the table and guiding me to my feet. "Good night, you bastards."

CHAPTER SIX

When Khiral, Alaric, and Thalanir had excused themselves to head to bed, Mithraan took my hand and led me out onto the deck.

The Tírian crew was still hard at work to ensure our ship was moving swiftly enough to evade any pursuers—and from the looks of it, our escape had been a success.

"I don't know how you managed it," I told Mithraan as we both leaned against the ship's railing, looking out to the moon's reflection upon the waves lapping in our wake. "I'm impressed that you managed to best Kazimir so easily. But I'm glad...not to mention relieved."

"I'll be properly relieved when we drop anchor in Kalemnar," Mithraan replied, and for the first time, I detected a hint of concern in his voice. "Until then, I will trust nothing of what I see on these waves."

"So..." I said with a pang of shock. "You didn't think you could pull it off—did you?"

Mithraan looked vaguely sheepish as he frowned subtly—an unusual expression to see on his beautiful face. "When we chose to come after you, I knew one thing—that we must find you and get you away from that monster. He has been responsible for any number of atrocities, and I despise him more than I can say. But I know how powerful he is. I know how brutal he can be." He turned to look me in the eye. "I'm not being modest when I say Kazimir is more powerful than I am, than Thalanir. He is—they say—the strongest Fae in Aetherion. Which means there's no reason it should have been so easy to take you from him. Had he wished to, he should have been able to break free of the spell that held him in place. It was not some ancient dark magic, after all—it was a simple freezing spell."

"Then why didn't he?" I asked, and when Mithraan just shook his head, I added, "What are you thinking happened? Why would Kazimir fail on purpose?"

"I can't say. I don't understand why Kazimir did not fight— why he allowed his Lightbloods to be harmed, when I know full well he could have blasted me from the sky with one shot. He went to the trouble of traveling all the way to Domignon to claim you, brought you back across the sea, then let me have you back?" He ground his jaw for a moment. "It simply makes no sense. Something else is at play here, and the only question is *what*."

"We're together now," I consoled him, trying in vain to keep my voice from trembling with quiet fear. "That's all that matters. We can do so much good, you and I—we'll return to Tíria. We'll begin rebuilding your lands."

"*Our* lands," he corrected, reaching out to tuck an errant strand of hair behind my pointed ear. "Don't forget what you are, Lyrinn. The granddaughter of a Fae High King. It is your land as much as anyone's. I would argue, in fact, that you hold more claim over Tíria than even I do."

His words hit me like a shock of cold water. So much had happened—so much madness had consumed my mind in recent days—that I hadn't yet fully processed the transformation that had occurred inside my body and mind. I hadn't given full consideration to my status as a Tírian High Fae, descendant of Rynfael.

I was royalty. I might one day inherit the throne of Tíria.

The thought was enough to send my mind reeling.

But I had yet to fully understand my new powers, to hone and develop them into anything particularly useful. At the moment, I felt like a foal on brand new legs, still learning to walk.

And as much as I would have loved to meet my grandfather, the thought was beyond daunting. Like Kazimir, he was a High King. And like Kazimir, he was probably terrifying. He had lived for the last thousand years in isolation in Tíria's north, trapped in his own lands just as his fellow Fae were. Separated from the daughter he loved, his fury against her captor growing year by year.

It was entirely possible that by now, he was coiled as tightly as a snake, itching to strike the first victim to come along.

"What are you thinking?" Mithraan asked softly.

"I'm thinking, 'How can my grandfather possibly want to meet me?'"

"How could anyone *not* want to meet you?"

"I'm serious, Mithraan," I moaned. "My mother was exquisite, like Leta. They say she was Gifted and powerful, too. She was a wonder. But me...I'm a failure. I didn't prove myself in the Trials; I barely *survived* them. It was pure luck—and your help—that kept me alive. I may have summoned those Light-Beasts, but Kazimir was the one who put an end to it all."

"Never call yourself a failure." Mithraan kissed me gently. "You have brought new hope to a land that was once lost. It is only because you ventured into Tíria from Dúnbar that I managed to find my own way out—that I broke through the

Mist and freed our people. Tíria may soon see a rebirth—not because of me, but because *you* are their savior."

"I didn't do anything but climb some stairs against my better judgment," I said with a cynical chuckle. "As much as I'd love to take credit for Tíria's rebirth, it's all thanks to you."

Slipping a hand onto my neck, he trailed his fingertips along my skin, sending me into a spiral of desire and need that threatened to unravel me. "Tell me something," he said, his eyes fixed on my neck as he traced the dark lines that had appeared there the day he healed me in the Taker's Lair—the day my true nature was revealed. "Have you ever heard of the Elar?"

I was about to say no. But then I remembered something Kazimir had said:

By the Elar's wings...

He had spoken the words like a curse, though I hadn't known what they meant.

"Sort of. What is it?"

"It's not so much a what as a *who*. She is an Immortal—a Fae, selected by an Order of High Priestesses to oversee the realms. One who is granted a title and power greater, even, than that of High Kings. Some even say she has in her the essence of a goddess, which she passes down to her Successor when she fades."

"Fades?"

"The power bestowed upon the Elar steals life from her. Over time—thousands of years, usually—she begins to wither, her life drained from her, and so she is replaced."

"So, you're saying there has been more than one Elar?"

Mithraan nodded. "Many, as far as I can tell—though I believe the current Elar has been in power for thousands of years—but she is fading quickly. According to Thalanir, a new Fae will be chosen soon, and named in what the Order calls the Succession Ceremony in the far North of Aetherion."

"Is that where she—the goddess, or whatever she is
—lives?"

"They say she dwells in a place known as the Broken
Lands," Mithraan said softly. "And if she's as powerful as they
say, she will have the potential to help create a promising future
for our lands. Of course, she also has the potential to destroy us
all."

I laughed nervously. "That's quite a responsibility to take
on. I can't quite imagine aspiring to those heights."

Mithraan nodded. "There are a few motivating factors," he
said softly. "You heard Alaric mention the days when all High
Fae had the power of flight."

"I did," I said. "But honestly, I thought he was joking."

Mithraan shook his head, continuing to trail his fingertips
along my flesh. "Some say that wings were a gift granted to the
High Fae by the first Elar many long years ago. That one of her
Successors took the power away when she grew angry with her
subjects for allowing themselves to be corrupted by greed. But
when their wings were taken from them, resentment began to
brew. High Fae began to cast blame in all directions. Troubles
that already existed between Tíria and Aetherion grew in those
days—and all bonds between our races became forbidden. Each
side blamed the other for the loss of flight, and the animosity
only flourished and festered as the centuries wore on. Of course,
that was many thousands of years ago now. If ever High Fae
really *could* fly, there is no sign of it. For all I know, it's nothing
but a folk tale."

"But *you* can fly," I said with a half-smile.

"Only with the wings of an eagle, not those of a Fae," he
laughed, kissing me. "Ironically enough, I still don't have the
power to summon the wings that would once have sprung
naturally from my back—supposedly." Mithraan sighed deeply.
"In ancient times, the High Fae were sentinels—watchers over

the lands of human and Immortals alike. Now, there is a perpetual struggle for power over the realms, a quiet war between Lightblood, Tírian, and mortal. Some say the next Elar is the only one who can bring lasting peace—others say she will bring despair and ruin."

His expression looked grim, his eyes narrowed with doubt and cynicism.

"You don't sound convinced by either possibility."

He looked me in the eye and said, "I believe we craft our own fates, Lyrinn Martel—just as you and I are doing right now. It isn't up to some powerful entity to determine our futures. It's up to us."

I studied his eyes for a moment. There was so much about him that I had yet to learn. So much about my kind and our history that I didn't yet know. "Still, tell me—do you believe she's as powerful as they say?"

He shrugged. "I have never seen true evidence of such a being even existing," he said. "But then, I have never met one of the High Priestesses of the Order. I suppose I'll believe all the stories when I see proof."

"I'm curious now," I said with a slow exhalation. "She sounds like a tyrant who hoards Fae gifts for herself—though it sounds like many regard her as a goddess."

"Perhaps she is nothing more than a judgmental angel," Mithraan said, letting out a huff of derision. "As far as I'm concerned, the only goddess in all the realms is you."

"I'm no goddess," I protested with a bashful snicker. "I'm the farthest thing from it, in fact."

"Oh, I don't know about that." He slipped a hand onto my collarbone, then let his fingertips slide slowly downward. "Tell that to this exquisite body of yours," he breathed as his fingers grazed my nipple through my blouse, his eyes flashing bright with desire. My breath sealed itself inside my chest when he whispered, "I've tasted you. Each day that passes, I wake with your scent spinning through the air around me, tormenting me with desire. I would argue that only a goddess could possibly leave me with the insatiable cravings that eat away at me every minute of every day."

He pushed my hair back and leaned in to kiss my neck, sending the same deep need pulsing through me as I'd felt so many times in his presence—one that felt dangerous, uncontrolled...yet utterly delicious.

"Come," he said softly. "Let me show you my cabin, which until this moment has been the loneliest place on all the seas."

CHAPTER SEVEN

WITHOUT ANOTHER WORD, Mithraan led me toward a door that brought us into an elegant room filled with bookshelves, paintings, and a massive wooden desk positioned at its center. Off to one side, I spied a large bedroom through an open door, a vast bed at its center draped in cream-colored silk.

But before I could take in all the details of the well-appointed stateroom, he shut the door behind him and rushed to embrace me. He kissed me deeply, his tongue stroking its way over mine as an ecstatic moan escaped my throat. I had nearly forgotten the sensation of heat swirling in the pit of my stomach and somewhere below, a tightening throb as my mind conjured imagined scenarios wherein that tongue would find its way down my body, taking in every inch of me, every nerve, until at last, it found its way between my legs and claimed me.

He lifted me off my feet and, laughing with the purest joy, I wrapped my legs around his waist. For the first time, it struck me that we were free. Free to be together, to love one another. Free to be happy.

I was free of Corym, of the Blood Trials, free of Kazimir. At long last, we were headed home to start a new life together.

Instead of carrying me to the bed, Mithraan brought me to the desk, setting me easily on its top before tearing my blouse apart with two quick, expert swipes of his silver talons. The garment split open, and then the Fae's hungry lips were trailing their way down my neck to my shoulder as I writhed under the sensation. His hand cupped my breast greedily, his thumb coaxing my nipple to a rock-hard peak...and it was all I could do not to throw him down and climb atop him, showing him the Immortal strength that had amassed inside me since our first meeting.

Mithraan went lower, lower, until his lips were on my nipple, his tongue delighting, tormenting, destroying...all at once.

"This," he whispered against my skin, his tongue lashing at the bundle of nerves he was so mercilessly teasing. "*This* is what I now live for. Every inch of you to be worshiped as many times a day as there are hours."

I moaned again, tossing my head back as he lifted my hips and pulled my trousers down until they fell to the ground, leaving me wearing little but a pair of leather ankle boots and the shredded shards of blouse that draped over my shoulders.

He slipped to his knees, moaning with bliss as his fingers pulled me apart and he inhaled my scent, taking it in as if it brought him new life. His tongue trailed up my thigh, so slowly that my hips bucked in anticipation of what was to come. He pulled his chin up, looked me in the eye then stroked his tongue over me once, twice, driving me mad with his calculated slowness, as though he could read every tingle of my nerves as he inflicted his sweet torment on me.

"I want you," I breathed, a burst of heat searing my insides.

"You have me," he replied, lifting himself to his feet and undoing his trousers, splitting them open to release his steel-hard length. "I am yours, and I will never belong to another."

Slipping over me, he pressed the swollen head against me, tormenting me with the promise of what was to come.

I reached for his hips to pull him closer, aching brutally for more—for everything.

"No. Not yet." He smiled. "I'm not done tasting you."

As if in mockery, he fell to his knees again, his tongue flicking over me once, twice. *Torture. Sweet torture.* His hands gripped my thighs and I knew he could feel me convulsing under his touch—I could tell he was enjoying making me twitch with the extraordinary pleasure on offer. He enjoyed the power of it, the dominance.

The fact that I was entirely at his mercy.

A finger slipped inside me, working in synchronicity with his tongue, and I began to wonder whether the wooden walls were enough to prevent the entire crew from hearing my cries of delight.

Then again, I wasn't sure I cared.

I raked my fingers through his hair, taking control and demanding that he keep working me, tormenting me until I fell over the edge of the world to tumble downward until my entire body tingled with bliss.

He understood, his tongue and lips driving me to the place from which there was no return, until the climax overtook me, my hips jerking upward reflexively, demanding still more.

I throbbed with desire for him. Pulsed with an agony that could only be satisfied by one thing—and if he didn't give it to me soon, I would go mad.

The call for mercy escaped my lips as two simple words:

"Now...*please*..."

He rose to his feet and with one hard thrust, pushed himself deep inside me. I gripped the desk's sides as I locked my eyes on his, watching his struggle against the sensation as he moved his hips slowly, reveling in our bond, in the hold my body had over his...and his over mine.

When he sped up his pace, it was all I could do not to scream my ecstasy to every member of his crew. To express to each of them my pleasure, my arousal, my utter certainty that never had any being experienced a more delicious sensation than I was now—the agonizing, shattering feeling of Mithraan's perfect length tearing me apart.

I wrapped my arms around him, palms flattened on his back as I drew in his scent—one I had grown to crave as water or air. Tears streaked my cheeks with the joy I felt at our union. And when I sensed him struggle against the coming explosion, I understood that he, too, felt pure joy...

But I also sensed fear. And I knew exactly where it came from.

How long would we be together before someone tried to pull us apart again? When would we finally be free to love each other—to live as mates?

Was this really it?

Seeming to sense my thoughts, he pulled back, looked deep into my eyes, and, as he sheathed himself inside me again, he said, "I am yours for all the days to come, Lyrinn Martel. Whatever may come—whatever pain may be inflicted—I am yours. We will craft our own destinies, however hard others may try and destroy us. Do you hear me?"

Tears welling in my eyes, I pulled him tighter to me, my lips pressed into his neck to stifle a sob.

With a final thrust, Mithraan unleashed at last, and this time, it was he who cried out. A feral, relentless snarl of bliss and desire that reverberated through every bit of wood that surrounded this chamber—and that must have been audible to each and every Fae on board. The amalgamation of all he and I had been through since our first meeting. Our struggle against desire, our perpetual fight against succumbing to forbidden attraction...

Near loss. Heartbreak.

And now...

I collapsed backwards, my chest heaving, droplets of perspiration cooling me as Mithraan leaned down to run his tongue over the curve of my breast.

"Will they catch us?" I asked, throwing an arm over my eyes to avoid meeting his gaze. I couldn't bear to see the honesty in his face just then, if he were to reply with bad news.

"I don't know, *Vaelan*," he said, kissing his way down the valley between my breasts. "And right now, I don't care." He nipped playfully at me, eliciting a cry and a laugh, and my fear faded quickly away.

"Vaelan," I repeated. "What's that?"

He lifted his chin to look into my eyes. "An old Fae word—it means 'Little Wolf.' You remind me of one—stalking quietly as you observe those around you with keen eyes. Waiting for your chance to pounce...but biding your time—because you understand the consequences of impulsive moves."

"Little Wolf. I like that."

Mithraan pulled me up and looked at me, the shredded blouse still clinging to my shoulders.

Barely.

"This is a good look," he said, teasing my nipple with the knuckle of a curved finger. "I'd like to bring you out on deck and show you off to the entire crew like this."

"Would you, now?"

He sank to his knees, taking a nipple in his mouth and taunting me again with gentle snaps of his teeth. "I would," he said, his voice vibrating against me. "I may be powerful, but perhaps my greatest feat will be to render every Fae aboard so envious that he throws himself into the sea."

Leaping to his feet, he hoisted me up, carried me to the bed, and laid me down gently, pushing my thighs apart with a decisive hand.

"I'm not leaving this chamber until I've claimed you at least seven more times," he growled, his hand slipping possessively to the place between my legs, then following its trajectory with his mouth as he slid down the bed. "It is a High Lord's duty to please his Lady." He spoke these words into my flesh, the movement of his lips making me squirm with pleasure.

I reached down and cupped his jaw in my hands, pulling his face up to say, "Thank you. For finding me."

With a kiss to my thigh, he replied, "I will always find you. Come what may—whatever enemies we face—I will never let you go. If ever we are separated again, you have my vow that never in this lifetime will I stop hunting for you."

I looked into his eyes, and I knew it to be true.

But those beautiful eyes quickly disappeared, and I found myself letting out a quiet, desperate howl of delight.

Little wolf, indeed.

CHAPTER EIGHT

For three days and nights, we sailed east.

And for three days and nights, Mithraan and I deepened our bond, spending every possible waking moment in one another's arms—claiming and reclaiming each other's bodies as if we were two people who knew the world would end imminently.

Despite my happiness and the absolute perfection of our time together, a worry began to gnaw at me as we drew closer to Kalemnar—one that I couldn't shake, however hard I tried. Almost every hour of every day, I found myself wondering how Kazimir could possibly have given up his hunt. How—or why—such a Fae would ever have accepted defeat at the hands of a Tírian High Lord and headed home empty-handed.

It seemed entirely contrary to the High King's nature—not to mention a simple impossibility.

Still, by all accounts given by Mithraan's crew as I interrogated the Tírian Fae on board, it seemed that was exactly what had happened.

I even asked Thalanir at one point to tell me his opinion.

"You've encountered Lightbloods before," I said. "Do you think there's any chance Kazimir simply changed his mind?"

Thalanir had been perusing my face, his weapon-like eyes feeling like blades teasing the surface of my skin, and I was uneasy as he said, "A High King does not show weakness… unless it is for reasons of strategy. Weakness is death for sovereigns—and Kazimir, as we all know, is far from weak. Which leaves strategy—though what his might be, I could not begin to say."

The words were enough to turn me away from Thalanir, forcing me to retreat quietly to the shadows of our cabin, fear consuming my insides.

When Mithraan and I spent time alone together, I allowed the worries to fall away. Our nights were spent tangled blissfully together, our bodies one perfect, ecstatic entity. Many daylight hours, too, were spent in moments of stolen intimacy away from the crew's watchful eyes.

We dined each morning and evening with Alaric and Khiral, who were beginning to feel like the brothers I'd never realized I wanted. Ever since the incident in the woods near Domignon when I had found Mithraan so near death, they had begun to accept me as one of their own.

And now that my bloodline had come to light, Khiral, always stubborn and sullen in the past, had turned almost friendly, if such a thing were possible. I had grown fond of his honest-to-a-fault, surly nature.

Thalanir joined us on occasion, always observing from a calculated distance. My repeated attempts to penetrate the armor that was his mind proved fruitless. He was always polite, but irritatingly mysterious. Charming and cold at once.

On occasion, I would see Mithraan or the other two talking quietly to him in some dark corner or another, their heads together as they appeared to strategize about some unseen future dilemma. Once, I watched as Mithraan handed him a small, tied sack made of leather. *Payment,* I thought. *For what, I'm not certain—but at least Thalanir is on our side...*

For now.

On the third night, after Mithraan and I had made love three times in the space of a few hours, I drifted into a deep sleep, my mind overtaken by a vivid dream.

I was standing on a hilltop overlooking much of Kalemnar, though I couldn't quite understand how I could see so far into the distance. I spied the River Dún near my home, the Onyx Rise to the north, the far-off realms of Belleau and Domignon.

My eyes were still scanning the landscape when I spotted a winged creature soaring through the sky, its outline glowing bright against a thick cover of dark clouds.

At first, I assumed it was a bird—a large eagle, perhaps.

Mithraan?

But as it approached, I realized with a shock that the figure was female and human-looking, her body lithe and graceful. Her face was concealed behind a white veil, flowing and opaque—though I knew without question that it was no impediment to her sight.

A set of powerful silver wings laced with dark red veins reminded me of angelic figures I had seen depicted in Dúnbar's chapels over the years. Those creatures had always struck me as extraordinary and ethereal, but frightening in their way—creatures crafted by the minds of humans as a symbol of strength, of purity, of a power beyond mortal comprehension. They often exuded goodness, gentleness, their sole purpose to convey messages of goodwill.

But this being projected nothing but pure, unbridled chaos.

She flew madly about, casting violent spells that sent bolts of lightning crashing down toward the realms below. Forests and towns burned as I watched, and the distant river I'd known and loved all my life caught fire before my eyes, flames doing battle with water and reflecting angrily in its shimmering surface.

The Elar, I thought, looking at the monster who had started the conflagration. But why was she wreaking such havoc on Kalemnar? Why was she so...*angry*?

I told myself it was nothing more than a dream. I was not there—I was in bed with Mithraan. The Elar—if indeed she existed—was nowhere near Kalemnar, and our lands were safe.

Still, she felt eerily real as she swept down to earth and landed several feet away from me, her fingers tingling with the same crackling lightning she had hurled at the landscape below.

I stared at the veil that covered her face, desperate to see through it, to find her eyes and prove to myself that she had a heart. Though I couldn't see her features, I sensed a malice, a sort of toxic rage that seeped through every particle that formed her being.

"Why are you doing this?" I asked, my voice manifesting all the innocence of a young girl. "Why are you destroying everything? My home...my land..."

"The world is a cruel place." Her voice was raspy and jagged as broken glass as it echoed through the air around me, seeming to glance off the land itself. "It is time to renew the realms—to bring back the days of glory before Fae and mortals turned corrupt and ambitious beyond reason. But before rebirth must come death—and so, the lands and those who occupy them must die."

"But—you can't do this!" I cried. "You're talking about

killing innocent people. Children will suffer. It's not right. It's a cruelty beyond measure..."

"Perhaps you should stop me, then, *Highness*," she said disdainfully with a bow of her head. Though I couldn't see it, I sensed a wicked smile in her tone. "Stop me, and save your precious world."

"I can't!" I protested. "How could I possibly stop a being such as yourself?"

"There is only one way," she said, but when I opened my mouth to ask her to explain, she flew off at enormous speed.

Helpless, I watched as distant lightning crashed down in bolts of venom and torment, leaving a black trail of smoking destruction in her wake.

I jolted awake, convinced that I could taste the acrid smoke I had seen in my dream on my tongue—that the dream was somehow based in reality.

I shot up to a sitting position, reaching for Mithraan, desperate for comfort.

But all I could feel was a mass of crumpled sheets where he'd been.

Smoke billowed through the air, wafting into the cabin through its open door. I listened for cries, for warnings from Fae crew members—but the night was eerily silent.

I leapt out of bed and threw on a silk robe that hung over a nearby chair, darting toward the door.

As I stepped out onto the deck, I heard voices. Deep and intense, they sounded disturbingly calm. I found myself walking toward the sound slowly, carefully, asking myself if I was still dreaming. Clearly, the ship was on fire, though I could see no flame.

How could anyone sound so stoic when they were in so much peril?

I strode half the length of the ship before a figure emerged from the smoke, stepping toward me, then another—and another. They were tall, broad-shouldered...

And silver-haired.

Lightbloods.

On instinct, I reached for my blade, seeking to defend the Tírian ship against these night-time invaders. But with a curse, I remembered that I hadn't had a dagger in hand since the Blood Trials.

I found myself helpless.

Except...

You're a Fae, damn it, I chastised, and as two Lightblood guards took a step toward me, I raised my hands into the air.

"Where is the crew of this ship?" I asked. "What have you done with them?"

"They're exactly where you left them," one of the Fae said. "Perfectly safe—just as the High King ordered."

I shook my head violently, trying to force myself out of this strange nightmare. "If they were here, then their leader would be standing between you and me, his talons ready to tear you apart. What have you done with him?"

"Nothing at all," the guard said. "Come, now. The High King would like a word with you."

"I will not speak to the High King under any circumstances," I growled. "Tell him so."

"I'm afraid you have little choice in the matter, Highness."

My jaw tensed, rage boiling in my veins. "Do *not* call me that."

Despite my protestations, they were still moving toward me.

Out of desperation, I raised my hands higher, sealed my eyes shut, and called forth creatures of shadow, as I had done in the Blood Trials—a trick my mother had apparently mastered many years ago.

In my mind's eye, feral beasts rose up around me—a small lion, a bear, a wolf—each of them made of light itself. I opened my eyes to watch the summoned creatures stalk toward the Lightbloods, snarling and baring their teeth.

"Attack!" I commanded silently.

But before they could do my bidding, a tall, powerful figure emerged from the swirling smoke, stroking a hand easily through the air.

My Light-Beasts vanished, as did the smoke—and Kazimir grinned, his teeth gleaming white in the darkness.

For the second time, he had decimated my conjured forces.

Bastard.

"Enough, Daughter. You've enjoyed a few days and nights with your lover. I'm afraid that was all I could afford to grant you. But now, it's time we moved on."

"What have you done with Mithraan and his crew?" I asked. "Where *are* they?"

"As my guards said, they're alive and well. And believe it or not, they are on the Tírian ship, going about their business. In fact, Lord Mithraan is sleeping in the bed you just left."

"No, he isn't. I reached for him—he wasn't there. I..."

Kazimir lowered his chin and gave me a dubious look. "You *do* realize I can make you see what I *wish* for you to see, do you not? I can take your mind in hand and move it this way and that, bending your thoughts to suit my needs. You will eventually learn to combat such a simple spell, of course. But until you have honed your Immortal mind into something useful, you are still malleable, suggestible. A mental weakling."

As if Kazimir were trying to prove his words true, a fierce jolt of piercing pain shot through my head. I pressed my palms to my temples and let out a wail of agony.

The pain passed after a few seconds, but his point was taken.

"I can break you, Daughter. You and anyone you love. Always remember that."

"Did Thalanir help you?" I asked in an almost feral growl. "Did you pay him to spy on Mithraan? To turn me over to you?"

"Thalanir?" the High King asked. "I'm afraid I don't know any Fae by that name."

I glared at him, frustratingly unsure whether or not he was telling anything remotely close to the truth. But I told myself not to trust the sell-blade if ever I should see him again. Someone—or some*thing*—had brought Kazimir across the sea to our exact location—and I knew already that Thalanir could be bought for the right price. He'd confessed as much, after all.

"This is a cruel joke," I hissed. "If Mithraan were here on the ship, he would strike you down. He would not simply sleep the night away. You've put him somewhere—below deck, perhaps..."

"You're absolutely correct," Kazimir said. "Your Tírian would certainly try to take me down—of that, I have no doubt. But you give the High Lord far too much credit, and me far too little. Mithraan *is* sound asleep, I promise you. It is simply that you are too far from him to feel the absolute truth of it."

Scowling, I turned and raced back toward the cabin. I would thrust the door open and confirm for myself that I had not gone mad. I would prove Kazimir was lying through his sparkling white teeth...for all the good it would do me.

But as I raced toward the door, a sickening feeling overtook me.

CHAPTER NINE

THE DOOR that stood open before me was nauseatingly familiar —but it was no Tírian design. And when I glanced up to examine the ship's sails, it was the sigil of a flaming sword that met my eyes.

Not a silver eagle.

As bile churned in my stomach, I recognized the entrance to the cabin where I'd been imprisoned when I had first awoken after the Blood Trials—the cabin on Kazimir's ship.

Letting out a cry of rage and frustration combined, I scrambled toward the railing and watched helplessly as the thick mist parted, revealing open sea. Flat and calm, it stretched as far as the eye could see.

There was no sign of Mithraan's ship. No sign of the vessel where I'd spent the last few days in a state of happiness and peace.

"No," I whispered, letting the railing go and racing first to the prow, then the stern, sweat beading my brow. I hunted everywhere, my eyes scanning the horizon, but there was no sign of the Tírian ship.

There was *nothing* on the horizon, in fact, except...

Oh, gods.

A large mass of land rose up in the distance—one with jagged white cliffs, the sea crashing in waves against its coastline.

I had never seen Aetherion. But I knew without asking that I was now staring directly at it.

"Do you really think, Daughter, that I would have allowed a Tírian lord to steal my eldest child from me and sail back to Kalemnar with nary a struggle? Do you think me as weak as that, after what I did at the Blood Trials?"

I spun around to stare daggers at Kazimir, who let out a laugh. "I'm sure Lord Mithraan was very pleased with himself, thinking he'd accomplished such a momentous coup. But he is not so talented as he suspects. In your three days of jolly holiday, you were never more than a few miles from Aetherion."

"But..." I said. "We *left* you. I saw how fast we were moving. We were far from here, across the sea. Some of your Fae nearly died trying to stop us!"

Even as I spoke the words, I knew them to be false. Mithraan and I had both expressed our doubts, our worries that we were living a beautiful, precarious dream—one that was ready to crash down upon us at any moment.

"My Fae, nearly die?" he asked with a smile. "Or did you simply imagine such a thing?"

I scowled, my palms twisting into such tight fists that my nails dug like sharp, vicious crescents into my flesh, cutting into it as if to prove I was still alive.

"If you're telling the truth," I growled almost under my breath, "then why didn't you stop Mithraan taking me in the first place? Why play this game at all?"

Kazimir's face softened temporarily, just enough so that he almost looked sympathetic. But in an instant, his eyes had hardened again, his features unreadable.

"It may surprise you to find I'm not entirely immune to empathy," he replied dryly. "And not entirely cruel. You wished more than anything to know if Mithraan was still living, and something told me you would not rest easy until you knew. So I allowed you the truth—that he is very much alive. I promise you, *he* was not an illusion, nor was anything that occurred on his ship during your time together."

My cheeks burned as he spoke the words. I didn't wish to know if he was aware of all that had occurred between Mithraan and me during my time on the ship. I couldn't bear the thought, in fact.

"However," Kazimir continued, "I'm afraid he and his crew are now battling a fierce storm out at sea—one that will rapidly push their ship perilously close to Kalemnar's shores. They will not find the winds blowing in their favor anytime soon. For the time being, at least, you are mine...Daughter."

I scowled at Kazimir, enraged almost beyond words. To allow me a taste of the life I might have had, then snatch it away from me—it seemed one of the greatest tortures he could have chosen to inflict.

"Why can't you just leave me be?" I cried, tears staining my cheeks as I succumbed to my ire. "I was happy. I was going home. Why is it so damned important to you that I end up in Aetherion? You may be my father by blood, but you don't know me. You don't even *like* me, for the gods' sake."

He shook his head, clicking his tongue in mock compassion. "Come now, your arrival in Aetherion is not so important to me as it is to *you*, my dear," he said, his voice a slow-working poison in my mind. "When you see what awaits you—the fate that is calling to you—you will understand. Of that, you have my word."

"Just let me go," I said quietly, wishing I possessed Prince Corym's and Kazimir's own capacity to bend minds. If only I could make him obey me and set me free... "Let me leave. I want—"

"Do you think for a moment that I care what you want, Daughter?" he hissed. "I allowed the Tírian to defile you for a few days. I gave you what you desired. Perhaps you would do well to consider what *I* want, for a change. For years, I held back and waited while you were raised by a mortal man. I soothed myself with the knowledge that you would one day return to your rightful home—the kingdom you will one day rule if the gods be good. But ruling is a duty—not a privilege granted to those who wish for it. And so, your days of doing as you please have come to an end. The Tírian ship will not come for us again —and I will not release you, however you may try and manipulate me."

Something in me snapped with those words. Any fear that I had, any sorrow, was gone.

All I felt now was a rage so profound that my skin seemed to have caught fire.

"I do not want anything to do with your realm. I do not wish to rule Aetherion or any other kingdom. You have stolen me—snatched me away from the life I was meant to live—just as you did to my mother so many years ago—and I hate you for it. There is nothing you could say or do to change that."

For a moment, he merely stared at me. Then he said, his voice uncharacteristically gentle, "I did not snatch your mother away. If you only knew how much she wished to come with me—how much she begged me to take her to Aetherion, to leave her life behind...you might not think so ill of me."

"Liar!" I bellowed. "I've seen her memories. I know what you are—you're cruel and selfish. That much is clear, whatever lies you tell."

"Your mother's memories are not reality!" Kazimir snarled.

"And though you might convince yourself that she is an angel, believe me when I tell you she—"

He stopped himself, running a frustrated hand through his white hair and pushing out an angry breath.

"You—not my mother—have stolen my life from me," I growled.

Kazimir snickered. "*Life?*" he repeated as though the word were foul on his tongue. "You would have died, had I not extracted you from your little 'battle' in the Blood Trials. Corym was going to kill your Mithraan—and he would have taken *your* life, too, and your Gifts—the Gifts of Lightblood and Tírians alike. If you think for a moment that I would have allowed that mortal bastard to steal away what the gods granted you—what your mother and I gave you—"

I laughed—a clipped, derisive snicker. "Corym wouldn't have killed me. At the worst, he would have taken me for his wife so that our children would inherit both our Gifts. But he would not have murdered me in front of many witnesses for his own purposes."

"You're wrong. He would have done it in a heartbeat, Daughter. Do not forget—Corym's father rules Kalemnar. He can alter the Trials' rules anytime he likes—which means he could easily have sliced your head from your shoulders and commanded the Taker to extract every last one of your Blood-Gifts."

I wanted to reply, to tell him he was wrong...but the truth was, I couldn't come up with a single counter-argument. King Caedmon had proven himself a liar, as had Corym. It was possible they were even less trustworthy than Kazimir himself.

"Perhaps you recall that Corym has an eye for your sister, Leta," Kazimir said. "He is quite taken with her, in fact. And she with him. He has been planning for some time to take her as his bride."

At that, I laughed. "Another lie. Leta has hardly spent any time in his presence. She doesn't know him in the least. Besides, by now, she's probably seen his true nature. If she watched the final battle—if she heard the vicious things Corym said—"

But then I remembered what Khiral had said—that, although the audience could see the battle unfolding, they couldn't hear what we were saying. For all they knew, Corym was trying to save me from the evil Mithraan.

Leta might have perceived an entirely different battle from the one I was actually part of.

"I've seen enough of Leta to know she is weak in the presence of powerful men," Kazimir said. "And you seem to be forgetting that Corym is a talented mind-bender. Do you not think he is able to work his influence on your sister, particularly if she believes her older sibling has run off with a Fae lover and deserted her?"

I was about to protest again when a feeling of roiling sickness overtook me. Leta *might*, in fact, be easily swayed—especially if she thought Mithraan and I had fled together. If she didn't know the truth about Corym, about the Trials...she might think I had simply broken down and fled.

In her mind, I was her last living family member. I was all she had.

She didn't know Kazimir was our father...

She didn't know he had taken me.

"She will be heartbroken by now, given your abandonment," Kazimir said, clicking his tongue mournfully. "In fact, why don't we see for ourselves how she's faring?"

CHAPTER TEN

Kazimir pulled a stone from his pocket—flat, perfectly smooth and white, though unremarkable in almost every other way.

"Take it," he said, handing it to me. "It's a Seeing Stone. Seek her out."

"What do you mean?" I asked in a sullen drone. I was so angry that I could barely see his face in front of me, let alone imagine seeing Leta from all the way across the sea.

But the thought of laying my eyes on my sister, if only in my mind's eye—of seeing her beautiful face somewhere out there, and knowing she was safe—it was enough to abate my rage, if only briefly.

"The stone is a means to find Leta. It will allow you temporary access to your sister. Command it, and it will obey."

I wondered for a moment if it was a trick—some cruel joke he was playing for his own entertainment. But I closed my eyes and clenched my hand around the stone, trying desperately to picture Leta in my mind.

Where is she? I asked silently. *Show me.*

At first, the vision only came to me in bits and pieces, like a dream that wasn't entirely sure of itself.

I saw a wisp of a green dress, then a flash of a face. And then, a mound of twisting, curling red hair.

Leta was standing in a courtyard I recognized, in the palace at Domignon—a sight that only confirmed what Mithraan and the others had told me.

My sister was being held there by Caedmon and Corym. Whether she believed it was her choice or not, the fact remained that she was, without a doubt, a prisoner between their walls.

But what was even worse was the sadness in her face. Tears stained her cheeks. Her shoulders slumped uncharacteristically. She looked heartbroken, and I could only guess why.

As I watched, someone walked toward her—a young man, tall, broad-shouldered. His own cheeks were accented with angry, deep red slashes—the vicious wounds Mithraan had inflicted on him during the final battle of the Blood Trials.

Corym. Hatred heated my blood. *You vile, lying bastard.*

He was no longer quite so fresh-faced as he had once been, though admittedly, he was still handsome. He looked like a man who had been to war and survived only to come out the other end jaded and bitter—a man scarred by his enemy, weakened by his insecurities, and fueled by rage.

He walked up to Leta and laid a hand gently on her shoulder, lowering his chin as he spoke.

"My Lady," he said softly. "Please, don't be so sad."

I shuddered to hear his voice. That awful voice—one that had at times soothed me, charmed me, consoled me—now felt like sand being rubbed into an open wound. How had I ever thought him kind? How had I not seen him for what he was—a manipulative, mind-bending ass?

"Why did she desert us?" Leta lamented. "Why would Lyrinn leave like that? I never got to say good-bye—and *you*—you poor thing—"

She looked up into his eyes with genuine tenderness that made me want to scream a warning at her.

"I was taken in by her charms," he said sadly. "I was deceived, as was everyone. I didn't know she would run off with the Fae lord. Who could have guessed your sister was so...corrupt?"

I suppressed my ire just enough to keep watching, though I wanted to fling the stone far from me, to scream, to rant.

"Lyrinn is not one to be impulsive," Leta lamented. "It's not in her nature. It doesn't make any sense."

"People do strange things for love," Corym said with a shrug. "It's one of the world's harsher truths. You're young yet —but you will learn this hard lesson one day."

People, he'd said. Of course. As far as Leta was concerned, I was still her human—*mortal*—sister. She didn't know the truth about our bloodline. She had no idea her mother was a Fae, or that her father was Aetherion's High King.

She didn't yet understand what blood flowed through her own veins, and when she learned of it, she would be as shocked as I was. Leta would soon face her Coming of Age, just as I had, and it would be a horror unless I could be there to hold her hand.

Just as Mithraan had done to ease the pain of my own transition.

She has no one, I thought. *No one to guide her. To explain what will happen and the pain of it.*

"My sister would never leave her family behind," Leta said again. "Is she so love-sick over the Fae that she can't see reason? How can she be? How—"

I felt the pain in her voice like a blade in my side. Leta had always worn a shield of iron around her heart, and seldom had I ever seen her reveal her vulnerability. To see her like this—

wounded and pained by what she perceived as emotional mutiny on my part—destroyed me.

The prince stepped closer and, to my horror, wrapped his arms around her, pulling her tight to his chest. She wept, holding him close—something I had only ever seen her do with our father.

Our *true* father. The blacksmith in Dúnbar—the man known only as Martel.

"Let me go to her," I pleaded, turning to Kazimir. "Turn the ship around, and I'll beg her to come with us back to Aetherion. Please—if there is any goodness in you at all, you'll let me speak to my sister. I cannot stand watching her with him. She can't stay there."

"You have no choice in the matter, I'm afraid," Kazimir said coldly. "She must stay in Kalemnar for now. But don't worry, my dear. You both have many lifetimes ahead of you, and I have no doubt that you will find your way back to one another one day. In the meantime, however..."

He held out a hand, silently demanding the return of his precious white stone. I wanted so badly to hold onto it, to preserve my tenuous connection to Leta. But I wasn't certain I could stand to watch anymore, to witness her descent into a pit of self-destruction at the hands of the devious prince.

"Come, now. There's something you and I must do," he said.

I handed him the stone and held back tears as I half-whispered, "You're not intending to hurt Mithraan, are you?"

"I am not intending to go anywhere near Mithraan," Kazimir said. "He is a free Fae—I told you as much."

Kazimir reached a hand out and pressed it to my cheek. "Take comfort in the knowledge that you will soon be home, Daughter," he said quietly. "Your true home—one where you have always belonged. I understand your fear, and even your anger. But please know that this is for the best...for everyone."

Though I wanted to flinch away from him, his touch was gentle and strangely comforting. Against my will, I found myself sinking into the sensation. My body seemed to go limp, tumbling to the floor as though my muscles had surrendered to a force beyond my control.

For the second time in recent memory, my mind, twisted into a raging storm, emptied, and the world fell into bleak darkness.

CHAPTER ELEVEN

MITHRAAN'S FAMILIAR, beautiful voice floated through my mind.

"Lyrinn," he breathed softly. "*Vaelan...*"

I could feel his fingers slipping down my neck, slowly, gently caressing me into consciousness.

It was just a dream, I told myself. *Kazimir—the smoke, the ship, my vision of Leta—it was all a dream. All part of the same horrific nightmare that had begun with the Elar...but it's over now.*

I reached an arm out, straining for Mithraan, seeking him in the depths of the inky darkness surrounding me.

"Are you there?" I asked, my voice muffled, sleepy. "Am I—"

I narrowed my eyes, eager to find his exquisite face, to discover that my torment was truly over.

But when I shot up, expectant and blissful, Mithraan was nowhere to be seen. The air smelled of flowers and chocolate, fruit and pastry. For the first time in days, the world felt solid beneath me, the gentle rocking of the sea at an end.

I was no longer aboard a ship but lying in an enormous room with white plaster walls inlaid with swirling silver patterns reminiscent of snaking ivy. To one side of the chamber was a set of glass doors that appeared to lead out to a small marble terrace. The ceiling was impossibly high, and the bed impossibly broad.

There was no denying that my surroundings were sumptuous, luxurious. But I knew without thinking twice that this was not Kalemnar. It was not Tíria, where I had so wished to end up.

I had gone from Kazimir's ship to an exquisite, pristine prison cell.

Hardly an improvement.

"What is this place?" I moaned, the opulence of my sleeping quarters doing little to quell the feeling of loss that was overtaking me more violently with each passing second.

Hearing the soft shuffling of feet, I turned toward the glass doors only to see Kazimir stepping into view from the terrace, an awful smile rippling along his lips.

"You're in Thera, my girl. The royal palace in Aethos, capital city of the realm. You're home at last, on the southeast coast of your true homeland."

A sob rose up in my chest.

So far from Kalemnar. From Mithraan. From Leta. And the last place in the world I had ever wished to end up.

Mithraan's ship had not caught up to us this time, not that it mattered.

Even if it had, I understood now that Kazimir had too many tricks up his sleeve. My blood-father had teased me with the cruelest gift—a brief, sweet taste of a life with Mithraan that would never come to be.

I was impossibly far from home and from those I loved. There was little hope that I would ever see Mithraan or Leta again. An army of powerful Lightbloods now separated us, and the High King of Aetherion—one of the most powerful Immortals in all the kingdoms of the world—would use all his substantial strength to ensure that I would never again feel the touch of Mithraan's lips.

"What do you think of your quarters?" Kazimir asked as if he hadn't just destroyed my life, his eyes roving about the bed chamber. "Beautiful, no?"

Rage simmered in my veins. This monster had stolen me, just as he had stolen my mother so many years ago. *Selfish, arrogant bastard, convinced that he has the right to the ownership of women.*

I will kill him for this.

My hope had faded to nothing.

I had nothing left to lose by speaking my mind.

"What gives you any right to bring me here, you prick?" I asked, my ire barely contained in my chest.

Not that the question needed to be asked. Kazimir was a purveyor of chaos. It was he who had severed Tíria from Kalemnar's mortal lands for so long. It was Kazimir who had unleashed the poisonous mist known as the *Breath of the Fae* to keep our people separate.

It was Kazimir's magic that had torn the souls from so many Fae and turned them into the creatures of shadow and bone known as Grimpers. And it was Kazimir who had murdered the two Fae Champions in the last Blood Trials a thousand years ago.

It was Kazimir who was crushing my soul now.

"Your bloodline has a history," he said by apparent way of explanation, ignoring my insult. "One that is rich far beyond your imagining. It is one that you have only barely tapped into —and that will reveal to you a world you never dreamed of. In Kalemnar, you would never have lived up to your full potential, Lyrinn—you couldn't have. But in this land, you will flourish as you were always meant to. Your Gifts will be revealed to their fullest extent, and with my guidance, you will come to see what you're made of." He began to pace the room slowly, eyeing this corner and that as though searching for some unseen set of

eyes. "I will ensure that you receive the instruction you need—
and one day, you will thank me for it."

"I could not possibly care less about my so-called *potential*,"
I retorted. "I'm not ambitious, nor have I ever been. I never
wanted to participate in the Blood Trials, to marry a prince.
Never wanted any of this. I only want M—"

I want Mithraan.

But why share my innermost desires with this beast of a
Fae? He didn't deserve an ounce of my mind, of my soul.

He deserved only death.

But perhaps death would be too easy and light a sentence.

I wished for Kazimir to be tortured for eternity, so he could
experience one *millionth* of what he had inflicted on others.

"You wish for your sister, of course," Kazimir said with a
dose of false kindness. "And the other one, too—that vile
Tírian. Well, I'm afraid he's in Kalemnar by now, and honestly,
he is most likely moving on with his life. He knows better than
to try and bring an army of his ilk to my shores."

"And if he did come to Aetherion?" I asked, my jaw clenching. "What would you do to him if he landed on your precious
shores?"

I expected Kazimir to revel in his answer, to give me a
sadistic retort about all the ways he would torture Mithraan.
But instead, he simply said, "I would treat him with the respect
he deserves, of course."

My flesh burned with his judgment—his vile, sexist scrutiny. It was no business of his what I did with my body—no
business of his whether I chose to give myself to my mate.
Because that was what Mithraan was—my *mate*. I felt the bond
as acutely as I felt my arm, my lungs, the heart beating in my
chest.

"So then, I take it you are intending to trap me here for the
rest of my life?" I spat.

At that, Kazimir finally stopped pacing. His hands rolled into fists at his sides, the tendons in his neck tensing in apparent solidarity with his fingers.

The first time I had laid eyes on the High King—before I knew who he was to me—I had thought him extraordinary. He was one of the most beautiful creatures I had ever seen, with his silver-white hair and bright eyes. He was ageless, yet his face had seemed to contain all the wisdom of the universe. He was cunning, yet had the ability to appear naive at times...as though the world were still new and interesting to him, able to surprise him at every turn.

But even in that first moment, I had known that he possessed a great capacity for cruelty, for hatred. Some part of him felt like a tightly coiled device ready to spring open and explode malice over the entire world.

I could feel that malice growing in the air now—a palpable anger, an utter hatred for this world and all its miserable inhab-itants—and I couldn't help but wonder if that hatred included his own people.

Perhaps Kazimir had lived too many years. Perhaps he'd seen too many cruel beings, too much death. Perhaps after all, there was some explanation for his vileness.

Or else I was trying to make excuses for him—because I couldn't fathom the notion that my father by blood was simply evil.

"You are not a prisoner here, Lyrinn," he said quietly, releasing his fists, his shoulders relaxing slightly as he turned to look at me. His eyes flared slightly, reminiscent of Mithraan's when he was half-divulging a secret to me, opening his mind to mine. "But I do ask that you give Aetherion a chance. See the place a little; experience it before you judge. Look out over the city of Aethos and rejoice in its beauty. Explore the palace. I promise you, before this day is through, you will be very glad to have come—and your desire to flee will fade."

"Unless you tear my heart from my chest, that desire will never fade," I replied, my voice seething. "Even if Aetherion is the loveliest place in the world, it will remain vile to me so long as you rule the lands between its borders. Everyone I love is far from here, or dead—and it's your fault. All of it."

"*Love*," he repeated with a sort of half-amused smirk. "Ah, but I am sorry for you, Lyrinn, that you feel that cursed emotion with such acuteness. It is a weakness—a scourge thrust upon inferior beings. I had hoped that your Coming of Age would harden you against such mortal fragility."

Immediately, I regretted confessing the emotion. It was folly to reveal vulnerability to this brutal being. Love, in his eyes, rendered me pathetic...and the last thing I wanted to seem was weak in the eyes of one such as Kazimir.

He would feed off my pain like a parasite.

But to my surprise, he didn't look at me with disdain. Instead, he slipped toward me and seated himself on the edge of the bed as I pressed myself back against the headboard. "Despise me all you like, but I'm telling you now that not *all* those you love are in Kalemnar." He spoke in as gentle a tone as he could muster. "For now, you will need to trust me on that front."

Against my will, I let out a quiet laugh. "Trust *you*," I said. "Do you know how ridiculous you sound when you say those words, after all you've done to me? I could never trust you, not even if you kept me here for ten thousand years."

The High King's eyes flared again, and, moving toward me faster than I could register, he raised a hand as though to strike me.

I raised my chin and challenged him with a glare, wondering if my irises, too, had brightened to meet his rage.

Do it.

Strike me.

I'll wear my bruises with pride. I'll walk the halls of your palace and show your servants what kind of a beast you really are.

But instead of following through, he lowered his hand. No doubt he could do far worse to me than a mere slap—after all, his cruel magic and twisted manipulation were worse than any beating I could have sustained.

Worse even, in some ways, than death.

With a deep breath of exasperation, Kazimir rose to his feet and made his way to the door.

"One of my servants will arrive soon to show you around the palace a little," he said, his back to me. "You will wish to flee, but trust me when I tell you you won't get far. And after today, you won't want to. In the meantime, you're free to explore."

"What's happening today?" I asked, though I knew the question was pointless. Short of bringing both Mithraan and Leta to Aetherion to live by my side, there was nothing that could possibly make me want to stay in this place.

Kazimir turned to face me, one hand gripping the door handle. "I will be presenting you with a gift," he said. "One that will bring a smile to that beautiful, sullen face, and make you realize you have no desire ever to leave this realm—whatever you may tell yourself at this moment."

With that, he left, closing the door behind him.

CHAPTER TWELVE

WHEN KAZIMIR HAD LEFT, I leapt out of bed and rushed to the door, grabbing the handle with all my strength and pulling.

It wouldn't budge under my touch.

What a surprise.

I am not, in fact, free to explore.

With an exasperated groan, I strode over to a tall wooden wardrobe that sat against the far wall and opened it to discover a series of white garments of various styles—dresses, tunics, cloaks, trousers, anything I could desire—but oddly, no color to be seen. I wondered if the Lightbloods traditionally dressed in white while at home in Aetherion, though Kazimir himself did not.

Perhaps someone was trying to render me conspicuous as I wandered the palace halls. The pristine princess, as pure as a perfect flake of unmarred snow.

After a quick sponge bath using the ewer and bowl sitting on the dresser, I selected a pair of linen trousers and a tunic, slipping them on then studying myself in the full-length mirror that stood against the wall next to the window.

My eyes looked unusually bright, and I wondered if it was

this land that had made them so, or simply a reaction to my Coming of Age and all that had occurred since the night when I had turned nineteen.

More shocking, though, was that my hair, dark and thick, was streaked with gleaming strands of silver. Smooth and shiny, they intermingled with the rest of my hair like vines encroaching on other vegetation.

I had heard that young Lightbloods were often born with dark hair which turned white over time. I was beginning to look like one of them—to look like Kazimir's offspring.

And I hated it.

My first instinct told me to tear the hairs out and trample them into the floor. They were nothing but marks of the Fae who had imprisoned my mother. Of all the lies Leta and I had been told growing up—of a cruelty inflicted so harshly upon Tíria.

But they were also marks of strength, I told myself ruefully.

Everyone claimed the Lightbloods were powerful, and after all, my greatest hope of escaping this damned place was to overpower the High King—though I had no idea how I could ever hope to accomplish such a thing.

I twisted a few of the silver strands of hair around my fingers, my emotions doing battle inside me. I didn't hate the hair itself; it was actually quite beautiful. What I despised was the thought that Kazimir was getting his wish. I was becoming a Lightblood, through and through.

"Not exactly a badge I can wear with pride," I said under my breath as I pulled my hair back and wove it into a braid, exposing the twisting black patterns that now adorned my neck where deep, angry scars once lay. I was relieved, at least, to feel at liberty to display my tipped ears, which had shown themselves for the first time when Mithraan had healed me in the Taker's Lair.

In Aetherion, at least, there was no need to conceal my true nature. For the first time in my life, I was beginning to feel comfortable within the confines of my own skin.

Just as I finished dressing, a knock sounded at the door. Before I'd had a chance to react, a female Fae with long white hair, large eyes, and a pretty smile stepped into the room. She wore a silver dress and matching shoes that clicked on the marble floor as she moved. Her skin was bronze, her eyes light gray, and though instinct told me to distrust her for being a Lightblood, there was something in her face that I immediately liked.

"Princess Lyrinn," she said. "How nice to make your acquaintance."

The words were gentle, even warm. Yet they collided with my mind like a blunt weapon.

Princess. Lyrinn.

I cringed to hear the title spoken aloud.

"I'm Riah," the Fae continued when I said nothing. "I'm hoping to get to know you in the coming days, and eventually to show you around the city of Aethos. But for now, the High King has sent me to guide you around the palace and bring you to the dining chamber."

"And what if I don't wish to accompany you?" I asked, my tone icy.

With a shrug, she replied, "You don't need to come with me, of course. You can sit and stew in your room for as long as you like." Peering over my shoulder at the largely empty chamber, she added, "But I'd recommend you get to know me a little before you decide I'm unworthy of your company. I can be quite a pleasant companion, and a loyal friend. Perhaps one day you and I could pop into the city for a pint, even."

I stared at her, surprised at the familiarity in her tone and her words. Against every effort to the contrary, I found myself smiling slightly. I cursed her for putting me at ease—the last thing I wanted was to enjoy the company of any Lightblood.

But I supposed if I had to be subjected to one of their kind, it may as well be one who understood my enjoyment of ale.

"Meanwhile," she continued, "I should probably tell you…"

With that, she vanished into the air.

"…that the palace is very beautiful," her voice continued from somewhere behind me.

I spun around to realize she had somehow moved to the other side of the chamber, her movement so quick that I hadn't registered it. She was standing by the doors leading to the terrace, looking out at the view.

I found myself bracing for a conflict, my mind spinning as I searched for a spell to cast in self-defense in case she was planning to attack. Someone so quick was a danger, surely.

As it turned out, there was no need to concern myself.

"I didn't mean to frighten you," Riah half-whispered, stepping toward me with her chin low. "It's only that this view is one of the loveliest in the world. Even so, Highness, you would be missing out if you simply stayed in your room. So please— just let me show you around a little. Instead of telling yourself this palace is a prison, try and think of your time here as a holiday away from home. Who knows? Perhaps one day, Aetherion will begin to *feel* like a second home."

"That will never happen," I snapped, though my voice was rapidly losing its hostility. Riah was proving quite interesting, not to mention a much-needed calming presence.

"Never say never," she replied with a shimmering laugh, then turned back to face the glass doors. She pulled them open, gesturing to the terrace. I realized as she did so that I had not yet taken the time to look upon the land that was holding me prisoner with such a fierce, hostile grip.

"Come on," she urged. "Take a look. Surely even you can admit it's lovely."

Hesitant, I stepped toward her and peered out at the palace grounds below—sweeping gardens, elegant courtyards—and the scenery beyond.

All around us, I could see the white marble fortifications of the castle. Long, high walls enclosed the grounds. Delicate and strong at once, narrow watch-towers were carved with interlacing patterns of stone that met in pinnacles pointing impossibly skyward. The structures seemed to grow like rooted vines from the ground itself, tall enough almost to reach the clouds.

In the distance beyond the palace grounds were vast green fields dotted with trees blossoming with flowers of every color imaginable: purple, red, blue, pink, orange, yellow...

Riah was right. It was just about the most beautiful place I had ever seen.

But I told myself with a grimace not to allow it to seduce me. This place was toxic. Poison, trying to drive its way into my veins and to weaken me, inch by inch, until I fell for its charms.

"Thank the gods Aetherion's south is still intact," Riah said, her voice tinged with gloom. "Kazimir has shielded us from the rot that has festered in so many other parts of our lands."

"Rot?" I asked. "What do you mean? I was under the impression that Aetherion was perfection—or was that another lie on the High King's part?"

Riah sighed, seeming to ignore my quiet accusation. "It *was* perfection. Once, long ago. But something happened many years ago to destroy forests and valleys, entire towns. Some say it was the Elar—that she did it out of vengeance for a wrong committed against her. But...well, we all have our theories."

My vivid nightmare flashed through my mind. If the Elar was real, there was no question that she was vengeful, malicious. A murderer of innocents.

"Did you know," Riah said, "that the central part of Aetherion is known now as the Barren Lands? They say nothing grows there—not even birds dwell in those lands anymore."

I stared at her, conflicted. Part of me wanted her to explain, to expand. What had happened to destroy entire swathes of land, and why had Kazimir not retaliated, if indeed it was the Elar who had torn Aetherion apart?

But another part railed against the idea of showing an ounce of interest in this place. Why should I care, after all, if it fell to pieces, or sank into the sea? I hated everything about it. This land and its borders were keeping me from Mithraan, from Leta...

No. It wasn't the land that was holding me.

It was my bastard of a so-called "father."

"Look," Riah said, sensing my growing irritation. "I meant what I said. You'll be bored to tears in this chamber after a matter of mere hours. Besides which, there's something you need to see, and it's at the opposite end of the palace. It would be best if you accompanied me."

At that, I narrowed my eyes. "What if I should refuse? Will the High King kill me? Torture me? He's already doing the former slowly and the latter very effectively."

Riah pursed her lips, then let out a quiet, frustrated chuckle. "If I may offer you some advice..." She paused, waiting for some kind of reaction.

When I nodded, she continued.

"Whether you like it or not, it is in your best interest to please your father while you're his guest."

"I believe you mean *prisoner*."

"Fine, then. Prisoner. I know he can be sharp-tongued, but I speak from many years' experience when I tell you he *is* a fair and good leader."

When I looked like I was about to laugh, she added, "Oh,

I'm the first to admit he enjoys bluster and intimidation. He likes wielding threats as a weapon, just as all leaders do. But he is not nearly so evil as he often pretends to be. If he sees you putting forth an effort, I can assure you he will mirror it and do his best to keep you content. After all, there is a reason he remains High King after so long on the throne—despite the events that ravaged our lands. He is strong—and he has given much of his strength to our Fae through many hardships. It may be difficult for you to believe, but for the most part, he is very well-respected in Aetherion."

I threw her a dubious glance. *For the most part. I wonder who, exactly. Who doesn't respect him?*

I'd love to have a drink with them.

I searched her face, but I could feel nothing malicious in her. Even if she was deceiving me, I could not find my way past the clear façade of friendliness. She felt *good*—which I had long assumed was an impossibility for a Lightblood.

Perhaps, I confessed to myself, I was wrong about their kind. Perhaps my blood-father did not represent every one of them. After all, the Lightbloods on Kazimir's ship had not seemed like monsters.

Then again, it wasn't as if I'd managed to have a conversation with a single one of them.

I spoke calmly, though my quiet ire was growing with each passing moment. "I can only assume that by 'respected,' you mean Kazimir is 'feared' in this land."

"There is little difference," Riah replied with another shrug. "Fear, in small doses, is an effective means of governance. If the subjects do not fear their sovereign, the likelihood of rebellion grows. Trust me when I tell you High King Kazimir has learned that particular lesson the hard way. He understands how and when to wield his power—and when to sit back and observe."

I wondered what she meant when she said he had learned

the lesson the hard way, but chose not to ask. I had no desire to feel an ounce of empathy toward the Fae that had brought havoc crashing down on my life and made such a concerted effort to destroy my happiness.

With an exhalation of defeat, I finally gave in.

"Fine, let's go," I said. "I may as well have a look around before I persuade the High King to let me leave."

Riah laughed, stepping lightly toward the door. "No one persuades the High King. And no one leaves Aetherion unless it is with his blessing. But perhaps one day, Princess...you will give him a reason to let you go."

CHAPTER THIRTEEN

RIAH GUIDED me out the door into a broad, bright hallway adorned with works of art that hung along its walls in a series of exquisite gilt frames. As we strode along, my eyes caught depictions of Lightbloods casting spells of pure light, summoning objects, weapons, and creatures from thin air, fighting battles against mortals and beasts alike.

One of the works—a large painting, at least eight feet across —showed a small army of Lightblood doing battle next to a castle that looked eerily familiar.

"Is that...is that Fairholme, in Tíria?" I asked, stopping to examine the image. I had spent time Mithraan's home, which now lay in ruins atop the Onyx Rise. I had eaten and slept between the half-destroyed castle walls.

But never had I seen it whole, except via an illusion cast by Mithraan's extraordinary mind.

"It is, yes." Riah nodded, stepping up next to me. "This was a battle fought many centuries ago, when High King Kazimir was but a boy."

Soaring in the sky above the castle was a flying beast, an

eagle or other bird of prey seeking to take down its foes, and I wondered if it was one of Mithraan's ancestors.

But a tremor of apprehension worked its way under my skin as I looked closer, making out the vague, shadowy shape of a female Fae attached to those powerful wings. I recognized the creature I'd seen in my dreams.

Except that this version of her looked...different. She wore a gown of rich emerald green, and rather than silver and red, her wings were the same deep purple as the grapes used in Castelle for wine-making.

"That is the Elar, in case you wondered what she looked like," Riah said, following my gaze.

"Was she really there?" I asked, knowing the question likely sounded naive. There was a long history between the Lightbloods and Tíria that I could not begin to comprehend. One that stretched for thousands upon thousands of years. But never had I heard of a flying quasi-goddess taking part in their battles. "I mean, is she even real?"

"I am not exactly a follower of the Order," Riah said quietly. "Whether she's real or not, I can't say—but I will tell you, there are many who believe she is. They say she is the reason Lightbloods and Tírians despise one another—that she drove a wedge between our realms many thousands of years ago. Some say our two lands were once connected, but that the Elar split them and drove the sea between them to keep our kinds apart—that she will never let us be allies, so long as she lives."

At that, I let out a quiet laugh, and my fear seemed to fade to nothing. Nightmarish creature or not, the Elar was beginning to sound like every other fictional invention of disgruntled rulers.

"A winged terror sounds like a convenient excuse for Fae to murder one another and call it war," I said with a snicker.

"Blaming a woman for all the world's ills is hardly a new concept, so I don't know why it surprises me in the least."

"Myths are often used to excuse the poor choices of men and Fae," Riah concurred. "Perhaps the Elar is nothing but a conjured scapegoat for every war, every bad decision ever made by High Fae Lords. Who knows? It's not like anyone I know personally has seen her in the flesh." She looked hesitant for a moment before adding, "Forgive me for saying so, but you really don't know much about our kind, do you?"

My eyes still locked on the painting, I shook my head. "I was raised human—mortal," I told her, trying my best not to sound apologetic. "Those words sound so bizarre to me now, I'll confess. But the truth is, I still *feel* human, more or less. It's difficult for me to absorb what I am at this point, and I'll admit I don't know a great deal about the Fae and their history. Most of what I learned as a child turned out to be lies meant to scare my sister and me into staying far away from Tíria."

Riah turned to face me, drawing my eyes to hers. She smiled kindly when she said, "Let me put it simply, Princess. What you are is, well, a miracle. Lightbloods and Tírians have long been forbidden from bonding—be it by the Elar or by those who rule on thrones of stone. I don't know of another hybrid now living, other than you and your sister."

"But why should it matter if I'm a hybrid?" I asked. "Other than the fact that my parents broke some arbitrary law, I mean? I don't see what makes me any more special than any other Fae. I'm *certainly* no miracle."

"Put it this way." Riah glanced around, checking to see if we were being watched. "There is an old prophecy—one that says if a Lightblood High King produces an heir with a Tírian Fae, a tumult will flow over the lands like a massive wave. That a new Elar will rise, and war will overtake all the realms, mortal and Fae alike." She let out a deep breath before adding, "The High

King may not be devout, but I have to wonder if he wants you close to protect you from that prophecy coming to pass."

"That sounds more like a curse than a miracle," I said. "As for Kazimir wishing to protect me—I find that hard to imagine. If it's true, then what about Leta, my sister? He should have brought her here, too."

"I know nothing of your sister, and I can only guess at the High King's motives," Riah said. "But for all his quirks, his Grace does little without reason."

I bit my cheek to force back the choice words I wanted to utter about the High King and his so-called "reason." I'd never seen anything in him but greed, hostility, and a conspicuous lust for power. He didn't strike me as protective of anyone, not even his own kin.

"Do you believe in the prophecy?" I asked, my tone dripping with cynicism. I'd heard many predictions in my life—of cataclysmic events that never came, of wars that never materialized. Most of those so-called predictions were akin to fearmongering and nothing more.

Riah sucked in her lower lip, pensive for a few seconds, then looked me in the eye and said, "I believe there is a reason you're here. I feel it in the air—I feel a change in our realm already. I see goodness in you, Princess—and I feel certain that when the time comes, you will choose to help our people—whatever that may mean."

Her words were kind—complimentary, even. But something in them felt intrusive, too.

Who was she to explain my own nature to me?

"With respect, why would I help those who have done harm to so many?" I asked, my voice tinted with subtle hostility. "Kazimir stole my mother from her home and from her father, High King Rynfael. He decimated Tíria and left it in ruins. It's nothing but the charred remains of a once-beautiful land. Not to mention that he ripped me away from my life only to force me across the sea against my will. I have wished him dead more than once—and I still want him dead." I leveled her with a look of quiet animosity when I added, "So tell me, do you still think me good?"

Riah nodded gravely. "Believe it or not, I understand your ire." She pulled her chin up when she added, "But you don't know everything, Princess. You don't know the good that your father has done. You don't know how *she*..."

She stopped speaking, biting her lip as if to prevent a thought from escaping.

For the first time, the light seemed to leave her eyes. When she finally spoke again, it was with a deep sadness. "The High King was instrumental in Tíria's isolation. But he had his reasons for his actions. Perhaps he was misguided—maybe he should have taken a different path. All I know is that our own land has suffered for a long time, and his Grace is doing what he can to salvage it. He has already sacrificed a great deal in order to keep what is, at best, a tenuous peace between Aetherion's own borders. Look—there are things you will learn soon enough. And perhaps once you begin to learn what has occurred, you'll start to understand your father a little better."

"I'll believe this land suffering when I see it," I sneered. "All I see are blossoming trees and green hills—and I know this is no illusion on Kazimir's part. I can smell the freshness of the air. I can *taste* it. Your land is faring far better than that of the Fae across the sea."

"You have not seen the Barren Lands," Riah insisted. "You have not seen the island to the northeast known only as the *Scald*. Not all of Aetherion is flourishing—and you would be wise to see it before you make assumptions."

"Then perhaps Aetherion is in need of better leadership," I

said icily. "Perhaps a king who is willing to let his lands perish slowly is no king at all."

"And perhaps her Highness would do well to remember that the High King has eyes and ears in all corners of this palace," Riah retorted in a hiss of warning. "I realize you were raised a commoner, but you must watch your tongue, for your own sake. I am more than happy to get to know you—to befriend you, if you'll have me. But I cannot protect you from a Fae as powerful as him. And there are others between these walls— some even more dangerous than the High King himself."

When she began walking again, I accompanied her in stony silence, her words echoing like alarm bells in my mind.

I cannot protect you from him.

An admission of what he was—what he could do to me.

After a time, we passed a narrow alcove, and out of the corner of my eye, I was certain I saw a pair of bright eyes staring out at us from the shadows. But when I turned to look, they were gone.

I glanced at Riah, who kept her eyes fixed on the distance.

"You will find that there are some in this palace who take a keen interest in you, Highness," she said a moment later, her voice softer than before. "Most of us have your best interests at heart."

"You'll forgive me if I tell you I find that hard to believe."

"Understandable," she said as we turned to make our way down a long, broad corridor flanked on either side by floor to ceiling windows. "Tell me something, Princess—are you glad that the Blood Trials never fully concluded? I believe it's the first time in history that no victor was declared."

"You know what happened, then," I said. "You know about the Trials?"

"It's not so much that I heard about the Trials themselves. But I have certain...talents. I am cursed with feeling the emotions of those around me, and I can feel much conflict in you—your heartbreak, your despair. You long to be reunited with those you love—and there is something more, as well. A deeper loss. But somewhere in there, I sense relief, as well. I can only assume where it comes from."

"I'm relieved not to have been forced to wed Prince Corym," I confessed. "Relieved not to have seen more death than I did. But my sister, meanwhile, is still with Corym, who is a vicious monster. And..."

"And there is one other you were forced to leave behind," she said, nodding gravely. "Perhaps he is the first Fae you have loved."

"He is the *only* Fae I have loved—and the only one I can ever imagine loving."

"Come now, you have a long life ahead of you, my dear," Riah said, reaching for my arm and touching me only briefly before pulling away. It seemed as though she realized it was inappropriate to touch a princess uninvited—though something told me she meant no disrespect.

"A long life I wish to spend with him," I replied. "Even if I should live ten thousand years or more, I don't want to waste a single day separated from him. And yet, the High King has seen to it that I have no choice in the matter."

"You will find love again soon enough."

She spoke as though Mithraan was nothing more than a necklace I had lost in the sand—something replaceable, trivial —and I had to grit my teeth to contain my irritation.

For someone seemingly empathetic, she certainly had a way of being dismissive.

"And trust me," she added, "when I tell you a bond with a Tírian is inadvisable. They are more deceitful than you may think—or so I am told."

"He never deceived me," I said, though I knew my own

words to be a lie. In the early days of our fraught relationship, Mithraan told me plenty of falsehoods. He misled me many times, in many ways—and there was a time when I hated him for it.

But I knew now that he told those lies in order to protect me. He did it because he loved me.

"He charmed you," Riah replied calmly. "Convinced you of his undying affection and loyalty. That he will follow you to the ends of the earth, whatever may come to pass. Am I right?"

She stopped walking and turned to me, and as I faced her, I found my features freezing, stone-like, as I attempted to conceal my irritation.

The worst part of it was how right she was.

But then, she was describing any being who loved someone. Anyone devoted would have made the same vows.

"Why would you say that?" I asked.

"Because in my very limited dealings with Tírians, I have heard the same story more than once. But why shouldn't yours be sincere in his declarations? You are, after all, miraculous. You are powerful and beautiful, and if I were a Tírian, I would do everything in my power to get you on my side. Because one thing is certain."

"Which is?"

"You, Lyrinn, are a Fae the likes of which the world has rarely seen. You are more valuable to both Aetherion and Tíria than all the jewels and precious metal in the world. You're a weapon of war—one that will soon be used to win a conflict that has been raging for thousands of years. How you will be wielded, however, remains to be seen. And for your sake, I hope you come out of it in one piece."

CHAPTER FOURTEEN

I TRIED my best to let Riah's words sink into my mind as we walked on, but the truth was, there was no absorbing them.

Everyone who had ever thought I was some powerful being had been proven wrong.

I had proven during the Blood Trials that I was mediocre, at best. I had failed at almost every turn. I barely made it through the Labyrinth on the first day. I was gravely wounded during the Hunt, and I would have died if Mithraan hadn't saved me. I was too weak-willed to take down the silver stag—too weak, even, to kill Prince Corym, a mere mortal—though at least I had tried.

But whatever Riah might think, I was no weapon of war. I had no killer instinct, despite having carried a blade strapped to my thigh for the better part of my life.

Whether or not my powers had the potential to grow, the truth remained that at this moment, I was nothing and no one.

But if wielding power meant turning into a monster the likes of Kazimir, I was happy to remain no one.

Power corrupts souls...and I do not wish for my soul to be tainted by malice.

I didn't offer up any arguments or protests as Riah and I made our way down yet another series of corridors.

Let her think I'm some powerful being. Let them all. It's the best defense I have in this awful place.

I tried to memorize the route, telling myself I needed to learn the castle's footprint as quickly as possible. But after a while, each white hallway began to flow into the next, with no distinguishing features. I was starting to wonder if it was by design—if its visitors were meant to be disoriented in this maze of a prison.

A few times, I found myself turning to look over my shoulder, hunting for the bright-eyed shadow I had seen in the alcove earlier. Once or twice, I was certain I saw a flicker of movement as a dark cloak swirled away. But I told myself it was merely my imagination—a curtain swaying in the breeze, the shadow of a tree on a terrace outside. Nothing more.

I said little to my guide, and instead chose to eye the carved pillars or ornate windows leading out to various courtyards as we moved.

I took in their delicacy and beauty with reluctant admiration. There was no denying the skill of the Lightbloods or their appreciation of exquisite architecture. They understood beauty as no mortal did, and their artists were gifted beyond measure. I only wished the beauty surrounding me didn't feel so oppressive, as though it had wrapped elegantly manicured fingers around my neck and was squeezing every shred of life and spirit from my body and mind.

With a smirk, I reminded myself that Mithraan's ruined palace, Fairholme, had once felt prison-like to me. Ironic to think that I would now give anything to find myself back there.

"Perhaps one of these evenings," Riah finally said, breaking the silence between us, "if you feel up to it, I could take you into the city for a brief adventure. It's lovely, and I think you may enjoy its sights and sounds, Princess. It would also mean a brief escape."

I glanced at her, surprised that her tone had reverted to such effortless friendliness, given that I had challenged her at nearly every turn.

"I'll think about it, if you'll answer one question," I replied with a twisted smile, appreciative of the offer. "How many pubs *are* there in the city?"

"Fae are nothing, if not devout drinkers," she laughed. "There are loads of pubs, and I know one in particular that you'd enjoy, if I'm reading you correctly. Dark lager, in a pewter stein. Am I close?"

"You're spot on, in fact."

For the first time, I was starting to suspect we understood one another, and I resolved to give her a chance. After all, if I was to be trapped here for any length of time, I could use a friend.

At long last, Riah led me to a set of broad white double doors carved with intricate, bone-colored patterns reminiscent of the towers I had seen outside my bedroom window. They twisted and ebbed like intertwining snakes, carved impossibly delicately from wood so dense that it resembled stone.

There was no denying their beauty, and even my anger at having been dragged across the sea to this place could not subdue my quiet appreciation for the skill behind their creation.

I wondered with an internal sigh how Kazimir could live in such a lovely place and still seem so bitter—so vicious.

There has to be more to him than meets the eye, I thought, recalling all that Riah had said about his even-headed leadership. *He cannot simply be a walking manifestation of cruelty.*

As we approached, the doors opened to welcome us into a

long, bright dining chamber. At the far end was a row of glass doors, all of which opened to a large terrace beyond. Outside, I could see a long table covered in colorful fruit and pastries that reminded me with an angry churn of my stomach how hungry I was after the strange and difficult journey.

"The High King will be out to join you soon," Riah said, laying a hand on my arm to stop me. Her voice lowered to a near-whisper as she added, "Go out there. Enjoy the view. And most of all, try your best to settle in here. Trust me when I tell you that when you see what's on offer, you will not want to leave, however powerful you may soon become."

"You say I'm powerful," I replied in a whisper. "But if that's true, why can't I simply escape? Where are the shackles holding me here?"

I saw a look of fear flash across her features, and I looked down to realize I had grabbed hold of her wrist and was gripping her tightly—far *too* tightly.

More frightening still, my hand was glowing with a blinding white light.

I yanked my arm away, pressing it to my side and lowering my chin in silent apology.

Riah stiffened, rubbing her wrist, and replied, "There are no shackles, Princess. Not literal ones, anyway. Please, I beg of you —try to enjoy yourself, if you possibly can. Whatever may happen here, you will not be returning to Kalemnar anytime soon. There is a force at work in this place that will compel you to stay, whether you like it or not. That is all I can say. I'm sorry."

"I won't let him take control of my mind, if that's what you're implying," I hissed. "I am not so weak as—"

But she shook her head. "That's not what I mean. It's not a matter of mind control."

"Then tell me what you mean," I replied, my whispered voice pleading. "I don't understand what in all the world could make me wish to remain here."

"It is not for me to say. I hope to speak to you soon, to get to know you better." She nodded toward the terrace. "But for now, go out there. Wait for him. It will not be long now until you have your answers."

With that, she turned and left me alone in the chamber, the doors slamming shut behind her.

My feet heavy, I wandered out to the terrace, which overlooked the rugged coastline and the sea that lay to the east of Aetherion. Crashing waves far below reminded me how far I was now from Kalemnar and of the many miles of raging waters that lay between me and Mithraan.

The terrace was framed by stone balustrades and railings crafted as expertly as the rest of the palace. Its floor was made up of slabs of polished white and gray marble. The table, carved from some enormous, ancient tree, reminded me of the Taker's Lair in Kalemnar—the place where I had nearly died and then been reborn a Fae.

I was reminded once again of Mithraan, of the moments we had spent together in that strange subterranean dwelling. Of the bond we had shared all too briefly...the bliss I had felt with the touch of his fingers, with his words, his lips.

His tongue.

A surge of heat poured through me like liquid from a vial, and I told myself that for all her talk, Riah knew nothing about Tírians. Mithraan had not charmed me for his own amusement. His feelings for me were as real as mine for him.

He had taken enormous risks to be with me...and I had given myself to him freely.

Willingly.

Happily.

I had fought my attraction to him for all too long before succumbing, and he had done the same.

Still, the smallest, most insidious doubt had begun to creep its way into my mind. Mithraan *had* toyed with my emotions when I had first encountered him. He had tested me, teased me, tortured me. There was, undoubtedly, once a part of him that enjoyed playing with my heart.

But he would never do so again. He was mine now, and I was his. Our bond was sacred and pure—and it was absolute.

I shook my head, scolding myself for listening to a Light-blood—even one who seemed as well-meaning as Riah did. Those who dwelt in Kazimir's palace under his watchful eye would do whatever it took to convince me I was better off here. They couldn't risk their High King growing angry with them, which meant they couldn't risk my unhappiness or any attempt on my part to escape—or they would have to face his wrath.

I consoled myself with the knowledge that, if indeed I was as powerful as Riah claimed, I could one day bring their world crashing down upon them, beginning with the High King himself.

I was pondering that thought when a deep voice echoed through the chamber, coming from somewhere behind me.

"Lyrinn, Daughter."

I winced so, so hard against the second word. How I hated it, coming from his lips. The audacity of the High King to call me such a thing when he'd had no hand in raising me—when he had forced my mother to flee for fear of what he might do to Leta and me if he were given the chance to raise us.

I had only ever had one father, and he had died at the hands of a Grimper. He had been a good man, and a kind one.

Enraged, I turned to meet Kazimir's eyes, my jaw set in a hostile sneer.

"I am here," I said. "What do you want?"

He threw me a look of exaggerated injury, as though I had wounded him to the bone. "I want to spend time with you, as if it should be any great mystery," he replied in a tortured voice that made me want to roll my eyes in disgust. "You *are* my kin, after all."

My voice was ice cold when I replied, "You told me you had a gift for me. I wish to see it."

"Ah, yes. The gift." Casually, he stepped out onto the terrace to join me, inhaling the air. "Is it not extraordinary to breathe in the sea itself?"

"Is that your gift? Air? Because I could have inhaled to my heart's content in Kalemnar. Air is not exclusive to this land, you know."

Kazimir let out a laugh before taking a seat at the table and reaching for an orange. He began to peel it as he spoke, his eyes fixed on the brightly-colored skin. "My gift is far more pleasant than mere air, Lyrinn. My gift to you...is blood."

A jolt of fear pulsed through me at those words. Was I to be subjected to more violence, more cruelty? Another battle for his amusement? What?

"Explain," I said, swallowing my fear and raising my chin in feigned defiance.

"Words will not be adequate, I'm afraid," he said, turning to look toward the doors at the dining chamber's far end. "So instead, I'll show you." He raised a hand, palm out, and the doors flew open.

Moments later, a figure stepped into the room, dressed entirely in black. A female Fae, I guessed by the grace with which she moved. Though it was hard to tell at first, as she wore a thick veil through which I could see no distinguishing features.

I gazed at her curiously, my heartbeat racing against my will.

He said he is gifting me blood, I thought. *Could it be...*

I hardly dared hope, but still, the question spun around in my mind like a child's toy.

Have his Fae underlings brought Leta to Aetherion? Could one wish of mine be coming true?

No, I thought, my heart sagging. *She's with Corym. I saw her —I know I did.*

Still...

"Come," Kazimir commanded to the slow-moving figure. "She is eager to see you, and I suspect you're just as eager, my love. This will be a beautiful reunion—one long in the making."

Reunion? A reunion implies that we've met before—that we're...

*It **has** to be Leta.*

Nervousness roiled inside me, along with a feeling of grim disquietude.

But why the veil? Why the secrecy?

When the enigmatic figure was close, she stopped in her tracks. Slowly, she turned to face me, pale hands clasped obediently before her.

"Come now, lift the veil," Kazimir commanded, his patience waning as he popped another piece of orange into his mouth. "We don't have all day."

The figure pulled her hands up, her fingers trembling, and did as the High King asked, drawing the veil slowly back over her head.

As each inch of her features revealed itself, I held in my breath, my mind reeling with questions. Her chin, her lips, her nose—all of them were familiar, as though I'd seen them many times in my dreams.

But it was only when her flame-red hair showed itself—and her bright, large blue eyes—that I understood why.

She looked so much like Leta.

But so different.

My lips barely moved when I uttered the two syllables, the word trapped inside me in a place I hadn't dared venture in years.

"Mother."

CHAPTER FIFTEEN

"You see?" Kazimir asked, a fist slamming down on the table. "I have given you your own blood, Daughter. Do you not think it the most splendid gift?"

My legs threatened to buckle under me as I stared at the woman I knew as Alessia—the name she had assumed years ago—the name my father had known.

The assumed name of a princess in hiding.

My only memory of her face came from a tiny portrait my father had kept in a small drawer in his bedroom. I had no recollection of her touch, her scent. Of ever being held in her arms.

And yet, I knew I must have been, as she made the long voyage from Domignon to Dúnbar.

"But..." I breathed. "My mother...didn't she..."

Die.

For years, Leta and I had been told that the fire that had scarred us both had taken her life.

But no, I told myself. There was no fire. It was all a lie.

I have seen some of her memories—I watched her leave us

in Dúnbar with the man who raised us. I saw her desert us and disappear, seemingly forever.

I've only *assumed* she was dead.

If she was alive, why had she never returned to us? Why had she never so much as attempted to communicate with Leta or me? No mother would abandon their children like that. No mother would be so cruel.

Except I knew perfectly well that many mothers left their children, as did many fathers.

Whatever the case, whatever her nature, here she was, standing before me like a ghost clad in the obsidian shade of those who mourn.

"Yes, yes, your mother lives," Kazimir said, gesturing to her as if she was nothing more than a piece of furniture. "She has always lived, despite what lies your smith father may have told you."

"But...where have you been all this time?" I asked her, my heart torn to pieces inside my chest, trying hard to mend itself even as I grasped the truth. In spite of my shock I was overjoyed to see her face, so much like Leta's. She was beautiful—wondrous.

But the feeling of betrayal that assaulted me as I looked into her eyes felt like a thousand blades carving away at my soul.

Her chin was low, eyes fixed on mine...but she did not speak. She was expressionless, cold, as though her mind were entirely under Kazimir's control, and I found myself wondering if this had been the extent of her life since she had last seen me. It would explain a great deal, if the High King had kept her under some kind of cruel spell of isolation.

"Speak, Wife!" the High King shouted, pounding his fist on the table once again. "You have waited so long for this moment. Haven't you got anything to say to your daughter?"

My mother stepped forward obediently, opening her

mouth. At first, all she let out was a quiet croak, and I watched as a steady stream of tears trailed down her cheeks.

She looked as helpless, as torn, as I felt.

Yet I didn't know what to do.

Should I run to her? Throw my arms around her?

Or chastise her for deserting us?

We had never bonded. I had no real knowledge of her, other than what I had seen in my conjured visions of her memories. But even those now felt like a distant dream.

I wanted to hear her voice. To understand who she was—who she always had been.

"Lyrinn," she finally managed in a half-whisper, her lower lip quivering. "Can it really be you?"

I nodded, but the small exertion proved too much for my already weakened body. I sank to the cold stone of the floor, my legs too unsteady to hold me up any longer. I was certain I would not find the strength to rise until I knew she was real—that she was not some illusion conjured by the cruel being who called himself my father. I had been deceived too often and too maliciously to sustain another brutal joke.

"It's me," I said. "I...I always thought...Leta and I...we didn't know if..."

Kazimir interrupted with a coldness that made my blood freeze. "You didn't know if I had murdered her. What a low opinion you have of me, Daughter. Well, here we are, all together once again. A family. Isn't this nice?"

His bitterness—his ruthless disregard for my mother's feelings—made me hate him all the more. I glared at him and, energized by rage, pushed myself to my feet. As broken as I felt, I did not want to feel vulnerable in his presence, *or* weak.

I refused to allow him that pleasure.

"You have kept her locked up here all this time," I spat. "Just as you intend to do to me."

"Actually, she returned to Aetherion of her own volition after you and your sister were born," Kazimir replied. "I did not chain her to a bed in some dingy attic, contrary to whatever you might assume."

I looked to my mother for confirmation, and she simply offered up one quiet nod.

"And yes," Kazimir added, "I asked that she remain here in this realm—but with the promise that her eldest daughter would one day join her. She has been allowed to travel the lands to her heart's content over the years. She has been well looked after, allowed to do as she pleases, and kept safe. Isn't that right, Alessia?"

My mother turned to him, and I was certain I detected a flare of hatred in her eyes before she subdued it and nodded. "I have been given delicious food. I have had a comfortable bed. I have...survived." She stopped there and cleared her throat, turning back to me, and reaching her hands out to take mine. "I am so very glad to see you. I can't begin to tell you what joy it brings me."

"Do you know what?" Kazimir bellowed, clapping his hands together. "I think I'm going to leave you two alone. You can catch up all you like, exchange stories of dead blacksmiths and fake fires and whatnot. I'm sure you both have a good deal of weeping to do."

I glanced at my mother as her husband spoke, squeezing her outstretched hands. I could see the pain in her face when Kazimir mentioned my blacksmith father. I could feel a tightness in her fingers, her cold, shaking hands. After all these years, perhaps she still longed for the mortal man she had only briefly known. The man she had barely had a chance to love before she had returned to the High King's side.

When Kazimir had gone, I pulled away and sat down in one of the chairs at the terrace's broad table.

"What happened to you all those years ago?" I asked. "Did they find you?"

"Did Kazimir's Fae find me in Dúnbar, you mean?" she replied, taking a seat opposite me. "No. I didn't let that happen. I couldn't, for your sake and your sister's."

"Then what? Why did you leave us?"

She let out a slow breath. "The truth is, I never intended to stay long in Dúnbar. I wanted to go home to Tíria—to bring you and Leta with me. The Breath of the Fae would not let me through, however, and even had I managed to break the spell, I feared that doing so would alert Kazimir as to our whereabouts. So I left one night, while your father was sleeping. I left him a note, of course."

"I never saw it."

"No," she said. "I don't suppose you would have. He probably knew it was best that you not try to find me when you grew older."

"There were two pendants, as well," I said, pulling at the dangling silver object around my neck to reveal a small dragon etched onto its surface. "Leta found them, after Father died."

At seeing the pendant, my mother winced as if the sight of it brought her pain, and I shoved it quickly back under my tunic. "I'm sorry," I said. "I didn't mean to upset you."

"They were from my father's court," she said slowly, her eyes turning dull. In her tone I thought I could hear a bitterness, almost anger. "The Dragon Court, in the north of Tíria. I don't know where your father acquired them."

"They weren't from you? I thought—"

"No," she said curtly. "They were *not* from me."

I stared at her, trying to assess what about the small piece of jewelry had set her off. Had our father stolen them? Had he acquired them illegally?

"It doesn't matter," I said, my voice quivering slightly. "I didn't want a pendant. I wanted a *mother*."

"I didn't want to leave. You must believe me when I say it. I didn't want to leave you or your sister. I felt terrible doing what I did to Martel—to your father...but..."

It was clear that she wanted to say more about him, but couldn't find the strength. His death was probably as raw a wound on her heart as it was on mine.

"I know," I said. "But...did you not have a choice? Couldn't you have stayed in hiding with us?"

She shook her head. "Kazimir was never going to stop his hunt," she said. "I knew his Lightblood Fae were searching quietly for me—I could feel them coming closer. They combed the countryside and grew ever nearer to Dúnbar with each day that passed. I knew if I stayed, they would have taken us all captive. They would have killed your father, and you and Leta would have been in grave danger."

At that, my eyebrows arched. "Are you saying Kazimir wanted us dead?"

As awful as he was, I wasn't sure I was ready to believe that just yet.

She shook her head, though the effort was unconvincing. "I'm saying he is a volatile Fae—he's unpredictable. He might have hurt you to punish me, and it was a chance I couldn't bear to take." She let out a quiet, pained sigh before adding, "I knew that if I went to Kazimir of my own volition, I might be able to persuade him that you and Leta had succumbed to the elements. You were small and frail, after all, and the journey from Domignon to the north of the river was perilous, even for Fae younglings. You had no powers—you were little more than mortal babes at that point. It was a plausible enough tale."

"Kazimir believed you, then. He thought we were dead."

My mother let out a breath that felt like it held all the

weight of a thousand years of sorrow. Looking into my eyes, she smiled faintly. She looked so much like Leta—only, a broken version of my sister. One who had endured endless hardship.

If I hadn't before, I now understood what she had given up when she left us. I could feel it in the air between us. It was a sacrifice greater than anyone should ever have to endure.

"Yes," she said. "I suppose Kazimir saw the heartbreak in my face when I told him I'd lost you and had no choice but to believe I was telling the truth. He even had Riah question me and study my emotions to ensure that I was indeed devastated enough to satisfy him."

Her tone was bitter as she spoke, and her pain summoned a fire inside me that made me renew my silent vow to end Kazimir's life.

Someday. Somehow.

"He brought me back here," she continued, "and made sure I would never again be able to leave. When he says I'm allowed to roam, he speaks the truth—I can roam. But I cannot leave these lands."

"Why not?" I asked, swallowing hard. I didn't want to know the answer, but something told me I needed it.

She held up her left hand. On her third finger was a silver ring, and at its center was a gem of pure, glowing white. The ring itself was made of ornate, hair-thin strands of silver wrapping around one another and then coiling—it seemed—right into her finger and the back of her hand, burrowing like roots, deep under the skin.

"A ring of impediment," she told me, pulling her eyes to stone at the center of the strikingly cruel piece of jewelry. "It is alive, and filled with malice. The ring itself is twisted into the bones, veins, and nerves of my hand, the Fae Silver melded with my mind. So long as I am forced to wear it, I cannot cast a spell

—and Kazimir holds dominion over me. Should I try to remove it, I would most likely die of blood loss, if nothing else."

A grim weight planted itself inside me, heavy and grotesque, dragging me down toward the terrace and beyond. I finally understood what Riah and the High King had meant when they said I wouldn't wish to leave once I saw Kazimir's "gift."

Now that I'd found my mother, the last thing I wanted was to leave her here to contend alone with the High King's cruelty. Yet I could not take her with me without risking her life.

She was ensnared by a ring...and I was ensnared by my loyalty to her, to my father, to Leta. To a life I had never been allowed to live and a past that had been stolen from me the day I was born.

I would never be able to leave this realm so long as my mother lived.

CHAPTER SIXTEEN

"If I were to leave this place—to go seek help from Tíria," I asked, "What would he do to you?"

My mother laughed then, and the sound chilled me.

It was the cackle of one so bitter, so jaded, that I wondered for a moment if she was even the same woman my father had loved two decades ago. I couldn't blame her—after all that Kazimir had done to her, it was impossible to imagine she would be anything but filled with perpetual ire.

"You know full well what he would do to me," she said. "He would kill me slowly and painfully. For that reason alone, I am a shackle around your wrists, my girl, and for that, I am so sorry. Much as I have longed for years to lay my eyes on you again, I never wished this for you."

I shook my head, tears welling in my eyes, and reached for her hand. I took it in my own, squeezing, feeling the jagged edges of the vile ring pressing into my flesh and trying in vain to take her pain away. "It's not your fault," I said. "You did what you needed to, and you made an enormous sacrifice. You gave Leta and me years of freedom to live normal lives. Years with our...with our *true* father." My voice was catching now, to think

I had hesitated for a moment about what to call the man who had raised Leta and me with such care. "You gave us an incredible gift when you gave us to him."

She smiled, and this time, it held in it all the warmth of a hearth on a cold winter's day. "I've always hoped the sacrifice I made was worth something," she said. "I have thought of you so many times over the years. I tried to connect to you—to see your mind—but I could not. This *damned ring*—" She stopped, staring at her hand, and added, more to herself than to me, "And after all of that, as great as my sacrifice was, it seems it was not enough. Not enough..."

I pulled back and stared down at my hands, which I dropped into my lap. "I looked into your mind—your memories," I said softly. "I didn't want to—but I needed to understand what was happening to me when I came of age. I'm so sorry for what he did to you."

My mother looked out toward the sea and simply replied, "How much did you see?" Her voice was cold again, distant.

"Not a great deal. I was told...I was told someone had veiled your memories. Shielded them, manipulated them. That it was either you or someone else."

"It was me," she said in that same, far-away voice. "I had my reasons. I offered up just enough for you to see what I needed you to, should you ever come looking."

"I needed to know who I was. Where I had come from. Why the scars..."

She turned and leaned toward me then, tucking a strand of hair behind my ear, and stroked a finger along the pointed ridge at its tip. "I'm sorry for the deception," she said. "I'm sorry to have taken away your identity for so long—to have asked your father to lie to you. But you understand why I had no choice, don't you?"

I nodded. "Of course. Had I known what I was, I would have

yearned to join my kind—I would not have been able to reach them, with Tíria cut off as it was. It would have been torture. I still yearned for the Fae in my own way for all those years. I just didn't understand my desire to...to know them. I told myself they were long gone. But..."

"But in the end, fate forced your true identity upon you, as I always knew it would." She cupped my cheek in her hand, then pulled away and looked out to the sea once again. "Strong is the bond that ties Fae to our homelands. And whether you like it or not, you have two of them: Tíria and Aetherion. This land is one you will get to know a little, and a part of you will fall in love with it, while another part may well despise it. It is a place of beauty and horror at once—but one that I'm afraid you must see, in order to understand who and what you are—and how important you are to its future."

I shook my head and scoffed. "No. I have no intention of getting to know Aetherion. I plan to leave. I'll take you with me. I'll find a way. I'll—"

"Lyrinn."

Her voice had a hard edge as she said my name, and I tightened under the sound as though I'd been slapped.

"You cannot leave," she said, softly this time. "Please don't torture yourself with fantasies. For hundreds of years, I tried to find my way out of this place, and you know what happened to me when I finally did. Do not try to convince yourself you have the power to outwit Kazimir. It will only lead to pain and suffering for us both. Settle in here. Try to make it your home; you'll be better for it."

"I *have* to leave," I said with a hard shake of my head, tears streaking my cheeks. "I must. Leta needs me. And..."

But I stopped there. I was a young woman of nineteen, and if my mother had any sense, she would tell me that no one—

not even a Tírian High Lord—was worth risking my life and hers.

"You love someone deeply," she said softly. "I, too, have loved. It is a difficult thing to let it go—particularly when it is in the early stages, where the craving is so strong it feels like you will break if you cannot be with the one who has claimed your heart. It feels like a death each time you think of him, each time you imagine his touch. Don't think I don't understand, Daughter. I am all too familiar with heartbreak, and with the hole it leaves in its wake. I relive it every day, even all these years later."

"Then you should wish me gone," I half-sobbed. "You should wish for me to be with him—but you must know that I will not leave without you. Tíria is your home, too. It needs to be reborn, rebuilt. You need to be reunited with your father, the High King. His joy at seeing you again would be enough to renew his strength, I'm sure."

"My father," she said as though the words were distasteful to her. But she smiled woefully and looked into my eyes. "Tíria will never be rebuilt. Not unless..." She stopped speaking and gazed toward the dining chamber's distant doors, seemingly fearful that we would be overheard. "No matter. Kazimir will never allow it. He understands your value, and he will do everything in his power to keep you here, so long as you are of use to him."

"Of use?" I echoed. "How am I of use? He's already pointed out on more than one occasion that I'm weak, that I need training and instruction. He knows I am no warrior—I'm not some miracle."

My mother's expression went from sad to broken when I spoke those last words, and she lowered her face when she said, "I'm afraid you *are* a miracle, Daughter. It pains me to say it— you must believe me. But now that you're here, your fate will hold you in its clutches until you have fulfilled your purpose. In the meantime, please—for me—try to be happy. Embrace each day as though it were your last."

"What purpose could I possibly serve?" I replied hoarsely. "Why am I any more special than any other Fae?"

She shook her head, her jaw tightening. "When the time is right, you will learn all of it. I can't tell you—not because I don't want to, but because we would both suffer for it. You must live —you must breathe in the air and experience your days and nights to their fullest. And, when the time comes, you will come to understand how profoundly crucial you are to every realm in this world."

I hesitated for a moment, then said, "If I'm so special, then Leta must be a miracle as well. Why didn't he steal her, and bring her here with me? Then at least we could all be together. If she knew you were alive…"

"That is a question you'll have to ask Kazimir, I'm afraid. He could easily have brought Leta back with him. He's a fool for leaving her there. A fool. Had he only brought her…"

A flash of flame burst in her eyes, and for the briefest moment, I felt her power in spite of the ring that was holding it inside, trapped somewhere she couldn't access it.

With bile rising in my throat, I recalled the sight of Leta with Corym. My horror at seeing the trust in her eyes, the heartbreak in her features, convinced her sister had deserted her to run off with a Fae.

"I can only hope Leta comes to understand what a monster Corym is before it's too late," I lamented. "He'll do everything he can to take her powers from her, once she comes of age."

"Perhaps," she said, the fire leaving her eyes, and she took my hand again. "Do not surrender to hopelessness, Daughter. I am not here to discourage you—only to tell you to exercise patience. Fleeing will only bring Kazimir after you, and it will certainly endanger others, including your sister. You can be happy here. You will find you have friends in this realm, believe it or not. It is not all bad."

Her words seemed to etch themselves into my flesh, and for the first time, I found my shoulders lowering, my body relaxing. I looked around at the beautiful terrace and the castle, at the rough landscape stretching out along the sea. I savored the exquisite loveliness of the place and told myself that I must find a way to be happy here...if only temporarily.

I would only ever manage to escape this place, this inflicted fate, if I had a well-crafted plan. And that plan had to entail more than mere flight. I had no ship, no means of escape. Even if I could manage to find my way beyond the palace walls, I wouldn't last long on the open sea.

Regardless of how desperate I was to return to Mithraan, it wouldn't do to get myself killed before I had some minute chance of success.

"I'll try," I said with less resolve than I'd hoped. "I'll do my best."

"You can come to me anytime you like," my mother said. "And make sure you explore the palace. There are corners within the castle that are quite wonderful. Learn your way around—and learn to use the shadows to your advantage."

"To hide myself, you mean."

My mother's eyes narrowed cunningly, and she nodded. "Privacy is not easy to come by in this place. Kazimir has small spies—sprites who flit about the palace and report to him with news of goings-on. There are few places where they cannot venture, and an ally of mine will tell you where you can find sanctuary. He has already promised to place a warding spell on your bed chamber. You will not be spied on there."

As she spoke, the sound of flitting wings met my ears. I turned sharply to my left only to see a flicker of quick movement...and then it was gone. I was certain, though, that I'd spotted the delicate features of a faerie on a tiny face, its lips pulled into a conniving grin.

I had never seen a sprite, though I'd heard of their existence in my youth. I had always believed they'd disappeared along with the Fae, gone long before my birth. But apparently I was misled about them just as I was about so many other truths.

"I'll be sure to find quiet escape as often as I can," I said, suddenly irritated. "It will be a relief to get away from all the watchful eyes in this damned place."

When my mother frowned, I reached a hand out to wrap my fingers around her wrist. "I didn't mean it like that," I said. "I'm overjoyed, of course, to find you here—to find you alive. It's the greatest gift imaginable. But I despise Kazimir, and I don't care if his spies hear me say it. You of all people must understand why."

"Of course I do. And it goes without saying that your presence here is the greatest gift for me, as well. The only thing that would make our reunion sweeter would be to have your sister here." In her voice, I could hear another flash of anger.

Finally, she said, "Kazimir has told me he intends to have you trained while you're here—to seek out your Gifts and hone them into something extraordinary. He is intent on preparing you to rule."

"And I've told him I have no desire to rule."

To my surprise, she replied, "Even so, you *must* train, Daughter. Train, and let your Gifts flourish. Show the world what you're made of—your value. There is one here—the ally I mentioned, a Spell-Master. His name is Erildir. For a thousand years, he has been my teacher and my closest confidant. He is a Sidhfae—one of an ancient race from a place far beyond Aetherion's North. You can trust him, Lyrinn. He will help you develop your powers, as he helped me for so many years before my spells were stolen from me. He will guide you toward your destiny."

Toward my destiny.

It was a strange turn of phrase, unsettling and final.

I will craft my own destiny, Mother—just as Mithraan said.

"Does he, by chance, have light blue eyes?" I asked, recalling the being I had seen while walking the corridors with Riah.

My mother nodded. "I am not surprised that he's already watching you. He told me some time ago that he anticipated your arrival." She sighed, adding, "His is a sad tale, but it is not mine to tell. Suffice it to say that he and I have more than a few things in common. We were both taken from our homes and our people at too young an age. But with his help, you and I will both find a way to attain our goals—I can feel it even as we speak."

CHAPTER SEVENTEEN

My mother and I had only a few more minutes to sit and talk before the dining chamber's doors opened and Kazimir strode in again, this time with two Fae guards in tow. Each was dressed in strong-looking silver armor, as though the High King were convinced my mother and I might try to take them on.

I braced myself, thinking at first that Kazimir's sprite spy had overheard me speak of my desire for escape, and the High King now intended to escort me to a prison cell—or worse. But the guards simply positioned themselves to either side of the chamber's doors while Kazimir joined us on the terrace.

"Catching up?" he asked, looking first at my mother then at me, a broad grin on his lips. It was impossible to tell whether he was genuinely content to see us together, or merely pretending to be capable of actual joy. "I'm sure you two will find much more to talk about over the coming months."

Months.

The word spread bitterness through the depths of my mind.

Months spent away from Mithraan. From Leta. *Months,* for Corym to sink his claws into my sister's mind—not to mention what he might do to her body.

Kazimir may as well have inflicted a life sentence on me. I may recently have learned of my own Immortality, but knowing I might live for centuries somehow made time slow to a crawl.

Still, my rage diminished when some small, selfless part of me wondered if it might be for the best if Mithraan stayed away as I plotted my escape. As much as I longed for him to come and steal me away from this place, a Tírian High Lord venturing to Aetherion would be folly, given what Kazimir had threatened.

Yes, I told myself. As much as I loved him—as much as I craved him every waking moment—I needed to be patient, at least until I could solve the problem of how to free myself without endangering my mother.

"We discussed the beauty of Aetherion," my mother said quietly, hardly daring to look at Kazimir. "Among other things."

"I see," the High King said in a casual, indifferent tone. "Tell me, Lyrinn—how are you feeling now about being here?"

I smiled—a forced, friendly smile meant to disarm any foe—and said, "I can't say I came here of my own free will. But had I known I would find my mother after all these years, I would have been far happier about my fate. I do wish you'd told me."

Kazimir let out a stifled laugh. "Now, where would be the fun in that? But perhaps you're right. I could have saved myself—and you—some anguish. I do hope your desire to flee has diminished, at least a little."

I nodded. "You have my word that I will not. I intend to stay by my mother's side."

A bold-faced lie—at least the first part. *The second I have a plan in place, I intend to tear my mother from this land and get as far away as I possibly can.*

Kazimir studied my eyes for a moment, assessing me for honesty in the same way Mithraan had done so many times. Seemingly satisfied, he nodded. "Very good. In that case, I give you free rein to roam and get a feel for the place. In fact, I encourage it. You will learn to love the landscape around here—and I hope that soon, you will get to see more of Aetherion. Who knows? Perhaps you will even forge some...*friendships*."

He said the last word suggestively, and I got the distinct and awful impression that he was hoping I would take a Lightblood lover.

You'd like that, wouldn't you? I thought. *You think I could so easily forget Mithraan, so long as some silver-haired fool takes his place.*

"I have my doubts about friendships," I said bitterly before forcing a smile onto my lips. "I mean, I've always been a solitary person. I don't make friends easily."

"Well then, perhaps you will be a solitary Fae," Kazimir replied, as if allergic to the insinuation that there was anything human in me. "But that doesn't mean you don't need a circle of close allies. I know perfectly well, Lyrinn, that the coming weeks and months will not be easy for you. Believe it or not, I want you to be happy."

How benevolent of you, your Grace.

"There are Lightbloods in this realm," he continued, "who would stun you with their exquisite beauty and their Gifts." He moved closer and, in a conspiratorial tone, said, "And you may be interested to hear that there are Witches in our lands."

At that, my mother shot him a look of irritation.

"Witches?" I repeated, wondering if he'd meant it in a derogatory manner.

"Not actual ones, of course," he replied, looking sideways at my mother. "Female Fae who call themselves Priestesses. Those who belong to the Order of the Elar."

My heart skipped a beat at the mention of the powerful Immortal I'd seen in my nightmare. The creature of cruelty, of pure malevolence who had assaulted the lands I loved so well.

"They may be fanatics," Kazimir added, "but they are adept

in the ways of spell-casting. We have a Priestess residing on our grounds, even. Perhaps it would amuse you to meet her one day, Lyrinn. She spends most of her time in our temple." He raised one mocking eyebrow as he added, "Your mother spends a good deal of time there."

I looked to my mother, who lowered her chin, clearly not wishing to speak of it.

"The High Priestesses are skilled magic users," Kazimir added when neither of us replied. "I intend to send you north sooner or later, Lyrinn, to learn from them. It would do you good."

I resisted the desire to tell him once again that I had no intention of sticking around long enough to be sent north, or anywhere else. But I simply nodded, forcing another smile onto my lips. "I must admit that I am a little surprised that you genuinely want me to improve my spell-casting, your Grace." *Given that I want you dead.*

His eyebrows rose comically. "Of course I do. You are my daughter. You are the grand-daughter of the Tírian High King. There is no sense in wasting your Gifts—not when you could be of great use to us in the coming days. You have the potential to be our greatest weapon, and I would not squander an opportunity to use you."

I bristled at his words.

There it is.

I was nothing more to Kazimir than a weapon. *His* weapon —one he no doubt hoped to use against Tíria when the time came for war.

He still hadn't grasped that I would never fight for his side —never go against Tíria's Fae.

But if I could learn—if I could harness my Gifts and grow powerful enough to to fight one such as Kazimir...

Then perhaps I really could find a way out of here.

"I would be honored to learn," I said with an artificially reverent bow of my head. "I would love to understand the true power that comes with my bloodline."

"Then learn you shall," Kazimir said with a clap of his hands. "And you will be taught by the best." He turned to my mother then, acknowledging her existence for the first time in what felt like hours. "Did you tell her about your special friend?"

My mother bowed her head and nodded, and once again, I saw how he had broken her piece by tiny piece over the years. Belittling, trivializing, cutting her down and reducing her to shreds of what she had once been.

"I mentioned Erildir," she said. "Your Grace."

"Ah, good. He can teach you the Old Ways, Lyrinn. He is a master who will guide you toward your fate."

In a moment of defiance, I raised my chin. "And what fate might that be? I keep hearing of it, yet no one seems able to fill me in."

Kazimir leveled me with a hard look. "The throne, of course. And by the time Corym has wedded and bedded our dear Leta, we will have the two greatest weapons known to Fae-kind at our disposal—assuming Domignon remains allied to us."

At his mention of Leta marrying the prince, a swell of nausea threatened to make me double over.

"No wedding will take place anytime soon," I said. "She's young yet."

"She will be eighteen years old before you know it," Kazimir said. "Or are you forgetting that your dear blacksmith of an adoptive father lied to you both about your ages? Leta is perilously close to adulthood."

"The coming of age of a Fae takes place at *nineteen*," I protested.

"It does, normally," he replied. "But if the Fae finds his—or *her*—mate earlier, it can be accelerated. A Fae who has bonded can come into their powers as early as their eighteenth birthday. Didn't you know?"

My nausea only intensified with his words. *Corym, that piece of goat excrement, needs to keep his hands off her.*

And if he doesn't, I will murder him.

But a sinking feeling overtook me as I reminded myself I was in no position to confront the prince. Leta was across the sea...and on the verge of losing everything.

I spoke as evenly as I could as I pushed myself to my feet and locked eyes on my mother. "I'm afraid I must excuse myself —I'm suddenly quite tired."

I nodded to my mother and spun around, marching as quickly as I could toward the dining chamber's doors, which flew open violently as I approached.

Nothing could have compelled me to turn back, to let Kazimir see the tears streaming down my cheeks.

He may have spoken the truth about Leta, or it may have been another lie.

Either way, I hated him more than ever.

CHAPTER EIGHTEEN

W<small>ITH NO GUIDE TO</small> lead me through the palace this time, I strode quickly down corridor after corridor, uncertain of my destination.

Tears still stung my eyes as I stormed past artwork and twisting columns until I discovered an open door leading out to a small cloistered courtyard. I walked through, grateful to have found a place of remoteness and solitude.

I flinched when I heard the door seal shut behind me, but didn't move to open it again. I didn't want to see Kazimir, whether by accident or otherwise. I didn't wish to be anywhere near that monster...or even my mother, who was still little more than a stranger to me.

My head pounded with a rush of confusion brought on by all that had occurred in the last hour.

Everything—*everything*—I had believed all my life had been a lie.

I had already come to terms with what I was—what my body and mind could do. I had accepted that I was an Immortal Gifted with powers that I had never known or understood before my nineteenth birthday.

Not only that, but I had swallowed down the bitter pill that I was a forbidden creation—one who was both reviled and sought after.

My true father was a High Fae. A cruel one, at that.

My mother—a mother I had silently longed for all my life—was alive. Yet I didn't even *know* her. I had spoken to her today, I had looked into her eyes, felt her touch, listened to her voice... yet I had no real understanding of who she was.

And Mithraan—the one being who could possibly have granted me the smallest hope for any sort of future—was many, many leagues away from this fortress protected by an army of Lightbloods and their grim-faced, vindictive leader.

I was entirely alone now, with no hope of happiness.

When I came to a stone bench set among a series of tidily trimmed shrubs, I seated myself, struggling against the desire to thrust my face into my hands and weep.

Forcing down my emotions, I stared out at my surroundings, telling myself to breathe. After a few moments, I was pleasantly surprised to realize I was beginning to feel calmer. I could inhale again without wanting to scream, now that I was far from Kazimir.

I was basking in my thoughts, my eyes fixed on a statue at the courtyard's far end, when a shadow moved next to me.

Turning to see who had so silently invaded my surroundings, my eyes veering to a figure in a long silver cloak, a hood pulled over his head.

"You have chosen well," a masculine voice said. It was sweet and lilting, neither particularly low nor high, but somewhere exactly in between. There was kindness in it, but something sharp-edged, too, as though he didn't care to have his emotions read by the likes of me.

It was the voice of experience, both good and ill. A voice of wisdom.

"Chosen?" I asked, turning to see that the door I had come through was still closed. *How did he get in? Was he already here when I arrived?* "What exactly did I choose?"

The figure turned my way, and now I could see his eyes— the same bright, aqua-colored eyes I'd seen in the shadows when Riah had shown me around. His cheekbones were sharp, angular, his lips thin and his brows keenly arched.

Erildir.

The Spell-Master my mother had mentioned.

"You hand-picked this courtyard," he said, gesturing to the space around us. "And you were wise. It is shielded by deep magic that not even High King Kazimir can break through. You cannot be watched here, Highness. But perhaps a part of you already knew as much when you walked through the door."

"No." I straightened, suddenly nervous at feeling so isolated with this stranger, and said, "I didn't know, I assure you."

"I cast a spell on it several hundred years ago, for the sake of your mother. She comes here frequently to escape, to find peace. This place and the temple are her two sanctuaries."

"I see." I spoke cautiously when I said, "You're Erildir. Aren't you?"

"Am I?" he asked with a smile and a twinkle in his eye.

"My mother told me about you. She said that you've helped her during her time spent in this...palace."

It was all I could do not to say *prison*.

With a nod, he replied, "I am very fond of your mother. But it should be said that she has helped me, too."

I managed a faint smile. "She's fond of you, as well. And grateful for all you've done for her." My tension dissipated a little as I spoke. Something in his face, his quiet contentment, was mesmerizing and pleasant at once. It was as if the most delicate sensation of drunkenness had overtaken me; I felt fully relaxed for the first time since my arrival in this place, and though part of me wanted to push the feeling away, I found myself embracing it, holding on for dear life for fear that apprehension would return.

"Did she happen to tell you anything of me?" he asked.

I half shook my head when I replied, "Only that you're a...Sidhfae?"

He nodded. "So, you know of our kind."

"Only a little. My mother also told me you've protected her over the years. I'm grateful to you for that. As my sister would be...if she even knew our mother was alive."

"Your sister," he said pensively, nodding. "I am deeply sorry that you have been separated from her. The High King had his reasons, but still, it would have been better had she been here with you. There's no denying that Kazimir can be a cold bastard."

I glanced around, shocked that he would dare use such language to describe the High King. "Aren't you afraid he'll find out you said that?" I whispered, my chin low. "The sprites—"

He smiled again. "I'm not afraid in the least. Though it may be considered treasonous to say it, my spell-casting is more powerful than Kazimir's. In truth, the High King fears me as much as most Fae fear *him*. But none of that matters, given the protections I have in place for this courtyard."

I wanted to ask why Kazimir would keep Erildir around, if that were the case. The High King hardly seemed like the sort to welcome one more powerful than himself into his circle. Erildir had to be a threat of some kind—and yet he had been permitted to stay by my mother's side, a loyal friend for so long?

It didn't make any sense.

"You're wondering why the king doesn't dispose of me," the Sidhfae said.

"No," I lied. "It's just—"

"It's quite all right," Erildir laughed. "I suppose Kazimir

keeps me around for my various...uses. Otherwise, you're quite right—I'm sure he would kill me himself."

"Your uses?"

His gaze turned distant, an odd expression taking over his features. "I should mention that I come from a land far from here. One from the ancient days before the realms separated, when Fae were allowed to mingle with other races. I was born in Naviss, beyond the Northern Seas. The realm where the Elves once resided."

The pitch of my voice betrayed my shock. "I didn't know Elves were *real*. I only ever heard of them in tales told by the town elders when I was growing up."

"Oh, Elves are very real," he replied. "At least, they once were, many lifetimes ago. I have knowledge from those days that few possess, and your father the High King has always considered me an asset for that reason alone. I am a walking library of recorded history—and my mind contains memories of every spell ever cast by the magic folk. Lucky for me, I suppose, to be such a font of useless knowledge. It keeps me alive."

I had so many questions that I didn't know where to begin. "You taught my mother, didn't you?"

He nodded. "Of course, that was before you were born, well before her brief escape to Kalemnar." With a sigh, he added, "I do miss those simpler days."

I studied his face. His skin was smooth, poreless. His hair was light blond, but not as pale as the Lightbloods', accentuating those extraordinary eyes that swam with the depth of an ocean and the lightness of the sky. He was beautiful in the same way a swan was—graceful, elegant, intriguing, quiet. A creature forged from the mind of a master storyteller.

"May I ask what happened to your kind?" I was unsure as to whether it was a cruel question.

"Who knows?" he said with an abrupt finality. "Many thousands of years ago, our land was cut off from this one and disappeared across the sea, like a ship sailing toward the horizon. I watched it vanish—along with many Lightbloods. They say it was the Elar's doing. She separated all the lands, the Fae said, so that she could control them—so that she could keep our races apart. Of course, that was so long ago that I couldn't tell you how many moons it's been—even if I had counted each and every one of them."

My body went rigid. The Elar—whether real or imagined—was sounding more and more awful with each morsel of information I gleaned about her.

"Why would the Elar be so cruel?"

Erildir shrugged, as though responding to a question about whether or not it might rain. "She works in mysterious ways," he said. "She is a power unlike any other. She forms and reshapes the lands; she steers our lives in ways we cannot see. For me to question her is like asking why air exists. It is simply the way of our world—at least, so the Priestesses say."

"You don't believe in her?"

"Oh, I believe she exists," he replied. "I've seen evidence with my own eyes. Whether or not she is as cruel as they say, I don't know. But it doesn't matter. Soon, another Elar will rise. One who will reunite this land with Naviss." He looked away when he said, "I look forward to the day when I will once again be able to look upon my people."

All of a sudden, I didn't wish to hear any more about the Elar. Something about the creature had made me uneasy since I'd first heard her name uttered on Kazimir's lips. Though I was certain I would never lay eyes on her, the very thought of the Elar was beginning to feel like a malevolent force at work.

"Tell me," I said, trying to ask the question with some delicacy. "Do you...*like* the Lightblood Fae?"

Erildir let out a pleasant laugh that sounded so sincere that it melted my hostility of this place a little. Something about him was so disarming, so...*honest*...that it was impossible not to feel at ease in his presence. He felt like an open book, inviting me to read his pages without a moment's hesitation.

"When I was first brought here, the Lightbloods were kind to me. They kept me alive when my land disappeared. They gave me food and shelter when they could have forced me into servitude, or worse. There was a time when I thought very highly of them indeed."

"And now?"

His smile faded as he pulled his gaze to the arches on the far side of the courtyard. "Many are kind, or at least fair. But I suppose my opinion of them altered when one of their High Lords took it upon himself to ensure I would not produce offspring."

"What?" The word flew from my mouth like an arrow shot from a crossbow.

Erildir nodded solemnly. "When I had nearly come of age, his surgeons stole a part of me in order to ensure my bloodline would end. In order to preserve the purity of *their* bloodlines, or so the High Lord told me. And before you ask—no, it was not Kazimir who inflicted such cruelty on me."

My breath hitched as Erildir's full meaning assaulted me. "You mean to say—"

He nodded. "To put it bluntly, animals are not the only creatures the Lightbloods castrate. Never underestimate how cruel creatures can be when they feel someone might pollute their clean waters."

"How could anyone do such a thing?" I asked, my voice tight.

But then I remembered that my mother's and Kazimir's bond had been forbidden, too. Tírians were not allowed to be with Lightbloods, and all Fae had known it for thousands of years.

Then again, it wasn't as if they were going about castrating one another to prevent the bond.

"Power comes more easily when one's enemies are hobbled," Erildir said, "and the greatest way to hobble an enemy is to destroy their race entirely." He let out a sad breath. "For all I now know, my lands are gone forever, and I am the last of my kind. The Lightbloods have ensured that with my death comes the possible end of my people."

I sealed my lips tightly against the question that invaded my mind. There was no tactful way to ask it, no way to frame it that wouldn't be potentially hurtful.

"You still wish to understand why they kept one lone Sidhfae alive," Erildir said, "why they wouldn't simply end me instead of cutting me and keeping me in their lands."

"Am I that transparent?"

"It's the question everyone has on their minds when they meet me. 'Why allow the magical castrato to live—is he not bitter? Does he not pose a threat to us all?'" He let out a quiet snicker before continuing. "The truth is, I am quite content. And I am grateful to be alive to see this day in particular, as I have long been waiting to meet you, Lyrinn Martel."

My cheeks turned fever-hot. Surely, after thousands of years of life, encountering *me* was not a highlight of the Spell-Master's existence.

"I come from a long line of magic users," he said. "But it is you I have looked forward to most out of all my potential pupils over the centuries. You pose a unique challenge, and I suspect we will both enjoy peeling back your layers to see what lies inside."

I searched his face to see if there was any sign of threat. Was there any reason to think Erildir meant me harm? Was he befriending me at Kazimir's bidding?

But I could find no particular reason not to trust him. There was nothing in his eyes but kindness and patience—traits no doubt practiced over thousands of years in his dealings with the Lightbloods.

"I would like that," I said. "It seems the High King would, too. He's far more excited about my training than I could ever be, though I can't fathom why."

"The High King knows how special you are, though perhaps he has a strange way of showing it."

"Well...good luck, I suppose."

"You say that now, but you may change your mind," he replied with a laugh. "I can be a harsh and demanding teacher."

"A harsh teacher doesn't frighten me. Teach me to escape this realm, and I'll—" I stopped speaking and froze with the realization of what I'd said. *Damn it. I'm too comfortable with him.* "That was foolish of me. I'm sorry. I...didn't mean it. I have no intention of escaping. I don't know why I—"

"Ah, but you did say it," he interrupted, laying a hand over mine for only a moment. In his touch, I felt warmth and calm at once. A healing touch, that's what it was. "It's all right, Highness. It's no surprise to me that you would rather be far from this place. Your heart lies elsewhere—believe me, I know the feeling all too well. But please, do not worry that I will betray your confidence. You have my promise that I will protect you with my life while you're between the palace walls. Keep your word to your mother—stay in Aetherion—and no harm will come to you here."

His final demand took me aback for a moment. How did he know what my mother and I had discussed? Why was he so intent on my remaining here?

But I told myself I was being unnecessarily distrustful. He

was only protecting my mother—looking out for her, given Kazimir's threats.

"Thank you," I said, sensing deep in my soul that he could take on an entire army, if it came down to it. I hadn't seen him in action, but something told me he was as powerful as he seemed.

Perhaps his greatest power lay in convincing me that he was powerful.

"Now," he said, grasping the edge of the stone bench and pushing himself to his feet, "I will leave you. But first—" He turned to look down at me and smiled fondly, and all of a sudden, I felt as though we had known each other for a hundred years. "Keep your eyes open for Lark. He is small, but he is mighty. I believe you two have already met, albeit indirectly— out on the dining chamber's terrace."

"Lark?" I asked, and when Erildir didn't reply, I said, "The sprite. The one watching my mother and me—he's...*yours*?"

"Not mine, no. No one can claim ownership over a sprite," he replied with a chortle of amusement. "Be sure never to imply in Lark's presence that he serves me, or anyone else. He and I are simply...acquaintances. Should you ever come under threat, you will find him a quick and effective protector. He owes your father a debt—one from many years ago. He has promised the High King to look after you, and will do everything in his power to keep you safe."

More likely he promised to keep an eye on me and make sure I don't try to escape.

Still, I almost laughed at the image of the tiny entity I'd seen out on the terrace fighting a fully-grown, powerful Fae.

"Should I really trust an ally of my father's?" I asked.

"Perhaps not. But I will say one thing for the High King— for better or worse, he values you, Highness, above all his wealth and property. He sees you as the future of this realm.

And he will do everything in his power to keep you from harm."

"Even lock me up," I said bitterly.

"Even lock you up, yes." Erildir let out a long breath. "Meet me here tomorrow, after breakfast. We'll begin our training then, and see what you're made of. If all goes well, I won't subject you to too many sessions."

I glanced around at the well-manicured shrubs, delicate-looking statues and the braided silver and stone of the court-yard's benches. All very lovely, but the location didn't exactly scream *training ground*. "Isn't there a better place to—"

Erildir shook his head. "The courtyard is warded, remem-ber. We need privacy, you and I, for what I have planned. Best not to let anyone watch us."

I narrowed my eyes suspiciously. "Why is that, exactly?"

He let out a laugh. "*So many questions*," he said with a shake of his head. "I intend to keep you alive long enough to fulfill your purpose, Lyrinn, Princess. For now, trust that I have your best interests at heart."

"You're not the first to tell my he's looking out for my inter-ests," I replied, recalling that Kazimir had insisted on exactly the same thing.

"The difference," Erildir replied, "is that when I speak those words, they're true. You have been blessed with a fate that will bring change to the world—and I will do everything in my power to see it fulfilled."

CHAPTER NINETEEN

I WANDERED the palace aimlessly for what felt like hours.

Perhaps it was pathetic of me, but my thoughts had shifted away from terrifying, winged Fae and training sessions to evolve into a deep, sorrowful longing for Mithraan.

I had never missed anyone as I missed him. Never felt a cratering chasm inside me as I did now with his absence. But the worst of it was not knowing if I would see him again—not knowing if I would ever again feel his touch.

There was something brutal in the feeling—and deep—like a knife wound in my side.

Lamenting my loss and my loneliness, I wandered until I found myself at the base of a spiral staircase.

Without thinking, I climbed until I came to a small, narrow window. I pressed my hands to its stone sill to peer out at the city far below, my heart pounding with a nostalgia I had never expected to feel.

There was no denying that the city of Aethos was beautiful. Its streets were an iridescent blue-gray cobblestone, its buildings made of pure white that reminded me of Domignon—yet felt entirely different. Instead of being crafted by the hands of men, the structures felt as though they'd been built with nothing more than pure magic. Effortless and weightless, their roofs peaked up into twisting spires of silver and white.

The Lightblood Fae wandering the streets far below me wore light colors as if to match their surroundings—though none were clad in the pure white wardrobe that had been forced upon me.

I watched as Aethos' population moved gracefully about, wandering into shops and other buildings at a pace that seemed easy, relaxed. Here and there, I spotted Fae children—some with hair almost as dark as my own—with their parents.

By some miracle, I found myself smiling at the sight. Something about watching young Fae filled me with hope and the promise of a better future.

Perhaps, one day, there would be peace between the realms.

Perhaps, if I *were* crowned queen...

No.

I pushed back against the quiet, insidious ambition working its way into my mind like a parasite. *No. I don't want to be Queen, or even Princess. I simply want my life back. I want to be left alone—so long as I can be with Mithraan.*

As I looked down on the city and reminded myself of the life that had been cast upon me like a curse, the flitting of wings met my ears.

"Highness," a deep voice said from somewhere eerily close by.

I spun around to see the small sprite I had spotted briefly on the terrace. The look of mischief in his eye had disappeared, and instead, he looked solemn as he stared back at me. One hand was on the hilt of a tiny sword, the other across his abdomen as he bowed.

For a moment, I studied his wings. Delicate and beautiful,

like silk drawn over bone, they were exactly what I had always pictured when I thought of Fae wings.

Yet in my nightmare, I had seen something entirely different...

"Are you Lark?" I asked, forcing my mind from the memory.

"I am," he replied. "It is a pleasure to make your acquaintance at last."

"I saw you outside when I was with my mother. Why didn't you introduce yourself then? I thought..."

"You thought I was spying on you."

There was no denying it. Even Erildir had said Lark was allied closely with the High King. "Weren't you?"

"I was watching over you," he said. "But if your concern is that I will report what I heard back to His Grace, the answer is no. He asked only that I protect you. He does not want you feeling any more oppressed than absolutely necessary."

I let out a laugh. "Forgive me if I find that a little hard to believe. Kazimir seems to enjoy imprisoning the women in his life."

"The High King is less tyrannical than you think," Lark said. "But you may discover it for yourself one day. In the meantime, I will keep an eye on you, as promised. The High King fears that there are some in Aetherion who see you as a danger to this realm."

This time, I fought to stifle my laughter. "I'm no more dangerous than you are," I said. "With all due respect."

With that, Lark shot faster than my eye could register over to a small stone statue set in an alcove in the tower's wall. With one quick stroke of his saber, he sliced its head from its shoulders. He was back to hovering next to me before the head even hit the ground, falling with a *thunk, thunk* as it careened down the spiraling staircase.

"I stand corrected," I said with a shallow curtsey. "That was impressive, I'll admit."

"Sprites are not weak, Highness," he said. "Our size does not determine our capacity for mayhem."

"As you've just proven. Well, then..." I turned and began to head back down the tower's stairs. "I feel we should set a few rules, if it's all right with you."

"Rules, Highness?"

I smiled as he accompanied me. Though I wasn't sure I was keen on being watched, followed, or defended by someone I had only just met, there was something about Lark I liked immediately. He felt honest, though I couldn't entirely say why.

"Rules," I repeated. "Number one: Don't watch me while I sleep. Actually—don't watch me in my bed chamber at all. Unless you have reason to believe someone has infiltrated it with the intention of murdering me."

"A reasonable demand. What else?"

I padded down the winding stone stairs, trying to think of other requests. "Keep an eye on Kazimir," I said. "Please warn me if you think he's up to anything."

"You're asking me to defy the High King."

"I'm merely asking you to protect the daughter he told you to protect. I don't see it as a conflict. Do you?"

Lark let out a low chuckle and replied, "Good point. Well then, two rules should suffice for now. If you'll excuse me, I'd like to fly ahead to make sure your chamber is secure. Is that acceptable?"

"I can live with it."

Lark disappeared instantly, the flitting of wings fading quickly into the distance. I made my way toward my chamber, pleased to have memorized enough of the castle's floor plan to find my way there without too many detours.

As I rounded the final corner, Lark suddenly appeared before me again and I jumped, my palm pressing to my chest.

"Gods, you startled me!" I said with a laugh. "You're lucky I don't carry a dagger these days."

"I'd be impressed indeed, if you managed to strike me with it before I evaded," he replied with a grin. "But I do apologize. I came to find you because your mother, the Queen, would like to see you in your chamber."

I expected Lark to leave me then, but he continued along until we reached my door. "If you should ever need me, simply whistle low. I will always come."

I studied him again, eager to understand his mind. "Why are you so loyal to the High King?"

"He saved my family once," he said simply, "from a pack of Northern wolves. It was many years ago—but I owe him several lives. I am a sprite of honor, and I will serve him until one of us comes to an end."

Part of me wanted to ask if he was certain we were speaking of the same Kazimir—the one I knew didn't seem like someone who would ever lift a finger to help anyone, least of all a family of sprites.

But instead, I simply smiled and pushed open my chamber door.

My waiting mother was seated at the large wooden desk by the far window. Her face lit up as she rose to her feet, and in return, my smile grew.

"Lyrinn," she breathed, clasping her hands together like she'd been holding in the two syllables for years.

"Hello, Mother," I said, the word foreign and slightly uncomfortable in my mouth. "Are you all right?"

She nodded. "I'm very well." Stepping toward me, she took my hand in hers and guided me to the edge of the bed, where we both seated ourselves. "You've met Erildir," she said. "I wanted to check in and see how you got along."

"I have," I nodded. "He's...unique."

She let out a quiet laugh. "He is wonderful, isn't he? He has all the greatest hopes for you. I just know he'll be such a help to you while you're here."

"*While I'm here*," I repeated. "Are you implying that there will be a time when I'm no longer here?" Trying to suppress my excitement at the thought, I leaned toward her. "Do you know something I don't?"

She winced slightly when she said, "I didn't intend to give you false hope. I only meant while you're in the palace. One day, perhaps you will find a home elsewhere in Aetherion."

"Or in Kalemnar," I said without thinking. My chamber was supposed to be warded, but I wasn't entirely certain I was safe from eavesdroppers. "I'm sorry. I'm angry with the High King just now for taking me away from..." I looked away, not wishing to mention how brutally I ached for Mithraan.

"I know, my dear. You may think I don't, but I understand completely—which brings me to the second reason I came by." My mother looked ponderous for a moment, then reached into a pocket and extracted a blue silk bag cinched with a yellow ribbon. She opened it to reveal a tiny glass vial of clear liquid, which she handed it to me. "One of Erildir's creations. Before you go to sleep tonight, take two drops on your tongue."

"What is it?" I asked, taking the vial from her.

"A sleep draught. One that allows your dreams to meld with those of others. You will be able to see the one you love, if only from a distance. You will be capable of speaking to him, of touching him, even—and it will feel as real as though he were here with you."

I stared at the vial, wondering if it could possibly be true. I had seen Leta from across the sea with Kazimir's stone. Could the draught bring me close to Mithraan, if only for a few moments?

"Only if he's asleep, though," I replied. "Right?"

She nodded. "Best to wait until nightfall to take it—to give yourself the best chance," she said. "The draught has never steered me wrong. So use it tonight, and other nights. Seek him out, and let him know you're safe. Speak to him. Gain comfort from his presence. It will give you peace of mind, at the very least."

A surge of frustration bit into my mind. "I'm not seeking peace of mind. I want—" I stopped and looked into my mother's eyes, which seemed to hold all the pain in the world. "I want out of here. But I won't leave—I promise you that. It's only...I never intended to find myself here, across the sea. I want to help Tíria. Your home."

At the mention of Tíria, her smile faded, but she nodded. "If you want to help Tíria," she said mysteriously, "You'll work with Erildir. Put your faith in him. Learn from him. He will open up your mind and show you what you're capable of. If you wish one day to find your way out of this place, he is your greatest hope."

She rose to her feet and glided toward the door, her black dress trailing behind her. "You must be tired," she said, turning back to face me. "If you like, I'll have dinner sent to you later—and then, perhaps you'd like to turn in early." With that, her eyes moved to the draught still clenched in my hand.

"Yes," I said. "I think I would like that. Thank you."

With a final nod and smile, she left me to my thoughts...and my eventual dreams.

My mother was right—I was feeling tired. But it was early yet, and I was determined not to allow myself to rest until nightfall. Mithraan would be awake, wherever he was. Awake and plotting a way to come to Aetherion, no doubt, and extract me.

I must tell him I can't leave, I thought. *I should warn him against coming—tell him to hold off for the time being.*

But the most selfish parts of me didn't want any part of that. All I wanted was to feel his touch, to hear the promise that he would be here soon—that we would be together, even if we had to do it in secret.

I need to get out of this place...and I need to bring my mother with me—whatever it takes.

For the next few hours, I found myself restless, bored as I anticipated the night to come. I paced my room, stalking out to the terrace more than a few times to look out over the country Kazimir was convinced I would rule one day.

In a small desk at the chamber's far end, I came upon a pleasant-looking book filled with colorful painted maps of Aetherion's various regions. I rifled through it, staring at the artists' renderings of the lands, from Aethos in the southeast all the way up to Nordvahl, the snowy realm in the North.

Along the center of Aetherion was a strip of land that looked scorched. The Barren Lands, it said. The lands Riah had told me about that had been decimated—though by what force, I didn't know.

As I flicked through the pages, my eye was drawn to an image that appeared entirely out of place. To the east of Nordvahl, sitting in the sea, was what looked like an immense, shattered stone wheel, with the title "The Broken Lands," and no further explanation.

The map showed no topography, no terrain whatsoever. Nothing but a symbol.

As I stared at the page, a memory flitted into my mind of Mithraan saying the Elar lived in those lands.

With a quiet shudder, I closed the book, telling myself artists enjoyed inventing fantastical landscapes, and the Broken Lands were just that—a figment of some painter's imagination.

I was delighted when dusk fell and as my mother had promised, a delicious meal appeared at my door. Fish, vegetables, and all the bread I could want to consume in a lifetime—not to mention a flask of wine. I ate and drank hungrily, grateful not to have to look Kazimir in the eye this evening. For the most part, I avoided the wine, telling myself I wanted a clear head for the dreams I hoped to enjoy when the sky darkened fully.

When I told myself I couldn't eat another bite, I washed up and prepared for bed, moving with deliberate slowness. Hoping that by the time sleep took me, Mithraan would be sleeping somewhere, too.

The last step before I crawled under the covers was to take two drops of the draught my mother had given me, sealing the bottle tightly to preserve it.

I tucked myself into bed, closed my eyes, and allowed sleep to take me.

CHAPTER TWENTY

My DREAMS MEANDERED for some time, nebulous and frustrating. As if I had found my way outside my own body, I watched myself wandering through woods and valleys that shifted and ebbed, changeable as clouds.

Stepping through the landscape in a loose, flowing dress of green silk, I called Mithraan's name over and over again, but the sound simply flitted away into the distance like a lost songbird.

For a long time, there was no response.

It was only when I found myself standing inside a dark cavern, a damp chill prickling goosebumps into my flesh, that I began to feel a tenuous sense of hope.

The cave was dreary and dank and smelled of salt air. I was standing close to the sea—I had to be. I could feel a breeze coming from the cavern's mouth, and though my surroundings were unquestionably dark and unwelcoming, nothing compelled me to leave.

And then I found myself lying on my back, eyes locked on the cave's ceiling which glistened with moisture.

"Are you here?" I asked quietly. "Have you found me?"

"Lyrinn..."

My name came only in a whisper, yet I knew it was him.

I sprang up and looked around frantically, narrowing my eyes at the thick, inky darkness. But I was certain the cave was still empty, with no one to be seen. Beyond the mouth, I saw the sea lapping steadfastly at the shore.

"Close your eyes," he said. "Lie down again. Wait for me."

As I obeyed, my heart began beating wildly. Whether part of the dream or waking life, I could not tell.

Mithraan was here. I could...I could *feel* him.

Yet he was nowhere near, not really. This I knew deep in my soul. He was an entire sea away from Aetherion—unreachable, untouchable.

"That's it," the voice said quietly as I sealed my eyes shut, and for a moment—a blissful, anticipatory moment—I wondered if I would soon feel his breath on my skin, inhale his intoxicating scent.

"I am here," he whispered with the first touch of his fingers as they slipped down my neck.

I reached for his hand, needing to know he was real. But at first, I felt nothing.

"Do you trust me?"

"Yes," I whispered. "I trust you."

"Good. Tell me—do you remember when we were in the Taker's Lair, and I brought you to another place—only we never actually left the lair?"

I nodded, then let out a quiet laugh. "Of course I remember," I said. "It was..."

The best moment of my life.

We had become one in that moment, and I had committed every sensation, every kiss, every touch, to eternal memory.

"How did you do it?" I asked. "Bring me to that place?"

"I called it up in my mind's eye. And you came with me. We journeyed outside of ourselves to live a waking dream. And now, we have wandered into one another's minds. We are one again."

"But where are we?" I asked. "Why did I find you in a cavern?"

"We are in the Mouth of the King," he said softly.

"The...what?"

Mithraan chuckled. "There is a jagged headland near Aethos called Khithar Head. It was named for a great Fae king who lived many, many centuries ago. Legend holds that a cavern at its base looks like the mouth of one who cries out for his love, lost at sea. I suppose it makes sense that I should find you there, after..."

After all that has separated us.

"But I want to see you," I said. "I need to—"

"Picture the cave in vivid detail—as though you weren't dreaming. Know that it is real. Can you see it? Feel it?"

I did as he said, conjuring an image of a rounded ceiling, walls, a solid layer of rock beneath me.

"Yes," I replied. "I feel the cold. The damp. I can smell the sea."

"Good. Now—open your eyes. Can you see me?"

With a sudden, desperate feeling of need, I realized the hand was no longer touching my neck. I inhaled, sitting up, and opened my eyes.

A faint shadow lingered a few feet away. Unfocused at first, it began to solidify as Mithraan's words resonated through my mind.

Can you see me? A transparent voice asked the question again, and I panicked momentarily as I stared at the flickering shade, afraid I was losing him before I had a chance to be near him.

"I...I don't know," I replied, desperate. "I..."

"I am here," he said. "It's all right."

The shadow stepped forward, his face growing clear in a sudden burst of light, bringing the entire cavern to life. Intense amber eyes, exquisite cheekbones.

Perfect lips.

"You're really..." I whispered. "You're here with me. This isn't just a dream."

"Not just a dream, no. Lyrinn, I will come to you, love. Watch for me where you least expect me."

"But Mithraan, you can't—" I needed to tell him something —something of great importance...But as I grasped for it, my mind went blank, as though the thought had simply vanished into thin air.

He moved closer. Tentative, fearful of destroying the tenuous link between us, I pushed myself to my feet, stepping toward him. When I laid a hand on his chest, I was certain I could feel his heart pounding under my palm.

I pulled closer, tears stinging my eyes, and kissed him delicately, fearful that he would disappear under the merest touch of my lips. When he kissed me back, my mind swirled and delighted in the sensation—his tongue finding mine, the deep moan that emanated from his chest.

I pressed myself tightly to him, a quiet need telling me I had to feel every inch of him against me. He reached for my hair, combing his fingers through, urging my head back just enough so that he could slip his tongue up my neck. Shivering with pleasure and desire, I was desperate for him—desperate to feel him inside me again, to prove to myself that he was real and whole—that we were still one.

Regardless of my imprisonment in Aetherion, he was mine, now and always.

"I will come for you," he said again as he slipped his lips softly over my neck, one hand cupping my breast through the delicate white silk, his thumb stroking its way over my nipple.

"And when I do, I will claim you again, with my mouth and every part of me. We'll find our way out of that forsaken land. We will build our lives together, Lyrinn. I promise you that."

I tightened with his words, though I wasn't sure why. There was a reason I couldn't leave—a reason I couldn't simply climb onto a boat and sail across the sea with him...but in that moment, I couldn't remember what it was.

As if the memory had been stolen from my mind, I found myself helpless with sadness and joy at once.

But I told myself to hope. I wanted this dream—this pleasant, perfect connection of our minds—to continue as long as possible.

Mithraan pulled back just enough to look into my eyes, stroking a thumb over my cheekbone.

"Don't go. Not yet," I whispered. "Please."

"I will never leave you," he said, falling to his knees before me. His lips wrapped themselves around my nipple despite my dress...

No.

There was no dress.

I was naked before him, and his tongue was working its way down my belly, his hands gently urging my thighs apart.

I ached fiercely for what was to come, and I parted my legs eagerly, throwing my head back when his fingers slipped inside me, then pulled out to seep over the sensitive bundle of nerves that drove me to madness.

When he bowed down and his tongue followed suit, I braided my fingers in his long hair, cursing the gods under my breath for denying me this pleasure for so long.

"I am yours," he spoke against my flesh, driving me to the edge of a blissful precipice. "I am yours, and nothing will ever change that truth...Vaelan."

The cool air lapped at my skin, forcing goosebumps to its

surface as I pleaded with the gods to preserve this moment. Heat tore through my veins like wildfire, my heart beating wildly as I raked my fingers through his hair, silently urging him to keep going.

Don't stop. Never stop.

And then...

He was gone, and I was awake.

I was lying in the bedroom in Aethos once again, naked, my core throbbing with a deep ache for the explosion that never came.

He said he is coming for me. I lay back and closed my eyes again. *Watch for me where you least expect me...*

I shot up, my heart suddenly racing with the memory of what I meant to say to him.

You can't! You can't come—because if you do, I will want nothing more than to leave with you...

And my mother will die.

CHAPTER TWENTY-ONE

IN THE MORNING, I found myself in no mood to lock eyes with Kazimir. So instead of heading down for breakfast, I remained in my room and ate a little of the leftover bread and butter from the previous night's dinner.

As I prepared myself for my training session, a sharp, brittle knock sounded at my door.

"Princess?" Lark's voice called from the other side.

I sighed, "Come in." Motivating myself for the morning's training session was proving difficult after my pleasant—but frustrating—dream.

"Are you ready?" the sprite asked as the door creaked open —an impressive feat, considering Lark's diminutive size.

"Ready as I'll ever be, I suppose," I told him with a half-hearted smile.

"Come, then. I'll escort you."

We headed for the small cloistered courtyard with me leading the way, as determined as ever to memorize the castle's map.

"You seem a little down," Lark observed as we made our

way along hallway after hallway, my pace unfaltering and determined.

"I suppose I'm distracted. It will pass." There was no way I was about to reveal what had set me on edge—the cravings that had renewed themselves inside my mind and body. Much as I liked Lark, I barely knew the sprite. For that matter, there was not a soul in the world I would have talked to about my desires, other than Mithraan.

"I hope so, for your sake," he said. "From what I understand, Erildir is demanding—and distraction is not an excuse he'll happily accept in a training session."

I grimaced. "I still don't understand why I'm in training to begin with," I said. "Kazimir speaks as though he intends for me to take the throne eventually. Do I really need to learn to do battle, if that's the case?"

Not that I intend to stick around long enough to find out.

"Fae training is not about battle, necessarily. It's about gaining control over your powers. Trust me when I say you don't want to take a seat on the throne if you are not as powerful as you can possibly be. There are many Fae who would happily tear the royal title from under you, given half a chance."

I wanted to retort that I would happily hand the throne over to any Fae who asked for it, but instead, I smiled and said, "I have a question for you."

"Yes, Highness?"

"Speaking of power...are you able to control the volume of the sound of your wings? I would think a spy would be capable of being a little...quieter."

He let out a laugh, and I eyed him sideways to see a broad smile on his small face. "If I desire, I can shield myself from all eyes and ears," he explained. "Even those of Erildir. It is a Gift that only Shadowlings possess."

"Shadowlings?"

"Those who are able to vanish without a trace. I am one of their kind—a trait inherited from my grandfather on my mother's side. They say that we could conceal ourselves from the Elar herself."

"Yet I saw you flying around when I was sitting with my mother on the terrace yesterday..."

"I revealed myself to you alone—but only because I want you to trust me. You may have noticed that your mother did not see me."

"You aren't as intent on my mother trusting you, then?" The question was half joking, though I was genuinely curious.

"I don't know your mother well," Lark said, speaking slowly as if calculating the potential repercussions of his words. "But if I'm to be honest, I prefer to focus on you alone."

I contemplated that for a moment. "Fair enough," I said. "So, you say you can disappear at will? If, say, someone you despise walks into the room?"

"Yes. Exactly."

As we arrived at the courtyard's doorway a few seconds later, I turned to him and asked, "Is it wrong of me to tell you I'm highly envious of that ability?"

"Not at all, Highness. It comes in quite handy at times."

Erildir was waiting for us in the courtyard, dressed in his silver cloak and elegant armor of thick, embossed black leather.

As I examined him, I felt woefully unequipped, having put on a light-weight white sweater and matching linen trousers. I could only hope the king's people would eventually equip me with something a little less pristine and more useful.

"Highness," Erildir said, bowing his head slightly as we approached.

"Please, in our training sessions, call me Lyrinn," I replied. "I don't need formalities. Nor do I particularly enjoy them."

"Fair enough...Lyrinn." He lifted his chin slightly. "Tell me, did you sleep well?"

It wasn't a particularly unusual question, but the way the Sidhfae posed it made me redden, stiffening uncomfortably under his suggestive gaze.

"I did," I replied with a curt nod. "Quite well, thank you."

"You visited the Kalhern," he said confidently. "The Cavern of Dreams at the Mouth of the King. There, you saw your lover."

He spoke the words as though commenting on the weather —not at all as though he had just revealed that he had spied on my mind, invading my deepest fantasies in the night. It was the only explanation, after all; I hadn't told anyone about the dream, and my mother only knew she'd given me the draught —not what it had done to me.

My awkwardness turned quickly to irritation, and my brows met in annoyance. For a moment, I contemplated leaving the courtyard and requesting another trainer.

Or, better still, none at all.

Don't be stubborn, Lyr. Don't be proud. Just...deal with it. He's a Spell-Master. It's his job to prove his mettle.

I looked the Sidhfae in the eye and, instead of denying what he had stated, asked, "How do you know about my dreams?"

He laughed. "Come, now. Who do you suppose gave your mother the sleep draught?"

When I didn't crack a smile, he added, "I promise you—I wasn't spying on you. I was only guessing based on experience. Those who take that particular draught almost always end up in the Kalhern. It is the place where minds—and bodies— connect. The cave is a sort of channeling chamber, resonant and magical. If ever you should make your way in on foot, you will feel its power firsthand."

My shoulders relaxed slightly, and I finally allowed my trust to renew itself. "The cave is near here, yes?" I asked. "Mithraan said—" I stopped short of saying anything more. Best not to give away our conversation. "Come to think of it, I don't know how he knew about the cavern."

"It sounds like your bond with your High Lord is strong. And yes, the cave is just a little ways from the palace grounds. You have seen it in your dreams, and the cavern now knows your greatest desire—as if there was ever any doubt. You wish for Mithraan to come here, to you. And who knows? You may have your wish one day soon."

"I may," I said, wondering if I should really admit as much. "But there's little hope of it, right? And even if he did come, it's not as though I can leave with him. He would be a prisoner here, just as I am."

Erildir offered up a distant smile. "Perhaps. But maybe being imprisoned together is preferable to living free, but a world apart."

"Living freely but together would be my preference," I said, surprised that I was being so candid with the Spell-Master.

"Ah, what a world it would be if we could all have the thing we most desired...*Vaelan,*" Erildir said, sending a shiver along my skin.

"What did you call me?" I asked, hostility tinting my voice as my defenses raised again.

"A term we use frequently in these parts—Aethos is surrounded by woods. And in those woods are many wolf packs. I'm sorry—should I not call you that?"

I threw him a quick, skeptical smile. "It's fine," I told him, though I didn't mean it in the least.

The term of endearment was too intimate—too familiar.

And ultimately, it was proof that he had access to my innermost thoughts.

"Well then," he said, "what say we begin our training session?"

CHAPTER TWENTY-TWO

"We'll start with a simple assessment," Erildir told me, gesturing with a broad sweep of his hand to the courtyard. "Show me what you can do."

I froze at the demand, my body and mind stunned into nervous silence. *What I can do* felt like a broad spectrum—yet all too limited.

"Do?" I asked, glancing around. "With what?"

"Cast a spell. I know you've done so before. Show me what you know."

I felt suddenly foolish, standing there as I was in front of the Spell-Master and Lark, who had retreated into his invisible mode. Both of them were far more adept than I was at casting spells. I was nothing more than a novice who had been fortunate enough to survive the Blood Trials—with a good deal of help.

"During the Trials," Erildir said with an exasperated sigh, "You must have had to fight a little."

"You didn't watch them through bird-sight?" I asked, but then recalled that Aetherion had little interest in the competition, which was, after all, a battle for supremacy over the realms of Kalemnar.

"I did not," he said. He took a few steps backward, his expression indecipherable. I told myself he was disgusted with me. Disappointed, too. The daughter of the great Kazimir and grand-daughter of High King Rynfael of Tíria, too indecisive to come up with a single spell.

"Lark," Erildir called out, and the sprite appeared instantly, darting through the air to his side.

"Yes?"

"I think Lyrinn needs to start simply—perhaps with a little target practice. Are you up for it?"

"Target?" I asked. "I don't see a—"

A horrid thought struck me as Lark eyed me, his chin high as he hovered in mid-air, his wings moving impossibly fast. "I'm ready. Are you?"

"We'll soon find out," the Spell-Master replied with a crooked grin.

When the sprite began to zip rapidly around the courtyard, I started to understand exactly what was being asked of me.

Erildir padded a few steps to his left and said, "Every Light-blood has a common Gift. They are, each of them, capable of harnessing pure light. There is no reason you should not be able to do the same, given your bloodline."

"Which means what, exactly?"

"It means you can summon energy—the sort of energy that can blow realms apart, if focused correctly. But we're not setting out to do that today. All I want from you is a simple conjuring. You have summoned Light-Beasts before, yes?"

I wondered how he knew that, given that he hadn't watched the Trials.

"Yes," I replied. "But it felt almost accidental—I had no confidence that it would work."

Erildir moved swiftly toward me, took me by the shoulders,

looked me in the eye, and said, "I am not here to make a warrior of you, Lyrinn. Only to keep you alive long enough to fulfill your destiny. Still, the High King asked me to train you a little, so that is what I am doing."

His tone was strange and cold, his eyes distant, and I was struck with the realization that this Erildir was not the one I had met the previous day—the warm, smiling Sidhfae who had seemed so friendly.

Perhaps this was his instructor personality—maybe he simply became standoffish when teaching. But something had felt off since the beginning of the session. Something fundamental had changed between us, and I was beginning to wonder if I had offended the Spell-Master in some way.

"Do you see Lark?" he asked.

I looked over to see that the sprite was shooting manically from one shrubbery to the next so rapidly that my mind could barely register him.

I nodded.

"Stop him," Erildir said.

"How?"

He pointed to my hands. "You have seen the light that dwells inside you. I know you have. You've been witness to your own veins glowing brightly under your skin. You've felt the power of your bloodline. Now you must harness it. Harness the light, and use it to your advantage."

I still had no idea what he meant, but I focused my eyes on Lark and, watching him move left, then right, up, then down, I told myself to trust in my powers.

As I watched the sprite intently, he seemed to slow down—though I was quite certain that it was my mind that was speeding up. For the first time, I could see his trajectory clearly. He was moving in a pattern. *Up, down. Right. Left. Up.*

I thrust my hands out and, without thinking, shot what looked like a sharp blade of pure, bright light toward him.

Horrified, I cried out a warning.

But I was too slow.

The projectile clipped Lark's foot as he tore sideways, and he stumbled, letting out a sharp cry...but managed to regain his balance.

"Good," Erildir said. "Very good. Don't kill him, though. He's one of your few allies in this place."

"I'm sorry!" I called out.

"It's all right," Lark replied, landing on the back of a nearby bench. He grabbed his injured foot and turned to Erildir. "But perhaps you could work on something else while my foot stops throbbing."

Erildir looked like he was about to respond when the court-yard's door cracked open. A young female Fae in a gray linen dress stepped quickly over and whispered something in his ear.

The Spell-Master nodded once, then said, "Thank you" to the visitor and watched as she left. Turning to Lark and me, he said, "I'm afraid I need to cut our session short today. We will resume here tomorrow. Same time."

With that, he offered up a quick bow of his head and, sweeping his silver cloak around him, left without another word.

"Who was that?" I asked Lark. "Our visitor, I mean."

"A servant of your mother's," Lark said. "I don't know her name."

"My mother? Why would she send a message to Erildir in the middle of our session?"

Lark shrugged. "Perhaps she wanted to make sure he wasn't working you too hard—she's familiar with his techniques, as you know. I imagine she wants him to go easy on you."

"Yes," I said. "That must be it."

I ate dinner in my room that night, as well as breakfast the following morning. I was in no mood to speak to Kazimir, or even my mother. My experience with Erildir had unsettled me —his prying, invasive insinuations, and the way he had cut our session short had both left a bitter taste in my mouth.

After breakfast on the second day, I went back for another session, and again, Erildir asked me to shoot conjured projectiles at Lark—an endeavor that was beginning to feel downright cruel—and then he left without another word.

This continued for days, during which I occasionally ran into my mother in the dining hall. She was always cheerful, curious to know how I was feeling about remaining in Aethos— but never asking about my training or about Erildir.

Frustration was quickly building inside me. All I had desired since being taken by Kazimir was to get away from him, from Aetherion. To find a way to bring my mother home. But if Erildir didn't teach me something more effective than a basic combat spell, I would be trapped here for years, if not decades.

Erildir didn't seem to care much about my obvious frustration, and when I grumbled in my sessions, he simply told me that until I had perfected the first skill, I would not move on. I wondered silently if he would insist that I kill Lark before he deemed me impressive enough to advance to the next level.

Each night, seeking escape, I took the sleep draught my mother had given me. But not once did I find Mithraan again. Instead, I found myself alone in the Kalhern, disappointed and empty as I lay on the cold ground, gently calling for him.

And each night, my dreams would shift from that vision to nightmares of the Elar, screaming through the sky as she burned the world below. Her wings of silver and red glowed bright as the stars, and though I told myself over and over that this...this *monster* was not the true Elar, some force in my mind warned me that she was very real indeed.

Finally, one morning after my session, I asked Lark to bring me to my mother's room so I could seek some answers. The sprite guided me down what seemed like miles of unfamiliar hallways until we reached a beautiful white door inlaid with swirling silver patterns.

I realized as my eyes grazed the designs that they looked remarkably like the markings on my skin. Marks left behind when my scars had healed—marks that I now found beautiful but mysterious.

As we approached the door, the patterns shifted and twisted until they had reconfigured themselves into something that looked like braided vines snaking their way down toward the floor. I wondered if I had only imagined the change—if it was some trickery on the palace's part—or if it was a spell cast by the High King, one of his twisted games.

When I stepped close, the door opened inward to reveal an enormous, bright bedroom larger than most of Dúnbar's houses.

I wasn't sure what I had imagined my mother's room would look like—but this was the farthest thing from what I would have envisioned for her. She had not struck me as the type who wished for a lavish lifestyle—yet the space screamed wealth and privilege.

She is the queen, after all, I told myself. *Kazimir's chamber is probably far more opulent.*

To one side was a huge bed laid with silk bedding of rich gold, its headboard made of bone-white wood inlaid with more swirling gold. At the room's far end was a set of glass doors like the ones in my own chamber, and like mine, they led out to a broad terrace.

At its center I could see my mother standing, her red hair blowing in the breeze as she stared longingly out at the sea.

I stepped into her room and cleared my throat. Lark vanished as I took a second step, and I wondered if he had made his way back through the open door to leave us to our privacy.

My mother turned and smiled when she heard my footsteps, gesturing to me to join her outside. I could now see that a broad outdoor table was laid with food and drink, as though she'd anticipated my arrival.

"Come, Lyrinn," she said. "Have something to eat. You must be hungry after your session with Erildir."

So, I thought, *at least you acknowledge that we have daily sessions—useless though they seem.*

I stepped out and took the seat she offered me as she pulled up a chair for herself.

She looked rested and content. The color that occasionally left her face had returned, and I wondered if she, like me, had managed to evade Kazimir for the last several days.

"Are you well?" she asked, leaning toward me and taking my hands in hers. Her touch was warm and affectionate, her smile so filled with quiet joy that I couldn't help reflecting the sentiment back in her direction.

"I'm fine," I replied. "Training was a little—difficult, as always. But brief. Which brings me to why I'm here, actually."

She let out a quiet laugh. "Erildir's got you shooting at the sprite, doesn't he?"

My eyes widened with surprise that she knew, then I chuckled. "Poor Lark," I replied. "Yes, that. But it's all I've been doing for days on end. I would have thought we'd move on to something else by now."

Something that could help me take down Kazimir...

"Ah," she said, her voice as soothing as a warm caress, "Back in the day, Erildir and I spent many an hour—many a *year*, actually—working on my spell-crafting." She sat back with a sigh and added, "I was quite good at it, you know. Light-Beasts weren't the only tool in my arsenal. But it took me a long, long time to move beyond the basic spells, Lyrinn. You must be patient—it is one of the most difficult things in the world, I realize. Erildir will not push you beyond what he feels you're capable of, so you must work your way there."

I watched her, convinced there was more going on behind her eyes than she was letting on. "During our first session, a servant of yours came to deliver a message to Erildir. Do you have any idea what that was about?"

Her eyes widened, and she shook her head. "Not a clue," she said, taking hold of a nearby tea pot and pouring herself a cup. "I suppose she had a message for him from someone in the kitchens. Erildir often conjures food for the palace, you see. Perhaps it was an emergency."

I sat back, relieved and annoyed with myself for having been suspicious. Of course—I was hardly the center of the Spell-Master's universe. He had many responsibilities in the palace, and I was simply one of them.

"I must say," my mother continued, "I envy you the early days of training. I miss them."

Looking into the distance, she played idly with the cruel ring that cut so deeply into her hand.

"When your spell-crafting advanced," I said, "What else could you do? I mean, other than summon Light-Beasts."

A sigh. "What *couldn't* I do? I was a High Fae, the daughter of a High King. I was able to create walls of pure, thick ice. Occasionally, I would cast them around myself inside my chamber, just so I could be left alone. Sometimes, the walls took days to melt, much to Kazimir's annoyance. For my part, it didn't matter much, as I could conjure food and drink with a mere thought. It was my way of isolating myself from him."

I found myself staring at her in admiration. I had no idea my mother was capable of such high magic—and such a variety of spells. But I should hardly have been surprised; her reputation had preceded her, after all.

For the briefest moment, I allowed myself to hope that I would be capable as well, one day.

"How does one conjure food?" I asked.

"A powerful Fae has only to think of it, to call it up as you might a weapon of light, of ice, of fire." She gestured to the table. "Come, try it now. See what you can do."

"Really?"

She laughed. "What harm could it possibly do?"

She was right—I wasn't the greatest spell-caster in the world, but I had summoned before, at least—and thanks to my repetitive lessons with Erildir, I was growing more consistent in the calling up of light-blades.

I closed my eyes and pictured a bowl of apples, ripe and shiny, sitting on the table before me.

The jangling of dishes met my ears, and my eyes shot open to see that I had forgotten about the tea cups laid out on the table. The apples—which had obediently shown up—had done so on top of the fragile porcelain on the table.

Laughing, I moved the bowl, grabbed hold of an apple, and took a bite.

"What else could you do?" I asked, genuinely curious.

"I conjured weapons—blades, projectiles—as you've been doing. There was a time when I could have taken down a small army. A happier time, when Kazimir and I got along somewhat better than we do now. Once he deemed me a true threat, of course, he took it all from me." She blew out a puff of air and gazed down at the ring, then smiled again. "But you, Daughter —you will have far more opportunities than I ever did. Your father, the High King, *wants* you powerful. He wants you strong. It's only a matter of time before you prove the full extent of your Gifts."

Time. Something I have in droves—but ironically, the last thing I want.

"I'm not sure why. Kazimir is awfully confident, considering..." I began.

I was about to say *considering I want to kill him*, but a voice on the air warned me against uttering those words in this place.

"Kazimir has always been confident," she replied. "It will prove his downfall. Just as your goodness will prove yours."

My eyes shot to hers, only to see that they were glowing with flame—and once again, I could feel her power...in spite of the oppressive ring that clawed at her hand.

"Mother?" I said meekly. "What do you mean by that?"

The fire in her eyes faded, as if my voice had brought her from some distant place to the present, to here and now. She smiled sweetly, pouring me some tea, and said, "What's that, dear?"

I stared at her—gawked at her, trying to piece together the combination of that strange, faraway voice and the feeling that something had just occurred between us—something irrevocable and profound.

Yet she seemed oblivious to the fact that she'd said the very thing that had sent my blood running cold in my veins.

With shaking hands, I took a sip of tea and said, "I...I must have misheard you."

As if nothing out of the ordinary had happened, she said, "I meant to tell you—Erildir thinks it would be good for you to see the city at last, and I am in agreement with him. Aethos is beautiful, and can be quite exciting. I used to enjoy it thoroughly in my younger days."

The words set me a little at ease, and I managed a nod. "Lark suggested a while ago that I take Riah up on an offer to escort me into town. You don't think Kazimir would lose his mind? I've never been convinced he's comfortable with my leaving the castle grounds."

"No. You're probably right." My mother shook her head, her red waves falling loosely about her shoulders. "Why don't I deal with him? If you ask his permission, chances are that he'll say no." She pulled close to me, laid a hand on my cheek, and said, "I want to see you happy, Lyrinn. I know you're in pain—I know you miss...*him*...terribly."

She didn't need to say Mithraan's name. I was an open book to her—and it felt like a relief. It was good to have someone around who understood just how much my heart ached for my mate.

"Tell me," she added. "Have you been able to make use of the sleep draught?"

I chewed on my lip for only a moment before replying, "Once. Since then, I've taken it nightly, but when I drift to sleep, I can't find him. I can feel him out there, but somehow, I can't reach him." I stopped short of telling her about my dreams morphing into horrid visions of the Elar—as a believer, I couldn't imagine she would care to hear me speak ill of the Immortal so many Fae worshiped.

"Sometimes, when one person is on the move—traveling or restless—it proves difficult to connect. It could be that your Mithraan is on his way back to Tíria. Or, better still, that he is on his way here."

I sat back in my seat, stunned at the suggestion. "You think that's a possibility?"

A knowing grin took over her features. "The sea is no impediment to love," she said. "I wouldn't be surprised if he showed up here one of these days."

"But..." *I couldn't leave with him. It would be an endless cycle of frustration and torment.*

"Let's just say that if ever it happens, I will do what I can to help keep him safe," she said, reading my thoughts once again.

"*If it ever happens,*" I said, allowing the faintest light of hope to pour into my soul. I pressed my hands to the table and rose. "You know, I think I'll take you up on your suggestion. I'll ask Lark to bring Riah to me, and see about an outing in the city."

"Good," she replied. "I'm so glad to hear it."

As I smiled down at her, the accumulation of nineteen years without a mother assaulted me. I had told myself all my life that I was happy with just my father and Leta, that our small family was perfect, and that you couldn't miss what you'd never known.

But I couldn't help wondering how different our lives would have been if only our mother had been able to spend those years with us in our small, thatch-roofed house.

"Come see me on occasion," she said. "Keep me apprised as to your progress. I realize it can be frustrating, but you're working toward a goal more noble than any other. Your purpose here is more important than any spell you could possibly cast."

My momentary bliss crashed to earth, shattering to pieces. She had to be talking about the throne of Aetherion—not a goal I desired, and certainly not a "purpose" I relished. If that was to be my destiny, I would rail against it until I was spent. Hell, I would be only too happy to sabotage my training sessions, if it meant convincing Kazimir that I should never rule over any realm.

"I'll try to remember that, Mother," I said with a weak upturn of my lips.

As I turned away, my mother said, "Lyrinn..."

"Yes?"

"The coming days will be difficult for all of us. Whatever comes to pass, I want you to know that I *am* fond of you."

The way she said the words—the strange, distant calculation and coldness in her voice—they felt like they came from one incapable of emotion, yet trying all the same to convey it.

I walked away, saying nothing, and telling myself that over the course of one thousand years under Kazimir's thumb, anyone's heart would turn to ice.

CHAPTER TWENTY-THREE

LARK REAPPEARED the moment I stepped into the corridor outside my mother's chamber, flapping along in obedient silence as I began to walk.

I didn't ask if he'd overheard our conversation. I didn't want to know. Best, I told myself, not to think too much about it.

"Would you do me a favor?" I asked when we had nearly arrived at my bed chamber.

"Of course. I am at your disposal, Highness."

"Fetch Riah for me," I said. "Bring her here."

Without another word, Lark took off, disappearing into the shadows of the long corridor, and I made my way into my room.

A few minutes later, a timid knock sounded at the door.

"Riah," I said when I'd summoned her inside and sealed us in. "I'm so glad to see you."

Her chin was down, her posture submissive, and I cursed myself for my treatment of her during our first exchange. It had been days since it had occurred. But in the interim, a deep loneliness had set into my mind—and I realized that my coldness to her was unwarranted. She had tried to offer me advice and friendship, and I had rebuffed her at every turn.

The truth was, I needed a friend. A companion. Someone I could trust implicitly.

"Come in," I said. "Listen…"

She lifted her chin as she stepped forward, her pace trepidatious at best.

"I apologize for being hard on you during our first meeting," I told her. "I was untrusting, and it was wrong of me. I didn't know…"

"You didn't know your mother was here," she said, her eyes lighting up just a little. "You didn't know there was any good in this place at all, and you felt that I was just another Lightblood trapping you here. I understand—believe me, I do."

"That's true," I conceded. "But it doesn't excuse my behavior. I wanted to apologize in person."

"It's all right, Highness," she said, and at last, I could see her straighten up as though a heavy load had been removed from her shoulders. "Really."

"I thought perhaps I could take you up on your offer to take me into town. Tomorrow night—if it's all right with you."

At that, her eyes lit up and a smile transformed her features. She took a step toward me, stopping herself before she was too close. "Really, Princess?" she asked.

"You'll have to refrain from calling me that for the duration," I laughed. "But yes. I'd like to go into town as a regular Fae—a normal, everyday Lightblood, if there is such a thing. But I'm not asking you to break any rules. As long as we don't leave the city limits, we're not defying the High King, correct?"

"Exactly," she replied with a wave of her hand. "My only concern is dressing you in something appropriate. Your wardrobe, it's…"

I was wearing a white dress of thick silk that flowed down to the floor, and realized, casting my eyes downward, that it was a little ridiculous. "Too formal?" I asked.

"Too...white. You'd stick out like a sore thumb among the town-Fae. Come—I'll lend you something. I should also make sure Lumen and Kierin are available to meet us, for an extra layer of protection."

"Lumen?" I asked. "Kierin?"

"Two High King's Guardsmen—friends of mine. High King Kazimir *would* have my head if I took you into town without protection. I'll make sure they're waiting for us at the pub."

"Great," I said with a forced smile, relieved, at least, to know she wasn't trying to set me up in some sort of awkward romantic pairing.

"I'll make all the necessary arrangements," she said, her voice high-pitched, excited, and I could sense her desire to bounce up and down with giddiness...though she was good enough to suppress it. "I'll return to you tomorrow when night falls. I'll dress you like a commoner, just to be on the safe side."

As evening neared the following day, a knock sounded at my door. I had barely left my chamber since morning, apprehensive that Kazimir would learn of my plans with Riah and lock me inside, if only to spite me.

I'd managed to avoid him for days on end; it would be terrible indeed if today was the day we came face to face.

"Who is it?" I called.

"Lark," the sprite's deep voice replied.

When I pulled the door open, I saw that he was dressed in a small suit of armor, his blade sheathed elegantly at his side.

"You're all dressed up," I said.

"It's a special occasion."

Smiling and leaning against the door frame, I crossed my arms. "Go ahead. Tell me why you're here."

"Because I want to give you some advice."

I gestured for him to continue. "Please."

There was no smile on his lips when he replied, "When you head into the city tonight, be wary."

"Wait—how do you know about my outing, given that you aren't allowed in my chamber except in emergencies, and Riah and I definitely made those plans in this very room, with the door closed?" I poked him in the stomach and laughed. "Or do I even need to ask?"

Lark fisted his small hand, pressed it to his mouth, and let out an awkward cough. "Just a guess."

"Tiny spy," I retorted.

"Enormous Fae," he shot back.

"All right. I deserved that. And your advice is duly noted. I will pay attention to my surroundings and try not to do anything reckless. There—are you satisfied?"

"I'd be happier if you didn't leave the palace at all."

"Hmm...that sounds like something a certain High King would say."

Lark narrowed his small eyes at me. "I assure you, I have not discussed this with the High King."

I assessed him for a moment, then said, "Fine. I believe you. Now, if you don't mind, I need to get ready."

With that, I shut the door, knowing full well that was not the last I would see of Lark tonight.

By the time Riah showed up on my doorstep, I had already eaten the dinner the servants had brought me. I was pacing my chamber, restless and excited.

Riah held out a pair of black leather trousers and matching boots, a cream-colored blouse and a long coat of worn brown leather. "It gets chilly in the evenings." She spoke quickly when she added, "You'll be happiest if you wear layers. Oh—and I suggest you wear your hair down."

"Why's that?"

She took my hand and dragged me in front of a long mirror, pulling my dark waves back and gesturing to the markings on my neck. "You do know what these are, don't you?"

"They were left behind when I was..." I began, but realized how long a story I would have to tell to explain the wounds I'd suffered as a young child and how Mithraan had healed me. "When I discovered I was a Fae."

"They are called *Morfi*. Some say they're patterns that alter and change as a High Fae moves toward their fate, their eternal destiny. Not all have them, but they're a target on your flesh for anyone curious to seek out a powerful Fae...such as a princess."

As if on cue, I watched my reflection as the twisting spirals of black on my skin began to unfurl, curling up into new configurations. I recalled the doors on my mother's chamber, the way their swirling patterns had shifted as I approached, and wondered if there was any connection.

"That's..." I was about to say *impossible*. But if my life over the last few months had proved anything, it was that nothing was impossible.

"I know," Riah said. "It takes some getting used to. I didn't know about Morfi for most of my life. Most High Fae who have them keep them hidden, in case they contain some secret message or other—though no one really seems to know what they mean. Legend holds that only devout followers of the Elar and her High Priestesses can read them."

"Really?"

Riah nodded. "Truthfully, I'm still not sure I believe in any power higher than the High King," she said. "But there's been so much talk about the Elar lately and the coming Succession. There are plenty in the city who worship her—which is why you should probably keep the marks hidden. They're a target on your flesh you don't want to show off."

"Well, I have no intention of showing any part of me off," I said. "All I want is a flagon of ale, honestly. And to breathe a little. I feel like I've been pacing my room for months—like I've forgotten what it is to live outside a pretty cell."

"I'll see to it that you have a pint with your name on it the second we sit down," Riah laughed. "Come—let's go look after that craving of yours."

Just outside the stables, we found a small carriage of plain, unvarnished wood awaiting us. Utterly lacking in opulence, it looked like something a Fae commoner might have in their possession—and meant we would be unlikely to attract unwanted attention before our arrival, at least.

"Kierin and Lumen will meet us there," Riah said as we climbed inside. "They walked into town earlier."

I nodded. "You said they're High King's Guard. Are they...old?"

"Lumen is. He's in charge of the new recruits—the younger Fae, looking to prove themselves in service. He's worked for the High King for many years. Kierin is young, but he's extremely enthusiastic and loyal. To say he was bouncing off several walls at the chance to spend time with you is barely an exaggeration."

Laughing, I asked, "And you're friends with both?"

As I seated myself opposite her, Riah let out a self-conscious chuckle. "I'm friends with almost everyone," she said. "It serves me well. Easier to extract information from allies than enemies, I suppose."

"Oh?" I asked as the carriage lurched forward. "And why would you want to extract information?"

For a moment, her amusement faded as though she realized she'd said too much. Then she smiled and replied, "I work as a Watcher for the High King—don't worry; he doesn't know about tonight. But there is an ongoing threat in this land—one that grows year by year. An evolving conflict between Lightbloods, the believers and the non-believers."

"You're talking about the followers of the Elar?" I asked quietly.

She nodded. "The thing is, some who believe in her don't want the Succession to come to pass. They're afraid—of what, I'm not entirely sure."

I pulled my eyes to the window, pushing away thoughts of my nightmares, of the horrible winged apparition and her destructive nature. If others had been subjected to the same dreams, I could only imagine how desperately they were willing to fight against the Elar's followers.

"I've heard that she's chosen by the order of High Priestesses," I said. "Maybe we should be reassured by that."

I hoped the words would reassure Riah and me both, but they fell entirely flat.

"Maybe," Riah said. "Still, the whole thing is eerie, if I'm to be honest. I've never liked the notion of a being who controls our fates from afar—particularly not one who is chosen by a bunch of faceless women so powerful that they could easily destroy our world."

As the carriage slipped under the portcullis that led out of the courtyard, we made our way down a long, steep cobbled avenue flanked by narrow white saplings. The sky was growing dark, the clouds glowing purplish-blue in the dusk, and as we moved, lights began to flicker to life in the trees' branches.

"Magic?" I gestured to the sight.

Riah looked out and shook her head. "Sprites. Each evening, they light the trees for us. Take a look."

I stared out, narrowing my eyes as we passed one tree to see a number of sprites perched on the branches, tiny torches in hand.

"Why would they do that?" I asked, horrified, though admittedly the street looked beautiful, ethereal, even magical. "Did the High King command it?"

"No! It's their way of thanking him," she said, laughing. "For saving their kind from extinction many years ago."

I raised an eyebrow, shocked. "Saving? From what?"

I recalled what Lark had said about Kazimir saving his family. But surely my father hadn't gone around over the years, rescuing thousands of sprites from feral canines.

"When the sprites' territory in what is now known as the Barren Lands was burned and decimated long ago," Riah explained, "the High King invited the sprites to Aethos, to live. He gave them homes and employment and saw to it that they were able to earn fair wages. No ruler had ever done such a thing for them, and they have never forgotten it through many generations. In the old times, the sprites were largely considered menaces. Parasites, feeding off Lightblood land, wreaking havoc on livestock. To be fair, they do tend to behave like tricksters."

My eyes darted around the carriage's inside as I wondered if

Lark was hiding in a dark corner, listening to what Riah was saying.

"The only sprite I know seems honest, and honorable," I replied in a slightly defensive tone.

"Oh, yes—I don't mean to imply that they're horrid little creatures," Riah said. "I've always enjoyed their company. But most Lightbloods have been less than courteous to their kind. High King Kazimir changed that when he granted them their food and homes in return for their loyalty."

I found myself stunned to hear such a thing about Kazimir —that he had the capacity for such generosity. But I couldn't help asking myself if generosity given in return for loyalty really counted...or was it simply a negotiating tactic?

"Honestly," Riah continued, "it's tragic what happened to the sprite lands. The Barren Lands were once known as Levath. Long ago, that territory was green and lush, covered in flowering trees and beautiful, crystal-clear ponds. Waterfalls, lakes. For the sprites and many Lightbloods, it was a wonderland."

"Why did Levath fall?" I asked, a note of apprehension in my voice. "Who destroyed it?"

"Some say it was the Elar...but I've heard other rumors," Riah said, glancing at me before pulling her eyes quickly away. "The truth is, I don't know."

As the road continued its descent from the castle grounds, we passed by someone—a female Fae in a white cloak who stopped, turned, and stared as the carriage passed.

When her eyes flashed briefly red, locking on mine, I found myself cowering against my will.

"Don't mind her," Riah whispered, leaning in close. "I swear, her kind loves to sow fear. They enjoy playing with us."

"Her kind?"

"She's a Priestess of the Order of the Elar. And she's not even one of the high-ranking ones—just a Novice. You can tell by the white garb. There's only one High Priestess around here —the one who presides over the temple on the palace grounds."

"I'm confused about something," I said, a vertical crease forming between my brows. "If the Elar is responsible for the destruction of so much of Aetherion, then why is a Priestess even allowed to worship on the palace grounds? I would have thought Kazimir would have kicked their kind out long ago."

Riah shrugged. "A fine question, and one I've asked myself for a long time. Some think the High King is curious to know their ways—to learn if there's any truth to the stories about the Elar. Others suspect he just doesn't care—that, like most of us, he thinks the whole thing is a fairy tale told by a bunch of fanatics, and that the lands were ruined by some other force entirely."

"Something tells me you have other ideas."

Riah let out a deep sigh. "I'm not sure the Elar is all she's reputed to be. But if she is, then I believe it's best to leave the Priestesses be and to live our lives. Look, the fact is, Aethos is thriving. Right now, it's a happy place, with happy Fae and happy sprites. But Kazimir is ambitious, and always has been. He'd like to extend his reach to the North, which means embracing the Order of the Elar and its many followers. The High Priestesses run Nordvahl—one in particular, a Fae named Cassia. They call her the Gray Lady, and I've heard she has a direct link to the Elar—that she is the only one capable of communicating with her. I've heard rumors that she will be coming south in the very near future—though why she would come so close to the Succession, I can't say."

Without knowing why, I shuddered. "It sounds to me like they're a bunch of religious fanatics trying to hold onto their lands as long as they can. Perhaps they burned the Barren

Lands themselves to separate the North from the South—to keep themselves isolated."

"Maybe." Riah half-grunted. "There's a rumor, and I don't know if it's true. But it's always puzzled me."

"Which is?"

"That long ago, the Elar took the wings of all High Fae from them."

"Yes, I've heard that."

"The thing is, they say the High Priestesses *have* wings. That the Elar grants them to those who serve her loyally."

"Have you ever seen any proof of that?" I asked as the carriage pulled to a stop.

"No proof," she replied. "But I've heard that Varyn, the Priestess who presides over the temple in the palace, has them. I can't bring myself to enter that place, but you should venture in one of these days—you might actually find it interesting." She winked at me when she said, "Maybe you could report to me with your findings."

The carriage's door opened, the driver waiting for us to descend.

With goosebumps rising on my skin, I recalled the apparition who haunted my nightmares—the Fae with red-veined silver wings who reveled in chaos.

Under my breath, I said, "I would be just as happy never to see the wings of a Priestess."

CHAPTER TWENTY-FOUR

WE FOUND ourselves standing under a pair of white trees, their branches intertwining overhead like an elegant arbor, the sprites lighting them up in an exquisite display.

Riah led the way toward a broad wooden door, turning as she moved to speak over her shoulder. "Welcome to the Flask," she said as she pulled the door open to the sound of singing, laughter, and semi-intoxicated voices shouting in mock argument.

As we stepped inside, my nose was greeted by an assortment of familiar, comforting scents.

Pipe weed. Burning wood. Fresh bread. Flagons of ale.

But that was where the sense of familiarity ended. The pub's interior was unlike any I'd ever seen in Dúnbar. Instead of the warmth of dark wood and a soot-stained hearth, this place was bright, almost glowing with a warmth that I could scarcely bring myself to describe. Here and there, small bursts of light flickered in mid-air, but there was no clear source of luminosity. No lanterns, candles, or torches brightening the space.

Instead, it appeared almost as though it was the Fae themselves who brought the light to our surroundings. It wasn't that the Lightbloods were glowing, exactly. Only that in their presence, darkness...disappeared.

As we walked in, I didn't feel my usual self-conscious desire to hide, to tuck myself away. Instead, I felt light, comfortable, and at home, welcomed by an unseen force.

"Lightbloods don't just get our name from our hair," Riah said, turning to watch me wonder at the strangeness of the place. "We thrive on brightness. Feed off of it. It's why so many fear caves and dark places—and the North, where it's dark for so much of the year."

"It's strangely calming," I admitted. "I've always been drawn to darkness—yet this feels like...comfort."

Riah laughed. "Come on, let's go sit with my friends."

Taking my hand as though I were her oldest friend, she guided me across the pub until we'd come to a large, light wood table where two Lightblood males stood to greet us. One of them—his cheeks freckled, his eyes dark green—grinned at me. The other, a dark-eyed Fae with bronze skin, assessed me as if trying to work out whether or not he should kill me on the spot.

"You must be Lumen," I said to him as I met his gaze with a hard-edged stare.

"I am," he replied without addressing me by my title, for which I was grateful.

"And this is Kierin," Riah said, gesturing to the freckled young Fae, who stared in wonder at me.

"It is an honor," he half-whispered, leaning in a little too close, his breath smelling of ale. "I can't believe I'm meeting the...I mean, *you*. Honestly. It's like a dream."

"Sit down, you wank," Riah told him, pointing to the nearest chair. "Don't act so reverent. We're meant to be friends out for a quiet evening, not some bizarre fanatical worship party."

Neither of the Fae wore a uniform, though Lumen's tunic

bore a small silver pin that indicated he was a member of the High King's Guard.

Riah glanced toward the barkeep, a tall, thin Fae with long braided hair, and held up two fingers. "Wait until you experience Lightblood lager," she said. "It's unlike anything you've ever had."

I glanced around the room, curious, and noted that none of the pub's Fae denizens looked intoxicated—though most of them did look genuinely content and relaxed.

Here and there, a sprite flitted about, darting this way and that. A few tables down, two of them were engaged in some sort of mid-air fisticuffs, which brought an amused smile to my lips.

I spotted Lark perched on a bottle of wine two tables over. He was watching me intently, his small hand on the needle-like blade sheathed at his waist. I wondered silently why he looked so concerned...but quickly pulled my attention to the others.

"So, you two," I exhaled. "What's it like to be in the service of my father?"

Lumen still had the same look of scrutiny in his eye when he replied, "I would think you would know perfectly well. He's your father, after all."

"I barely know the High King," I retorted. "We aren't exactly close, in case you haven't heard."

"The High King's Guard is phenomenal," Kierin said enthusiastically. "Truly. Such an absolute thrill. A dream, really."

"Is it?" I asked, laughing. "Why is that?"

Part of me simply wanted to hear him speak—something about the young Fae was so effervescent, so enthusiastic and positive that I couldn't help but find him charming. But part of me was genuinely curious as to how it could possibly be pleasant to serve such a beast as Kazimir.

"He's a legend," Kierin replied. "Just an *absolute* legend. He's

helped so many Fae. They even say he will restore our land—
that he will soon vanquish—"

"Shut your weedy little food-hole," Lumen hissed, his brows
meeting. "How much lager have you had, you fool?"

As he spoke, the barkeep laid a pint in front of Riah and one
in front of me. I took a sip and quickly realized Lightblood Lager
was unlike anything I'd ever consumed. Instead of the usual
feeling of warm, slow intoxication that alcohol provided, it
filled me with an instant feeling of clarity, of strength.

Confidence.

Far too much of it.

"I've had half a pint, that's all," Kierin replied defensively.
"Besides, I'm off-duty 'til tomorrow."

"No matter. Don't go talking about rumors about the High
King. It's against every protocol. He'd have your head for far
less."

"Wait," I said, reaching for Kierin's arm, which inspired a
smile to curl his lips. "Tell me more." Shooting a look at Lumen,
I added, "That's an order. Tell me who the High King is
allegedly going to vanquish."

Riah issued me a *Trust me, you don't want to hear this
nonsense* warning, but I persisted.

"I'm curious, that's all."

Kierin leaned toward me, lowered his chin, and in all sincer-
ity, he said, "The *Elar*."

Riah made a scoffing laugh and said, "Ridiculous. There are
just as many rumors circulating that Lyrinn is the next Elar."

I slammed back in my seat, staring at her. "What?"

"Now *that's* insane," said Lumen, his hard veneer breaking
as he burst into laughter. "She is not a High Priestess. Everyone
knows Sisters of the Order must have served faithfully for
centuries before they'll even be considered."

Riah shrugged. "Maybe—maybe not. Look—I'm just saying rumors are stupid. They mean nothing at all."

"Fair enough," Lumen agreed, then waved his hands next to his face and added, "Or...maybe Lyrinn really *is* meant to be Elar. Maybe that's why she was brought to these shores."

I couldn't help it. I let out a loud laugh that drew a few eyes from those around us. I quickly cupped a hand over my mouth and slouched back in my seat. "Sorry," I said, staring at my drink. "I have no idea why I found that so funny. What in the realms is in this lager?"

"All good things," Riah said with a chuckle. "But watch yourself. It can hit hard the first few times."

"Well, the good news is that it seems our princess isn't too concerned with prophecies," Lumen added under his breath before clinking his glass against mine and whispering, "I commend you for that, Highness."

"Prophecies are nothing more than a convenient excuse for gossip," I replied before taking another swig. "Besides, I can't help but point out that not a single soul has bothered to ask me if I would ever have any *interest* in becoming the next Elar."

"Would you?"

"Hell no," I replied with a chuckle. "Power is all well and good, but...no."

We continued our conversation and ordered another round of lager, laughing our way through the evening. After a while, the drink had dulled my senses and inhibitions enough that when Kierin asked what it was like having Kazimir as a father, I leaned toward him with a grin.

"Well," I said, taking another long sip of ale. "Let's just say that one of the first things he told me was how he poisoned the two Tírian Champions at the last Blood Trials. So it's been...interesting."

"Wait—he told you *that*?" Riah said, and out of the corner of my eye, I saw Lumen looking equally baffled.

I chastised myself. *Gods. Why would I say that out loud?*

"I—"

I was about to tell them it was just a tasteless joke when Riah said, "It's not that we don't know what happened—every Lightblood knows it was the High King who was behind the actual killing."

I breathed a quick sigh of relief, as mad as it was to be pleased that my father had actually murdered innocent Fae.

"The thing is," Kierin said with a grin, "It wasn't *really* him. Everyone knows—*Ouch*!"

He glared at Riah, who had apparently kicked him under the table.

"Wait just a minute," I said, my tongue slightly swollen from the effects of the ale. "I saw Kazimir do it. I watched him."

"It was a thousand years ago, and you're what, nineteen?" Kierin scoffed. "You can't have watched him."

"I did," I insisted. "Through my mother's memories. I saw what happened."

Riah and Kierin exchanged a knowing glance, while Lumen's face went blank.

"What aren't you telling me?" I said, feeling suddenly awkward.

"Ancestral memories can be...unreliable," Riah said quietly. "Depending on whose mind you're accessing. It's easy to alter them or to veil them. Otherwise, we would all know our relatives' deepest secrets, and that would be bloody awful."

"But—are you saying those two Champions weren't poisoned? I told you, Kazimir was more than happy to own up to it."

"No—it's a well-known fact that they were. I'm only saying it may not have happened as you saw it in your mind. Look, even if no one messed with your mother's memories, they may have ebbed and changed over the past thousand years. We sometimes convince ourselves we saw things that weren't there —or fail to see things that *were* there."

I wanted to reply that it sounded an awful lot like they were making excuses for murder, but I thought better of it. I shouldn't have been speaking of such things in a public place, anyhow; it was folly.

"On another topic," I said, looking at Riah, "Tell me why the hell my clothes are all white. Like, every single garment in my possession in that damned palace. Whose idea was that?"

There was no smile in her eyes when she said, "Your mother's, actually."

My eyes widened. "Really? Why would she—"

Again, she and Kierin exchanged a knowing look. "Should we tell her?" Kierin asked.

"I don't see why not." Riah gestured to him to go ahead.

"It's one of the reasons the rumor is circulating about you being the next Elar," he said. "White is the color of the Succession—many of the followers of the Order wear it in the days leading up to the ceremony. There are some who have seen you wandering the palace who call you the White Priestess."

I laughed again. "Why anyone would use that title for me..." I tried to finish, but for some reason, this time I convulsed into fits of howling. I tried to picture what Mithraan would think if he knew anyone around the palace called me by such an absurd name. "The day I become a follower of the Elar is the day—"

My smile disappeared instantly as I noticed a solitary Light-blood sitting a few tables away, her gaze locked on me. She was dressed entirely in form-fitting black leather garb, including a jacket with a high collar that brought out a set of yellow eyes.

She was studying my face, her expression set in a strange sort of accusation, though I had no idea why.

"I'm being watched," I muttered, pulling my eyes away from her.

Riah turned and glanced at the Fae. "She's probably just admiring you. You do stand out a little, with your hair—though many younger Lightbloods don't come into their white hair until their twenties, at least. It's not like it's that unusual."

I pulled my chin down to stare at my hands, which were now intertwined nervously in my lap, glowing white as if in warning. Quietly, I glanced around in search of Lark, but I could no longer see him.

"Just ignore her," Riah said. "Seriously. Lightblood ale makes some Fae hostile and cocky. She could be looking for a fight, and you do not want to give it to her. Just pretend she's not there, and she'll leave you alone."

I pulled my attention back to Kierin and Lumen, who were arguing quietly about some topic or other.

"I want to hear more about the Elar," I interrupted. It wasn't entirely true, but I desperately wanted to take my mind off the yellow eyes I'd seen a moment ago. "I take it you two believe she exists?"

Kierin's eyes shot to mine, opening saucer-wide as his eyebrows flew upward. "You don't believe in her?" he asked, and immediately I regretted what I'd said.

"I don't know what to believe," I replied. "I've only just arrived in this place—and in the mortal lands of Kalemnar, we never so much as heard of her. I didn't mean to offend."

He nodded. "When I was young..." he began.

Lumen chuckled. "Young? You're still a mere toddler, by my standards."

"Fine. When I was young*er*," Kierin corrected, "my mother took me to meet a Priestess in the Barren Lands. There is still a temple there, about halfway to Nordvahl. I don't remember why we were so far north, but I'll never forget her—her face, her eyes. But most of all...I remember her wings."

"You saw them?" Riah said, pressing her elbows to the table, keenly interested.

He nodded. "They were extraordinary. Made of pure light, but so strong that you could *feel* the power emanating from them. She told me they were a gift from the Elar—that all those who served loyally were granted flight. Ever since that day, I have believed. They were the only Fae wings I've ever seen— though they say that Varyn has wings as well—the Priestess at the palace."

"You only believe in the bloody Elar because you want wings of your own," Lumen scoffed. "I have news for you: that bitch doesn't gift wings to males."

"Well, maybe she will one day," Kierin replied.

"And maybe dogs will fly."

They glared at one another, then both burst into laughter. "Okay, maybe that's a shite reason to worship an unseen entity," Kierin admitted. "But I'll admit it—I want what my forebears had. I want the powers we Fae once lost."

"You're not even a High Fae, you twat," Lumen scoffed. "You wouldn't have had wings, even in the old times."

"In the old times, I would've been *king*," Kierin protested, puffing his chest out like a too-proud rooster.

As Lumen shifted the subject back to their service in the High King's Guard, I continued to listen, downing my pint quietly and being careful not to say too much. Before I knew it, a servant came by with more drinks and laid them in front of us.

I had just reached for my own when I felt a sharp jab in my shoulder that prompted me to drop it. The cup hit the table with a hard *thump*, sloshing so that it almost spilled.

"What the hell was that?" I gasped. I looked up to see a sprite shooting across the pub away from me.

"Lark?" I breathed.

"Oh!" Kierin said. "Someone bought you a Faeberry Twist!"

Without asking permission, he grabbed my cup and downed half of it, then let out a loud belch.

"Kierin!" Riah chastised. "Rude!"

"It's fine," I said, laughing nervously. "But I didn't even order another drink. Where did it come from?"

I glanced around the pub, and as I did so, Lumen, suddenly wary, rose to his feet and reached for something at his waist. It was then that I noticed a small, elegant silver hilt—a dagger tucked into a white sheath.

I spun around, alert and nervous, and looked to see if we were still being watched. But the Fae who had been staring at us earlier—the one dressed in black—was gone.

As my eyes scanned the space for her, a sickening thud met my ears. I turned to see that Kierin's head had hit the table.

He wasn't moving.

The whites of his eyes had gone red, and out of his mouth trailed a horrific white froth. His skin, rosy-cheeked just seconds earlier, was gray and patchy.

"The drink," Lumen said. "It was meant for her Highness. Get her the hell out of here!"

Without a word, Riah grabbed hold of my arm and dragged me toward the door. I spun around, horrified, trying to see if there was any hope for young Kierin.

I knew without asking that he was dead, and whoever had killed him had used a potent poison to do so.

Desperate, I leapt back to him and held my hands over his slumped form, calling on the healing power I had once possessed to bring him back to life—but if it still surged inside me, it wasn't enough to counter the gruesome toxin the Lightblood had consumed.

"Your Highness," Lark's deep voice spoke from beside me. I

wiped away a tear as I turned to trudge toward the door. "I tried to pursue the assassin—but she's a dark-wielder. She disappeared into the shadows. Forgive me."

"It was you who jabbed me in the shoulder," I said. "You stopped me from taking a sip."

"Yes, but I was a fool—I should have spilled the drink instead. Your companion—"

"I know. But...you saved my life, Lark."

Riah led me to our carriage and we climbed in, with Lark still hovering outside. "I am so grateful," I said. "No one could have known Kierin would..."

I couldn't bring myself to say more. The guardsman was so young, so vivacious and good-humored.

And now, he was gone.

"We must get you back to the palace," Riah said. "Before anything else happens."

Lark said, "I'm going to search for your assailant. Head straight to the palace, and do not stop for anything."

Tight-lipped, I nodded silent thanks and watched as the driver shut the door.

"My father will kill me and finish the poison's job," I said woefully. "When he finds out about this."

CHAPTER TWENTY-FIVE

As THE CARRIAGE passed under the portcullis into the courtyard, I could see that several members of the High King's Guard awaited us in full armor, helmets and breastplates gleaming in the moonlight.

"Hells," Riah said under her breath. "Damn it all. Lumen must have sent a sprite ahead to report the assassination attempt to your father. Not that I can blame him for it—but I'd hoped we wouldn't have to deal with it immediately on our arrival."

"It wasn't just an *attempt*," I pointed out with a morose shake of my head. "One of the High King's guards is dead—so I can hardly blame Lumen. It's not his fault...though I can only imagine what the consequences will be when Kazimir learns I was in town without his express permission."

The last thing I wanted right now was to speak of what had just occurred. What I had seen.

What Kierin must have endured in the brief moment between life and death.

I wanted to retreat to my bed chamber and lie in secluded

darkness, hiding from this realm that was becoming simultaneously more and less welcoming by the day.

I glanced over at Riah to see that her fear appeared even more intense than my own. But of course—*what a fool I was*. Kazimir might punish me harshly, cruelly, even. But she was the one who had taken me into the city without first asking the High King's permission. She was a Watcher—and she had failed to see the threat coming for us.

For all I knew, he might order her killed.

"I won't let him hurt you," I promised. "Whatever happens. He's the one who wanted you to make me feel at home, remember."

"You might not have a say in my pending demise," she replied. "Your father is far more powerful than either of us—and he can do as he wishes."

"No matter," I murmured, my jaw clenched resolutely. "If he touches you, I'll kill him. I swear it."

Riah shook her head in silent warning, but didn't utter the words I knew she was thinking.

Never, ever threaten the High King's life.

I turned away, pulling my eyes to the door as a guard yanked it open.

"The High King wishes to see you both in the throne room, Highness."

I reached for Riah's hand and took it protectively, stepping down from the carriage and, holding on tightly, followed the guard toward the nearest set of white doors.

We walked in silence for what felt like several tense minutes until we reached a large, imposing chamber. Flanked with ornate white columns crawling with expertly crafted vines of delicate silver, the room's centerpiece was a single, enormous throne displayed at its far end.

Like so many things in Aethos, it was beautiful, pristine, forged of white stone veined with silver.

Only one throne, I thought. *Does my mother never sit on one of her own?*

As we approached, Kazimir slipped out of a side door and made his way to the throne, a crown of silver perched atop his head. It was delicately forged by the Lightblood smiths, its tendrils intertwining into what almost looked like an array of organic greenery but for its metallic sheen.

The crown glinted in the flickering light, reflecting every torch in the room. But more than that, it seemed to glow with an ethereal light, as if its source were within the silver itself. It was a beautiful piece, and one that exuded untold power.

I wondered with a quiet sigh if it was that same crown I would one day wear, should I be forced to take the throne. Against my will, part of me ached for it. Craved the power that came with such a symbol.

Another part was disgusted by its very existence.

When we were near enough, the guard signaled us to stop. I glanced over to see Lumen, now in full silver armor, standing some distance away and watching me, his expression icy.

You're in pain, I thought. *I don't need Riah's empathy to know it. You lost a friend, and I am sorry for it.*

"Is it true, Daughter, that you were in the city this evening?" Kazimir asked, his voice echoing through the chamber.

My bones shuddered, but I held my chin high when I nodded. "It's true," I said. "I wished to see something of this realm and its inhabitants."

"I see," he replied. "Without my permission, you chose to accompany Riah to the Flask—a public house frequented by miscreants. Without so much as considering the possible repercussions of it, you foolishly entered an establishment without adequate protection."

"It seemed an innocent enough excursion," I retorted. "I wore the clothing of a local. I—"

"Did I ask you to speak?" Kazimir snapped, pulling his focus to Riah. "And *you*—what the hell were you thinking, putting my daughter in danger in such a way? She was nearly killed. I lost a new recruit because of your recklessness."

Riah bowed her head. "I take full responsibility, Highness," she said. "It was foolish of me. I..."

As she spoke, I caught sight of a shadow moving quickly to the left side of the throne room. I glanced over to see that Erildir and my mother had stepped into the chamber and positioned themselves near a few of the High King's Guardsmen. Their faces were impassive, unreadable, but I could only imagine they were as disappointed in my foolishness as the High King himself.

"You endangered her life," Kazimir scolded, his eyes still locked on Riah. "My guards are hunting for her assassin as we speak—and I have a team of sprites doing the same. But even if we should catch her, there is no telling how many others might be out there who now know Lyrinn's face. Do you know the risk you took? Do you have any idea how important the princess is —not only to this land, but to me?"

"To *you*?" I snarled, stepping forward to position myself protectively between Riah and Kazimir. "You don't even know me! You've never had so much as a normal conversation with me...*Father*. Every time we've spoken, you've treated me with disdain, with disgust. How can you sit there and pretend I'm important, when all you've done is abuse me?"

Kazimir studied me for a moment, his jaw set, the veins in his neck jutting out in barely suppressed rage. "You have no idea what you're talking about," he said slowly. "Nothing in this world is more valuable to me than you...and your sister."

"So why is Leta in Kalemnar still?" I asked. "Why would you

leave her behind? Why separate us? You're cruel beyond words. The one time I dare to step outside the palace walls to see a little of Aetherion, you act as though I've committed some wretched sin. I was fulfilling your wishes, your Grace. I was learning to call this place a home."

"Back away, Daughter," Kazimir said, rising to his feet and stepping down from the throne. "I wish to address Riah."

"No," I snapped. "I will not."

"She needs to suffer consequences for what she has done."

"Punish me, if you're going to punish anyone. She has done nothing wrong."

"Believe me, I'm contemplating throwing you in the dungeons as we speak. Now, move, before I ask a guardsman to do it for me!"

Out of the corner of my eye, I saw my mother step forward as if she wanted to throw herself between us. But Erildir put his hand on her arm and held her back with a small shake of his head.

"I will not let you hurt Riah," I said, pulling my full attention back to Kazimir. "She is my friend."

Immediately, I knew it was the wrong thing to say.

Foolish.

Stupid.

I had just admitted her value. Made her a weapon Kazimir could use to injure me, to manipulate me. He knew it would hurt me to see her harmed, and I had no doubt he would use that pain.

"Move aside, Lyrinn," Kazimir said again.

I shook my head, but Riah laid a hand on my shoulder and said, "It's all right."

"No. It's not." I held my ground.

"Move, or I'll move you myself," Kazimir growled. This time, he raised one hand into the air. His fingers glowed a blinding white, and the power beneath his flesh was palpable in the chamber as every Fae in the room anticipated its unleashing.

My legs trembled with fear, my heart pounding in my chest to feel such power. But instead of cowering, I raised my own hand, mirroring his motion, and stared into his bright eyes.

"You. Will. Not. Harm. Her." My words were clipped, percussive. As though it was someone else entirely who spoke them.

Kazimir chuckled. "What exactly do you think you're going to do to stop me?" he asked, turning to Erildir with a laugh. "Have you taught her some trick you haven't told me about, Spell-Master? And here, I was under the impression that you had done very little in your sessions but force Lyrinn to pursue a sprite. Am I to be taken down by some secret skill?"

"No, your Grace," Erildir said. "I have taught her nothing that should surprise you."

"Well, then. It's time for this nonsense to end." Kazimir flung his hand toward me, fingers splayed.

Without knowing why, I imitated his motion again, thrusting my hand back toward him with the same violence.

A terrifying, swirling ball of pure blue flame flew at me from his outstretched hand. But in the same moment, a perfect mirror image of the projectile thrashed through the air to meet it. They collided with a blinding explosion and a sound like a thousand shattering windows as every Fae in the room—even the High King—thrust an arm over their eyes.

The fragments tumbled to the ground, disappearing in fading shards of light.

Gasps rose up around me. It seemed even the guardsmen were shocked to witness what had just happened.

But no one was more shocked than I was.

I could hear Riah breathing hard behind me, and I turned to

see Erildir's face twisting into an expression of shock mixed with what almost looked like...fear?

"A Thariel," someone said. "She...she is a Thariel!"

"Yes," Erildir moved toward the High King. "It would seem she is."

"Did you know about this?" Kazimir asked angrily. "Did you lie to me?"

"I did not," Erildir replied morosely. "Though I suppose it comes as no great surprise, given her bloodlines."

"Well, then," Kazimir said, his grimace turning into a smile. "I am delighted to know she's more Gifted than I ever imagined."

I winced as I watched them speak of me like some prize pig. I wanted to ask what a Thariel was, but I was too baffled as to why the High King seemed so pleased.

Why in all the realms would he be happy that I had fought him off so easily?

"Do you realize what this means?" Kazimir asked, his eyes on Erildir.

Erildir nodded. "I do." Turning to me, he added, "The High King's power—the Azure Fire—is one that only he possesses. Which means you, Lyrinn, are a mimic. In the old language, a Thariel. It means that any spell that is thrown at you, any power of any Fae or other magic user in your presence, is one you can replicate, even amplify."

I got the distinct impression that he wasn't as pleased about the revelation as Kazimir was.

"Ah, Daughter," the High King said, stepping toward me and taking my chin in hand. "You are even more valuable than we ever could have predicted." He studied my eyes for a moment, then turned away, and with a wave of his hand he said, "Go to bed, all of you. And Lyrinn—tell me, the next time you wish to go on some foolhardy adventure. I'll send a taster along to sample any food or drink before you. But at least I won't have to worry that any Fae will best you with their spell-crafting."

At that, he turned and strode out of the room, seemingly gliding on a cloud of delight.

Stunned, I turned to look for my mother, but she and Erildir were rapidly making their way out of the room as if they were hoping to evade some deadly threat.

I turned to Riah, my shoulders relaxing for the first time since we'd been in the Flask. I took her arm and guided her out of the chamber, my breath held tight in my chest until I was certain we were safely away from the High King.

The evening had been one of the most bizarre of my entire life. I was relieved to have survived it—relieved that Riah was free. But I still wanted to weep for Kierin, for the life he could and *should* have lived.

I would blame myself for his death until the end of time.

As we made our way toward my bed chamber, I found myself eyeing every Fae we passed suspiciously. Guards I had seen before were now potential enemies. Sprites, flitting rapidly through the air, were new threats.

When I came to my chamber, I let out a low whistle, relieved when Lark appeared.

"Riah, will you be all right?" I asked.

She nodded. "I'll be fine, thanks to you. Is there anything you need before I head to bed?"

"No—thank you. Bar your door tonight, if you would."

"Of course," she said, bowing her head and disappearing down the corridor.

I was about to open my door when Lark told me to stop. "Please—let me go first."

I pushed the door ajar and Lark flew in before me, looking around for any sign that someone had been in the room. "One thing is certain," he said as I stepped inside, confident that we were alone. "Your father and Erildir were right—if you're a Thariel, you would be *very* hard to kill. Even in your sleep, your magic will remain awake and on high alert. The only thing that could possibly stop you is a ring of impediment."

A ring like the one my mother wears each day of her life, I thought.

"Highness," Lark added, turning to me as he hovered at eye level, "Be wary. You are strong indeed—but a determined killer can take down the greatest adversary. Don't trust anyone—not even me."

CHAPTER TWENTY-SIX

When I first awoke in the morning, the sun beaming into the window in joyful rays, I had all but forgotten the previous night's drama. But it all came barreling back into my mind in one swift gust of memory and pain.

Kierin, dead before I even knew him.

My father the High King, delighted for some incomprehensible reason to discover that I was his equal in strength.

All I could think was *I could overpower Kazimir.*

The full meaning of those words was only now beginning to sink in—the knowledge that I could kill my captor, if I so chose. I could take his life and his throne in one fell swoop. Take control of this entire realm.

The trouble was, I had no desire to do so. As much as I hated Kazimir, I wasn't quite ready to call myself a murderer. *King-killer. Traitor to the Crown.*

Not to mention that I hadn't woken this morning with the sensation of strength flowing through my body and mind. I didn't feel invincible. If anything, I was frightened of my newfound power. A small mouse cowering in a dark corner, praying that the local cat failed to spot me, to claim me as its lunch.

With a hard breath, I climbed out of bed and dressed, looking around for any sign that Lark was still around. I couldn't see any evidence of it, but then, Shadowlings didn't exactly thrive on making their presence known.

Ignoring the possibility that he was watching me more closely than usual, I dressed and headed down to the dining hall for breakfast.

When I found no one there, I grabbed a pastry and made my way to the door, pondering my strange new existence as I walked.

I was so very far from Lyrinn Martel, a mortal with a life expectancy of forty years.

I was Princess Lyrinn—a Fae of unspeakable power, and one who might live many thousands of years.

More than ever, I found myself longing for Mithraan's presence. To tell him what had occurred. To hold him, kiss him, make him mine all over again.

Tonight, I told myself with a smile. *Tonight, I'll take the sleep draught again. I will find him, whatever happens—and I'll forbid myself waking up until we have driven each other mad with pleasure.*

By now, the palace's labyrinthine corridors had become second nature, and as I made my way toward the courtyard we used for training purposes, I found myself pausing here and there to take in paintings I hadn't noticed before. A landscape showing rolling green hills with snow-capped mountains in the distance.

A portrait of Kazimir, looking regal, handsome, and terrifying as always.

A portrait of the Elar I had never noticed before. This one was clearer than others I'd noted around the palace. For one thing, she didn't wear a veil this time—and I could clearly see a pair of translucent violet wings, seemingly made of pure light, so delicate and fine that they looked as if they could never support a grown Fae's weight.

I stopped and stared at her. At the face, heart-shaped and beautiful, and a pair of eyes that seemed to alternate between kind and intimidating as each second passed.

She wore a long white dress, and on its chest was embroidered a serpentine symbol—a swirling pattern that looked similar to the marks on my neck, only with more curls and another twisting line striking its way through it. Random and ordered at once, it was strange and beautiful, and as I stared, I was certain it shifted and altered before my eyes.

With a shiver, I turned and continued to walk.

I found Erildir in the courtyard, seated on a stone bench. His eyes were locked straight ahead as if he were immersed in deep meditation.

"I take it our training session is on?" I asked as I approached.

But Erildir shook his head. "You proved last night that you don't need me to train you," he said, gesturing to the bench. "Have a seat."

I sat down, surprised and confused. Did he really think I had nothing left to learn from him?

"The High King is expecting the arrival of a party of visitors today," he said, raising an eyebrow as if testing to see if I already knew. "Guests from the North—honored ones, including the head Priestess of the Order of the Elar."

"Lady Cassia," I said with a nod. "Yes, I'd heard. I—didn't realize she was visiting so soon."

"I only learned of it last night, myself. It seems the High King and your mother have kept it quiet—probably out of caution. It wouldn't do to let all of Aethos know Lady Cassia will be in the palace."

I nodded, still absorbing the news. The last thing I wanted was to encounter more strangers—to have to put up a façade of friendliness around a daunting Priestess like the one I had seen on the street the previous night.

"Be mindful of them," Erildir said. "Get to know them, be friendly and as open as you can. I know you lack trust in strangers, Lyrinn, and I don't blame you for it. But it is my hope that you will get along well with these ones—particularly Adhair, the High Priestess's son."

My heart sank and I felt a familiar curdling sensation in my belly. "Please tell me you're not hoping he and I will marry, because—"

Erildir chuckled dryly. "No, I would not force such a commitment on you. But I'm hoping you will learn to trust him. And that, when the time comes, you will venture north with us for the Succession Ceremony, when the new Elar will be named."

"North?" I blurted out. "I don't...I have no reason to..."

Erildir raised a palm and said, "Please, don't decide right this second. Just...think about it. I think you might find the experience enlightening. The Priestesses would be honored to have you among them. You are somewhat more special than you know, Lyrinn—as you may now realize, given that you were targeted for death last night, and then managed to fight off one of the most powerful Fae ever to live."

I went quiet for a moment before asking in a whisper, "Why *did* someone try to kill me? What am I, that someone would send an assassin to take my life?"

To my surprise, Erildir shrugged. "There are any number of reasons," he said. "You're the daughter of the High King. You're a forbidden hybrid between Tírian and Lightblood. And now, as it turns out, you are a Thariel. That makes you a threat beyond the imagining of most."

"I don't see why. My father already sits on the throne. If I were to take over his reign, nothing would change."

"Perhaps it's your father who has deemed you a threat."

At that, I went rigid, my heart throbbing percussively against my ribcage. No—that theory made no sense. My father had seemed genuinely surprised and angered—protective almost to the point of violence—to learn I had headed into the city last night.

Then again, he was nothing, if not a talented liar. Perhaps it was all a façade.

"No," I finally said with a shake of my head, my long hair falling about my face. "My father could easily kill me himself."

"You proved last night that's simply not true. You are very capable of taking High King Kazimir down with a simple flick of your wrist. Had you fired off a spell after the explosion, he would lie dead on the throne room floor."

He looked like he was almost savoring the thought when a door opened at the far end of the courtyard, and one of the High King's Guardsmen strode in.

"We are not to be interrupted!" Erildir called out. "This courtyard is off-limits to the King's Guard!"

The Fae stopped before us, offered up a quick bow, and said, "Apologies, Spell-Master. The High King sent me to inform you that the would-be assassin has been apprehended and is now in the palace's custody. She is being held in a cell in the dungeons."

The guard turned on his heel and left.

"Did you know anything about this?" I asked Erildir, who looked surprised—even concerned—to hear the news.

"I did not," he said slowly. "You should stay away from her, Highness. Let the High King deal with her, whoever she may be.

In the meantime, Lark and I will do what we can to protect you. Won't we, Lark?"

I heard the sprite's deep voice say, "I will follow her Highness to the depths of this or any other world, if I must." I turned and looked to see that he was hovering just behind me.

"I know you will," Erildir said. "Now, Lyrinn—before you meet the High Priestess and her son this evening, may I suggest you take a trip to the temple at the southeast end of the palace? Perhaps it would be wise to get to know a little about the Elar before meeting the most high-ranking Priestess in the Order."

With a sigh and a sudden feeling of empowerment, I rose to my feet and said, "I suppose I may as well learn a little more about the ways of this land before I leave it for good."

"Leave it?"

I smiled. "Come now, Spell-Master. Someone is trying to kill me. I've just discovered I'm more powerful than the High King. So I'm more convinced than ever that I must find a way home—and keep my mother safe in the process."

Erildir shot me a mysterious look when he said, "If anyone can accomplish such a thing, Lyrinn, it's you. Just—do yourself a favor and don't make any plans yet. You would do well to wait a few days and see what our esteemed guests have to say for themselves. In the meantime, do go and see the temple. I believe it would do you good to meet one of the Elar's acolytes face to face."

"Perhaps you're right. I promise I will."

As I left the courtyard, I vowed to follow through on the vow.

But first, I had an assassin to visit.

CHAPTER TWENTY-SEVEN

THE DUNGEON, it turned out, was not easy to find, even after all the hours I had spent scouring the palace to memorize its copious nooks and crannies. I raced down corridor after corridor, searching for something—anything—that looked like an entrance to a forbidding underground passageway.

At first, I was wholly unsuccessful. Every door I tried was locked or simply wrong, and I found myself striding accidentally into more than one servant's chamber, apologizing repeatedly for the intrusion as I moved on.

"Princess!"

The sprite's voice came to me at the peak of my frustration. I didn't want company or help...yet I had to admit that I was in dire need of the latter, if not the former.

"Lark," I breathed, exasperated.

"You're seeking the dungeon."

"I am," I said, spinning around and starting to walk again. "I'm determined to find out why that Fae wants me dead."

"I'm curious myself," Lark said, flying along next to me.

"You're not going to try and stop me? Erildir would be furious if he knew what I'm up to. Not to mention my father."

"I am not here to serve Erildir or your father—I serve *you*."

I couldn't help but smile. "I knew there was a reason I liked you."

Lark pulled his weapon and pointed. "Head straight down this hallway. Then turn left, and it's the third door on your right. It leads to a stairwell—one that's innocuous enough that no one ever notices it. That's where you want to be."

"Thank you."

"I only ask that you let me come with you."

"Of course."

"And perhaps you should arm yourself, Highness."

"I don't intend to kill her. I just want to chat."

Lark let out a little sigh that was so adorable that I almost laughed. I forced it back, not wanting to offend him.

He continued to direct me as I came to the door he'd mentioned, descended the stairs, and then negotiated my entry with the guard, who had no intention of letting me by until Lark announced that as the High King's daughter, I was entitled to entry in any room, corridor, vestibule, or dungeon in the palace—and that if he wanted to take it up with the High King, he was welcome to do so.

That shut the guard up, and he immediately escorted us to the cell in question.

Lark vanished as we neared the door, but I could still hear the faint *flit-flit* of his wings as I approached, as if he were deliberately reassuring me with his presence.

When we halted, the guard looked at me and said, "Are you quite certain you wish to enter? She's a little..."

He didn't finish the sentence, but I could tell that he found the Fae somewhat terrifying.

I nodded, and with a gruff, "Suit yourself," he unlocked the door and pushed it open.

Inside, the Fae I'd seen in the Flask the night before was

seated on a straw cot, her spine straight. I could see her yellow eyes clearly, disconcertingly bright in the dim light.

On her right hand was an impediment ring similar to my mother's, digging in so that blood trickled from her finger. It was a relief, at least, to know she couldn't cast any spells.

But it meant I would not be able to reflect anything she hurled at me, either. Still—I had honed my skill of summoning light blades. Should I need to, I could probably end her quickly.

"My name is—" I began to say as the guard sealed the door behind me.

"I know your name, Highness," she said, venom dripping from the words.

"Right. Of course you do. So, perhaps I should get right to the point then. Why did you try to kill me last night?"

I was trying my best to keep my eyes locked on hers, but there was something so animalistic, so feline in her expression that I found myself glancing away repeatedly. "Because you are the *Calloc*."

That...was not what I had expected.

I stared at her now, puzzled. "Calloc? I'm afraid I don't know what that is."

The assassin's lip pulled up on one side as she began to sing, low and lilting, with the simplistic melody of a children's song.

"Only with the Calloc's death...

Shall the Elar rise again.

But if she should live,

The Elar falls..."

The melody was strangely beautiful...but the words made my skin crawl.

"Are you a Priestess?" I asked, wondering if that's why her eyes were so strange and her manner so...otherworldly.

She shook her head slowly, her eyes never leaving mine. "I

am a follower of the Elar—nothing more. A devotee, if you prefer."

A fanatic, you mean.

"You still haven't told me what the Calloc is, or why you think I'm her."

"The Calloc is a warrior," she said coldly. "One with the blood of two High Kings in her veins. You are a threat to the order of things, Princess. And you must be stopped."

At that, she pushed herself to her feet and rushed with terrifying speed toward me, grabbing hold of my neck.

Never had I longed so badly for my old dagger. I cursed Erildir for failing to teach me how to fight someone off at close quarters without a weapon.

By the time I'd cried out for the guard, one of the assassin's hands was already twisting in my hair. I could feel her cold fingertips tracing the lines on my neck, her breath on my skin.

"You are marked," she hissed. "Marked for death. There will be a great betrayal — a killing—a sacrifice. And with your end, the world will burn and be renewed."

She had just finished reciting the words when she released her grip and let out a high-pitched cry, grabbing at her throat.

The guard flung the door open and marched in, taking hold of the prisoner and throwing her back against the wall. I twisted around to see blood trickling from a small wound in her neck.

I stormed out of the cell and down the corridor back to the stairs, my heart racing, my skin clammy with sweat.

"Princess." The voice was Lark's. "Are you all right?"

I nodded, though I could feel the redness of my face, the panic in my expression.

"The blood on her neck..." I stammered. "Was that..."

"It was my blade. I couldn't bear her hurting you any longer."

"Thank you," I replied. "I should have cast a spell—I should have killed her. That thing she said...what did she mean, I'm marked for death?" My hands were trembling now. "Why would she say that?"

"Highness, she is a lunatic—a fanatical disciple of the Elar. Nothing more. One who uses her devotion as an excuse to hurt others. It's best not to try and find meaning in her words."

"Is it?" I asked. "Because she sounded pretty damned sure of herself." I stopped walking, having reached the top of the stairs, and inhaled a stuttering breath.

"It's all right," Lark promised, flying around to hover before me so that I could see his bright eyes staring into mine. "You're safe now, Highness. I promise."

I pressed a hand to the wall as I asked, "Can you promise to *keep* me safe?"

"I can promise I will give my life to protect you, should it come to that."

"Then here's hoping it never does," I said, spinning away to head for my room, determined never to come back to this part of the palace.

Once in my chamber, I threw myself on my bed, my breath coming hard and fast. I didn't know what was to become of the prisoner, nor did I particularly care. As far as I was concerned, Kazimir could have her hanged, and I would say good riddance.

I tried to tell myself to forget what had transpired—that she was insignificant in the grand scheme of things. My life would continue while hers did not—I would escape to Kalemnar, and I never, ever needed to learn what her rambling words meant.

But the longer I lay there—the longer I allowed the thoughts to roll around in my mind—the more I felt drawn to the palace's temple.

Perhaps if I spoke to the High Priestess there, if I spoke to her, I would find myself reassured.

I had seen the temple before as I wandered the palace's grounds, and it was easy to make my way to its doors via a series of cobbled pathways leading through a long series of well manicured gardens.

I didn't hear Lark's voice or the flutter of wings as I moved, but something told me he was watching me, concerned, from a distance.

From the outside, the temple looked like nothing more than a block of solid marble with a few stained glass windows set here and there. It had never struck me as very enticing, though I had always been a little curious about its interior.

I pushed open its large wooden front door to discover an arching silver chamber of spiraling columns. The series of stained glass windows, which looked dark from outside, were infused with sunlight, depicting the Elar in flight in various situations from battles to pastoral scenes of rolling hills.

As I walked slowly across the floor, I peered up at each carefully crafted image, my mind spinning with questions.

Occasionally, I found myself glancing over my shoulder nervously. Something about the temple felt unnaturally cold, beautiful as it was—and I asked myself if I'd made a mistake in walking through its doors.

"You will not see any assassins in this chamber," a smoothly echoing feminine voice said from somewhere in the shadows at the temple's far end. The sound ebbed and flowed, twisting through the air like a gentle breeze. "Only those worthy of the Elar's presence may enter here—and killers are not welcome in her sanctuary."

I turned to see a figure walking slowly, gracefully, toward

me. She wore a long cloak of deep red silk that clung to her form, and a matching veil over her face, concealing her features. Gloves of red leather coated her hands, as well, giving the impression from a distance that she was covered in a thick layer of fresh blood.

As she neared, she stopped, and though I could not see her eyes, I sensed that she was scrutinizing me with a deep curiosity, as if she wished to pull me apart and examine my inner workings.

A jolt of fear shot through my mind as I searched in vain for a set of eyes—for anything that rendered her more...*human.*

"I am Varyn, the High Priestess who presides over this temple. And you are Princess Lyrinn, daughter of Alessia."

"I am," I said, noting her failure to mention my father. "What happens to those who aren't worthy of entry into the temple?"

"They cannot cross the threshold," she replied. Her accent was one I couldn't quite place, and I wondered if she came from the North. "The Elar forbids the entry of hostile forces."

Against my will, a wave of relief swept through me. I had told myself I didn't believe the assassin—that her words were madness. That I was not the "Calloc"—if such a thing even existed. That my death would not result in some great rebirth. Still, the intensity in her eyes when she had spoken had jarred me into some grim sort of acceptance, some determination that she spoke the truth, however horrid it was.

But if indeed I was some warrior meant to kill her, the Elar would hardly allow me into her sacred temple.

Stop it, I told myself. *These are ridiculous thoughts. Absurd. You're getting swept up in folklore and nothing more.*

"I see," I said coldly. "And how, exactly, does she determine if someone is worthy, given that she's not here?"

The Priestess laughed quietly and said, "You doubt her power, Princess."

"I simply don't *know* her power. I mean no offense."

"The Elar sees everything. She sees through Fae as though their souls were written on a page, word by word, piece by piece. It is a power granted her by the force of her followers—by their devotion. Through the disciples, she is made whole. The Elar even sees the signs on your flesh, Princess." Varyn reached out and pushed my hair behind my ear, tracing a delicate fingertip over the markings on my neck.

"Aingil. The language of the Elar," she said. "Written on your skin."

I pulled my hand up to my neck, pushing her fingers away and covering the markings. The assassin's words came to me then, clear as the stars on a cloudless night.

"You are marked for death...With your end, the world will burn and be renewed."

"Do you know what the markings say?" I asked, trying and failing to conceal the tremor in my voice.

The Priestess took my hand and gently pulled it from my neck to study the swirling patterns again. "They say you will meet her one day soon," she replied. "You will find yourself in the Elar's presence. You will need to make a choice—and that choice will determine the fate of the world."

"I see." I hesitated for a moment before asking, "What... what is the Calloc?"

The Priestess pulled back violently. "Where did you hear that word?" she asked, her voice echoing so loudly around the space that I wanted to slam my hands over my ears.

I hesitated before saying, "The assassin—she told me..." I stopped myself before finishing the thought. If I told her the assassin had accused me of being the Elar's future killer, things could turn hostile rather quickly. "She said it was...someone who threatened the order of things, whatever that means."

"Ah," the Priestess said, seeming to settle. "So the legends say. Yet some have spoken in secret of the Calloc since the beginning of time, and never has anyone managed to harm the Elar."

I swallowed. "Have you ever...met..."

"Met the Elar myself?" Varyn said with a laugh. "Yes, of course. Every High Priestess does, in the moment when we are granted our wings. It is part of the ritual that leads us to our ascension." She stared at me, silent, through the thick veil before saying, "But you have seen her, too—in more than just the paintings and stained glass here in the palace. You have seen her manifested in your mind, have you not?"

My cheeks heated sharply, and I felt my chest tighten under Varyn's quietly disconcerting gaze. Too many in this palace knew my mind, my thoughts, my emotions.

And I didn't like it one bit.

"I've had a few dreams," I retorted. "Nightmares. The Elar I have seen is not the same one from the depictions."

"No," she said in that strangely lilting, faraway voice of hers. "You saw a future—one that you fear desperately. But it is not necessarily the future that will come to pass. The new Elar has not yet been chosen—and the old has not yet passed from this world. Fate is not etched in stone, Lyrinn, Princess—nor is it etched on your dreams."

My breath caught as she spoke the reassuring words. I nodded, then asked, "So, there's hope?"

"There is always hope," the Priestess said. "I cannot predict the future. I can only hope the chosen Elar is good and kind." She moved closer and lowered her chin. "Some say *you* are filled with goodness, Lyrinn. That you would make a fine Elar."

The words—the very suggestion of that fate—sent a

juddering fear through my bones. I had laughed at the thought the night before, but now, it felt like a curse. I shook my head. "I couldn't be Elar. I'm not a High Priestess."

Varyn clicked her tongue behind her veil and said, "Every rule has exceptions. Perhaps you should open your mind to what fate may have in store for you."

I shifted on my feet, suddenly wretchedly uncomfortable. The inability to see the Priestess's features meant I couldn't tell if she was serious. Surely, she couldn't be, after all. I barely believed the Elar existed. How would I ever *become* her?

"I...think I'll head to my chamber," I said, backing away. "Thank you for allowing me to see the temple. It's...lovely."

It was a lie. The temple had seemed pleasant enough at first, to be sure. But now, it horrified me as much as the twisted, yellow-eyed face of the Fae who had tried to kill me.

"Please, visit again soon," the Priestess replied, the smile still audible in her voice. "It is an honor, Princess, to have one so important as yourself in our presence. Before you go, may I offer you a word of advice?"

No. Please—no advice.

"Of course," I said with a tight-lipped smirk.

"Do not fear your role in the world. For better or worse, you are one key to a rebirth that is long overdue."

I nodded my head, turned, and made for the door, vowing never to return to the temple.

The Red Priestess had claimed she couldn't see the future— but something told me she knew far more about my coming days than she was letting on.

CHAPTER TWENTY-EIGHT

THE PALACE'S airy interior was a relief after the unsettling mood that had ravaged my mind inside the temple. I felt as though a heavy chain had been removed from around my neck, freeing me once again to tread lightly through the hallways.

I headed for my chamber, determined to rest a little before Kazimir's guest party arrived. It wouldn't do to be lightheaded and disoriented when they arrived, particularly if I was to contend with yet another High Priestess.

Find a way to keep your mind closed off, I told myself. *Don't let the Northern Priestess see your thoughts, whatever happens.*

Do not let her toy with you.

I had just begun to stride toward the marble staircase leading up to my bed chamber when I spotted a Lightblood guard standing at its base, his eyes locking on mine. He was tall, broad-shouldered, and dressed in a tunic that bore a sigil I didn't know—an image of a fierce-looking white bear.

I could only assume he was a guardsman for the visiting party. They were from the North, after all, and I had always heard of white bears in Tíria's northern reaches.

I nodded as I approached, intending to walk by him. But as I drew closer, he stepped in front of me, his eyes flaring bright. He looked me up and down, an odd smile twisting his lips. He was handsome to be sure, as all Lightbloods were. But in his expression there was something more. Something enticing, forbidden, and familiar—all at once.

I wondered if perhaps I'd met him before and simply forgotten.

"Can I help you?" I asked coldly, all too aware of how close he was now standing to me.

"Depends," the guard said in a low growl. "*Can* you?"

"I'm in no mood for games. What is it that you want?"

"What I *want*," he replied softly, moving still closer and breathing the words into my ear, "is the same as what *you* want...Highness."

I recoiled, stepping back and glaring at him. "I should have you thrown in the dungeon for such disrespect!" I scowled. "How dare you speak to me that way?"

"You could throw me in the dungeon," he replied, backing away, his smile intensifying. "But something tells me you won't."

I scowled. "If you speak to me like that again, I will have you taken to the bowels of this castle, and I'll command the dungeon-master to have his way with you. Understood?"

He nodded, but the devilish grin never left his lips as he offered up a low bow. "I'll do my best not to tell you what I'd like to do to that body of yours, then, shall I?"

I let out a grunt of disgust, but by now, part of me almost wanted to break into full-blown laughter. His come-on was so blatantly aggressive as to be comical. He reminded me so much of some of the young men I'd known in Dúnbar—the ones who had been my good friends in my younger years...young men who knew I would never take offense at their ridiculous one-liners and propositions.

As I climbed the stairs, I turned and looked over my shoulder to see him watching me, the sly, utterly inappropriate grin never straying from his lips.

And all of a sudden, all I could think was how much I missed Mithraan.

I had just awoken from a long nap when three aggressive knocks sounded at the door to my chamber.

"Who is it?" I called out, rubbing the sleep from my eyes as I climbed out of bed and made my way over.

"I have a message for her Highness, Princess Lyrinn," a low voice called out. "From Lord Adhair."

Adhair. Yes, Erildir had mentioned him. He was the son of the High Priestess—Lady Cassia, from Nordvahl.

"Come," I replied, straightening my dress and clasping my hands in front of me.

When the door opened, I found myself once again staring into the eyes of the Lightblood guard I'd encountered earlier— the same one who had made such ridiculous advances.

I took a step toward him even as he moved into the room. My chin was high, my eyes fixed on his, and I could only hope that staring him down would suffice to persuade him to back away.

"Highness," he said with a smooth bow of his head, his eyes never seeming to leave my own.

"What is the message?" My mood was quickly darkening, my amusement gone now—and had I been carrying a blade, I would likely have drawn it so that he could see how little interest I had in his company.

The guard looked around the room, scanning its ceiling and walls, the distant glass doors, and finally...the bed.

"Answer me," I said curtly. "Or leave."

His eyes locked on mine again when he said, "Lord Adhair is looking forward to dining with you this evening. He hopes you will wear something..." His gaze moved down my body, lingering far too long on my breasts. "Something that complements your lovely form."

"I see," I said as I reached out to grab hold of the door handle. "Well, please tell your lord I'm looking forward to meeting him and his mother—but that I will wear whatever I choose to wear."

I expected the guard to move out of the way so that I could seal the door, but instead, he positioned himself in the doorway and stared down at me, narrowing his eyes enough to make me feel utterly exposed to his scrutiny. "His lordship is a fortunate man if he gets to dine with you, Highness. I would give a great deal for such a privilege."

"If you don't move out of my way, I will take your head," I snarled. "Your lord may be a guest here, but *you* are not. You are not welcome in this corridor—nor are you welcome in my bed chamber. Do you understand me?"

He slipped into the corridor and gestured toward the door, his grin never wavering. As I slammed it shut, a familiar, enticing scent met my nose...and then it was gone.

But it was enough to stop me in my tracks, to force a wave of longing to wash over me against my will and my judgment. I turned and pressed my back to the door, breathing hard...and hoping with everything in me that I would not see that Fae again.

What the hell had he done to me? Why did I find him so intoxicating, so...desirable? Was it some trait of Northerners, some spell cast to test my integrity?

I had never wanted to consume anyone so badly, never felt so overcome with desire...except when it came to Mithraan. How the hell was I now feeling such a violent craving for some High Lord's servant, when I had a High Lord of my own back in Kalemnar?

CHAPTER TWENTY-NINE

I WAS DEEPLY relieved when Riah knocked on the door a little while later then popped her head inside, smiling.

"Are you all right?" I asked, striding over and gesturing her to come in.

"Just fine," she replied. "Thank you."

"After what happened with the High King, I wasn't sure what had become of you. I was worried—"

"I'm fine, truly, Highness," she insisted. "Thanks to you standing up to him as you did. I'm so sorry again about all of it. I still feel responsible. It was so foolish of me to trust that you were safe in public."

"Come now, you know I wanted a night out. I *wanted* to go into the city. Neither of us ever expected anyone to know it was me, let alone want to *kill* me. There was no way you could have anticipated it."

Riah simply smiled quietly, then said, "Would you like help getting ready for dinner with the guests?"

"Yes, actually," I said with a smile of appreciation. "That would be wonderful."

As Riah began to rifle through the wardrobe, I recalled what the guard had said about his lord wanting me to wear something "enticing." Part of me wanted to defy him entirely, to dress in something resembling a large, unkempt burlap sack. But another part—some deep, mischief-filled bit of my soul— wanted to tease that guard with just the sort of dress that would drive such a lascivious male wild. Perhaps I could taunt him from afar. Torment him by letting him know he could never have a Fae such as me.

I had no intention of going near him, of course. No intention of touching him, of ever speaking to him again. But the thought of driving him just a *little* mad brought me a welcome frisson of pleasure.

"I have a thought," Riah said, eyeing the vast assortment of white clothing. "A dress tucked away in this mess that I think you might like to wear on an occasion such as this one. You might be relieved to know there is one garment in your possession that isn't white."

I nodded gratefully and said, "Please! I'll take whatever you find." I watched her dig through the closet until she came upon a long silver dress that shone in the waning sunlight like a shimmering pond.

"How did I miss this?" I asked, laughing. "Clearly, I haven't spent enough time hunting through my wardrobe."

"I thought it might be suitable tonight. A silver dress for the future wearer of the silver crown."

I smiled as she pulled it out and held it up for me. I could see now that it was very low cut in front, with a belted waist. Revealing, yet simple, it wouldn't require me to be corseted inside some oppressive undergarment—not that I ever favored such constricting clothing.

"Perfect," I said. "Let's just hope it doesn't offend the High

King. I could see him sending me to my room with no supper for looking too—"

"Edible?" Riah laughed.

"Terrible. You said it—not me."

"Anyhow, I would have thought you'd *love* offending the High King," she replied with a wink, and I chuckled.

"You're not wrong about that."

When I'd dressed and Riah had helped me to tie my hair back in a loose knot, I glanced in the full length mirror that rested against the wall.

If only Mithraan could see me now, I thought, laughing quietly to myself as my eyes moved down my body, taking in every subtle curve and bit of exposed skin. I smiled at my strange new confidence, basking in the realization that I actually looked...desirable.

I had never felt desirable before I met Mithraan, even when my lips had met those of Dúnbar's various lecherous boys and young men. But the Fae lord had taught me what it was to experience a lover desperate for my scent, my taste, my skin...

"Will you be joining us for dinner?" I asked Riah, forcing my fantasies away as I turned and made my way to the door.

"No, but I'm looking forward to hearing about it. I've heard Lord Adhair is quite...pretty."

"I'll let you know," I laughed. "Though chances are, I won't find him nearly as pretty as..."

"As the one you love," Riah said softly as we began the long walk to the dining chamber. "No, I don't suppose you will." After a brief pause, she added, "Well, I must admit that I envy you a little. My opportunities to meet exciting males are highly limited."

I offered up a little smile, but didn't speak the words that were on my mind: *I have no desire to meet any alluring Fae. My heart is Mithraan's, and Mithraan's alone...regardless of what irritating charm spells Adhair's guardsmen may cast.*

"Riah," I said, eager to change the subject.

"Mmm?" she replied.

"I keep thinking about how in the pub, you and Kierin looked shocked when I said Kazimir had told me about poisoning the Tírian Champions."

Her face blanched, and I could see fear in her expression now, away from the courage bestowed by drink. "I...I shouldn't have said anything," she replied. "It was foolish of me. I apologize."

I took hold of her arm gently and pulled her gaze to meet mine. "It's all right. I just want to understand what you meant when you said I may have seen something other than the truth. What really happened?"

She looked for a moment as if she wanted to flee. But she cleared her throat, managed to meet my eyes, and said, "There... have long been rumors that your mother was the one who wanted the Champions dead."

At that, I dropped her arm, tightening with defensiveness.

"Why would anyone spread such a rumor? Even if her memories were a little skewed, Kazimir told me himself that he did it. My mother is a Tírian—those were *her* Fae, for the gods' sake."

Riah bowed her head, contrite. "It doesn't matter," she replied, glancing around like she was still seeking an escape route. "If the High King said it was his doing, then that is the final word. Now—I think we should get you downstairs for dinner."

"I think I'd like to go down alone, actually," I said, fighting to keep my voice in check.

"Highness, I—" Riah said, reaching a hand out.

"You've done nothing wrong," I told her. "I asked for the truth, and you gave it to me. You're a good friend. I just need a moment."

I meant every word. But right now, I couldn't bring myself to look her in the eye.

CHAPTER THIRTY

I HEARD the faint flutter of Lark's wings a few minutes later as I proceeded down the long, first-level corridor that led to the dining hall.

"Where have you been?" I asked.

"I'm sorry, Highness. I...fell asleep in a poplar tree."

At that, I managed a snicker. "That's admittedly adorable. But now that you're here, do me a favor and keep an eye on Adhair's guards. Tell me if you see anything odd."

"Of course, Highness."

When we neared the dining hall, nervous excitement wound its way through my insides. I was curious about Lady Cassia most of all, to learn if such a powerful Fae was secretive and quiet like my mother...or a brutal ruler like Kazimir.

With a deep intake of air, I pushed the chamber's doors open.

Kazimir was already inside with two Fae I had never seen—presumably our Northern guests—as were a few guards in Northern uniforms who stood against the chamber's walls. The High King wore his silver crown, and I couldn't help but note how regal he looked, how kingly.

As I strode into the room, I looked around until my eyes locked on those of the flirtatious guard I'd been unfortunate enough to encounter twice now. He was positioned against the same wall as the chamber's door, a weapon at his side, and he watched me closely.

I broke contact the moment I felt my cheeks heating, cursing him under my breath for drawing my focus.

"Ah, Lyrinn, Daughter," Kazimir called out, gesturing me over. I tried my best to glide elegantly across the floor toward him, my eyes roaming shyly to his well-dressed guests.

One was a small, slight female Fae—a mere wisp of a thing. Her hair was a fine, delicate silver-white, woven into what looked like hundreds of braids all tied into various knots on her head. A crown of iridescent flowers ornamented her brow, and she wore a stunning lavender-colored dress to match.

"This is Lady Cassia, known as the Gray Lady," Kazimir said. "High Priestess of Nordvahl, and Warden of the Northern Territories."

"It's a pleasure to meet you," I said, bowing my head in a reverent curtsey.

"The pleasure is all mine," she said, her voice musical and light on the air. "I have heard so many wonderful things about you—and, like many others, I have anticipated your arrival in Aetherion for some time."

At that, I shot an inadvertent look at Kazimir, who simply issued me a tight smile.

With a graceful gesture of her hand, Cassia acknowledged a young male Fae standing a few feet away.

He was taller than her by at least a head and a half. His silver-white hair was long and drawn back over his pointed ears in narrow, delicately woven braids, similar to his mother's. Dark lashes and arched brows framed his eyes, which were deep green, a delicate circle of gold around his pupils.

He was, without question, as beautiful as any Fae I had seen —and I now understood what had gotten Riah so excited about his coming.

"This is my son, Lord Adhair," Lady Cassia said.

"I—" I began, suddenly feeling entirely out of place. "It's a pleasure."

"The pleasure is all mine, Highness," he said, his eyes slipping down my body in a way that wasn't entirely disrespectful —but wasn't entirely *innocent*, either.

I recalled with a flush of my cheeks that I'd chosen to wear a far more revealing garment than I was accustomed to, which probably accounted for the fact that the impish guard on the opposite side of the room was still watching me, too.

"Will you come out onto the terrace with me?" Adhair asked, slipping over to the table to reach for two glasses of red wine. "We can get to know one another while we wait for dinner."

When we turned toward the broad glass doors, I was certain I saw a flicker of involuntary movement from the guard— though I was trying my best not to let on that I was watching him out of the corner of my eye. Why should he care if Lord Adhair was escorting me, anyhow? Adhair was his leader. It was a guard's duty to *protect* him, not to covet what he appeared to possess.

"My mother and I have been both curious and anxious to meet you, as you can imagine," Adhair said, handing me one of the glasses when I took a seat next to him at the table on the terrace. "We—and others—have been awaiting your arrival in these lands for some time."

"Oh?" I asked nervously. Too many people had offered me some variation of this same statement since Kazimir had dragged me to these lands, and it was beginning to weigh on my soul. "May I ask why?"

He glanced toward Kazimir and his mother, who were standing just inside the glass doors, engaged in what looked like an intimate conversation. He leaned in close to me, whispering. "There are some who say your coming was prophesied. That you will bring peace and prosperity to our lands. That you are—"

Before he had a chance to finish, his mother strode out to the terrace with Kazimir, her eyes locked on mine.

Cassia cleared her throat. "I am so excited to get to know you a little, your Highness," she said, smiling warmly at me. "I must say, you're the most interesting Fae to grace our lands in some long years. A hybrid in our midst is an extraordinary thing indeed."

I half-grimaced. "I don't know about extraordinary, my Lady," I replied with an uncomfortable laugh. "I'm really not particularly interesting, as you'll soon discover."

"Oh, I beg to differ. You are an anomaly, to say the very least. Unique. And, dare I say, beautiful as the sea and sky. But of course, it is no surprise that the daughter of Queen Alessia and High King Kazimir should be so lovely."

As if she had been summoned, the dining hall's doors opened and my mother strode in, wearing a long golden dress that trailed on the marble floor behind her. She slipped over to the table and took a seat, her eyes locked on the opposite wall.

Lady Cassia glanced sideways at Kazimir in a way that made me wonder if there might be more between them than a distant acquaintance. In her eyes, I sensed profound desire combined with a wistful sort of sadness.

Something compelled me to peer back into the chamber at the flirtatious guard, whose eyes were now firmly locked on my mother. At first, I wanted to punch him for being so vile—but after a few seconds, it occurred to me that his expression was more one of curiosity than lust.

Perhaps he, too, had heard rumors about Queen Alessia's involvement in the killing of Tírian Champions.

I wondered bitterly if every Lightblood had.

It doesn't matter. It's a lie, probably started to slander Tírians.

"I must go speak to your mother, Lyrinn," Cassia said, leading Kazimir back through the doors toward the table. "She looks so...lonely."

I watched as she took a seat, engaging my mother in polite conversation. Kazimir joined in, his eyes remaining firmly fixed on the Priestess. After a time, he laid a hand on hers on top of the table, and I let out a nearly-inaudible gasp, horrified that he would be so shameless about what appeared to be full-fledged infidelity.

I glanced at Adhair, and we both let out a stricken laugh at the same time.

"Apologies for the awkwardness," he whispered. "My mother and the High King...they go back many, many years. They were childhood friends, believe it or not."

I resisted the urge to ask if it drove him mad to see his mother with such a male, and instead said, "I can't quite imagine Kaz—the High King, I mean—as a child."

"No, neither can I." Adhair nodded in their direction. "Nor my mother. They are ageless, both of them. And both have been through a great deal in their long lifetimes."

"Yes, I imagine so," I said, trying to gauge whether the young Fae could be trusted. It was too soon to let him know I wasn't fond of Kazimir—that I had been torn from my life and brought to this place against every fiber of my being.

That there were moments when I contemplated murdering Kazimir and displaying his head on a pike for all of Aetherion to see...

"Your mother," I said. "Her voice isn't like that of the High Priestess I met in the temple here. I assumed they all spoke like that—in that sort of magical, distant way."

Adhair shifted in his seat as if slightly uncomfortable with the topic. "The voice only comes when the Priestesses are veiled," he said. "Mother's alters when she is presiding over Nordvahl's temple. They call it 'Elarrath'—the speech of the Elar. The devoted say it's how she speaks through her chosen acolytes. Others say it's a means for Priestesses to guard their anonymity; that they hide behind the voice, just as they conceal themselves beyond their veils."

I recalled the sound of Varyn's voice, a hard shiver tracing its way down my flesh.

"This whole thing must be so strange for you," Adhair said after a moment, easing closer to me, a smile in his eyes as he spoke. "I...heard what happened at the Blood Trials. I'm quite certain you did not expect to end up in Aetherion at the end of it all."

I thought then of Mithraan, of my hopes and fears, and of all that had happened to tear us apart. I found my eyes moving to the far end of the room, where the guard was watching me again, his eyes narrowed as if in judgment.

I forced my gaze back to Adhair and shook my head.

"No, I didn't expect it," I replied. "You're right about that. But...this land is beautiful. It's in my blood, of course—though I didn't know that a few months ago. Naturally, I'm grateful to be here in this lovely palace."

The lie came easily enough, though perhaps it shouldn't have. Had I spoken the absolute truth, I'd have told Adhair that I would have been perfectly happy never to step foot on this land—never to see Kazimir's home or, for that matter, to look upon his cruel face.

"The most wonderful thing, though," I added, pulling my eyes to my mother, "is learning that *she* is alive."

"Lady Alessia," Adhair said with a solemn nod of his head.

"That's right—you were separated from her when you were very young, weren't you?"

I nodded. "Yes. And I'm so grateful to the High King for reuniting us at long last."

Adhair pulled back, cocking his head to the side and eyeing me skeptically, a half-smile on his lips. He leaned toward me again. "You know, you don't need to lie to me," he whispered with a chuckle. "I can imagine what you're dealing with. I do know something of your history. Raised as a mortal, scarred, robbed of your bloodline and your birthright."

"Ah," I said, smiling wryly. "But I'm *not* a person. I'm a Fae."

"And what a Fae you are," he said, his eyes slipping down my body so that I found myself slouching away from his gaze. "If I may be so bold, Lady Lyrinn, you are as beautiful as Tomlin said you were."

"Tomlin?" I asked.

Adhair nodded toward the guard standing at the room's far end, his eyes still fixed on me. And once again, my cheeks caught fire. "He's been assessing you for me—and reporting back on his findings. I do apologize if he's been a little aggressive. It was by design, I assure you."

I let out a relieved laugh. "He really was testing me? Thank the gods—I was shocked at how ridiculous he was. Like a bull during mating season."

Adhair nodded, chuckling. "May I say, you passed with flying colors. Tomlin is a handsome Fae—but then, that's obvious to anyone who looks his way." He eyed the guard, adding, "He hasn't been in my service long, but he came highly recommended. A skilled fighter and a Fae of great honor, they say. Word has it that he has a way of charming all who encounter him. Yet you resisted easily."

*I wouldn't say **easily**.*

In fact, even in that moment as I sat next to the High Lord, it was difficult not to think of the familiar, intoxicating scent that had met my nose when I had shut the guard out of my chamber.

My cheeks flushed, and I found myself pulling involuntarily away from Adhair once again.

"I apologize," he said. "I didn't mean to make you uncomfortable."

"It's all right. It's just been...a strange few weeks. If I seem on edge, well, it's because I am."

"I'm sure."

He glanced over at my mother, who was sitting in stony silence once again, her eyes staring straight ahead.

"Did you know," Adhair said, noticing that my gaze had shifted, "that your mother lived for years in one of the Elar's convents? I heard that she even trained with the Order. Some say it's how she became so powerful back in the day."

I nearly spat out my wine. "A convent?" I whispered. "My mother? I knew she followed the Elar, and that she spends some time in the temple on the palace grounds. But...a convent?"

Adhair seemed baffled. "She didn't tell you?"

I shook my head, confounded and puzzled at once. "No. Though I have no idea why not."

Adhair shrugged. "Perhaps she assumed you would find it silly. Not all of us share her beliefs, after all."

"But..." I began. "Years ago, you said. When was it that she was in the North?"

"Oh, centuries ago, I think."

Centuries. Of course—that explained it. A few years, to a Fae who has lived over a thousand of them, are a mere drop in a pail.

"My mother told me about her once," Adhair added. "Something about your parents having a falling out, and your mother heading to the North for a time. Apparently she was a model pupil—attentive, faithful, everything a Sister of the Order should be. My mother thought very highly of her."

"But she returned to the South," I said, confused as to why she hadn't used the chance to flee. "To Aethos. She returned to the High King."

"I suppose she decided the Order wasn't a part of the life she wanted for herself."

"Tell me something, Lord Adhair," I half-whispered. "Do you believe in the Elar's power?"

I had given up asking anyone if they believed in the Elar herself. Enough Fae claimed to have met her that it was a pointless question at this point.

Adhair lowered his chin when he said, "My mother believes —and truthfully, that is enough for me. But even without her faith, I will tell you that I have *seen* her power—I have seen my mother's wings, and other evidence, as well. I have also seen the Elar drive Fae to madness."

Against my will, my eyebrows shot up in surprise. "Drive them to—really?"

Adhair nodded. "Some say she has even tormented your father these many years—that she has broken his mind more than once."

"It seems to me that my father broke his own mind without anyone's help."

Adhair sat back in his chair, staring at me. "You think him a tyrant, don't you?" he whispered just barely loud enough so that I could hear it.

"I..." I kicked myself for speaking ill of the High King to a virtual stranger. *Foolish, imprudent idiot.*

Adhair pulled his eyes to Kazimir and his mother, still locked in whispered conversation, their heads so close together they were nearly touching. "Good and evil are not absolutes," he said. "None of us is wholly good, just as none of us is truly evil. Your father has done what he can to keep Lightbloods alive, and to give his people hope even during times of great loss. I am grateful for his reign and to be honest, I dread its end. I don't know your father's mind—but I do know he has ruled Aetherion justly for a very long time."

I said nothing. Every time someone told me of my father's goodness, I found myself wondering if we were speaking of the same creature. Yet Adhair stared reverently at Kazimir as he spoke. Kazimir—the Fae who was now stroking his mother's cheek in front of his own wife, the queen.

Kazimir...who had no scruples whatsoever.

"If you'll excuse me," Adhair said, "I need to have a word with my guards. I'll be right back."

With a quick, friendly smile, he rose to his feet and slipped into the room to speak to the one he called Tomlin. The guard fixed his eyes on me as his lord addressed him, and I had to force myself to look away.

I could only hope Adhair had gone over to tell him there was no longer any need to test me.

CHAPTER THIRTY-ONE

With my head down, I whistled softly for Lark, who appeared instantly by my side.

"Tell me something. That guard—Tomlin." I whispered.

"Yes?"

"What do you make of him?"

Lark glanced toward the other side of the room with an exaggerated frown. "Handsome. Arrogant. Bit of a dirty bastard. And most certainly a Falach."

"Falach?" I repeated. "I haven't heard that term before."

"A liar," he replied. "More accurately, a deceiver—a shape-shifter. One who can fashion himself into whatever others wish to see. It's a dangerous power to have. Beware that sort—things with them seldom end well."

With a wince, I thought, *I know one or two Fae who are exactly that sort.*

"I'll steer well clear of him, then," I promised, though the truth was, knowing Tomlin was a shifter only made him more interesting. "But I don't think I have anything to worry about— Adhair admitted he has been using him to test me."

"Hmm," Lark grunted. "Disappointing, given that Lord

Adhair's reputation is one of an honest Fae. Not sure I approve of that sort of behavior."

With a laugh, I replied, "Me neither—but I suppose I can't blame him. He knows nothing about me; it was a quick and easy way to assess my character."

"Perhaps you should ask yourself why he needs to know anything about your character in the first place," the sprite said protectively. "I realize he is a guest, along with his mother—but something about them feels off to me. They're too charming, too inviting, yet I feel a chill coming off them both. Be wary, Princess. Northerners are notoriously difficult to read and have been cruel beyond words to my kind."

He was right—Adhair felt a little *too* comfortable, too easy to talk to. Too good to be true. He reminded me a little of Prince Corym, who had seemed kind, jovial, and protective...until he hadn't.

In a backwards way, I was beginning to appreciate Kazimir. At least he was glaringly awful. I never had to question his manner of thinking or his motives; I could always assume the worst, and chances are, I would be correct.

Adhair and his High Priestess mother were, both of them, all smiles and compliments. All charm and smoothness, without a trace of the coarseness of most living creatures. It was as if they had each studied for lifetimes to learn how to stroke others' egos, to draw them in and convince them to open their minds and hearts.

"Thank you, Lark," I said softly, and when the sprite flew off, I slipped into the dining chamber and took a seat across from my mother. I smiled when she pulled her eyes from the far wall to meet my own.

"How are you?" I asked. "When you left so abruptly last night after the incident at the pub, I wondered if you were upset."

Her eyes moved to mine, and she smiled, though it never quite reached her eyes. "Of course I was, Lyrinn. Someone tried to kill you. It was a terrible thing. I'm only glad they apprehended the Fae who did it."

I glanced over at Adhair to ensure he wasn't heading toward us, then whispered, "I went to see the prisoner—in the dungeon."

My mother's eyes flared for a moment, then the flame faded rapidly, snuffed by some unseen force. "Why would you do such a thing?" she hissed.

"I wanted to know her motives."

"And did she give you any information?"

"She said I was something called the 'Calloc.' That I was marked for death. None of it made sense to me. But you know about the Elar—does it mean anything to you?"

Her face was suddenly devoid of expression, cold and impassive. "You shouldn't listen to murderers," she said. "As for calling you the Calloc—rest assured that she was talking nonsense. That creature is an invented enemy of the Elar, nothing more. A creation of fanatics who hope to instill fear in the hearts of the Elar's followers and render them more devout. Now, we should drop it." She looked sideways at Lady Cassia, as though it was for her benefit that she wished to let the subject go.

I sat back, surprised that she was concerned about Cassia's feelings, given the Gray Lady's clear disregard for her own.

"Lord Adhair is a fine Fae, is he not?" my mother half-whispered, her eyes again shining bright for a moment—another shadow of the power she had once possessed. "Perhaps you will find him pleasant company when you venture to the North for the Succession."

"The Succession," I repeated. "Erildir mentioned the journey—but I'm not entirely sure I want to go."

"You must," she said. "The Succession is an event that occurs once in most Fae lifetimes, if that. It is one that you must witness. You are Princess of Aetherion, after all."

I stared at her, recalling what Adhair had told me about her living in one of the Order's convents.

"Do you know the Priestesses well?" I asked, looking sideways at Cassia, who was currently whispering something into Kazimir's ear.

"Some of them," my mother replied under her breath. "They have been very good to me—very kind." Turning to look at Cassia, she added, "She is an extraordinary Fae—and she's very impressed by you, Lyrinn."

I glanced over to see Cassia suddenly staring at me, her eyes bright and inquisitive—perhaps *too* inquisitive. I could feel her leafing around inside my mind, searching me for...what, I couldn't tell.

I looked away, my hands gripping the table's edge as I pushed her from me, shutting my thoughts away behind a wall of my own making.

She may be extraordinary, I thought. *But her power is terrifying.*

I was about to say something more when Adhair seated himself next to me again, a broad smile on his lips. "Everything good?" he asked, seeing the look in my eyes.

"Fine," I nodded. "May I ask you something, Lord Adhair?"

"Of course, Highness."

Smiling faintly, I said, "Forgive me if this seems a rude question—but why are you and your mother here in the South? With the Succession coming so soon, why come all this way for a casual visit? Unless...there is something more to this trip of yours?"

Adhair let out a quietly contained laugh and leaned in close. "You've found us out," he whispered. "Rumor has it that the next Elar may reside within the walls of this very palace—but you didn't hear it from me."

He drew back with a wink. At first, I thought he was joking... but a sickening surge was making the contents of my stomach swim.

Surely the rumor Riah had mentioned in the pub was not an *actual* possibility—that the High Priestesses were assessing *me* as a Candidate. Lumen himself had speculated that only other High Priestesses were to be considered—Fae who had served the Elar faithfully for years.

Yet there was something about the way Lady Cassia stared at me that sent a shudder of apprehension through my mind unlike any I had felt since I had been thrust into the Blood Trials.

Please, gods, tell me I was not brought to Aetherion to be forced into the position of demi-goddess.

The thought was almost enough to inspire an impromptu burst of panicked laughter from my chest.

I reminded myself with a reassuring exhalation that there *was* a High Priestess here in the palace—Varyn, whom I had met earlier. The one dressed from head to toe in blood red garments.

Was she really under consideration for Elar? If so, why had she not been invited to dinner?

"Princess?"

It was Adhair's voice again, and this time, he touched my arm ever so gently. I looked down at his fingers on my skin, and without knowing why, my eyes shot to Tomlin, who was still positioned across the room.

His eyes, too, were locked on Adhair's hand. If looks could send projectiles shooting through space, Adhair would have been pelted with a thousand daggers in that moment.

"I..." I stammered, pulling my gaze back to Adhair's even as I yanked my arm away and tucked my hands into my lap. "I'm sorry," I said with a pathetic attempt at a smile. "I suppose I'm just a little distracted."

I was relieved when, in that moment, Kazimir clanged a knife against his goblet, drawing the small party's attention.

"I would like to welcome our honored guests," he said, focusing his eyes first on Cassia then on her son. "To thank them for making the long, yet miraculously *rapid* journey from the Far North—" With that, Cassia and Adhair laughed as though both were included in some private joke. "And particularly for Lady Cassia's tireless work in the selection of the next Elar. I don't need to tell any of you that the Succession is a sacred process, and one that will shape Aetherion's future—as well as the future of all those living, be they Fae or mortal. I look forward to learning which deserving High Priestess has been chosen to succeed the current Elar."

"Thank you, your Grace," Lady Cassia said with a graceful bow of her head. "It need not be said that it is an honor to be here in your presence."

"No, it need not be said," Kazimir replied, slipping his thumb affectionately under her chin. "Because I am all too well aware of what an honor it is."

Dinner progressed with jovial conversation about the North, about the vast, magical temple there and the excitement surrounding the upcoming ceremony. I only half-listened, my mind wandering frequently to other thoughts, namely how to escape Aethos with my mother before the Succession.

Occasionally, I found myself glancing toward Tomlin, who seemed to manage each time to have his eyes locked squarely on mine, an intense, conspicuous hunger still palpable in his features. If Lord Adhair had indeed told him to lay off and stop testing my limits, it seemed the guard had chosen to ignore the command outright.

A few times, Tomlin stepped to his left to whisper conspiratorially with another Lightblood guard, who also shot me the occasional look. The two of them nodded or chuckled as they discussed secret topics, no doubt both lecherous and vile.

I strained my ears attempting to listen in, but my hearing was currently being assaulted by multiple simultaneous conversations as Kazimir and Cassia laughed about years past, and my mother and Adhair chatted about Aetherion's wildlife.

Finally, after dessert had been served and quickly devoured, I breathed a sigh of relief and pushed my chair back, rising to my feet.

"I think I'll excuse myself," I announced. "If that's all right. I'm quite tired, and could use some rest."

"Of course," my mother said, ignoring a glare from Kazimir, who appeared gravely annoyed that I had dared express a single desire of any kind. "Go—get some sleep. We'll see you in the morning."

When I'd said goodnight to Adhair and his mother and muttered a reluctant farewell to Kazimir, I headed back toward my bed chamber.

I was relieved, at least, to know I would soon be able to lay my head down and seal my eyes shut. I needed more than anything to rid myself of the invasive thoughts that had troubled my mind all evening—the apprehension of an uncertain future and a lurking, ugly sense of paranoia that had begun to eat away at me.

When I reached my door, I dismissed Lark, whose wings I'd heard flitting away behind me since I'd left the dining chamber.

"I'll see you in the morning," I told him. "Sleep well."

"And you, Highness," he said, then, more softly, "As I said before, be wary around the visitors. I don't like how Lady Cassia looks at you."

"Neither do I."

With that, Lark flew off, disappearing into the shadows.

I reached for my door handle, thinking only of the sleep draught I would soon ingest and hoping against hope that it would work tonight, after far too many failed attempts to connect with Mithraan.

"I need you," I whispered under my breath as I pushed the door open. "So much that it hurts."

When I slipped inside the dark room, it took a moment for my eyes to adjust and to realize a lone, threatening figure was standing silhouetted against the open glass doors that led out to the terrace.

I gasped, my heart racing with fear.

It seemed I'd dismissed Lark too soon.

CHAPTER THIRTY-TWO

"Who's there?" I asked, squinting into the darkness.

I should have been able to see the figure clearly, regardless of the oppressive shadows cast on everything in my chamber. I was a Fae, damn it. My vision since my Coming of Age was a hundred times more acute than that of a mortal.

Yet something—some powerful, aggravating interference—was keeping me from making out the intruder's features. A wall of shadow lay between us, and it was clearly his doing.

All I could make out was a flash of light hair, long and shining in the moonlight.

He's a Lightblood.

Which...doesn't narrow it down in the least.

"Answer me, or I'll call on the entirety of my father's forces," I announced. "I will have your powers taken from you and your useless body flung from the balcony—few Fae could survive the ensuing collision with the ground below."

"I would easily survive the fall," he said arrogantly, taking a step closer. A swell of apprehension ate at my insides as his face began to take shape among the shadowy depths of the room.

I could see his clothing now, the white bear sigil of the Northern Guard just visible on a linen tunic.

"It's...*you*." My voice softened more from shock than gentleness. "The one called Tomlin." Such an innocent name for such a devious creature. "But...I just left the dining hall. How did you get here so quickly?"

"I have my ways, Highness." The way he spoke the words was smooth, seductive...*dangerous*.

He was still moving toward me. Stalking, like a predator about to pounce.

I spun around, reaching for the door handle, but I was too slow. He moved with extraordinary speed, and the next thing I knew, his hand was on my wrist...and the door was still closed.

"I wouldn't do that if I were you," he whispered, his breath stroking my skin.

Fear wrapped itself around my chest and squeezed as the guard put a finger to his lips, warning me not to cry out. He pushed me back against the door, a hand slipping to the place just below my throat, and I gasped an inhaled breath, catching the air in my lungs in preparation for what was to come.

Cast a spell, I thought. *Cast a spell and tear a hole in his chest. No one could blame you for killing a Northerner if he attacks you first.*

But I did nothing. I simply froze as his eyes roved over my body again, down my chest as his free hand followed, slipping farther still to land on the dip of my cleavage, where it paused for a moment.

"What would you say to me, Highness, if I told you I still wish to taste you?" he asked. "If I told you I have craved you since the first moment I ever saw you? Would you threaten me with beheading again?"

"I would behead you myself," I breathed, though I wasn't entirely certain I meant it. That scent—that familiar, heady scent that had driven me mad before...it was back. But this time, there was something so recognizable in it that I wanted to fall to my knees and beg him to show me his true self.

I'm only imagining things. He's a Falach—a deceiver, just as Lark said. He's toying with me.

As if to confirm my suspicions, he reached down and lifted my dress, pulling it up so that his fingers grazed my bare thigh. I squirmed under his touch, struggling against an intoxicating, infuriating combination of confusion and desire.

"Please—stop. I love someone," I half-moaned. "I love him with everything in me. I would rather die than be taken by anyone else."

Tomlin stared into my eyes, easing closer still, and I tasted it on the air—that delectable aroma that sent my head reeling.

"Even Lord Adhair?" he asked in a low growl. "There are few who can resist that High Fae—he is handsome—charming. You would do well to seek one such as him to marry, Princess."

I recalled how Tomlin had looked when Adhair had touched me—how he had seemed to want to murder him for it.

I shook my head. "However handsome or kind he may be, he's not the one I want. No High Fae's appeal can force me to forget where my heart truly lies."

The guard finally dropped his hand to his side and stepped back, a satisfied smile on his lips.

"Did your sprite spy tell you about me?" he asked. "Did he say what I am?"

I nodded. "A Falach."

At that, Tomlin moved close again, and this time, he slipped his fingers onto my neck, touching me with a gentleness, a slowness that made me ache in a way I seldom had.

"Do these fingers arouse familiar feelings in you, my Lady?" he whispered, his lips brushing against my skin. "Do you wish for more...perhaps even for my tongue between your legs...*Vaelan?*"

Vaelan.

If I had any doubt left in my mind or body, it was gone now.

I pressed my palms to his chest and shoved him, and he went reeling backwards. Half stumbling, half laughing, his voice altered to one I knew as well as my own. "Hello, Lyrinn, love."

"Devil!" I hissed, though I couldn't hide the smile on my lips. "You deceitful, cruel..."

As I watched, his face altered, as did his hair. Silver was replaced by a twisting, churning sea of dark shades. His irises turned to amber. His shoulders broadened, his chest expanding until he was the Fae I had grown to love with every fiber of my being.

I understood now. Why I had wanted the stranger so badly —how he had managed to twist my mind into such desire in spite of myself, in spite of my loyalty.

"But—how can it really be you?" I asked, tears stinging my eyes. "You're..."

"Come, now—part of you has known since the first moment you laid eyes on Tomlin that it was me."

I only had to think about it for the briefest moment before I grabbed Mithraan and pulled him to me, my lips on his, my hands on his neck, feeling the throb of his pulse against my flesh.

"Why?" I asked against his mouth. "Why toy with me like that?"

"I'm sorry, love," he said with a deep chuckle as he pulled back. "The only way into the palace was to pose as a guard— and I couldn't pretend to be one of your father's. He would have known in an instant. Thalanir has connections in the North of

Aetherion—and he helped me to infiltrate Lord Adhair's Guard when they neared Aethos."

"Thalanir is here?"

I remembered with a hit of shame how I had suspected him of betraying us to Kazimir. The suspicion had long since faded, but the guilt still gnawed at me.

"No. He *was*—he came with me over the sea, in a ship that I charmed to grant it speed on the waves. But I have sent him back to Kalemnar on a mission."

"But Adhair must know you're not a Lightblood—he must suspect *some*thing, at least."

"I don't think he does," Mithraan said. "He's not so powerful as some seem to think—he's naive, inexperienced. I've only known him a little while, but I'm under the distinct impression that his mother has coddled him into thinking himself far greater than he is. I'm not sure he possesses the skills to see through my disguise. Still...all that matters is that I'm here now, and I need to get you away from this place—we need to go back to Kalemnar, you and I. Tonight."

"Kalemnar," I repeated wistfully. "What a dream that is. But I can't go, Mithraan—you know my mother is here."

He pulled closer, taking me by the waist. By now, I'd already forgiven him for the deception, the cruel teasing. All I could think was *You're here. You're really here...please don't leave.*

"We would bring her with us, of course. Look—there's a ship in the harbor that's ready to set sail any day now. I'll get you both on it, and—"

But I shook my head. "You don't understand—Kazimir put a ring on my mother's finger—one that robs her of her spells and keeps her trapped in this place. If she tries to leave, she will die."

At that, Mithraan looked stricken. Clearly, he wasn't prepared for me to say no to his proposal.

"It's not that I don't want to go with you," I assured him, my voice tightening in my chest. "If you only knew how I've dreamed of it—"

"I know, love," he said softly. "I don't doubt it."

"Leta is still in Domignon," I told him, "and I want so badly to get her out of there. But I can't leave my mother. I can't lose her, after everything that's happened. She's...well, she's been through a great deal."

Mithraan went quiet for a moment, then pressed his forehead gently to mine and said, "About Leta—"

I held my breath as I asked, "What about her? Have you heard something?"

"I told you that Thalanir traveled over the sea with me."

I nodded. "And you said you sent him back to Kalemnar on a mission..."

"I've asked him to help your sister. He'll find her, extract her from the palace, and get her to safety. You have my word."

A dart of cynicism hit me square in the chest. Why Thalanir? Why send a sell-blade for Leta, instead of Khiral or Alaric, both of whom I trust with my life?

"How much will that cost you?" I asked.

"It doesn't matter," he replied. "He's the best at what he does. He got me here to you, after all, didn't he?"

I frowned, but couldn't deny that he was right. "I am grateful to him for that—of course I am. And if he can help Leta, then I will take back every skeptical thought I've ever had of him. Promise."

Mithraan nodded, pulling me to his chest. "I would do anything for you, you know," he said softly. "Even hide myself behind a Lightblood face like a deceitful rat. Look—I'll stay here until we have a plan in place, and in the meantime, I will watch over you as closely as I possibly can. Speaking of which..." He slid his fingers down my cleavage, then hooked them into the thin fabric of my dress, threatening not so subtly to pull it aside. "Do you have any idea how much I wanted to leap over at dinner and tear this damned garment away from your perfect breasts? How much I wished to push you against the wall and claim you, regardless of who was watching? You were driving me absolutely mad with desire."

"How much *did* you want it?" I was barely able to breathe as I writhed with pleasure. "Show me."

"You really want to know?"

"Yes."

He backed away, and with both hands and little effort, he tore the top half of the dress apart, exposing me to the cool night air.

"*This* much."

He fell to his knees before me and cast a spell.

I found myself pushed against the door, though no hands gripped me. My arms were pinned over my head, my legs splayed, and I watched in wonder as his tongue traced the contour of my breasts, my nipples, teasing them into stone-hard peaks...and as he moved on, I remained frozen, unable to do anything but bask in the pleasure of every sensation he inflicted on me.

When he had satisfied himself by slipping his lips over every inch of my torso, he slipped a hand up my skirts to my inner thigh, watching my face—my head was the only part of me that I was able to lift away from the door—as he slipped a finger between my legs, then pulled it away to lick it clean.

"Two can play at this game, you know," I told him.

When he raised an inquisitive eyebrow, I mirrored his spell, shooting him full across the room so that he landed with a hard thud against the far wall.

He laughed heartily, stunned by my display of power, and

said, "My Vaelan has outed herself as a Thariel in my absence. Impressive."

I pulled away from the wall, now free of his spell, and strode over to him, the remnants of the dress falling to the ground around me.

And then it was I who was on my knees, pulling at his uniform—careful not to tear it as he would need it again in the morning. I yanked his tunic upward to kiss my way up his muscular stomach, reveling in each hard breath he took as he tried and failed to subdue his arousal.

Finally, I split his trousers open and taking him in my hand as he let out a low, exquisite chuckle of pleasure, struggling to free himself from my reflected spell.

"Not just yet," I said quietly, taking him in my mouth, my teeth grazing him just enough to elicit a moan, my tongue stroking over him so that he let out a low, drawn-out, "Please..." and I relented.

I rose to my feet and freed him, and he snatched me up, carried me over to the bed and lay me down, splitting my legs apart and thrusting deep, deep...and deeper still, until I had to reach for a pillow and cram its corner in my mouth to keep from screaming from the pure pleasure of it.

Mithraan snatched the pillow away to press his mouth to mine as he spoke my name, his hips moving slowly now, just slowly enough so that each thrust was a reminder of all I'd missed since we'd last been together—all I'd missed every second I had *ever* spent without him inside me.

"I love you," he said, pulling back to look me in the eye. "I have loved you since before I ever met you—since before I knew one such as you could possibly exist."

"I love you," I replied. "So much that I thought I would break apart these last weeks—months. I didn't dare count the days for fear that I would shatter."

"In that case," he said, speeding up his pace, "let's resolve to have no more days apart for at least a thousand years."

I smiled up at him, a hand caressing his stubbled face as I fought back gasps of pleasure and sorrow—and the question that I could not bring myself to ask...

Do I even dare dream of such a life?

CHAPTER THIRTY-THREE

IN THE MORNING, I awoke with Mithraan's powerful arm draped around my waist, the rising sun's rays warming the bed chamber. For one perfect, blissful moment, I lay still, a soft purr of contentment in my throat.

But the moment came crashing to an end as I remembered where we were. How dangerous it was for him to be with me in Kazimir's domain.

If the High King were to find him...

I couldn't even bring myself to contemplate what chaos would ensue. Mithraan was powerful, as was I—but an entire army of Lightbloods in their home territory was too frightening a prospect to contemplate.

"Mithraan," I said, stroking his arm with my fingers.

He snapped awake, seemingly as disoriented and surprised as I had been.

"They can't find you here," I lamented. "You need to disguise yourself and leave my room, or..."

"Or..." he repeated ruefully. "Or your father will take my head and put it on a spike to show the world what becomes of Lyrinn's suitors."

I slapped his arm playfully and smirked. "I wouldn't exactly call you a suitor," I scolded. "More like *impossibly desirable manipulator of tongue, and impressive grower of other bits.*"

"Oh? Is that to be my new title?" In one quick movement, he was over me, his hands pressed to either side of my head. "What else would you call me...Princess?"

"I would call you my *Everything*," I replied softly, staring up into his extraordinary eyes.

"As you are mine." He eased down, his chest against mine, and I moaned at the sensation of his hardness pressing against me, threatening to tear me apart all over again.

"If you don't go right now, I will climb on top of you and do unspeakable things until you scream for mercy," I whispered.

"That would be a shame. I don't know how I would survive such an ordeal..." he whispered back. But his thought was interrupted by the sound of footsteps in the corridor just outside my room.

We both pulled our eyes to the door, listening breathlessly until the steady beating had faded into the distance.

"Go," I said. "Return to me tonight, and every night until we figure out our escape."

"Night, day." He smiled. "I will find you every single time there is a chance to put my mouth on you, or my cock in you. That's a promise."

A flare of heat at my core threatened to drive me to impulsive behavior, but I curbed it, biting my lip, and said, "I'm serious. Leave, Tomlin of the Northern Guard."

He leapt out of bed and dressed in his stolen uniform, and only when he'd altered into his Lightblood guise did he lean down and kiss me again. It felt strange—almost a betrayal—to kiss the lips of the guard who had been flirting so relentlessly with me. But I reminded myself that it was still Mithraan who felt my touch—still Mithraan who had taken possession of my body and soul.

"I'll keep watch over you," he said. "And I'll be back tonight. In the meantime, do your best not to seem too happy, or the Northerners—and your beloved father—will grow suspicious."

"I'll act as morose and downtrodden as ever," I promised. "Don't worry."

"Good."

I watched him slip through the bedroom door, my heart full, renewed hope granting me life.

Perhaps my mother and I would find our way back to Kalemnar, after all. To Leta, to Tíria, and to a new home with a High Lord far more worthy than Adhair.

When I headed down to the dining hall, Adhair and Lady Cassia were already seated at the table alongside my own mother and Erildir, chatting amicably as they ate. Mithraan—in his Tomlin guise, stood by the door, his eyes focused straight ahead... though he issued me a brief glance as I wandered in.

"Highness," Adhair said, rising to his feet and offering me a quick bow. "We were just discussing our upcoming journey to Nordvahl and the Succession Ceremony."

"*Your* journey." The deep voice came from the direction of the doors, and I turned around to see Kazimir striding in, a resolute look in his eye. "Yours and your mother's."

My heartbeat accelerated to dangerous levels as I realized how close Mithraan now stood to my father—how dangerous the situation was.

"I don't want Lyrinn going north," Kazimir continued,

taking his seat at the table. "In case that wasn't clear. There's no call for it."

"No call, your Grace?" Adhair said with a polite, tight-lipped smile, his eyes flaring bright for a moment in defiance of his expression. "I thought you wanted Princess Lyrinn to experience Aetherion to its fullest."

"She can experience the North when its Priestesses are not in the midst of a contentious debate and a world-altering rite," Kazimir replied.

His jovial mood from the previous night was entirely gone —a change that I could only attribute to the lack of wine.

"There is no debate to be had," Cassia retorted. "The selection of the new Elar has been made already. It is only a matter of a formality at this point."

"Formality?" Kazimir snapped. "Which means what, exactly?"

"The chosen Successor must simply prove her faithfulness to the cause, in a rite that is as old as time. As I said, a formality."

"If, as you say," Kazimir replied, grabbing a pastry and tearing off a piece before popping it into his mouth, "it is all a mere formality, why bring my daughter all the way to Nordvahl for it?"

The rest of the room looked as surprised as I was when my mother responded.

"Lyrinn will rule Aetherion one day," she said evenly, a note of authority in her voice. "The Elar's Successor will be powerful. Do you not think our daughter should see what she is up against? Should she not meet the next Elar?"

Kazimir seemed to contemplate this for a moment. He lay the pastry down on his plate and turned to Erildir, who was seated to my mother's right.

"What say you, Spell-Master?" he asked. "Is my wife correct in her judgment?"

Erildir met his eyes and nodded slightly. "I'm afraid so, your Grace. I cannot fathom depriving Lyrinn of such an encounter. If she is to understand this realm—*truly* understand it—she must go north. She must see the Frozen Lands, and glimpse the territories between here and there. The trip needn't take long—you and I both have the skill to shorten the journey significantly. We can be there and back in a matter of two days."

Kazimir stared at the Sidhfae, and for a moment, I thought perhaps he intended to challenge him—to call him a traitor, even, for defying him by agreeing with my mother.

I watched Erildir, who had more than hinted that I would never wear the silver crown. Why, then, insist that it would be in my best interest to see Aetherion? What could I possibly have to gain, if I were never to rule?

Or did Erildir simply enjoy toying with my emotions as much as Kazimir did?

"Perhaps you're right," the High King finally said with a hard breath. "But if Lyrinn goes, I go, as well. If we are to make it a royal visit, we should *all* head to the Frozen City."

"I wouldn't want it any other way," Cassia said with a smile. "Yes, by all means—you should all come."

I glanced over at Mithraan, whose Lightblood visage was stoic—though I suspected he was grinding his jaw as the others spoke. The potential trip was an unwanted complication—a mallet tossed carelessly into any hopes we might have harbored for a simple escape.

But perhaps, I told myself, the trip would render escape easier by offering a distraction in the coming days—something to pull Kazimir's eyes and mind away.

A faint hope dared to blossom inside me once again. A mere dash of it...but hope nonetheless.

I will get you home, I thought, my eyes landing on my mother. *I promise.*

CHAPTER THIRTY-FOUR

When we were finished eating, Adhair turned to Kazimir and said, "I would love to see more of the palace grounds, your Grace. With your permission, I would like to ask that Princess Lyrinn accompany me on a stroll."

I glanced over at Mithraan, who managed to keep his Light-blood face stoic despite the request.

For my part, I couldn't imagine what Adhair and I would talk about on a walk—how we would entertain ourselves for any period of time. He was pleasant enough, I supposed, but far from a fascinating conversationalist.

Kazimir raised an eyebrow, then gruffly replied, "Yes, yes," with a dismissive wave of his hand. "Go anywhere you like. Bring a guard, though. An attempt was recently made on my daughter's life, and I don't wish to see that act repeated."

"Of course, your Grace," Adhair said with a bow of his head. He rose to his feet and offered me a hand. "I hope it's all right with you, Highness," he said. "I could use a breath of fresh air."

"It's fine," I replied. "A walk would do me good."

I was delighted when he signaled to Mithraan—Tomlin, rather—to follow us as we slipped out to the corridor.

"I was hoping we could take a tour of the gardens," Adhair said as we walked. "I noticed the hedge labyrinth out my window this morning—it looked quite exquisite."

"That would be...lovely," I said, glancing over my shoulder to see Mithraan behind us in full disguise, a mischievous grin on his lips.

I led Adhair outside to a large terrace overlooking what Erildir had once told me was Kazimir's pride and joy: an enormous maze of tall hedges, groomed to within an inch of their lives.

"The maze is changeable," Erildir had said. "Charmed. It shifts hourly to a new configuration so that the High King doesn't grow weary of staring at the same view from his chamber high in the palace."

Looking at it now, I could see why Kazimir enjoyed it so much. Something about the view was opulent, excessive, ridiculous even, yet comforting all at the same time. Not a leaf nor a branch was out of place, and I wondered if Kazimir had gardeners or if he simply cast a spell that created endless perfection out of the multitude of shrubs springing up from the ground.

"Shall we take a walk through this legendary structure?" Adhair asked as we approached.

But I was hesitant—I had heard that Fae occasionally found themselves trapped in corners of the maze when its rows shifted, sometimes taking hours to escape. The thought wouldn't have bothered me much, but for the fact that it reminded me of the Labyrinth in the Blood Trials—a deadly nightmare conjured by cruel overlords.

"I..." I glanced over my shoulder at Mithraan, who gave me a very slight, reassuring nod as if to say, "Don't worry—you're safe so long as I'm here."

"Yes," I finally said with finality. "Let's have a look."

As we proceeded through the maze's entrance, Adhair pressed toward me and said, "I must confess that I had an ulterior motive for asking you to come along with me, Princess."

My chest tightened. "Oh?"

"I thought perhaps you could use a break from your family. Your High King father can be rather..."

"Ornery?" I laughed, relieved that his motives weren't more nefarious.

"I was going to say 'intense,' but that'll do," Adhair replied with a chuckle. "But to his credit, it seems he wishes above all else to protect you. I can't blame him—if I had one such as you in my possession, I would feel the same way."

I bristled at his words, wondering if Mithraan had heard them, especially the word "possession," which stuck in me like an aggravating splinter.

I am no one's possession, Lord Adhair. Even Mithraan does not own me.

"My father is concerned about my welfare for the realm's sake alone," I said with a bitter tint to my voice. "Not that I ever intend to rule."

Adhair stopped walking as we came to a fork in the maze, then turned to me. "Tell me—what do you intend to do, then?"

I stiffened, looking briefly to my right to see Mithraan standing some distance away.

"I...I don't know," I said, bowing my head with the realization of my own recklessness. "It was foolish of me to say that. Of course I will take the silver crown when it is offered to me."

With a grimace, Adhair said, "I told you last night that you don't have to lie to me, Princess. I can sense your emotions—it's a Gift I inherited from my mother. You see, I too have a powerful parent. I understand what it is to live in their shadow. One day I will be expected to oversee the North, and I dread that day, truth be told. Still, duty is duty."

"Yes. I suppose it is."

We had walked and talked for several more minutes, following turn after turn, when we came to a fork in the maze. We both stopped, and Adhair said, "Right or left?"

I looked both ways. "Right."

When he proceeded, I turned to see if Mithraan was still close. To my relief, he was.

But by the time I turned to follow Adhair, a jarring sound met my ears—a sort of low grinding, as if the earth and stone beneath our feet were shifting.

Before I knew it, a hedge had sprung up between Adhair and me, cutting us off from one another. I spun around to see that I was standing in a long, narrow corridor of green with only one way out.

Ahead, and to the left.

Pivoting again, I realized I could no longer see Mithraan.

Where are you?

My silent question was answered when I began to walk briskly and he stepped around the corner to stand before me, pressing a finger to his lips.

"Princess!" Adhair's distant voice called. "Are you there?"

As I slipped closer to Mithraan, he shook his head and grabbed me by the belt, yanking me close. He was still in his Lightblood guise, but I didn't care for a moment, not anymore. His lips were the same ones that had kissed me so many times in so, so many different ways. His eyes, though a different color, were the ones that had peered into me over and over again as I opened myself to him, inviting him to dwell inside my soul— begging him to claim me.

He brushed my hair back from my face and cupped my cheeks in his palms. "Do not respond to the bastard," he whispered before kissing my jaw, my neck. "Don't say a thing. Let him hunt for you."

"But..." I whispered with a quiet laugh. "What if..."

Mithraan was working his way down, his lips on my shoulder now, then my chest...my...

"I can scent him from a mile away—and if you had worked on developing your senses as you should have done by now, you would be able to, as well." He chuckled as he chastised me.

"I've had other things on my mind, my lord."

"No matter. My senses are keen enough for us both."

He pulled at my dress, yanking the shoulders down until my entire chest was exposed to the sun, the sky, the breeze. I gasped as my nipples peaked with the cool of the air. Mithraan palmed my breast, a low, wild growl escaping his throat.

If Adhair found us like this...if my father saw us...

As frantic as I was, Mithraan's mouth was on my nipple now, his teeth biting at me gently as I stifled a moan of pure pleasure. I twined my fingers in his temporary silver hair, watching as he teased my flesh with his teeth, his tongue, slipping one hand up my dress to land on my inner thigh. He let out a sigh when he discovered I was not wearing undergarments, his fingers parting me swiftly, greedily.

The next thing I knew, his head was under my skirt, his tongue lapping at me, driving me rapidly to madness...

Gods...

"Princess!"

The voice was close now—so close that I leapt backwards and pulled my dress up to cover my exposed flesh, struggling to ensure that I wasn't still half-falling out of it.

"I'm here!" I called faintly, my voice shaking with laughter and horror combined. "Tomlin and I were separated from you when the maze shifted."

Adhair rounded the nearest corner and strode toward us, the smile on his lips intensifying as he came closer. I could still feel the wetness between my legs, and I wondered with a shock of fear if he was able to smell my arousal.

"Ah! I was worried that you'd been trapped, somehow," he said, clapping the Fae he called Tomlin on the shoulder.

Tomlin, his loyal guard, who was still wiping his mouth with the back of his hand, staring at me as though he had only just begun a feast that was nowhere near completion.

"Not trapped," I replied. "Just a little disoriented. I'm...sorry we lost you."

"No harm done," Adhair said. "Well, then, let's head back inside. I'd rather not get caught in another shift of the maze, to be quite honest. I think I've had my fill for now."

As we began to walk, I noticed him watching me out of the corner of his eye. I glanced up and laughed uncomfortably. "What is it? Do I have something on my face?"

"Not at all, Princess," he said. "It's...let's just say I'm very pleased to get to spend this time by your side."

The words were pleasant. Innocent, even. But something in his tone filled me with unease. There was a sense of entitlement there—a sort of one-sided, tacit understanding on his part... and I didn't like it one bit.

I was relieved when we found an exit that emptied the three of us out near the terrace. I didn't know what accounted for the quiet shift in Adhair's demeanor, but I wanted little more than to get as far away from him as possible

"I...should go speak with my mother," I said.

"Yes. Absolutely. Let me accompany you inside, and then we'll part ways...for now."

CHAPTER THIRTY-FIVE

WHEN WE WERE BACK inside the palace, I thanked Adhair for the walk.

He told me his mother and Kazimir were to spend the day together, and he was planning to dine with them that evening.

"Would you care to join us?" he asked.

I began to shake my head, but stopped with the realization that it might not be the best strategic move. Surely I could tolerate Kazimir's presence for a little, if it meant the chance to watch Tomlin across the room as his lips twitched uncontrollably into a varied assortment of sly grins.

"That would be...lovely," I said, poorly concealing the copious effort in my voice. "But first, I do need to see about finding my mother."

"I'll look forward to seeing you at dinner, then," Adhair said with a suggestive smile before turning to head toward his quarters. Mithraan offered me a shallow nod, then followed wordlessly.

I'll see you soon, I thought. *But not soon enough.*

I found my mother seated on a stone bench, a book in hand, in the small courtyard where I had often trained with Erildir. She looked up and smiled as I approached.

"Did you have a nice walk with Adhair?" she asked.

"I did. Very nice. It was good to get out and...breathe."

"Breathe, yes," she said with a knowing look. "That's one way of putting it."

As she spoke the words, a sound jarred me, and I turned to see that the door I'd walked through had sealed itself shut.

We were entirely alone. I could feel that even Lark was far from us, locked away from this private moment, and I found myself wondering if he'd watched Mithraan and me in the garden earlier.

"Sit, Lyrinn," my mother said, patting the bench. "I'd like to talk to you about something of a rather...*delicate* nature."

I did as she asked, struck by the conspiratorial tone in her voice.

"What about?" My voice was clipped—not that I had any objection to a moment of intimacy between us. I trusted her, after all. She was my family. My blood.

Then again, so was Kazimir. But I pushed him from my thoughts, undeserving as he was.

"I feel," she said, speaking slowly, her voice clipped and cool, "that I should warn you to be more careful."

"Careful?" I asked. "Look—if this is about the poisoner, I'm confident that—"

My mother raised a hand to stop me, issued a forced smile through tight lips, and said, "It's not about poisoners." She leaned closer and whispered, "I can smell him on you, daughter. I know you have been with the Tírian."

My cheeks heated and I pulled back, staring into her eyes.

"You know, then," I said. "That he's here."

Upon hearing my admission, an expression of giddiness passed over her face, so quick and fleeting that I wondered if I'd only imagined it.

"I do," she said, her voice smooth as silk. "But don't concern yourself too much. I am your mother—I am far more attuned to you than your...*father.*" The word came out accompanied by a wince. "I am delighted that your Mithraan is here. But if Kazimir were to find out what you've been up to, he would not be pleased, to put it mildly. I hardly need to tell you that—my point is that Kazimir would most likely kill him if he discovered him on these shores. Your High Lord might be strong, but he is no match for a palace full of devoted Lightbloods. Keep him secret, at all costs."

I wanted to deny it with every breath in my body. Or to tell her he'd gone, that he was far from us by now, on a ship back to Kalemnar.

But my mother was no fool. She had not survived this long under Kazimir's cruel and oppressive thumb by lacking observational skills.

"The thing is..." I began, but I had no defense to offer. Instead, I would offer the simple truth. "I love him."

My mother cringed at the words as though it pained her deeply to hear them. But she fought the momentary expression off with a nod. "I know," she said. "I feel it in you. And I am so sorry to tell you that it is that profound connection that will bring you the greatest joy—and the greatest sorrow—of your life."

"Sorrow," I repeated. She said the word as though she had looked into the future to see some far-off event, some cataclysm that would decimate my soul. "No. Mithraan will never bring me sorrow."

She reached out and took my hand in hers, holding it tight as she said, "Love is wonderful and beautiful...but love makes fools of us all. He will not bring you sorrow—but your love for him will."

Glancing down at her hand, at the ring that tore so fiercely into her flesh, her eyes narrowed with what looked like pure hatred.

No, I thought. *Kazimir and Mithraan are nothing alike. He would never do to me what the High King has done to you—never.*

"We need to leave this place," I whispered, glancing around cautiously. "I intend to get us both away from here. Mithraan can help."

She yanked her hand away almost violently when she hissed, "I cannot leave—I've told you so."

The change in her voice felt like a shock in the air itself.

"I know. The ring. But Mother—"

"I told you. I cannot leave!"

Ice hung from every syllable, and I found myself recoiling with the sort of fear one might feel of an unpredictable, wild creature baring its teeth in threat.

"Keep Mithraan's presence a secret at all costs," she said, and this time, her voice softened almost to its normal state. "Keep him close—but do not let your father learn he's here. I'll do what I can to help you—as will Erildir. You have my word. You must keep your High Lord close to you as long as you possibly can. He must stay in Aetherion until..."

She stopped speaking as though she realized she was about to divulge something vital and secret.

"Keep him here." She rose to her feet. "In the meantime, keep up appearances. Stay close to Adhair. Convince Kazimir that you are growing fond of the High Lord from the North, if that's what it takes to keep him content. Do you hear me?"

I nodded my head, feeling like a chastised six-year-old who feared the consequences of irritating the most important adult in their life.

With that, my mother left me alone, my thoughts a jumbled mess of worry and questions combined.

CHAPTER THIRTY-SIX

IN MY BED CHAMBER, I found Mithraan waiting for me, a ponderous frown on his lips.

I rushed toward him as soon as I'd closed the door. "What's happened?"

"Nothing serious enough for you to have so much worry behind those beautiful eyes," he said, kissing me gently. "Still— It's not good news. A pack of wolves has been disturbing the farmlands around Aethos."

A laugh burst from my chest. "From the look in your eye, I was convinced you were going to tell me Kalemnar had burned to the ground. Wolves are nothing. Let Kazimir's Lightbloods deal with them."

"I would, but it's not my choice, I'm afraid," he replied. "Adhair offered a few of his guardsmen to help with the tracking, me among them. I can't exactly refuse my lord and master, so I must go with the others."

My heart sank. "For how long?"

"One night. Perhaps longer, depending on how our hunt goes."

My heart sank deeper, a feeling of profound loss tearing at something inside me.

"Do you think..." I said softly. I couldn't bear to finish the question.

"Do I think he knows?" Mithraan asked. He shook his head. "Adhair is not the most perceptive Fae I've ever met, despite what he may say to the contrary. No—I don't think this is some mission he's conjured up to get me killed. If he wanted to do that, he'd simply tell Kazimir I've spent quite a few hours of late with my tongue between his daughter's legs."

I chuckled in spite of my concerns. "Fine, then. When do you leave?"

"Right now, I'm sorry to say," he replied, kissing me again before restoring his Lightblood guise. "I'm to be in the court-yard in a few minutes."

"Damnation. I was hoping your tongue could spend some time..."

"In its favorite place? Yes, me, too. When I return with a slew of wolf pelts, I promise we'll take up where we left off." With a final, deep kiss, he headed for the door, turning when he had his fingers wrapped around the handle. "You know, my Lady..." he added.

"Yes?"

"I must admit I'm enjoying all this sneaking around in defiance of a High King. I've all but forgotten my station as High Lord of Fairholme. I'm like a teen-aged boy, getting up to no good in the hayloft."

"With a serving wench?" I asked, laughing.

"With a *princess*," he replied. "Even better, if you ask me."

I watched him leave, my heart full even as my mind wallowed in worry. Was there a chance that Adhair knew who Mithraan was? Was he in grave danger? Was this some sort of ambush...?

I told myself my worries were silly. Mithraan was stronger than a few Lightblood guards. He could look after himself in any situation—not to mention that, thanks to a Gift the Taker had transferred from my mind to his, he could heal himself if something should happen.

I resolved to follow my mother's advice, as much as I disliked it. When dinner time rolled around, I would pretend to be far more interested in Adhair than I was, and never let on that a far more worthy Fae held dominion over my heart and soul.

As the sun began to set, I made my way down to the dining hall where I found my mother sitting alone, waiting for the others to show.

Like Mithraan earlier, she wore an expression of worry.

"What's wrong?" I asked as I entered the room.

She gestured me to come closer, then asked in a near-whisper, "Is the sprite with you?"

I hadn't heard nor seen any sign of Lark in hours, so I shook my head. "I don't think so," I told her. "What is it?"

"It's your sister," she said. "I'm concerned—I used a stone to see her earlier, thinking I would find her inside the palace at Domignon with the prince. But it seems she's escaped."

"Escaped?"

I thought of Thalanir then, of Mithraan sending him back to Kalemnar on his ship. But surely, he couldn't be in Domignon already—it had only been a matter of a day or so. Even if the ship was charmed for fast travel, it would be ambitious to think he could have gotten to Leta, met her and freed her all in the period since Mithraan had seen him last.

"Are you quite sure?"

"Completely," my mother said. "I saw her in the woods. Cloaked and hooded, she was making her way southeast. But where she was headed, I do not know. I lost the image soon after I found her, and...I'm worried about her, Lyrinn. What if..."

I hesitated for a moment, then said, "Mother...I suppose there's no harm in telling you this—" A sudden instinct commanded me to heed Lark's warnings about trust. But this was my mother. *Leta's* mother. She deserved to know. I whispered low, in case any sprites were nearby. "Mithraan sent someone—a friend—to find Leta and take her from Corym. To save her from the life she would have been subjected to in Domignon, since I can't do it myself."

I didn't know what I expected. Relief, perhaps. Gratitude for Mithraan's thoughtfulness, for the risk his friend was taking.

But instead, her eyes blazed with red flame as she stared me down, her voice a terrifying rasp.

"What have you done?"

Leaping to her feet, she grabbed hold of me and repeated the words. "What. Have. You. Done?"

Stunned, my heart thundering in my chest, I pulled away, watching a trail of blood seep from the wounds inflicted by her ring, which was clearly doing battle with her body and mind. I could feel power surging in the air around us. Waves of thrumming magic, aching to be released.

"Mother?"

My voice was mousy, almost pathetic, and if any stranger had walked into the room just then, they would hardly have known I was the powerful High Fae who could unleash a furious weapon of light at any moment, and my mother was powerless.

As if a sudden, brutal realization hit her, my mother pulled back, the flames in her eyes fading to embers then dying altogether.

"Lyrinn...I am so..." she said, falling back into her chair, her palm going to her forehead. "I'm sorry." She took a few deep breaths before saying, "I have these...spells. I think it's the ring. It's a sort of gruesome effect of my powers being leeched from me. I—I didn't mean to frighten you."

"It's all right," I said, taking a tentative step toward her. "I just want you better, Mother. We need to get that ring off your finger. To get you whole again."

"I know." She looked at the floor, her chin low, and spoke softly. "Of course it's wonderful that Leta will be safe. It's wonderful. I am very happy to hear it. All I want is for my two children to be well."

She spoke the words insistently, as if trying to convince herself of the truth in them.

I glanced over my shoulder to make sure no one had entered the room, then said, "If you saw her alone, she's probably not been discovered yet. The Fae in question—the one looking for her—he's probably far from Kalemnar still. Please, don't worry. Leta and I spent many nights in the woods when we were younger. She knows how to look after herself. And rest assured that she's probably safer on her own than with that wretched prince. I know his cruelty firsthand."

"You're right. From what I know of him, he's not worthy to lead Kalemnar."

"The prince is not worthy to own a cat," I replied bitterly.

"Still," my mother said by means of explanation, "I suppose I had hoped your sister had found a home—somewhere she could settle. Perhaps a royal life would suit her. And who knows? Maybe she would have been a good influence on Corym."

"Corym is not a man who is open to influence," I snapped,

more harshly than I intended. "I mean—he's not likely to listen to a woman, not under any circumstance. Leta is better off without him. And..."

I was about to say Thalanir seemed like a far better ally to Leta than the prince could ever be when the sound of a door opening made me freeze.

"My wife and daughter, together!" I sealed my eyes against Kazimir's voice, irritated by the intrusion. "What a beautiful sight."

"We are enjoying one another's company, your Grace," my mother said meekly, moving her hand to mine and taking hold.

"Yes, we are," I added, opening my eyes and turning to see Kazimir standing in the wide doorway, along with Adhair. I smiled as pleasantly as I could, hoping it was enough to mask my annoyance. "Even after all this time, we still find we have many years of catching up to do."

"*Nineteen* years, you mean. A mere drop in a vast cauldron, in the lifespan of a Fae," Kazimir insisted. "You will one day find that the first years of your life were meaningless, forgettable. All that occurred before your Coming of Age and your ascent to power will prove trivial in comparison to what is yet to come."

"I will *not* forget those years," I snarled, ignoring for a moment that the Northern lord was standing with Kazimir. "I will not forget my father or my sister, regardless of how badly you might wish for me to try."

At my utterance of the word 'father,' Kazimir's eyes narrowed, but he managed to resist an angry outburst. He remained silent for a few moments before saying, "Adhair has informed me he's hoping to take you for a walk to the coast tomorrow. I think it's a splendid idea."

"The coast?" I asked, locking eyes with the High Lord. "Where, exactly?"

"I thought we could wander toward Khithar Head and look out at the sea. I've heard the views are stunning."

"Khithar Head," I repeated. Where the Kalhern lies—the Cavern of Dreams, where I found Mithraan one night in my mind's eye...

"That sounds wonderful," I replied.

"I'll find you after breakfast tomorrow, then."

I wondered with an internal groan if I would be gone when Mithraan returned—if I would miss his arrival.

Not that I had any choice in the matter. If I was to carry on this charade, I needed to convince both Adhair and my father that I was perfectly content to spend time with the Northerner.

"You have my blessing to move about as you wish," Kazimir said. "And provided you remember what's at stake if you were to disappear on me, Lyrinn." With that, he fired an aggressive look at my mother. His eyes felt like projectiles tearing into her with a threat that was deafening despite its silence.

"I am all too aware of what's at stake," I replied with frost on my tongue. "I will not desert this place so long as my mother is here. You have my word."

"What a good daughter you are."

"Besides which," I said with an exaggerated, suggestive glance at Adhair, "this palace is beginning to grow on me."

Better to divert Kazimir's attention in that direction than to let him dwell on thoughts of bringing harm to my mother.

"Good," Kazimir said. "Because one day before too many years have passed, you will find yourself wearing the silver crown—and you will learn the meaning of the word duty. That begins with understanding your place."

Smiling, I told myself I already understood all of it.

Still, as far as I was concerned, I had only one duty: I would rid this world of Kazimir. I didn't know how, or when.

But I would find a way.

CHAPTER THIRTY-SEVEN

Sometime in the night, Lark's frantic voice awoke me.

"Highness!" he called out, a small hand shaking my shoulder. I surged awake, shooting upward with a shock of confusion.

"What is it?" I asked when I saw that we were alone in my room. "Has something—"

Has something happened to Mithraan?

"It's your mother. Erildir said you must come quickly to her chamber. She's..."

"She's what?"

"She's been stabbed, Highness."

I leapt out of bed, quickly throwing a robe over my nightclothes, and ran out the door and toward my mother's chamber with my heart in my throat. I was too panicked to cry, too frightened to ask the question that plagued my mind.

Is she alive?

"I'll keep watch outside her door when you go in," Lark told me as I ran. "In case the attacker should return."

Erildir greeted me at the door to my mother's room, a grave look in his eye.

"Is she..." I mustered, but he shook his head, gesturing me inside and closing the door.

"She's alive. But the blade used was doused in poison. She needs Blood Magic if she is to survive this."

"Blood Magic?"

"Come. I'll explain."

I raced over to my mother's bedside to see that her face, normally rosy-cheeked, was gray and coated in perspiration. A large crimson stain had spread over her white nightgown where the blade had pierced her side.

She let out a quiet moan as I took her hand, but her eyes were glazed over, her mind a thousand worlds from us.

"She will not bleed to death," Erildir explained. "But I cannot heal her against the sort of poison her assailant used. It's almost as though..."

"As though what?"

"As though they knew there was only one person in this palace who could help her."

He stared into my eyes, and a deep understanding wove its way through my mind.

"What do I need to do?"

Erildir reached for a blade tucked at his waist—one he didn't normally wear—and pulled it from its sheath. "Your mother needs your blood. The blood of her kin. It will cleanse her, drive the poison from her veins. You are—truly—the only one who can do this, Lyrinn."

"Cut me, then," I said, my eyes veering down to look at my mother. I couldn't lose her—not like this. I had accepted my fate, my imprisonment in Aetherion, all to protect her. I was not about to surrender to fear now. "Do whatever it takes."

Erildir reached down and tore the nightgown open just enough to reveal the wound. It was clean, at least, but the veins surrounding it had turned gray and dark as the poison worked its way through her body.

"Give me your hand," Erildir commanded.

When I did as he asked, he sliced into my palm deeply enough that I knew the scar would likely last me the rest of my life.

"Press your hand to the wound," he said. "Hold it there until I tell you to stop. Understood?"

I nodded silently, wincing against the pain.

I pressed my palm to my mother's side. After a few seconds, something began to move under my hand—as if tendrils were reaching for my veins, intertwining with them to draw my blood from my body.

"Who did this to her?" I asked, my voice strained as I looked up at the Spell-Master.

"I don't know," Erildir said softly. "Though I have my suspicions. We will have to ask her when all is said and done."

I closed my eyes and held my hand steady for what felt like hours on end, saying a silent prayer to unseen gods, to the Elar, to any entity who would listen, to ensure that my mother lived. As I did so, Erildir whispered an incantation in a language I didn't understand.

As his words caressed the air, I asked myself who would do this, and why. Who could possibly benefit from my mother's death? Was the assassin still in the dungeon? Had she escaped, perhaps, and gone after my mother when she could not find me?

The questions were still circling my mind when my mother let out another quiet moan, then a word, spoken clearly.

"Daughter."

I looked down to see her smiling faintly at me, the brightness returning at last to her large blue eyes.

Tears streamed down my cheeks, my shoulders shuddering,

and I found myself wishing more than anything that Mithraan was here with me in this moment.

"You may remove your hand now," Erildir said, a length of clean white cloth in his own hand as he prepared to wrap my wound.

"Mother," I replied, reaching down to cup her cheek with my other palm. "Are you all right?"

"I..." she said, looking up at the Spell-Master. "It hurts a little—but I am fine."

I looked down to see the dark veins fading from her wound, the flesh sealing itself shut, leaving behind nothing but a fine white line as though the stabbing had occurred many years ago.

"Who did this?" I asked, my voice eggshell-thin. "Who would hurt you?"

Even as I spoke the question, I realized how naive it was. One Fae alone had been hurting her for centuries.

Why should now be any different?

"It was Kazimir," she said, confirming my theory. "I...I think it was my fault. I argued with him about you, after dinner. I..."

I shook my head violently. "No. It wasn't your fault. There's nothing you could possibly have done to ask for such a punishment."

"He feels that I am growing too close to you," she said mournfully. "He doesn't like the attachment we've formed. I think he's afraid..."

"Afraid of what?"

"Afraid I'll destroy your ambition. That I will discourage you from wearing the silver crown."

"So he tried to *kill* you?" I spat. "Why would he do that? If you died..."

If you died, there would be nothing to keep me here, and Kazimir knows it.

It made no sense. A stupid, foolish move on my father's part. And, worst of all, he had nearly succeeded.

"We *have* to get you out of here," I said. "Away from Aetherion, back to Kalemnar. We need to escape."

She pressed her head back into the pillow, her eyes meeting Erildir's for a moment before pulling to mine. "Perhaps you're right," she said weakly. "But for now, I believe the Spell-Master wants me to rest."

"She's right," Erildir concurred. "She needs to recover. Her blood is fighting the poison still, and it wouldn't do to try and move her just now."

"Of course," I replied, stroking my hand through my mother's red hair. "I'm just...I'm so happy you're all right."

She grabbed hold of my hand, pulling it to her lips. "I should have been protecting you all these years, my girl. Yet here you are—saving me. How can I ever thank you?"

"You can start by recovering. Nothing will agitate Kazimir more than seeing you healthy at breakfast tomorrow."

She let out a little laugh, then her brow furrowed as she turned her gaze to the Spell-Master.

"Lyrinn—you must say nothing of this to anyone," Erildir warned.

My brows raised. "Why shouldn't I? Kazimir should suffer consequences for his actions. We all know I can take him on if I choose to. He's gone too far—surely you must both see that."

My mother shook her head weakly. "He will only feel empowered by your anger. And if he learns what we've done— that I have your blood in my veins—it will not go over well."

"But why? What could possibly bother him about our blood intermingling? You're my mother, for the gods' sake!"

She exchanged another look with Erildir, who said, "Let's let her rest, shall we? She's been through an ordeal."

I gave him a curt nod. "I'll see you in the morning, then," I said softly, kissing my mother's forehead before leaving her alone with the Spell-Master.

I headed for my room, with Lark following me in silence. It was only when he whispered, "Princess?" that I even remembered he was there.

"What is it?" I asked softly.

"Forgive me, but there's something about your mother's account that puzzles me."

"You heard through the door, then."

"I did. The thing is—the High King cannot have stabbed her."

"Why not?" I asked in a hiss. "He's done worse things in his life."

"Because he has been in Lady Cassia's chamber all night. A sprite who watches over him confirmed this for me just a few minutes ago, while he was patrolling the corridors. The High King has an entire team of Shadowlings at his disposal, all of whom remain close at hand while he sleeps—it's the only way he manages to rest. None saw him leave the room."

"You're telling me there were sprites inside Lady Cassia's chamber while he slept with her?"

"Among other...activities, yes," Lark said, understanding my full meaning. "Look—I don't envy them their duties. But I believe them, Highness. They would not tell another sprite untruths, not even to protect his Grace. We are loyal to one another above all else."

"If that's the case, then—"

It was the obvious question. *Why would my mother lie?*

But perhaps she hadn't lied. Maybe she'd seen a light-haired shadow in the night and *assumed* it was Kazimir. Maybe it was one of his guards, or an outsider. There were any number of possibilities, after all. In the dark of night, Lightbloods could be difficult to distinguish from one another.

She must have been mistaken, that was all. That, or Kazimir had cast a spell to convince the sprites he was still in bed when the attempt on my mother's life had occurred. He had, after all, convinced me I was still on Mithraan's ship when in fact I was on a Lightblood vessel headed for Aetherion.

All I knew was that it would now be impossible to accuse him of the crime—not without great risk. If I meant to escape alongside Mithraan and my mother, it would be best to remain tight-lipped and bide our time until we had a chance to flee.

After a few minutes, Lark and I arrived at my chamber door. "I suppose all that really matters is that she's alive," I finally whispered. "Thank you, Lark, for waking me."

"Of course, Highness. Anything for you."

CHAPTER THIRTY-EIGHT

I RUSHED to breakfast the next morning after throwing on a long white dress and a pair of leather-soled silk shoes, taking no time to style my hair into anything remotely passable—or any other part of me, for that matter.

I had not forgotten that I was to walk to the shore with Adhair, but all I cared about in the moment was to make sure my mother was all right.

To my relief, I found her seated at the dining table with Erildir by her side. Kazimir, on the other hand, was nowhere to be seen.

"Are you well?" I asked as I took a seat next to my mother, taking her hand in my own. I had removed the Spell-Master's bandage the previous night to discover my wound mostly healed, a surprise I could only attribute to him.

"Very well, thanks to you and Erildir—and Lark, of course," my mother said.

"No need for thanks," I replied with a surge of joy. "I'm just so pleased to see your cheeks looking rosy once again."

She did look wonderful. Healthy and vivacious—perhaps even more than before.

"Your blood is a wondrous thing," she replied with a laugh. "If I had doubted your power for a second before last night, I don't doubt it now."

Adhair walked into the room then, his mother at his side. He slipped over and took a seat next to me, his eyes fixed on my mother.

"Queen Alessia," he said. "How are you this morning?"

"Yes," Lady Cassia added. "How are you feeling?"

I glanced quizzically at them both. Had someone told the visitors about the attack?

"Perfectly well. Thank you." My mother shot me a glance of quiet warning to say nothing about it before adding, "Adhair— are you and Lyrinn still intending to go for a walk this morning?"

Adhair smiled. "If Princess Lyrinn is still keen, I certainly am."

Glancing at my mother, I said, "I..."

"Go," she said with a wave of her hand and a meaningful glance that told me she didn't wish to draw attention to herself. "Enjoy yourselves."

Adhair stood and offered me his arm. "Shall we, Highness?"

I rose to my feet, searching the air for the sound of Lark's wings. He'd vanished some time earlier, but now I could hear him faintly, and I nodded. "Yes, let's go. I could certainly use some sea air."

Once in the palace's main courtyard, Adhair led me toward a doorway I had never noticed.

"The High King told me this is the way," he said. "Apparently, there's a long path that leads right down to the headland."

I nodded, not entirely sure I wanted to walk any distance. Instinct told me to stay close to the palace in case my mother should need me again...or Mithraan should return with the hunting party.

But instinct also told me the attacker wouldn't be foolish enough to try anything so soon after the first failed attempt—and Erildir would keep an eye on my mother, as he had done for hundreds of years.

"I've called my guards back from the woods," Adhair announced as we walked.

My arm tightened around his, my heartbeat accelerating. "Oh?"

"I thought perhaps the palace needed the extra protection more than Aetherion's farmlands do."

Keeping my voice even proved a struggle. "Protection? From what?"

Adhair leaned toward me. "I know what happened to your mother last night—I know an assassin broke into the palace, then made their way into her chamber. I realize it's a secret—but she divulged it to my own mother, and we seldom keep anything from one another."

So, my mother had told Cassia that an intruder, not Kazimir, had done this.

I told myself it was sensible—arousing the High King's wrath would not be wise.

Still—why tell her at all?

We walked for some time, making our way past sweeping greenery, wispy trees, and ancient ruins deeply embedded in the rocky landscape. Finally, we arrived at the top of tall, sandy rise, its long, scraggly grasses swaying in the breeze. Adhair gestured toward a wall of white stone jutting out toward the sea. A narrow path led downhill from where we stood to its base, beckoning and lovely.

"Khithar Head," he said. "They say there's a cave down there where dreams come true."

"Is that right?" I asked, trying my best to sound as though I genuinely had no idea.

Adhair turned to face me, his eyes roaming down my body. All of a sudden, I regretted the choice to wear this dress—one that was made of thin, almost translucent silk, and showed off my every curve for all the world to see.

He probably thinks I wore it for his benefit.

If he only knew how little thought I put into it...

"You look extraordinary, Princess," he said, his eyes moving slowly along every inch of me. "I meant to tell you so earlier. It is a wonder to look upon you each day. An absolute pleasure."

"Thank you," I replied, flushing. "I...have a limited wardrobe here in Aetherion. Not much choice, I'm afraid."

"Well then, I am all the more honored for being the one who gets the privilege of seeing you in this particular garment."

"You flatter me."

"Flattery has little to do with it." He took a step closer to me, and I backed away, quickly turning my eyes toward the headland.

"Would you do something for me?" I asked.

"Anything," he said with that smile of his that managed to seem friendly and repulsive at once.

"After what happened last night to my mother, I could use a moment alone...just to breathe, to seek a little peace. Would you mind if I headed down to the cave—just to see if it really is as soothing as they say?"

"Of course I wouldn't mind," he said cheerfully. "I'll sit and admire you as you walk there and back again. Just—don't be too long. I wouldn't want to die of unfulfilled longing."

He said the last sentence with a flirtatious wink that nearly made me gag with its obvious intent, but I managed a smile. "Don't worry—I'll be back soon."

Adhair took a seat in the tall, swaying grass, and waved an

eager hand at me. I smiled, nodded, and headed down the path, summoning all my willpower not to charge headlong down the hill away from him.

The Northern Lord was quickly becoming more than a mere inconvenience. Despite my mother's advice, I was beginning to regret showing any interest whatsoever in him; he reeked of desperation, of a need for companionship—and I was the last person he should be looking to if he wished for either.

When I reached the sandy beach below, I looked up once to see that he was still seated high above me among the grasses, his eyes locked on the distant horizon.

Good, I thought. *Stay.*

I slipped toward the cliff face, searching its base for the cave that was supposed to open out to the nearby waves. It wasn't until I rounded a curve and padded perilously close to the crashing whitecaps that I finally spotted it. A hundred feet or so ahead, the cave's mouth called to me, set as it was beyond the mayhem of the raging sea.

Mithraan's words came to me as I beheld it. *Legend held that a cavern at its base looks like the mouth of one who cries out for his love, lost at sea.*

The description was apt, and I understood why some found the cave frightening. It was grim and dark...and yet I felt not only at ease, but perfectly content to move toward it.

I strode forward, only realizing as I approached how large it really was. Its mouth was tall enough that I could step inside without hunching over, and I did so, curious to see the interior after visiting so often in my dreams.

Behind me, I heard the quiet flitting of wings, and I smiled.

"You still with me, Lark?" I asked without turning around.

"Of course, Highness. I'll stay outside, if it's all right with you. We sprites aren't so fond of caves."

"Absolutely," I replied. "Keep an eye on Adhair. Signal me if he should come down the trail."

"Will do."

When I'd made my way deep into the cave, I inhaled deep, craning my neck to stare up at the rounded ceiling of smooth stone—one that I had beheld night after night as I waited, hoping, for Mithraan to arrive.

"Beautiful, isn't it?" a deep, echoing voice said from behind me.

"I thought I told you to—" I began to chastise Lark. But with a jolt of shock, I realized it wasn't the sprite's voice I'd heard.

"Mithraan," I breathed, spinning around to spy a tall silhouette a few feet away, standing between the cave's mouth and myself. "Is it really you—or is this another dream?"

"No dream, for once," he said with a low chuckle. "I heard you were headed for a wander with that Northern twat. I thought I'd see about intercepting you."

I leapt over and threw my arms around him, then pulled back to stare at his face, accentuated by shadow. It had only been a matter of a day since I'd last seen him, but I felt like I needed to memorize his features all over again. His eyes shone in the darkness...just as they had the first night we'd met. His cheekbones were sculpted as if by expert hands. And his lips...

My eyes stopped there, heat pulsing through me as instantaneous desire surged uncontrollably through my body and mind.

"He's at the top of the trail," I said softly.

"I know," he replied. "So we only have a few minutes."

"A few minutes...for...?"

His smile said everything words could not as he pushed me back, pinning my arms to the cold stone wall, kissing my neck, my jaw. There was no spell this time—nothing but his powerful hands holding me in place.

When his mouth met my own, I bit his lip, drawing a quiet cry of ecstasy from him even as he released my arms and slid down my body.

I reached down, pulling my dress up to reveal myself to him. "Since we have so little time," I said coyly.

"Gods, you alter the definition of perfection every single day, don't you?" he asked as his lips caressed my stomach, his tongue tasting my salt flesh, until he came to the place between my legs and let out a quiet moan, inhaling my scent.

"I have craved this since I last saw you," he said. "As I have never craved anything in my life."

Taking his head in my hands, I lifted my hips to meet his mouth, pulling one leg to hook it over his shoulder. I watched as he devoured me hungrily, closing my eyes to take in the sensation, a deep throb overwhelming every part of me.

He drove his fingers into me as his tongue worked in long, greedy strokes, and I lifted my face skyward, asking the gods how such a Fae had ever deemed me worthy of his perfect mouth.

I tried not to cry out, to allow the echoes of my desire to sound beyond the cavern walls, but it proved impossible as my climax rolled over me, my hips bucking as he let out a low moan against me.

Grabbing hold of his tunic, I pulled him up to kiss me again, tasting myself on his lips, his tongue. My hands reached greedily for his belt, my fingers scrambling to release its clasp and let his trousers drop, his extraordinary length freed from the shackles of his clothing.

He lifted me easily, my legs hooking around his waist, and I let out a euphoric moan as he pushed himself inside me, his eyes locked on my own. I took his face in my hands, all too aware of the soul-ravaging range of emotions that had assaulted me since we'd last spoken. So grateful for him, for his love, for his desire...for the gift of his extraordinary body.

He eased down to kiss my neck, pushing deeper inside me, and this time I let out a fierce cry then cupped my hand over my mouth, laughing as I forced myself into silence. It was almost an impossibility, my head spinning with pleasure and pain at once.

His mouth was still on my neck, his teeth threatening to tear through my flesh when the explosion rolled through his body, and he bit into me as he held back a roar of delight, fire and flame scalding us both at once.

I wrapped my arms around him, holding him close as long as I could. Releasing him meant saying goodbye, if only temporarily. Still, it felt like a grave loss.

"I do need to leave you," Mithraan finally said, his lips on my flesh as he spoke. He pulled back to look into my eyes. "I heard about your mother. Is she all right?"

I nodded. "Thanks to Erildir—and my blood."

He looked puzzled. "Your blood?

"She'd been poisoned. He said she needed her kin's blood to drive it out of her."

"I see." He looked puzzled, as if he'd never heard of such a thing. "I suppose the Spell-Master knows what he's doing, if it worked. In the meantime, we need to get her—and you—out of this damned place."

"I told her as much, but Erildir insisted she needs to rest." I bowed my head as Mithraan let my dress fall back down to cover me.

"She can rest on a ship back to Kalemnar. We must persuade her, Lyrinn. For her sake and yours both. There is something in the air in this place—I felt it when I was out hunting. A force is growing in this land, and I don't like what it may mean. Whoever—whatever—is selected as Elar, I feel a fore-boding on the air." He looked pained when he added, "I have had...visions."

"Of the Elar, you mean," I said.

He nodded. "In my dreams. I told myself it was only my imagination—but I'm beginning to wonder."

"I've had the same nightmares," I told him. "I—haven't spoken to anyone about them, because I thought I was losing my mind. Each night, I tried to connect to you, but instead..."

"Instead, you saw her." He nodded in understanding. "I've begun to think she is a force of destruction, and no benevolent demi-goddess named by the Order to bring peace."

"But the Succession means the current Elar will be gone," I said. "She's dying, after all—and will be replaced. Lady Cassia seems confident they've made the right choice."

"That would hearten me if I thought Lady Cassia was to be trusted," Mithraan said with a scowl. "But she feels like a lie dressed up in pretty clothing. Something in her is menacing, Vaelan—I'm sure you've felt it, too."

I couldn't deny that he was right. She had frightened me on more than one occasion—without so much as opening her mouth. There was a power in her that felt too much like that of the Elar I had seen in my dreams...too chaotic, too destructive.

I was going to ask if we could kill Cassia—if destroying the head of the Order would be enough. But something told me her demise would do nothing to stop the force that was coming.

"We can go home," Mithraan said, reading my mind. "That's all we can do."

We sealed our goodbye with a deep kiss, reluctant to part but aware of the consequences if we failed to do so...and I turned away to begin the long trudge up to find Adhair once again.

CHAPTER THIRTY-NINE

A STRONG BREEZE propelled me forward as I climbed the trail back toward Adhair's perch. With each step I took, I watched with horror as a smile spread wider and wider over his lips.

Not warm and friendly as usual, but almost...lascivious.

If I hadn't known better, I might have interpreted it as an expression of unspoken intimacy between us. A tacit understanding of things to come.

It was a look I'd seen on Mithraan's face a thousand times, and in *his* eyes it was the most beautiful sight in the world. In Adhair's, though, it felt off-putting to the point of near-retching.

It was the hungry, entitled gaze of someone who knew without a shadow of a doubt that he would get what he wanted —and it rendered me uneasy to the point where I wished I could disappear into my old cloak, hiding myself away in the shadows.

Oh, to be a Shadowling. If only Lark could teach me his ways...

Could Adhair possibly know what I—what *we*—had just done in the cave? Did he smell Mithraan on me, as my mother had? Or was this expression of his something else entirely—a promise my father had made to him, perhaps?

"I hope you found some peace," he said, still eyeing me as I approached.

I examined his face, searching for any sign that he knew what had transpired in the cavern. But I detected nothing in his features other than a quiet calm, like that of someone who had just awoken from a pleasant nap.

"I did, in fact," I replied coolly. "Thank you for waiting for me. I...I suppose we should get back, though. My father might not like me being away from the palace for too long."

"Of course," Adhair replied, rising and offering me his arm. "I'd be happy to accompany you. Very happy indeed."

His tone made my skin crawl.

You're too familiar, my Lord, and far too excited.

To make matters worse, when I took his arm, he placed his hand on mine, his fingers stroking my skin gently as we began to walk.

"I've told you I can sense emotion acutely," he said. "Though I must say, Princess—you are difficult to piece together. You shield yourself well from others, which is to be commended. But there are some things that even you cannot hide."

I tightened, horrified. Waiting for the accusation to come— the revelation that he knew everything that I'd been up to.

We had just come to a set of ruins some distance from the palace—an old stone farmhouse that had half crumbled to the ground. But a few of its walls were still intact, and as we drew near, Adhair stopped and turned to me, taking my hand in his.

Instead of calling me out for my crimes inside the cave, he pulled closer to me and said, "I have felt your desire for me more than once, just as I feel it now. And I want you to know that it is entirely reciprocated."

I was horrified to realize that he had now engineered a scenario in which my back was to one of the solid walls...and he was positioned between me and any reasonable chance of escape.

His hand reached up to stroke my cheek.

Don't react, I told myself. *Do not insult the Northern Lord. Do not let on that it's not him you want, or Mithraan's life will be forfeit.*

"Lord Adhair," I said, too meekly. "I..."

"I have wanted you from the first," he whispered, his lips entirely too close now. "I know, in spite of your attempts to conceal the truth, how desperately you want to be with me."

Revulsion filled me. *If you feel my emotions so acutely, surely you know how repulsed I am at this moment. Surely you know I do not want your hands or mouth on me. Surely...*

I pulled back, forcing myself flat against the wall, and assessed his features, hoping with everything in me that this was a poorly executed joke.

But his eyes told me he was entirely serious—and the way he licked his lips as I glanced at his mouth told me I was in deep trouble.

I knew in that moment what Lark and Mithraan had suspected from the first—he was a pretty, powerless fraud. He could no more read emotion than walk through a wall of solid stone. He had no idea how I felt; he was merely guessing based on my scent. Too many times, he had inhaled my desire for Mithraan and assumed it was aimed squarely at him.

Can you smell my disgust now, my Lord?

"Lyrinn," he said softly, my name doused in bile as he reached down and lifted my skirt, his hand running up my thigh, pushing itself higher, higher...until...

A piercing cry bit through the air, and a vast shadow swooped down from the sky, slamming into Adhair and tossing him sideways so that he flew several feet before crashing to the ground mere inches from a large block of shattered stone that could easily have cleft his skull in two.

And then the silver eagle was on him, tearing into his chest, its talons drawing a scream of pain from Adhair's throat.

A moment later, it was Mithraan himself who stood over him, silver wings spread behind him, majestic and thrumming with power.

Adhair looked...stunned.

"Bastard," Mithraan spat, rage coming off him in an aura of pure heat. "How *dare* you touch her?"

I wanted to cry out, to warn him of the consequences that would surely come. But it was far, far too late. Adhair had seen him now. He knew a Tírian Lord was on Kazimir's soil—one so possessive of me that he would risk his life to defend me.

"Who the hell are you?" Adhair asked, and I found myself gawking at him. It was no wonder Mithraan had infiltrated his ranks with such ease—he had absolutely no idea this was the same Fae who had been serving as one of his guards. For all his ability to smell my desire, he had entirely failed to recognize Tomlin's scent.

"I am Mithraan, High Lord of Fairholme." The words were a low growl, a guttural warning. "And if you ever so much as breathe on—or even near—Lyrinn again, I will tear your entrails out and present them to your lady mother without a second thought. Do you understand me?"

Adhair's face grew fierce, enraged. Feral, almost. But he nodded, and I knew unquestionably that he was the weakest High Fae I had ever seen. For all his mother's strength—for all her impressive presence—he was...nothing. A mere illusion of a High Lord, a shadow of the Gray Lady.

"The High King would have your head for this!" Adhair scowled, pulling his eyes to me. "Both of you!"

"Please," I said, but the word came out in a desperate whisper. "Please," I croaked again. "Don't tell my father. Don't tell the High King. He'll..."

Adhair shot me a look of ire, but as Mithraan raised a hand, silver talons flashing in the sunlight, he succumbed. "Fine," he muttered. "What would I tell him, anyhow? 'Your daughter rejected me in favor of a Tírian arsehole?' Not exactly something I'd be proud to report."

"Remember—I will gladly take your intestines from you if you break your word," Mithraan said, stepping aside.

We watched as Adhair rose to his feet, patted himself off, and began to stride rapidly toward the palace grounds.

"Do you think..." I began to ask, but Mithraan shook his head.

"He won't say anything. His entire life revolves around the image he has carefully crafted about himself—and it would shatter that image if he were to tell the world he was bested by a Tírian infiltrator."

Seeking comfort, I stepped toward him, and he took my face in his hands, pushing my hair behind my ear. "Go back to the palace. If Adhair returns too much before you, they'll grow suspicious. I will find you tonight. We'll talk to your mother. Tomorrow, we will find a way to remove her ring, and we'll leave—but we must do it quietly. Even Erildir must not know what we're planning. We cannot afford to stay in Aethos any longer, love."

I nodded, a lump forming in my throat, and turned away, my heart pounding so rapidly that I feared I would pass out before reaching the gates.

CHAPTER FORTY

I SPENT most of the rest of the day in my room, simultaneously pacing nervously and chewing on my nails.

Fear coursed through my veins with each sound I heard in the corridor beyond my door. Each footfall. Each creak or slam of a chamber door.

Would Adhair tell Kazimir what he'd seen, out of spite or hurt pride? As a punishment for Mithraan's assault? Or was Mithraan right when he'd guessed the Northerner would rather die than risk his manufactured reputation?

As the hours ticked by and no fist pounded violently on my door, I began, slowly, to relax. There was no word from Mithraan, no servants whispering about the Lightblood guard who had just been taken to the dungeons...just...

Nothing.

At dinnertime, a knock sounded at my door, and I smiled with relief when it was Riah's friendly face that peeked into the room.

"It feels like it's been an age," I said as I gestured her to come in, "though I suppose it's only been a day or two. How are you?"

"I'm well, your Highness," she replied with a closed-lipped smile. She looked like something was roaming untethered through her mind—something more than those few words.

"What is it?" I asked with a nervous laugh barely sufficient to mask my discomfort. "Has something happened that I need to know about?"

I wanted to be sick as I awaited her answer—but, to my relief, her smile didn't fade. She did not look like someone on the verge of delivering a deathblow of terrible news.

"I've heard the next Elar has been chosen," she said softly, conspiratorially. "That the Succession will occur very soon." Closing the door softly, she added, "Have you heard anything about it?"

"Not really. Only that they were close to a decision."

"It's such wonderful news," Riah said, then let out a chuckle. "I know I must sound mad saying that, when only a short time ago I doubted the Elar's very existence. But Kierin's stories of meeting Priestesses and so on—well, I suppose they gave me a faint hope that some good could come of it all."

"You really think this Successor will change things," I observed with a smile. It was nice to see someone feeling so optimistic.

She nodded vigorously. "I'm certain of it. I've *felt* it, Princess. Ever since your arrival in these lands, something has shifted—something immense."

"I can only hope you're right," I told her with a solemn nod. Anything had to be better than the creature I'd seen in my nightmares, after all. Surely the Successor would be less volatile, more level-headed...perhaps she would even be kind. "Though I don't suppose it has anything to do with my arrival. I still know very little about the Elar—and honestly, I don't care to know much. The very thought of her has always horrified me a little."

"Still—you arrived in Aetherion along with a tidal wave of excitement," Riah said. "I like to think that, if any good comes of this, it's because you're a good luck charm of sorts."

"Perhaps the High King and Lady Cassia will have news of the Succession," I said, nervousness creeping through my insides as I remembered that I would have to look into Adhair's eyes at some point this evening. "I...should probably head to dinner and get it over with."

"Let me know if you hear any exciting news, would you?"

"Of course."

Once Riah had left for her quarters, I made my way out the door and down toward the dining hall. When I was close, I blew out a low, quiet whistle.

Lark was next to me instantly. "Highness."

"Have you heard any rumors today?" I asked in a whisper. "Anything that should worry me?"

"About the Succession?"

I shook my head. "About me."

His small face betrayed confusion, and he said, "No...nothing. Should I have heard something in particular?"

"Not at all. I just..." Something occurred to me then. "Wait—you followed me to the coast this morning."

"I did—though I tried my best to grant you some privacy when you..."

My cheeks reddened when I said, "You must have seen what happened by the ruins."

"I'm afraid I did. I am sorry for it—but grateful to Lord Mithraan for protecting you so fiercely. Had he not done so, I would have slain the Northern Lord myself." Sheepishly, he added, "I apologize for my mistrust of Tomlin—but I'm sure you understand."

"Of course I do—you were looking out for me. But listen—I need to know if Lord Adhair has said anything to Kazimir.

"As far as I know, he has not," Lark told me softly. "I followed him for a time, after you were back in the palace. I believe you're safe."

I exhaled a relieved sigh, then dismissed him. A minute later, I entered the dining hall with a smile on my face.

As expected, dinner proved more than a little awkward.

I seated myself next to Erildir, with Adhair hunched and defeated-looking on the other side of the table, his eyes locked perpetually on his food—though he didn't seem particularly interested in eating it.

Kazimir and Cassia sat at the broad table's head, locked, as usual, in some intimate conversation.

On the other side of the room, Tomlin stood on guard as always. Occasionally, I caught Adhair narrowing his eyes angrily at him.

But never did he so much as mutter a word.

My mother was conspicuously absent, though I could hardly blame her for it. No doubt she was still recuperating in her room, as far from Kazimir as she could get.

I leaned toward Erildir after a time and whispered, "My mother—is she..."

"She's fine," he replied, his chin low, bright eyes glancing around to ensure the High King wasn't listening in. "Recovering well. But, as you can imagine, she had little desire to join us at the table."

"I'm glad to hear of her recovery." I shot a glance at Lady Cassia and Adhair, then added, "Have you heard the news?"

Erildir nodded once. "The Elar has been selected at last," he said. "I believe the High Priestess will be announcing something of it—ah. Here we go."

And as if on cue, Lady Cassia rose to her feet and held her wine cup aloft.

"I would like to inform you that a selection has been made," she said. "The Succession will take place in three days' time, in Nordvahl's great temple, when the portal to the Broken Lands will open for the first time in thousands of years. The Successor will pass through...and with those few steps, a new dawn will begin its rise over Aetherion and all the realms of the world."

Kazimir, too, lifted his cup. "Wonderful news, indeed," he said. "I'm sure you and the other members of the Order have chosen wisely, my Lady."

Cassia's eyes flared with light as she turned to look down at him. "By the Elar's wings shall Aetherion be renewed," she said. "Long may she preside—and long live the High King!"

With that, everyone seated at the table raised their cups—even me. Though it was all I could do not to scowl at Kazimir as I drank to his good health.

I watched Cassia as she drank, a smug glint in her eye. Part of me wondered if there was a chance she could have named her*self* Elar—but the thought seemed a little absurd, even for her.

Not that any of it matters, I thought, glancing at Mithraan across the room. *We'll be gone tomorrow. The new Elar—whoever she may be—is of no consequence to us.*

He seemed to be thinking the same, because a small, almost invisible smile took up residence on his lips before fading from sight again.

All of a sudden, I couldn't wait to finish dinner so we could go tell my mother of our plan.

Tomorrow morning at dawn, Mithraan would remove my

mother's ring and heal her. We would leave this place at last—
and we would never look back.

When our meal had concluded and the others had headed to
their bed chambers, I retired to my own, pacing in a relentless
back and forth as I waited for Mithraan to show.

It was only after two hours of wearing the stone floor down
with my soles that a knock sounded at the door. With a nervous
tremor in my voice, I called out, "Come."

Mithraan—still looking like Tomlin—pushed the door
open. "It's time to tell her," he whispered. "I'll head to your
mother's chamber. Wait two minutes, then follow."

I found him just outside her door five minutes later.

"Ready?" he asked, stepping close but taking care not to
touch me in case we were being watched.

I nodded, then knocked softly and pushed the door open.

My mother was sitting up in her bed, dressed in a nightgown and a white silk robe. She smiled when she saw me—but
when Tomlin followed me in, shutting the door behind him, her
expression wavered to apprehension.

"It's all right," I half-whispered. "He's with me."

She nodded. "Come in, then."

I noted an empty plate on the table next to the bed. She had
eaten her dinner, at least.

"This is..." I said, gesturing to the Northern Guard.

"I know who he is," my mother said, and I thought I
detected a quick flaring of her eyes as she looked at him. I
wondered with a jolt if he was the first Tírian she'd spoken to in
the last thousand years.

"Your Grace," Mithraan said reverently, shifting into his

natural guise and stepping toward her. "Lyrinn and I come with a proposal."

"Proposal?" she asked, turning sharply to me. "What is it?"

"After what happened last night—after the stabbing," I said, glancing at Mithraan for a moment. "We *must* leave this place. It's clearly not safe anymore. Not for you, not for any of us."

She shook her head. "No," she said irritably. "I cannot leave. I've told you as much more than once, Lyrinn. How could you think it wise to move me so shortly after what happened last night? And need I mention that the ring of impediment is—?"

I stopped her with a hand in the air. "I know what you're going to say—that the ring is holding you here, that it will kill you to remove it. But Mithraan has healing powers—strong ones. He will make sure no harm comes to you, I promise. Look, there is a ship leaving the harbor at dawn tomorrow. We need to be on it—all three of us. Once we leave Aetherion, Mithraan will see to it that no one follows us. Mother...it's time. You've been Kazimir's prisoner for far too many years."

She was about to speak again but seemed to give in when a rough sigh escaped her chest.

"My protests will be insufficient, won't they?" she said with a weak laugh. "You two are quite determined."

"I love your daughter with everything in my soul," Mithraan told her, his deep voice filled with affection. "I want nothing but to get her and you to safety. You should be away from this madness, and home in Tíria with your father the High King."

"My father," she said, a twist of bitterness in her voice. I realized for the first time that she and I had never really spoken of her bond with her father—of the relationship that had been severed when Kazimir had stolen her from Kalemnar and sealed Tíria off from the other realms. "What would my dear father say if he saw me again..." she mused with a dark edge to her voice.

"Are you all right, Mother?" I asked, shooting Mithraan a sideways look.

"Fine," she said, her smile rejuvenated as though the moment had never occurred. "Just remembering the old times. Tomorrow at dawn, then."

"Tell no one—not even Erildir," Mithraan said. "It's for your own good. We don't know who we can truly trust."

"I trust the Spell-Master," she retorted almost defensively, but she raised her hands and said, "I'll be silent as the grave. I promise."

"We will meet by the old smithy in Aethos's harbor," Mithraan said. "The ship leaves shortly after sunrise."

"Understood."

With a final nod from my mother, we left her chamber. Once outside with the door sealed, Mithraan, in his Tomlin guise again, whispered, "I'll come to your room in a few minutes." Glancing around before taking my hand, he kissed it gently. "I cannot express how delighted I am to be on the verge of a new life with you, Vaelan."

"You don't need to express it," I whispered back. "At least, not in words. Get to my chamber quickly, and we'll find other ways to convey our emotions."

CHAPTER FORTY-ONE

MITHRAAN and I spent the next few hours in a blissful tangle of limbs under the warm covers of my oversized bed, reveling in the knowledge that this would be the last night we ever had to spend in this place.

I felt renewal in the air, as though our lives, our future, had already begun with the mere promise of escape. And I could see it in his eyes, too, in the moonlit shadows of the room—in the flares of flame that lit up his irises when he looked down on me and called me *Vaelan*, or *love*...or simply *mine*.

It was after we'd made love for the third time that I slipped out of bed and walked over to the terrace, the nighttime breeze caressing my skin through the thin robe I'd pulled on.

I pressed my hands to the railing, looking down toward a small courtyard below where I saw two figures—one dressed in a long white robe, the other wearing some dark color—red, perhaps—from head to toe.

Varyn, the Crimson Priestess. It had to be. A veil covered her face and hair, and she was dressed just as she had been when I'd spoken to her inside the temple.

But who was the other Fae?

I watched as they spoke softly, then the Priestess stepped forward and a pair of glowing wings appeared, sprouting like two flaring torches from her shoulder blades. Crafted of light itself, they were white, with prominent blue veins...and I could feel their power from where I stood.

I had seen the Elar's violet wings in the palace's paintings. I had seen that other—horrifying—set of wings, silver with red veins, in my nightmares. But never had I seen a pair in person, and they were something to behold...more beautiful than I had ever dared imagine.

Even Mithraan, who had come to stand next to me, seemed stunned by the sight.

"Never did I think I would see such a thing," he said in a whisper. "The wings we High Fae should all possess—that were taken from us so long ago."

The Red Priestess slowly slipped down to her knees before the other Fae, taking her hand and kissing it, her wings fluttering slowly behind her. It was then that I spotted something gleaming in the darkness—a familiar silver ring—on the other Fae's hand.

"Your mother?" Mithraan said softly.

"The Priestess is probably offering her a blessing of healing," I whispered. "A spell, to precipitate it."

Silently, I wondered if my mother had told Varyn of our plan to leave. Perhaps we were witnessing a farewell of sorts.

Varyn rose to her feet, bowed her head slowly, then walked away, tucking her wings together before they disappeared as though they'd never existed in the first place. My mother pulled her head up and looked at us both, then turned to walk back into the palace.

A tremor overtook me then, and I wrapped my arms around my shoulders, seeking warmth.

"Come," Mithraan said, taking me by the hand to lead me

back inside, where I pulled off the robe and we climbed under the covers once again.

He rolled onto his back, his voice still low. "Are you confident that your mother will be on that dock at dawn?"

I propped myself up on one elbow and stared at him. "Of course I am. She wants to go home as badly as we do. She wants to see Leta—to be a family again. Her only hesitation was the ring...and we've solved that problem. Between my blood and your healing powers, there's no reason she should fear escape."

Mithraan nodded, but in his eyes I saw a faraway expression, as though some deep, insidious thought was robbing him of the hope we had both felt just a few moments earlier.

"What is it about her that you don't like?" I asked, a hint of annoyance in my voice.

Perhaps the question was unfair—he hadn't said anything about disliking her. But there was something in the air between us now, a tension I couldn't shake, that unsettled me.

"It's not a question of whether or not I like her," he said. "She's your mother—the one who gave birth to you. For that, I will always be grateful. I will always feel love for her for bringing you into this world. But—"

I glared at him, trying to figure out what he could possibly say that wouldn't hurt me deeply. She was my mother. *My* mother, who had endured a thousand years of hardship. My mother, who had suffered for so long between the walls of this palace, all in the hopes of seeing Leta and me again.

"But *what?*" I asked, my voice clipped.

"She left you, Lyrinn," Mithraan said, looking me in the eye. "She scarred you painfully, and left you and Leta behind, with a mortal—and yes, he was a good man, one who raised you and did what he could for you. But the fact is, your mother lied to you and asked Martel to lie to you as well. My question is— why? Why would she do that?"

"To protect us," I said. "We all know she feared Kazimir."

When Mithraan frowned, I said, "What is it? What's going on in that mind of yours?"

He slipped an arm around me. "I heard rumors once long ago about Princess Kaela, as your mother was known in Tíria—long before she took the name Alessia. Rumors that she had powers unlike our Fae had seen in centuries. She was as Gifted as the High King himself, they said. There were some who even found her frightening, given how powerful she was. But if that was true, why would she not have cast a simple warding spell over your home so that she could remain with her children? She could have protected you and kept you secret, all at once."

"She *was* protecting us," I snapped defensively. "Look, you know as well as I do that Tíria was cut off from mortal lands. She couldn't return to her father, but she delivered Leta and me to a place as near Tíria as she could get. She protected us from discovery—and she asked Martel to keep our Immortality a secret. I'm not sure what more she could have done."

Mithraan nodded solemnly. "Well, as strange as it is to say, Kazimir has also protected you—which makes me wonder what your mother was so afraid of."

When I looked like I was about to protest, he raised a hand. "I know, I know—he took you from Kalemnar, which hardly seems like an act of goodness. But he did so only when you and I were damn near death, Lyrinn. Corym meant to end us both, whatever anyone may say. You and I both saw the rage in his eyes—that was not a man in love with his future wife. As much as it still hurts my pride to say it, and as much as I still despise him, Kazimir kept us both alive that day."

Instead of arguing, I let out a long breath and contemplated what Mithraan was saying. All of Aetherion talked about Kazimir's goodness—about how he had saved countless sprites' lives. Was there any chance in the world that he really had brought me to Aetherion to shield me from Corym or some other threat?

"I suppose it's possible my father has some good in him," I confessed.

Adhair's words came to my mind then. Much as I disliked the Northern lord, he was right about one thing.

None of us is wholly good, just as none of us is truly evil.

"My mother, on the other hand," I said, "has been nothing but kind since my arrival. She's a little hard to read, it's true. But I can hardly blame her for shielding herself after all that she's suffered. I trust her, Mithraan. I have to believe she'll be on that dock."

Pulling me close, he kissed my forehead and said, "I feel protective of you. Of Leta, as well. What hurts you hurts me, and I suppose there's a part of me that has a difficult time forgiving your mother for the pain you've suffered because of her lies."

The thin layer of ice that had begun to form around my heart started to melt then, and I softened. "My pain is nothing compared to our mother's," I said. "She sacrificed a great deal to give us a life far away from this place."

"Perhaps it's only that I'm selfish," Mithraan said with a sigh, taking my hand and kissing it. "I want your happiness—because it is my own. I want your heart whole—because it is my own. And if your mother is the key to your joy, then I am happy and grateful for it."

"My heart will be whole when my mother and Leta are reunited. When my family is together, as we should be. And when you and I are safely away from here."

Mithraan pulled me close, kissing the crown of my head. "Just be wary, Vaelan. That's all I ask."

"I will."

It was with my cheek on his chest that I fell into a deep sleep, content to dream of the dawn to come.

CHAPTER FORTY-TWO

THE ROOM WAS STILL DARK, the moon high in the sky, when a deep, bellowing voice woke me.

"Rise."

Disoriented, I told myself I was dreaming. That my mind was recalling the first moment when I had looked upon Mithraan and his Fae atop the lands that overlooked Dúnbar.

It was the first word he had ever spoken to me, after all.

Rise.

I smiled, pulling the sheets tighter and tucking my body closer to his. *A little more sleep. Just a little. Then we'll leave for the harbor...*

The voice came again, this time more emphatic.

"Rise, Daughter."

With a shock of terror, my eyes opened. I shot up, the sheet still tight around my torso, to see Kazimir standing between the bed and the door with four guards surrounding him and several sprites fluttering in the air, lanterns in hand. The swaying motion of the light cast ominous shadows on the walls beyond. Long-limbed apparitions, come to destroy all hopes and dreams.

"Keep the sheet around you," Kazimir snarled. "I have no desire for my sprites or guards to lay their eyes on your naked form."

By now, Mithraan, too, had shot up. I could hear his breath, could feel the tension in his body as he contemplated the risks involved in defending me against one such as Kazimir.

Don't move. Don't give him an excuse to kill you. Please.

I wasn't sure if I said the words aloud or only in my mind, but Mithraan obeyed, holding fast.

Panicking, I searched my mind for a spell I could cast to stop this invasion in its tracks.

"Don't," Kazimir snarled, reading my expression. "You know full well that you are no match for me, and neither is your lover."

As if to prove it, he shot his right hand toward the bed and the sheets instantly tightened around my body, leaving Mithraan exposed to the cool night air. Taking it as a cue, he eased to his feet, casually pulled on his trousers, and then turned and took a step toward the High King, his shoulders back, chin held high.

He was not afraid of the Lightblood leader—which terrified me.

As he moved, I saw the glint of silver in the dim light—the distinct outlines of the talons he had used to tear Prince Corym's face during the Blood Trials. They were more than mere claws. They were part of his lethal power—a part of what made him terrifying, strong, brutal when he wished to be.

I knew without a doubt that, as powerful as Kazimir was, Mithraan would find a way to tear him to pieces if he threatened me. The High King's power was nothing when faced with the High Lord's protective rage.

"Mithraan," I said softly. "Don't."

He stopped, then held his hands up, his talons retracting.

"I will kill him if you ask me to," he growled. "I will not let him hurt you, Vaelan."

"I know," I replied. "But doing so would make you a king killer—and that is not a legacy you want to leave. The High King's life is not worth your reputation."

"I don't care about my reputation." His voice was menacing. "I would live a thousand lifetimes in exile if it kept you safe. You know what this prick is capable of."

"Yes," I replied, fighting to keep my voice calm. "I know."

My eyes were locked on Kazimir, my body rigid with harried anticipation. If he tried anything—if he cast a spell intended to hurt Mithraan—I would reflect it and kill him. I would destroy him.

I was a princess, but the title meant nothing to me.

Mithraan, though, was a High Lord, with Fae who relied on him. Fae who looked to him for leadership, for guidance.

My dream was to live with him in Tíria, far from this palace and everything it held. If I had to kill the High King—my own father—in order to live out that dream, I would do it.

"Tírians are forbidden under penalty of death from entering these lands without my consent," Kazimir growled, his voice threatening, his teeth bared.

Nausea roiled inside me as I realized I may as well be watching two rabid wolves stare each other down.

"Mith..." I said, but Kazimir held up a hand to silence me.

"Then again," he said, "the fact that you, High Lord, have been sneaking around under the guise of a Lightblood guard tells me you already know how unwelcome you are." He curled his fingers and stared at his cuticles as he added, "Hardly behavior befitting one such as you, is it?"

"As if you would *ever* invite one of my kind to this realm," Mithraan snickered. "You would sooner invite a monster into your lands to ravage them than a Tírian."

"Yes, because I know your kind all too well. Do not forget that I have been bound to one of your ilk for a thousand years— a millennium of hells that I was foolish enough to bring upon myself when I brought that bitch to Aetherion."

"Your *Grace*!"

My voice was shrill, enraged at hearing him speak of my mother so cruelly.

"Seize the bastard," Kazimir said with a sneer, nodding toward his guards. "I will decide what to do with him later."

Mithraan tensed, and my eyes moved toward his hands as his silver talons sprang to life once again. He pushed his way between Kazimir and me, shielding me with his body. As I watched, the silver wings of an eagle—broad and extraordinary —spread from his shoulder blades like an aegis separating me from any threat.

He leapt at the first guard who dared step toward him and with a quick swipe, he sliced through his tunic and mail, eliciting a sharp cry of pain as blood streaked down the Lightblood's chest.

He could destroy them, I thought. *He could kill them all.*

Except, perhaps, for Kazimir.

Kazimir—who stood to the side and calmly pulled his gaze to me as if Mithraan were no more of a threat than a gnat. "If your lover does not come peacefully, your mother will die," he said. "I promise you that."

The muscles on Mithraan's back were heaving with his breaths, his shoulders tight, arms taut and ready to strike again.

"Please," I said softly, unsure which Fae I was pleading with.

Mithraan's wings disappeared. His talons retracted and he turned to me, a look of quiet anguish in his eyes.

"Please," I said again, this time pushing my way forward to look Kazimir in the eye. "Don't take him. He was about to leave for Tíria. Put him on the ship and send him home. I promise, I'll stay here as long as you wish. Please..."

Kazimir's face remained entirely devoid of emotion.

At that moment, Adhair appeared in the doorway. He glanced first at Mithraan, then at me...then he stepped up to the High King and spoke softly into his ear.

Adhair...who had been so angry, so humiliated the previous day when Mithraan had stopped him from violating me. Adhair, who had shrunken to nothing before a far more powerful High Lord.

"*You* did this," I hissed, stepping toward him. "You told him."

Adhair turned to me with an irritating smile. "I assure you, Highness, that I don't know what you're talking about. I only came to tell the High King we are leaving for the North tomorrow morning. We have already arranged for a series of carriages—and don't worry; I will leave well ahead of you."

He issued Kazimir a quick, shallow nod, then turned to leave the chamber.

I found it difficult to believe Adhair would come looking for the High King in the depths of night to inform him of such a thing. But it didn't matter now who had reported his presence —Mithraan was caught, and I was helpless.

Wordlessly, two of the Lightblood guards took hold of his arms, and he did not protest when they dragged him away.

Tears streaked down my cheeks. I was powerful, they said. If I were so strong, I should have killed my father then and there and freed Mithraan from whatever fate was to be hurled at him.

And yet, I had no confidence I could defeat the High King. If I fought and failed, Kazimir would kill my mother—which meant I had no option but to accept that Mithraan was now his prisoner.

If I cooperated, there was a small chance the High King would be merciful.

"I am disappointed in you, though not surprised, Daughter," Kazimir said slowly, his eyes directed at the door. "I know how tempting their kind can be. Your mother seduced me a millennium ago—wrapped me around her little finger as if I was nothing more than a suggestible schoolboy. I am not blind to Tírian charms. They are pretty little parasites."

"I am half Tírian, in case you've forgotten—and you insult me when you speak of us as lesser beings."

"Apologies," he said with a biting chuckle, his gaze on mine again. "I did not realize you had so thoroughly embraced your bloodline. That is a good sign, at least."

I wanted to wrap my hands around his neck and squeeze, to watch the life drain from his face.

"I have not embraced the Lightblood in my veins," I retorted. "And I never will—not after what I have seen of you. And if you hurt Mithraan...I will *destroy* you."

"Your High Lord knows the laws of my lands. He chose to come here. To violate my palace, my daughter..."

"There was no violation," I replied. "I love him. I would give my life for him."

At those words, Kazimir took a long step toward me, his brows meeting, eyes darkening in the shadows. His sprites were still with us, still illuminating the room with their flickering, ominous lanterns. "You would do well to *stop* loving him," Kazimir said. "Tírians are cruel beasts. They take from us and from each other like leeches, until there is nothing left but a frail husk. You think you love Mithraan because he has cast a mask over your mind and tainted your view of our world—of this realm. He is nothing, Lyrinn. He is a pretty devil, that's all."

"He is everything. He is my life. And if you take him from me, you may as well sever my head from my body."

"Well, then. I am sorry to tell you by this time tomorrow, you may find yourself headless."

Without another word, he turned and left the room, the door slamming shut behind him.

I could hear the lock turning and feel the powerful thrum of an oppressive spell being cast around my chamber...and knew there was no chance of escape tonight.

CHAPTER FORTY-THREE

I WAS SITTING on my bed, my cheeks stained with tears, when the lock clicked and the door creaked open. By now, I was wearing a robe, at least, but I was hardly dressed for visitors.

"Highness," Erildir said, slipping into the room. "I've come to check on you."

I nodded wearily. "Come in," I rasped.

The Spell-Master walked over and seated himself on the edge of my bed, an unusually friendly move on his part.

It was a long moment before I managed to look into his eyes. I dreaded hearing what he had to say.

Was Mithraan dead?

If not, did I even want to know what fate would befall him?

"It's all my fault," I finally said, my voice quaking. "I should have sent him back to Kalemnar the second I learned he was here. I was selfish. I wanted so badly..."

"You wanted *him*," Erildir said, his voice smooth with sympathy. "You love him."

I nodded.

"Your father does not understand such desire, perhaps. But some of us do."

I pulled my eyes to his, and in them, I could see a depth I had not noted before—a wisdom in his expression that told me he understood what I was feeling better than I could possibly know.

"Who was..." I murmured. *He? She?*

He shook his head and let out a sad laugh. "I am not here to talk about love that was never to be," he said. "Let us just say I am not unsympathetic to your plight. I know what it is not to be able to find yourself with the one you need—the one who makes you ache for them. I am here as a friend—to support you and see if you require anything."

"Is Kazimir going to kill him?" I asked, bracing myself for his response.

"Ah. Well, on that front at least, I have brought you good news."

I sat up a little straighter, my eyes widening. I could accept whatever answer was coming, so long as it came quickly.

"Tell me," I said. "Please."

"Your father has agreed to release Mithraan—so long as he returns to Kalemnar immediately on one of the High King's smaller ships. I suppose he is in no humor to break his daughter's soul just now."

My heart soared. Surely he had to be wrong, though. Kazimir was not so merciful as to free Mithraan—to set him loose on the sea again. It seemed far too good to be true.

"I know," Erildir said as if reading my thoughts. "It's a shock. But Kazimir has assured me that Mithraan will be boarding the ship in an hour's time. In truth, it was a wise strategic move on his part."

"Strategic?" I repeated, puzzled as to his meaning. But I stopped there, telling myself to be grateful for this small mercy. "Do I have your word that Mithraan is safe?"

Erildir looked into my eyes for a moment, then smiled. "You

have my word that he is safe, yes," he said, and I finally breathed a sigh of relief. "Though he has been equipped with a ring of impediment—a preventative measure to keep him from spell-casting until he is safely home. It wouldn't do to have a Tírian High Lord take over the ship in the middle of the sea and kill its Lightblood crew. I promise, though—the rings don't do any lasting damage. The second they are removed, the wearer regains their full strength almost immediately."

I nodded. "I suppose I couldn't expect them to put him on the ship without shackling him *somehow*." I laid a hand on his, then slipped off the bed and said, "Erildir—thank you."

"For what?" he asked, rising to join me.

"I am certain you had something to do with the High King's mercy. I saw the look in his eyes—he would have loved to kill Mithraan on the spot. I have no doubt you worked some sort of spell on him. Whatever you did, I am grateful beyond words."

Erildir let out a laugh. "You read me so well," he said. "I did indeed."

"I will not soon forget it."

He looked long and hard into my eyes, then issued a final smile. "Seeing you looking happy is thanks enough," he said. "I look forward to our journey."

My brow wrinkled when I said, "Journey?"

"To the North," he replied. "Do not forget—the Elar's Successor is to be named in two days' time."

"Gods," I breathed. "I'd forgotten all about it. But I can't possibly go."

The Sidhfae looked taken aback. "May I ask why not?"

His tone told me he was not only disappointed, but for some reason, thoroughly displeased with me—almost to the point of anger.

"I simply can't," I insisted. "The fact is, I'm in no emotional state to make such a journey. The Succession should be a celebration, and even if Mithraan has been freed, I'm still losing him. I am in no state to celebrate a damned thing. I'll ask the High King to let me stay behind—he can have his guards watch me all day and night, for all I care."

Erildir sucked in his cheeks, and I could tell he was weighing his words carefully. "Highness—you *must* come. Your presence in the North is of vital importance." His voice was insistent, almost desperate, and I found myself narrowing my eyes as I tried to figure out why he cared so much.

I was no follower of the Elar. I had nothing to do with the Order or its Priestesses.

The only theory that sprang to mind was one I had pushed away a hundred times—the one Riah had raised in the pub that night.

There are just as many rumors circulating that Lyrinn is the next Elar.

I studied Erildir's face, seeking any answer that wasn't *that* one.

"Explain to me why," I said. "Why should I make such a long journey for a spectacle that will take, what, an hour or so? It's an absurd expectation. Even my father thinks so."

Erildir lifted a hand and lowered his chin, taking a deep breath. "The journey will be quick, it's true—and perhaps it's of little importance to you. Still, I was hoping you would keep me company in my carriage along the way."

I hesitated, then said, "Erildir—I am so grateful for what you've done for Mithraan. Really I am. In all likelihood, you saved his life, and I cannot possibly express my gratitude. But I'm simply not up for the journey. Not to mention that I assume my mother is to remain here, in Aethos. You can't expect her to travel so soon after the attempt on her life."

"Your mother is perfectly well," he said. "She intends to make the journey."

I considered that for a moment before saying, "Then I will see her when she returns. Now, if you'll leave me to it, I must get to the ship. I need to say goodbye to Mithraan."

Erildir looked as if he was tempted to block me from reaching for my clothing, and I wondered if I would have to fight him to get out of my room.

But he finally bowed his head politely and said, "Of course, Highness. I will have Riah escort you to the harbor."

A few minutes later, as promised, Riah rapped on my door. When I opened it, she rushed inside, almost frantic.

"Are you all right?" she asked, her eyes roving over me as if to check and see if I'd literally cracked. By now, I was dressed and ready to head out. "Erildir told me what happened. I'm so sorry. I must confess, I was wondering why you looked so… happy…lately."

"I was, briefly." My voice was bitter. "But it was a foolish risk we took. Look—there isn't much time. We need to get to the harbor now."

"Of course. Come, Highness," she said, taking me by the hand. She guided me swiftly downstairs and out to the main courtyard, where a small carriage awaited us.

"You won't find yourself in trouble for this, will you?" I asked. "My father…"

"It's fine," she replied, climbing inside and signaling to me to do the same. "Your father approved it. He's not entirely heartless, you know."

I want to believe that. But I'm not so sure.

My fingers fidgeted as the carriage took off down the road toward the harbor. My heart felt as though it had crept up inside my throat and was threatening escape. My body was tense, my foot tapping an irregular pattern on the wooden floor.

"It's all right," Riah assured me. "The ship won't leave before your arrival. Try not to worry."

I nodded, looking out the window toward the vast sea, lamenting the distance between us and Kalemnar. If I could only see his destination—if I could feel like we still lived in the same world...

It felt like an eternity before the carriage finally turned onto the narrow stone street flanked to one side by the sea, to the other by a series of fisherman's houses and shops.

The ship was moored there—a smallish schooner, elegantly crafted of ivory-colored wood. Like all Lightblood creations, its surface was veined with silver designs that glistened and beamed in the sunlight.

I looked for Mithraan, but at first there was no sign of him. The only familiar face I saw, in fact, was that of Erildir, who was speaking to a Lightblood Fae on the ship's deck.

"What's he doing here?" I asked, leaning toward Riah, who shrugged. "Probably seeing Mithraan off, just like you?"

"I suppose," I replied. "But it's not like they even know each other."

"You can ask him later. For now, let's find your Tírian."

Riah watched as I descended from the carriage, walking swiftly toward the ramp leading up to the ship's deck.

Erildir had already begun to make his way down, and he bowed his head slightly as he approached.

"Princess," he said softly.

"What are you doing here?" I asked under my breath. "Is everything all right?"

"Just fine," he said, glancing over his shoulder toward the uniformed Fae he'd just been speaking to, who was holding what looked like a sack of coins. I knew the bag...at least, it looked identical to one in my mother's possession. *Blue silk, tied with a yellow ribbon.*

"Is Lark with you?" Erildir asked, pulling my attention. I was about to say no when the flitting of wings met my ears and Lark appeared from the shadows.

"I'm here," he said. "Of course."

"Good. You may as well hear this as well." Erildir lowered his voice as he spoke. "I have paid the captain a tidy sum, and he has agreed to re-route the ship to Nordvahl."

"Nordvahl?" I repeated, baffled. "Why?"

Erildir glanced around cautiously. "I can't tell you much, Princess—but if you come North, I can promise to reunite you with Mithraan there. It will be easier for you both to flee your father from that port—he does not have much in the way of guards in that part of the realm. It is under the jurisdiction of the Order of the Elar—and they are far less likely to keep a close eye on you than the Southerners are."

With a flash of understanding, I nodded, smiling gratefully. "Was this my mother's idea?" I asked, recalling the small sack Erildir had handed the captain.

The Spell-Master simply smiled and offered me a quiet shrug, then turned to Lark. "When the princess goes north, you must stay in Aethos," he said. "For your own safety."

"What?" I asked. "Why?"

"Sprites are not welcome in the North," Erildir explained. "With apologies to Lark, they are reviled there."

"Then the Northerners are pathetic, and not worth a second thought," I replied. "Besides, Lark is perfectly able to hide himself from their eyes."

"Still, it would be unwise, Highness..."

"I will stay behind," Lark said decisively, his eyes locked on mine. "Erildir is right. It wouldn't be wise for me to accompany you."

"But..." I stammered. "If you stay..."

If you stay, I may never see you again.

"I know, Highness. But I must heed the Spell-Master's warning. He knows the Northerners better than I do."

A lump formed in my throat as I offered up a reluctant nod.

"Go," Lark said. "We'll see each other one day. I'm sure of it."

I wanted to hug him...but he was so small, so delicate-looking that I feared I would injure him.

"I'll miss you," I said.

"And I you. Now go and see your Tírian before it's too late."

"I've come to see Mithraan," I told a crew member when I had climbed on board. "I am Princess Lyrinn, daughter of Kazimir."

He looked me up and down with a scowl. "I'm not supposed to let anyone speak to him."

"I only want to say goodbye. Please—allow me that much." My voice was trembling now, and I could see that the discomfort of potential woman-tears was breaking the Fae's resolve.

"Five minutes." With that, he gestured toward a nearby guard, who strode over to a cabin door and opened it, indicating that I could enter.

Inside, I found Mithraan pacing the cabin, his expression one of abject rage. The second he spotted me, though, his eyes softened and he leapt over to take me in his arms.

"I should have stolen you away when I had the chance," he said. "Days ago. Come with me now—we can leave this place together."

I pulled back, shaking my head. "There's a better way—one that won't draw so much attention. Listen to me—Erildir has paid the captain to take you to Nordvahl. I will find you there tomorrow night. Kazimir will be there, too—but Erildir is confident you and I will be able to quietly find a ship to steal us away."

A hopeful glint lit up Mithraan's eyes, but he frowned and shook his head. "We've tried it before," he said. "There's no guarantee of success."

"No. But *not* trying means certain failure—doesn't it? Besides, my father won't know you're there, which will make it somewhat easier to flee."

At that, a bell began to clang in the distance, signaling the ship's imminent departure.

"Tomorrow," I said again. "I will find you. They say the High King's ships move rapidly on the water—when they're not being pursued by Tírians, at least. Hopefully you'll be in Nordvahl by the time I arrive."

He kissed me, stroking his fingers over my cheek, and it was only then that I felt something cold against my skin.

I reached for his hand, pulling it down to see the ring of impediment on his finger, a white gem at its center.

"Does it hurt?" I asked, pulling it to my lips.

"Not as much as you might think. It's more that it saps me of energy, of strength. I feel my power being stolen from me hour by hour. That said, it's better than death at Kazimir's hands."

The bell rang again, three hard *clang*s, and Mithraan kissed me one last time.

"I'll see you in the North, Vaelan."

CHAPTER FORTY-FOUR

SOMETIME IN THE AFTERNOON, I went to see my mother in her chamber and told her what had transpired—about Mithraan's departure to the North, about my coming journey.

"I am so glad you're making the trip," she told me, stroking a hand over my hair. "So very glad. You don't know just how important your presence will be at the ceremony, Lyrinn."

I stared at her, puzzled. "I'm not going to Nordvahl for the ceremony, Mother. You know that."

She looked equally confused when she pulled back, eyeing me as if I'd just told her I had seen a flying stallion. "Why are you going, then?"

It was as if she'd forgotten the entirety of what I had told her—as if she forgot, even, that she herself had paid to have Mithraan sent north.

"I'm going," I said, exasperated, "so that you, Mithraan, and I can free ourselves of this damned realm once and for all."

She waved a hand in the air as if that was a small detail. "Yes, yes—but only *after* the ceremony. I am a follower of the Elar, after all—this is as sacred a rite to me as to anyone. I must attend—it's crucial."

I stared at her, stunned. She and I had spoken of the Elar before, of course. But never had she seemed so tied to the idea of it—never before had I gotten the impression that she would place the Elar's Succession over my welfare.

"If...if it means that much to you, then I suppose our departure can wait," I said, my heart sinking. "Mithraan and I will do what we can to secure a ship once we're reunited—but we will have very little time to plot our escape. Kazimir does not intend to stay in the North for long, don't forget."

My mother smiled, an unwarranted delight in her eyes. "Wonderful," she said as if we were discussing a garden party rather than a plan that could easily lead to death for us all. "I couldn't be happier, truly. You don't know what this means to me, Daughter—to know I'll have you with me when the time comes for the new Elar's naming."

"When the time comes," I repeated, still baffled by her tone. "Why in all the realms is this naming so important to you?"

The light in her eyes faded slightly, and her expression turned serious. "Because I have awaited it for a thousand years."

At dawn, I found myself seated inside an elegant carriage, its interior upholstered in rich gray and black velvet. Furs of various shapes and sizes were strewn about, waiting to be draped over Erildir or me the second a chill invaded.

I had brought a long coat of leather and fur—white, like all my other garments, but I laid it on the seat next to me, not wishing to spend the next several hours sweating.

When Erildir climbed in to sit opposite me, a memory worked its way through my mind of the day when Mithraan had joined me in the carriage on the King's Road heading south to Domignon.

I had not welcomed the High Fae's presence then; I was grieving my father and the loss of my sister. I told myself I despised Mithraan, that he and I would never be anything other than enemies.

How things change.

Erildir came equipped with warm pastries, a pot of hot tea, and a wool blanket.

"We're heading to Winter Territory," he said. "You will find the air chillier by far than here. Best to keep warm from the start, I always say."

I nodded my thanks as I accepted his offerings and greedily devoured the pastry, then sipped the tea, grateful for its warmth.

"My mother," I said, peering out the window. "Is she joining us?"

"Ah. No—she's chosen to ride with Lady Cassia, actually."

A frown overtook my lips. "Why would she want to ride with her and my father, given that—" I began.

"She and Lady Cassia wished to discuss the upcoming Succession. Your father is traveling in his own carriage, for... obvious reasons."

I wasn't sure if he was implying the reason was my father's alleged attempt on my mother's life or his infidelity.

Neither was a wonderful choice.

As the carriage began to move, I looked out the window to see that we were making our way out of the city unnaturally fast. Erildir's spell of speed, I told myself. There was no other explanation.

"We will be at the midway point in a matter of hours," the Spell-Master said. "There, we'll stop for a quick break, then proceed. We will be in Nordvahl in time for dinner."

I sipped my tea, watching the landscape fly by at an extraordinary pace. Stunned that I did not feel the carriage jostling, or the horses tiring.

"I haven't had a great deal of opportunity to see your magic in action," I told Erildir. "I must say, it's impressive."

He smiled. "It's all I have on offer, Highness. But I do like to be useful."

"May I...may I ask you something?"

He raised his eyebrows. "Of course."

"My mother—how deep do her ties to the Elar go?"

"Highness? I'm sorry—I'm not sure what you mean."

"How devout is she?"

"Ah." Erildir pulled his eyes to the window. "She prays to the Elar nightly, Princess. She has for many years. Hers is a deep bond. The Order is a tightly-woven family. So, you can imagine why the Succession is important to your mother. To be able to be present when the next Elar is named—that is something extraordinary for one so devout."

"Yes, I suppose it is."

"But," the Sidhfae said with a sigh, "I fear she will find herself exhausted by the time we arrive. I don't suppose she'll be able to join us for tonight's banquet."

"Tonight?" I said. "I thought the *ceremony* was tonight."

"No. It takes place at dawn tomorrow."

Dawn. *Gods.* That meant I would have to wait around tonight—to bide my time until the Succession had concluded.

"I see. But..."

I was going to ask about Mithraan, and when I would be able to see him.

But Erildir spoke first. "The ship to Nordvahl may not arrive until tomorrow morning—so please, try to enjoy yourself. Revel in the Succession, alongside your mother. When the time is right, I promise—you will be reunited with your Mithraan."

As Erildir had promised, the carriage stopped after three hours of impossibly rapid travel, and I opened the door, hoping to stretch my legs.

"Princess," he said before I had a chance to climb out. "I must warn you—the landscape beyond that door is not a pretty sight."

I nodded, a sense of dread creeping through me as I stepped down from the carriage...but nothing Adhair could have said would have been sufficient warning for what I saw.

The air was bitter and tasted of ash. The ground was hard and lifeless. No breeze blew—not even a hint of one, and I found that my breath was shallow, my lungs already desperate to leave this place.

"Welcome to central Aetherion," Erildir said quietly, gesturing to the land so devoid of life—one whose patchy grass was brown and brittle, its trees blackened almost beyond recognition. "It may not be the most beautiful part of the realm, but we are more than halfway to our destination, at least."

"Do you know how this came to pass?" I asked, a hand over my mouth to avoid inhaling the particulate in the air. "How these lands were destroyed? I've heard stories, but I don't know what to believe, honestly."

"I assume you've heard it was the Elar's work."

"I have, yes."

"Some say it was another powerful Fae who did it—one who was angry with the High King long ago. But the Elar is the most obvious choice of culprit—there are few Fae living powerful enough to wreak this sort of havoc."

I stared out at the destruction, at the desolation. There was profound malice in the wreckage of this land—something far greater, it seemed, than a mere moment of rage. This was pure, unadulterated hatred, and all I could envision was the creature from my dreams, unleashing her bolts of lightning, flame, and cruelty toward the world below.

"Perhaps the Elar is frightened," I said, surprised at the gentleness of my own voice, given the nightmares she had inflicted on me for so many nights.

"Frightened? Of what?"

I pulled my eyes to Erildir's and said, "Of fading into a shadow and being replaced."

He shrugged slightly. "Every Elar fades—and is reborn. That's what the Succession is, after all."

"Knowing you will be reborn isn't enough to quell the fear of death," I said with a shudder. "Let us hope that the High Priestess who takes her place is kinder than she was."

"Yes," Erildir said. "Let us hope."

The Sidhfae wrapped his arms around himself and turned, hunched, back toward the carriage.

"Are you all right?" I asked.

"I am...tired, Lyrinn," he said, glancing around at the landscape. "For too long, I've resided in this realm, keeping watch and restoring the peace when I saw the need. But I long to return to my homeland...and at long last, I intend to do so."

He seemed vulnerable, pained. His cold instructor persona had entirely left him in favor of someone far more...real.

"How can you go home, when your land is gone?" I asked, recalling what he'd told me of his home the first day we'd met.

He pulled his eyes to mine then. They seemed to burn with a far-off desire when he said, "The Successor will have the power to help me—to help us all. That is why we're going north,

Princess. To celebrate the dawn. A new power is growing over these lands, and we would all do well to embrace it."

With that, he climbed back into the carriage, and I followed.

CHAPTER FORTY-FIVE

Our arrival in Nordvahl revealed a city of snow and ice, its twisting, blue-cobbled streets glowing with iridescent light and an inviting coziness that charmed me before I had so much as stepped out of the carriage.

From every chimney rose a merry plume of smoke, and each thatched roof felt as comforting as those in Dúnbar. Fae bundled in fur and leather strode up and down the streets, their faces alit with bright smiles. Each of them was dressed in white in celebration of the approaching Succession.

Unlike Domignon and Aethos, Nordvahl felt like a city built for its residents—a city of comfort, rather than gleaming opulence. There seemed to be no grand palace, no daunting structure towering over the lesser houses to remind the small folk of their station in life.

Large flakes of snow tumbled lazily toward the ground as our carriage rolled through the streets, moonlight bathing the glistening cobbles in a mesmerizing glow. In the distance, beyond the numerous buildings, I could just make out the faint outlines of white-capped mountain peaks surrounding the city on three sides.

"Beautiful, isn't it?" Erildir asked. "They may call it the Frozen City, but truly, it is as warm as any I have seen."

"It is," I admitted. "I must say, this is not what I expected from the home of the Order of the Elar. I suppose I foresaw icicle palaces and frightening-looking guards stationed on every corner."

"The High Priestesses do not need protection in this part of Aetherion, believe me," Erildir replied with a chuckle. "They are revered in this land—and those who do not revere them are expelled."

Expelled.

I shuddered.

It was the first crack in the city's welcoming aura. A reminder of what Varyn, the Red Priestess, had said to me inside Aethos's temple—that the Elar did not allow the undeserving to cross the threshold.

"The temple lies at the top of this road," Erildir said. "We will be staying nearby tonight, in the cells."

At that word, I balked. "Cells? As in...a prison?"

"Cells, as in rooms in a convent where Priestesses in training spend years learning humility and devotion to the Elar," Erildir laughed. "Think of it as an inn, with fewer comforts—but a wonderful view, at least."

I opened the window and jutted my head out to see a vast building of smooth gray stone in the distance. It appeared to be octagonal, its roof arching in an elegant dome. It was windowless, but I could see an enormous set of wooden doors facing us at the end of the road.

"*That's* the temple?" I asked.

"You were expecting high towers and stained glass, perhaps?"

"Well...yes, I suppose I was."

"It is somewhat more spectacular inside, I assure you. A

rotunda of sorts, with one large oculus in its roof so that one can behold the sky at any time of day or night—and so that the Priestesses may come and go without so much as opening the doors."

"By flying, you mean."

"Precisely."

I leaned toward the Spell-Master, taking care to keep my voice low when I said, "You told me I would be reunited with Mithraan here. Tell me—is his ship close?"

Erildir leaned back and smiled. "It is," he said under his breath. "And I promise, you will see him very soon. But for the time being, you must keep a brave face. Smile, comply—do all that is asked of you, and your wish to see him will come true sooner than you imagine. I swear it, by the Elar's wings."

By the Elar's wings.

I had never before known Erildir to utter those words, and something about hearing them from his lips unsettled me. Still, I nodded and sat back, sealing my mouth shut.

He was right—I had played a flawed version of the obedient daughter and princess this long.

Surely a few more hours wouldn't kill me.

We arrived at the temple only to be greeted outside its doors by Lady Cassia, who, like so many other Northerners I'd seen, was dressed in a garment of pure white. Kazimir stood by her side, the silver crown atop his head. I supposed he wore it as a ceremonial measure—a symbol of his status as High King, but also of the tenuous alliance between Aetherion's North and South.

Two Southern Guards flanked the large doorway—two

Lightbloods clad in silver armor with Kazimir's sword sigil etched into their chest pieces.

As I took Erildir's offered arm, I managed a smile and a reverent nod, aimed more at Cassia than my father.

I couldn't help but notice Adhair's absence, but I said nothing, grateful that he was nowhere to be seen.

"My son will not be joining us," Cassia said, reading my thoughts a little too easily. "The Succession tends to be a women-only sort of affair, with obvious exceptions for your father and Erildir."

Satisfied, I glanced around as we walked through the temple's doors, which had opened the moment we'd descended from the carriage. It was indeed impressive—much larger than it had appeared from the outside. Its impossibly high ceiling rose to a point hundreds of feet above our heads. An enormous, round hole—the oculus Erildir had mentioned—peered down at us from its center. Snow fell in light flakes through the opening to gather on the stone floor at the temple's center.

As Erildir had guessed, my mother was absent. Most likely resting after the journey, healing up in preparation for tomorrow morning's ceremony.

"Welcome to Nordvahl," Cassia said, gesturing to the space. "And to the Temple of the Elar—or, as we occasionally call it, the Temple of the Portal. We will dine here tonight—and in the morning, the portal shall be opened to the Broken Lands."

The building, as far as I could tell, was little more than this one large chamber—though there was a series of doorways along the walls that must have led to an outer corridor.

"It's an honor," I said, though in truth, my body was tight with an apprehension that came from some unknown place inside me. "Thank you for allowing us to see your beautiful city."

Cassia smiled. "I hope you feel welcome here, Princess. Your presence is much appreciated—and much needed for what is to come." With that, she turned and clapped her hands together sharply. Instantly, a door opened on either side of the enormous chamber, and a series of veiled Priestesses dressed in white walked through to gather in a semi-circle around Cassia.

"Now—it's time for the banquet!" she announced. "Let us transform the temple into something a little more welcoming!"

With her command, the chamber around us altered and shifted into a rectangular, white-walled great room. Torches danced along its perimeter, lighting the space in a cheerful glow. Beautiful, flowing music began to weave its way through the air from somewhere unseen—a voice wafting around us, accompanied by some sort of sweet-sounding flute. The words came in a language I didn't know—one that was both beautiful and unsettling. As much as I wished to enjoy the sound of it, something about the lyrics made me feel as though I was listening to a grim chant...something ominous and relentless.

As I watched in tense silence, a vast table appeared at the room's center, an enormous white cloth covering its surface. A roaring fire flared to life in a nearby hearth, warming the room so that I almost forgot the thick blanket of snow that was coming to rest on the nearby streets.

Cassia flicked her hand into the air, and on the table appeared enough food and drink for a large army. Thirty or more place settings arranged themselves tidily, as well as elegant gilded chairs for each of the guests, including the High Priestesses.

I stood in place, frozen by the apprehension that had been building since our arrival in Nordvahl.

Kazimir positioned himself by Cassia's side, looking smug as always—but I had the distinct impression that he was growing agitated with the lack of an invitation to sit.

"Well?" he said after a few seconds. "Shall we?"

"In a moment, your Grace," Cassia said, gesturing to three of the Priestesses to approach her. Eerily identical in their all-white uniforms, one approached the High King, one approached Erildir, and the other slipped over to stand in front of me. "There is something we must do before the banquet begins."

Confused, I stared at the Priestess who now stood in front of me and waited as she held out a fisted hand, fingers up, then opened it. The Priestess in front of Kazimir did the same. In both their hands I saw what at first looked like wriggling insects flipped onto their backs and helpless to escape.

"What is the meaning of this?" Kazimir asked.

I looked again only to realize they weren't insects at all, but rings of impediment like the one my mother wore.

"You mean to steal my power from me?" the High King barked, rounding on Cassia.

"It is tradition, your Grace," she said, her voice as supple as velvet. "In the temple, spell-crafting is forbidden by outsiders... particularly during the Succession."

My apprehension was beginning to evolve into something deeper, and an outright warning was now tearing at me.

If the Priestesses put the rings onto our hands, how could we trust that they would ever take them off again?

But I watched as Kazimir huffed and finally, reluctantly, held his hand out. The Priestess slipped the ring on and I watched as its tendrils tore into his flesh. Kazimir let out a quiet groan of pain before dropping his hand to his side and flexing his fingers irritably.

Serves you right, I thought.

Another Priestess slipped a ring onto Erildir's hand as the third pushed mine on. The pain of the tendrils digging in was not so wretched as I'd expected.

What was far worse was the sudden feeling of weakness overtaking my body and mind.

My Gifts had come on so gradually in the last weeks that I had not been entirely aware of just how powerful I felt as I went about my daily life, how strong I had grown. But the ring instantly sapped me of all of it. Even my eyesight and hearing dulled as I stared out at the sea of white-veiled faces.

I felt...*mortal* again, and with it came a sudden sensation of nakedness, as if I had no shield, no barrier between myself and any threat that might come at me.

Mithraan, I thought. *Where are you...*

When we seated ourselves, I found myself next to Erildir, who looked remarkably unfazed by everything that had just happened. If anything, he looked pleased, as though perfectly content to have his substantial power stolen from him.

He gazed around the table at the various Priestesses, an expression of pure satisfaction on his face.

"What's got you looking so happy?" I asked him with a faint hint of accusation. "I would have thought a Spell-Master would fight to the death to keep from wearing a ring of impediment."

"The ring is a mere inconvenience," he said. "A temporary pain. If I look happy, it's because I'm delighted with the Order's selection."

"You know, then," I said as I began to slice into the venison that had just appeared on my plate. "About their choice of Elar."

"I do," he said. "The Order has chosen wisely—just as I had hoped."

"Is it anyone I know?"

He glanced sideways at me and grinned. "You've met her once or twice," he said.

I glanced around, realizing there was no way to tell under all the white veils if Varyn, the Red Priestess, was here. And even if they each lifted their veils, I had no idea what her face looked like. All I had ever experienced of her was her voice, after all—and by all accounts, it wasn't even her own.

"Where is Varyn?" I asked.

"A fine question," Erildir said. "I believe we'll find out in just one—ah."

He gestured toward a door at the chamber's far end as it opened and, as if summoned by my question, she strode in. Her veil was down, but I recognized her robe and the way she moved across the floor like a gliding mist.

She slipped over to tower over Cassia, who took her by the hand and spoke low into her ear. Varyn lifted her veil then, and for the first time, I saw her face.

She was beautiful, her eyes dark, her skin olive-toned. She smiled as she looked down at Cassia, and something about her face, about her simple presence, filled me with profound relief.

For the first time, I admitted to myself that there was some small part of me that had feared the rumors were true—that I had been brought to the North to be named Elar—to be forced against my will to fulfill a wretched, alien destiny.

It seemed, however, that I was safe from that fate.

My destiny remains the crown on Kazimir's head, I thought, staring at its delicate, twisting silver. *A destiny that is everyone's choice but my own.*

Varyn took a seat to Cassia's left, and I watched as Kazimir issued her a faint smile and a nod, both of which seemed to take a great deal of effort. The High King was beginning to look disoriented, almost drunk—though I was fairly certain he hadn't yet consumed any drink or even food.

The ring, I thought. *Why is it affecting him so profoundly?*

After some time spent eating, Cassia rose to her feet and pulled her veil over her face. The music ceased, and every Priestess in the room turned her way.

"You know, of course, why we have gathered here. The

Succession of the Elar occurs once in a Fae's lifetime—if that. We are all privileged to be able to witness this moment, to embrace the Successor as she steps into the Broken Lands to be granted the essence of the Elar at long last. With her ascension will come a new realm—a new world. *A new order.*"

The last three words came in a voice I had come to recognize —one that echoed through the chamber as if channeled from someone other than Cassia herself.

It was the Elarrah—the voice of the Elar, spoken through the head of the Order.

Pulling the veil back up, she glanced down at Kazimir, and I was certain I detected a look of smug satisfaction in her eyes. "Gone are the days when High Lords dictate the Order's lives and impede our power. Gone is the need to conceal our faces, to hide from those who might threaten us. The Successor has vowed that the Order will be granted powers unseen in the history of Fae. From this day forward, we will take control of Aetherion. And with help from our allies, we will take the lands across the sea."

My mouth fell open and I looked at Erildir, who seemed as relaxed and calm as ever.

Kazimir's eyes shot to Cassia, a look of stunned rage over-taking his face. Any seeming disorientation faded instantly as he leapt to his feet.

"What is this treason?" he spat. "What do you mean by this madness?"

"I am simply relaying what the chosen Successor has declared, your Grace," Cassia said.

Kazimir pulled his eyes to Varyn, who was still seated. "Have you made any such promise?" he asked.

"No, your Grace," she said. "I have not."

His shoulders slumped in relief. "Thank the gods."

Varyn smiled at him and added, "You misunderstand me,

your Grace. The reason I have made no such vow is that I am *not* the Elar's Successor." With that, she rose to her feet and flicked a hand toward the far door, which flew open. "*She* is."

"What the hell are you talking about?"

Kazimir's question was answered when a veiled figure dressed from head to toe in gold strode in through the open door, a set of shimmering wings unfurling behind her like vast sails.

My mouth went dry even as a deep throb set into my hand where the ring dug into my flesh, its tendrils tearing at me even as I fought against their strength.

All I wanted now was to rip the wretched thing from my finger, whatever the risk, and to ask my strength to surge back into my mind, my body.

Every instinct inside me told me to hurl a deadly, unending barrage of flame and fury at the entity who had just set foot in the chamber. *She cannot be granted the Elar's title.*

She cannot be allowed to live past this night.

But I was powerless, and all I could do was stare.

"Those wings," I said under my breath.

"Yes," Erildir replied. "Are they not magnificent?"

No, I wanted to say. *They're as terrible as anything I have ever seen.*

They were silver...laced with deep, red veins.

The wings from my nightmares.

CHAPTER FORTY-SIX

I WAS ABOUT to blurt out a warning when Kazimir turned to face Cassia.

"What is this?" he shouted. "Some sort of sick joke?"

He had just begun to stride toward the Priestess in gold when she raised one hand elegantly into the air and the High King froze, falling to his knees before her.

"Ah. You're finally where you belong, Kazimir," an eerie, echoing voice spoke from behind the veil. "Just where you should always have been."

His hand went to his throat. When he tried to speak, nothing came but loud gasps, as if he was struggling for air.

"No one told us the Elar would be here," I said to Erildir through gritted teeth. My every instinct told me to run, to hide —to get the damned ring off my finger, even if I had to sever my hand to do it.

"That is not the Elar," the Spell-Master replied, seemingly unconcerned. "But she will be."

With a sickening comprehension, I remembered what Varyn had said only a minute ago.

I am not the Elar's Successor.

She is.

This—this creature I had seen so many times in my darkest nightmares—she was not the Elar, but the Successor—the Priestess chosen by the Order to ascend.

It was as Varyn had said—she was an apparition from a future I feared with every bone in my body. A future that now seemed inevitable.

"I've seen her before," I gasped. "Too many times to count. She's..." *Evil. Cruel. Maniacal.* "She's unworthy of the title."

"You're mistaken, Highness," Erildir said. "And I'm quite certain you will take back those words when her features are revealed."

I turned to him, assessing. Trying to figure out what he was playing at. His High King was on his knees, still struggling to breathe, and this Fae—this Successor—was responsible. How could Erildir be so nonchalant about it all?

I felt as though the Spell-Master was playing tricks on my mind, manipulating me into some illusion of madness. Either that, or...

No—I would never forget those wings so long as I lived. The vileness of them, like flayed flesh stolen from some animal and melded with precious metal.

"That's enough," Cassia called out. "Let him go."

The silver-winged Fae pulled her hand back, releasing Kazimir, and slowly he found the strength to push himself to his feet.

"Open the damned doors," he rasped. "I am leaving—and I'm taking my daughter with me. This lunacy has gone on long enough."

My eyes moved rapidly between him and the veiled Priestess in gold. I didn't wish to go anywhere with him...but everything in me was screaming a warning to get myself as far from the winged entity as I could.

"Come, Lyrinn," the High King said, turning my way, a hand outstretched. "We will find an inn and stay there tonight. In the morning, we'll head back to Aethos."

I glanced at Erildir, panicking. *I can't leave Aethos. Mithraan is here...*

"There will be no inns or comfortable beds for you, I'm afraid, your Grace," Erildir said, rising to his feet.

"Why the hell not?" Kazimir shouted.

"Perhaps the Successor would like to explain," Cassia interjected, glancing briefly my way as she spoke. "I believe your daughter would like some answers, your Grace. Most of all, perhaps she would like to know why you brought her to Aetherion."

"She knows why I brought her, damn it!" Kazimir growled. "She is my heir."

But Cassia shook her head, her beautiful hair moving in shimmering white waves that glowed in the light of the torches.

"She was drawn here by a force far greater than you, High King."

At that, the color drained from Kazimir's face. He looked like he was about to fall to his knees once again.

"Cassia—" he said, his voice almost pleading. "You and I have known one another for centuries."

Cassia pivoted toward him, her eyes glowing bright.

"She needs to understand her purpose, Kazimir," she said, her voice altering from the sweet smoothness I had come to know to something jagged, biting. "She needs to know the good that she is about to contribute to the world."

"I will not allow you to do this!" he said, his voice feral despite his failing strength. "You must understand—*she* is a monster!" With that, he pointed violently to the Golden Priestess who stood silently by the doors, those terrifying wings flickering like grim portents in the light.

"We both know it takes a monster to bring change to a realm—and this realm is long overdue. Sprites run wild in the South. Lightbloods have too much freedom, and have forgotten what they once were—weapons of war, powerful enough to overrun all the realms of the world. We are defenseless should Kalemnar attack us, and you know it. The Elar will render us powerful again."

"Kalemnar will not attack us!" Kazimir nearly screamed, the veins in his neck prominent with rage. "I have a pact with Domignon—it has held for a thousand years, damn it!"

"*You* do not have a pact," Cassia hissed, nodding to the Golden Priestess. "*She* does. She is the one who negotiated so long ago with the mortals of Domignon—or have you forgotten? Is your memory so skewed that you truly believe you're the one who orchestrated all of it—the coup at the Blood Trials, the siege of Tíria?"

I sagged into my chair, my mind twisting and reeling as if I were intoxicated. What were they talking about? Who was the Fae dressed in gold—the one who had invaded my mind so frequently? And how in the gods' name was she responsible for what had happened at the Trials so long ago?

Kazimir shot me an unreadable look, his jaw tightening. "It was me," he said. "I was responsible for all of it. We agreed to it then, and I have taken accountability for those actions for all these years, regardless of the consequences. My own daughter hates me for what I did..." He pointed again to the Golden Priestess. "To protect Lyrinn and her sister from *her*."

"Stop!" The voice came from the veiled Priestess in gold, who glided toward him with unnatural, horrifying speed.

The High King flinched, wilting before her like a flower that had been sprayed with acid.

"You have *always* known what I am," she said in that terrible, echoing voice. "*Who* I am. You have never doubted my ambition. And deny it as you might, you knew why I wanted you to bring our daughters to Aetherion. *Both* of them. Yet you failed me—didn't you?"

Our...daughters.

I choked on my own breath as I gasped, my body lurching with horror.

"No," I said softly, turning to Erildir to see if he was as terrified as I was.

Yet no surprise showed on his face. No look of horror, shock, anything.

Kazimir turned to look into my eyes, and on his face, for the first time, I saw a look of profound remorse.

The Golden Priestess made a quick gesture with her left hand and said, "Take him to the dungeon. See to it that he has none of the comforts of home. It's time the High King learned who truly wields the power."

Varyn, slipping over to stand before Kazimir, raised a hand in the air. A chain appeared from nowhere, shackling tight around the High King's neck like a constrictor. She took hold of the chain, but with one final burst of rage, he yanked himself backwards, trying to take her with him.

She simply let out a silvery laugh, then pulled gently on the chain, and he tripped after her as she led him from the chamber.

And, just like that, Kazimir turned into a submissive hound. His chin fell as though he no longer had the strength to lift his head—and with his shoulders slumping, the silver crown of Aethos tumbled to the hard stone floor and shattered into a thousand shards, scattering in every direction.

The High King of Aetherion had just been unseated. The realm was leaderless but for the Fae in gold—the one who had referred to Leta and me as "our daughters."

With tears in my eyes, I looked at her—at those gruesome

wings, still spread behind her, their tips twitching slightly as if assessing the air for threats.

"I am sorry, Lyrinn, child," she said softly. "No one should have to witness their father brought down in such a way."

With that, she finally raised her veil to reveal the features that I knew almost as well as my own. Her large blue eyes fixed on mine as I reached for Erildir, holding onto him to keep from collapsing entirely.

Seeing my mother's face framed by those cruel wings—it was like watching the slow death of someone I loved.

"I told you so many times," she said softly, "that I could not leave Aetherion. Now, you finally know why."

CHAPTER FORTY-SEVEN

"You...you're a High Priestess," I stammered. "How..." My eyes shot to Cassia's, seeking answers. "How is this possible? Varyn presides over the temple in Aethos!"

"A High Priestess does not have to preside over a temple to retain her title," Cassia said. "Your mother has served the Elar faithfully for many centuries. She has given of herself, prayed, and toiled—and now, she is prepared to make the greatest sacrifice anyone can make."

My shock was beginning to fade, to numb, and a brutal rage had begun to take its place.

"You never had any intention of leaving Aetherion," I said. "And not because of the ring—that *damned ring*. You kept me trapped here with threats that you would die, Mother. I could have left—I could have—"

I was beginning to wonder if the ring on her finger—the one she had worn for so long, and still wore now—was even real. After all, it had never seemed to incapacitate her as Kazimir's did—as mine was beginning to do now, draining the strength from me as it tore into my veins.

"You're quite right," she said. "I have never wished to return to that forsaken realm. I never wanted to see the Dragon Court again. Unlike you, I do not pine for my homeland." She smiled angelically at me, as if it was the most natural thing that we should both find ourselves surrounded by an army of silent, winged Priestesses who clearly wished to rule the world through some dark, malevolent force.

"Well, I do wish to return," I told her, barely mustering the strength to rise to my feet. "And since you have no intention of coming with me, I will leave now."

"Will you?" my mother asked. "Are you quite certain?"

I could barely look at her, at the backdrop of ghastliness that confronted me each time my eyes landed on her.

My voice was bitter, my quiet rage simmering toward a boil inside me. "Are you telling me I'm a prisoner here, just as I was in Aethos? Will you hold me here and tell me that my departure would mean your imminent death?"

"Of course not. But I believe you're forgetting something, Daughter. Your lover."

No. I had not forgotten Mithraan. All I wanted was to be by his side—to board a ship—*any* ship—together and sail to Tíria, never looking back upon this nightmarish realm.

"You sent him here," I growled. "Because you knew it was the only way I could be persuaded to come north. You paid to have him shipped here like livestock."

"That's true. I did."

"Why? Why did it matter to you so much that I witness—this?" I gestured to the space around us. "The High King's downfall? Your ascension to the level of absolute ruler of Aetherion's fanatics? Because I have no interest in any of it. As far as I'm concerned, you've all lost your minds."

A low laugh rose from her chest. "No—I did not bring you here merely to witness a power play of sorts, Daughter. You will learn soon enough why you're here—and you will see your

Mithraan. I promise you that." Clapping her hands together, she added, "But now, I believe it's time to rest. We have a big day ahead of us tomorrow, you and I. You will sleep in a comfortable bed tonight, Lyrinn—and when morning comes, you will see what true power is."

By now, my mind and body were devoid of feeling. As if I cared a whit about power—about the Elar, about my parents' twisted lies and their horrible, toxic relationship.

There was only one thing I wanted, and it seemed no one was going to help me obtain it.

"When I found you in Aethos," I said slowly, my voice ragged, "I thought I finally had my family back. You brought me so much joy, Mother. Your face—it's so like Leta's. But there was always—*always*—something hiding behind your eyes, and I never could quite place it. I had seen your memories. I was certain you were a victim, a downtrodden, abused wife, so cruelly treated by your domineering husband. So I chose to put my faith in you—to believe in you. Tell me—those memories—were those invented? Did you manipulate them to deceive me?"

For a moment, my mother looked aghast. "Lyrinn," she said sweetly. "No, my dear girl. Of course not. I showed you the truth—I showed you what I wanted you to see. Enough to make you feel something for me—which was all that mattered. I needed you to care."

"Because you needed me to remain here after Kazimir dragged me across the sea," I said scornfully. "But I ask again—why? Why do you need me here so desperately? You obviously have no real fondness for me—so it must be something else entirely."

"You are a part of me, Lyrinn," she said simply. "I am not complete without you. I need you because of our bond—and very soon, you will finally come to understand why."

"Unless I leave this place," I told her. "So give me *one* reason to stay."

"Fine." Her face hardened instantly at the threat of my departure. "Leave, and you will never see your Mithraan again. I promise you that."

"Lyrinn."

The voice was Cassia's, and I looked up through cloudy eyes to see her gazing down at me, a hand outstretched.

"You need to rest," she said gently. "You've learned some hard truths tonight, and it's best that you sleep a little, my dear."

I simply nodded and allowed her to take my hand and help me up, then lead me toward a set of large wooden doors which cracked open at my approach. I stepped through, disoriented, confused, weak. I was in a fog now, one brought on by the ring on my hand and my shock, my rage, my torment.

But mostly by the feeling of utter uselessness that permeated my every fiber. Without Mithraan, I could not leave. I was as trapped here as I had ever been in Aethos—but now, I had to live with the knowledge that my mother was monstrous.

"Good night," Cassia's voice said, and then I heard the temple's doors shut.

It took me far too long to realize Erildir was at my side, a hand under my arm to support me.

"The convent is a few doors down," he said quietly. "I'll guide you to your room."

"Mithraan," I replied in a whisper.

"Princess?"

I stopped moving and turned to face Erildir, inhaling the cold air deep into my lungs and summoning enough strength to speak clearly. "You promised I would see him soon. Were you lying to me?"

The Spell-Master looked shocked—pained, even. "Of course not, Highness. I would never lie to you."

"Where is he, then?"

"Lyrinn, I looked after your mother for centuries," he said. "Would I lead you astray now?"

"You served my father the High King, too," I retorted. "Yet now he is in a dungeon, his powers stolen from him. My powers, too, have been snatched away. Now answer my damned question. Where the hell is Mithraan?"

Erildir shifted in place for a moment. "He is safe," he said. "I promise."

"Fine," I snarled. "So tell me—why am I here?"

"Because you are instrumental in the new Elar's ascension. You're here to help your mother."

"*Help* her?" I nearly laughed. "I have seen those wings of hers many, many times in my dreams, Spell-Master. I have seen their bearer tearing the lands apart for sport. You think I wish to help that...*creature*...to destroy all that I love?"

"That 'creature' holds all the power now, or soon will." His voice was cold now. "And she has the strength to join realms, as well as break them apart."

A flame of understanding flickered then flared in my mind, and I stepped back, stunned. So many times, I had watched Erildir and my mother exchange meaningful looks—and so many times, I had assumed it was their close friendship that brought on those glances.

But I understood now that it was something more—a quiet promise made centuries ago. One that had granted the Spell-Master hope, and my mother an eternal protector.

"She promised you she would join Aetherion to your homeland...didn't she?" I asked. "To Naviss. She said you would go back to your people at long last, provided she ascended to the seat of the Elar and she was granted the powers that come with the title." I half-suppressed a bitter laugh. "Gods, you betrayed the High King—you facilitated his downfall—all so you could go home. Tell me—did Kazimir actually stab her, or was that another invention?"

Erildir fell silent, but I could see it in his eyes—the struggle against the lie he wished to tell.

This time, I let the laugh come. A maniacal cackle rising in my throat like the cry of a rooster. "You know, when I was younger, I heard stories about Fae—that they were incapable of lying. And yet, every Fae in my life has proven a liar of one sort or another. And apparently, Sidhfae are no better."

"I have waited thousands of years—" Erildir began, but I put a hand up, silencing him.

"I do not care about you or your suffering, you absolute bastard," I said. "I have no intention of helping my mother ascend. I will not be party to any more of this madness. Bring me to the harbor to await Mithraan's ship, and let's be done with all of it."

Again, Erildir shifted. "I cannot."

"Why not? You told me he was coming here."

"I said the ship would bring him to Nordvahl, and...it did. It arrived some time ago. But Mithraan is—"

I was exhausted, mentally and physically, but my growing rage had granted me new strength, and I found myself grabbing the Spell-Master by the throat. *I might be without powers, but I still have hands.*

My ire will have to be enough to subdue him.

"Tell me where he is," I snarled.

"He's...in the Broken Lands that lie beyond the portal," he croaked. "It is closed now, and only Cassia can open it—she is the only one with the strength to access those lands. She will only open the portal again when it comes time for the Successor to pass through."

My eyebrows met, my rage growing. "Get him back!" I hissed. "Get him away from there—away from these...these usurping *witches*!"

"I'm afraid it's beyond my power to do that, Princess."

My hand tightened around his windpipe, cutting off the air supply.

I had no doubt that he could have fought me off. Killed me.

But something told me he wouldn't dare. If I was as important as they said—as he and my mother insisted—he would never risk harming me. Not now.

"I should kill you right now," I hissed. "I should end you, you sniveling traitor. You knew—you *knew* what my mother was, and how she would break my heart—but you hid the truth of it from me. I will never forgive you for it."

"We thought it best..." he croaked, but I cut him off.

"Best to hide that she is a monster? Because in spite of what you may say, I *know*, Erildir. I have seen it—whatever power was granted to me when I came of age, I have seen the future. And nothing you say can persuade me otherwise. She will kill thousands of innocent people. Why?"

He tried to answer, but by now, his voice was nothing more than a tortured, grating remnant of what had been.

I dropped my hand to my side. "Why?" I asked again.

He spoke in a savage whisper when he said, *"Because she can."*

CHAPTER FORTY-EIGHT

It was clear that Erildir was powerless to get me to the Broken Lands tonight, and nothing I could do would change that. I was at the mercy of Cassia—which meant I had no hope of seeing Mithraan before morning broke.

So I surrendered at last and let him escort me to the convent to rest. I would need what meager strength I had, after all, for whatever tomorrow might bring. If he was telling the truth—for *once*—I would walk through the portal. I would see Mithraan. And there would be nothing more anchoring us to this awful place...so we would leave.

Together.

When Erildir had shown me to my "cell"—a small room with a narrow bed and tiny closet, where some servant or other had hung the clothing the High King's staff had packed for me —I seated myself on the bed, staring down at the ring that tore so viciously at my hand.

I tried to pull it off—yanked hard enough that blood trickled threateningly from the wounds, the tendrils digging in so deeply that it felt as though they were drilling into bone.

I could see no way to remove it without dire consequences. The ring felt alive and crawling with power, a leech sucking every ounce of strength from me, moment by moment.

I lay down and pressed my head back into the too-firm pillow and let the tears flow for the loss of the mother I'd thought I'd come to know.

The loss of my power.

The loss of my very soul.

For hours on end, I tried to sleep, but to no avail. All I could think of was Mithraan, trapped in the Broken Lands with no means of escape—imprisoned as no High Lord should ever be.

The Elar is there with him, I thought. *On the verge of death—a mere wisp of its former self. For all I know, they're the only two living things in that entire land...*

How gruesome it must be to coexist with such a creature. How desperately I wanted to free Mithraan from its clutches.

As I tormented myself with thoughts of the terrible entity, a deep voice penetrated my mind, pulling me out of my thoughts.

~Lyrinn.

It wasn't a sound, exactly, but something that spun and twisted its way through my veins. When it didn't come again for several seconds, I began to wonder if I'd only imagined it.

~Princess...

I shot up, my skin suddenly clammy, my breath coming in quick gasps. I had no power to summon water or to calm my heart into submission. This damned ring—

"Who's there?" I called out in a whispered hiss.

The flitting of wings came to my ear and an instant later, I saw it—a tiny, flickering torch, held in mid-air...but nothing else.

"Lark," I said. Though he was invisible to my eye, I knew full well that no other sprite would have dared follow me to these lands. "But—you said you were staying in Aethos! It's too dangerous here. You—"

~*I'm all too well aware of the dangers,* he replied bitterly, his voice still swirling through my mind. *Which is precisely why I told Erildir I wouldn't come. I've never trusted that bastard as far as I can throw him—and your father's imprisonment has only confirmed my suspicions.*

"Do you think it was Erildir's—"

~*Princess, it's best not to speak aloud. We don't know who might be listening.*

How the hell do I speak, then? I thought with a frantic, frustrated breath.

~*Just like that.*

You heard my thought?

~*I did.*

But—the ring...

~*Our thoughts are not spells, Highness. They are quite the opposite. The ring can't touch them. But—there is little time. I believe Lady Cassia intends to leave your father to die in his cell.*

Part of me wanted to say *Let him rot. Let him suffer as he has made so many others suffer...*

But for the moment, through some wild twist of fate, he appeared to be my only parent who was *not* intent on ruining my life.

~*He wishes to see you. He has information to impart.*

Suddenly, I felt tired beyond comprehension, my body sagging back into the bed, my mind shutting down. I could not fathom sustaining any conversation right now, or hearing any

warning of an ugly future. I had seen it all—I knew full well
what we were up against.

~*Princess, please. For your sake, you need to come with me.*

Fine. Take me to Kazimir.

Lark guided me silently through several dark corridors until we
reached one that descended sharply. A damp chill bit into my
skin through my clothing as we advanced, and I found myself
wondering if Kazimir had seen any of this coming when he was
back in Aethos, flirting shamelessly with Cassia.

We moved down a narrow, low-ceilinged passageway until
we came to a sealed stone door which opened on our approach,
almost as if it was awaiting our arrival.

Beyond it, we were confronted with a series of doors along
both sides of the hallway—each made of iron, with small,
barred windows.

A guard was standing next to one of the doors, his tunic
displaying the sigil of the white bear. He peered at me and
nodded once as I approached.

"I've come to see my father," I said, my chin held high.

I expected a protest, but the guard simply extracted a key
from around his neck, unlocked the door, and pushed it open.

"He's waiting for you," he grunted. "Go ahead."

My heart flipped in my chest as I stepped into the small,
dank cell to see Kazimir—the Fae I'd come to know as daunting,
beautiful, arrogant—seated on a dingy, stained cot on the far
side, his hair scraggly about his face, his chin pressed to his
chest.

He raised his face as I entered with Lark invisible by my

side. His eyes were red and wet with tears, and I found myself shocked to see such emotion on his features.

"You've come," he said hoarsely, pushing his hair back from his face.

I nodded once. "Only to find answers," I said.

"Then let us hope I can give them to you."

CHAPTER FORTY-NINE

I STOOD with my back to the wall, staying as far from Kazimir as I could. When I examined him, I saw that he still wore the cruel-looking ring of impediment that the Priestesses had inflicted on him.

Unlike mine, it was not crafted of light silver twining in tendrils around his finger and hand. Instead, it had turned glistening red and thick, its appendages tentacle-like, digging their way under his flesh in an invasive, horrifying display.

Noticing me eyeing the ring, he held his hand up and snickered. "Don't worry—I can't cast a single spell. It would be a little hard to keep me in here if I could."

"I wasn't worried."

"No," he replied with a smile. "Of course you weren't. You are far more gifted than I have given you credit for..." He eyed the ring on my own hand. "Even with that monstrosity tearing into you, I can feel your power from here. There is little doubt in my mind that you could cast it from yourself and strike me down, Daughter."

His honesty stunned me, and for a moment, I had no idea how to react. I watched as he pushed himself to his feet and began pacing slowly up and down the room, seemingly deep in thought.

"Did you know," he said, "that your mother has always been an ambitious woman? I'm talking about the days when I first met her—when she was barely twenty years old."

"I didn't," I said. "I never had that impression at all—though I'm beginning to realize that I am a terrible judge of character."

"You and me both, it would seem," Kazimir grunted. "Let me tell you a brief tale of a Fae king and a Fae princess who were born into two warring realms."

I sighed, waiting for him to get to the point.

"The king met the princess many, many years ago. He fell in love with her—deeply. Obsessively. Instantly, he wanted her above all things, and she seemed to want him, too. She told him about her life in the Dragon Court, in the North of Tíria—about her father the High King—about how she despised him more than any other living creature."

With that, Kazimir caught my attention. I eyed him, trying to figure out if he was lying, if he was seeking some sort of sympathy. But then, I had seen my mother's reactions at the mention of her father—the cold bitterness that overtook her voice, the immediacy with which she shut down any attempt to speak of him.

Perhaps Kazimir was telling the truth, after all.

"You see, the High King of Tíria did not want his daughter to inherit the crown. She claimed this was because her father was unjust—a tyrant, a cruel man who felt women incapable of ruling."

"Rynfael?" I asked in spite of myself.

Kazimir nodded. "Rynfael, yes. Your grandfather."

"But..."

Kazimir put up a hand and shook his head, indicating that

he intended to continue. "Together, the Lightblood king and the princess plotted to run off together—to flee to Aetherion and start a new life, each seated on their own throne. He vowed to her that she was his equal—that she would be a queen with all the power of a High King. He had told her of his land, of its beauty. Of the creature known as the Elar—an Immortal more powerful than any other in the world. The king was not fond of the Elar; in fact, he found her frightening. But she had been a part of the world since its beginnings, and he had come to accept that she would always cast a shadow on his land.

"When she heard of the Elar, the princess was intrigued, beguiled. She begged him to take her away from the life she hated so much—to teach her more of that creature and its powers. He vowed to grant her every wish—but first, they would both have to wreak a little havoc. A distraction, if you will."

"You're talking about what happened at the last Blood Trials," I said. "About how you murdered the Tírian Champions. Aren't you?"

He nodded. "When I told you long ago that I killed them for their arrogance, I wasn't lying. The Tírians *are* arrogant, and have been for many thousands of years. They thought themselves invincible, all because they were able to defeat a few pathetic mortals in a simple competition. The audacity..." He lowered his head and chuckled. "I will admit, I felt they needed to be put in their place. But it was your mother who wished them dead—she wanted Tíria to lose the hold it had had on Kalemnar for thousands of years. As it turned out, that impulse was only the beginning—the first sign of her cruelty. I was love-struck, and all I could think of was stealing her away. I failed to see what a monster she was—what a monster she made *me*. I was a fool, Lyrinn."

My throat went dry when I forced out the next question.

"What happened—to make her hate Tíria so much? I don't understand. I saw her speaking to her father in her memories—she looked so happy..." I recalled a red-bearded Fae who had spoken to her affectionately—and her voice as she had replied to him...Nothing in their interaction had spoken of hatred or hostility.

"Your mother always could smile and light up a room—and to this day, her beauty continues to serve her well. She is the most Gifted Fae I have ever encountered—a deceiver, through and through, with a rare talent for charm. Her father loved her —he tried so very hard to make her happy, and she was adept at convincing him of his own success. Still, he didn't want her to rule—but not because he thought less of women than of men. It was because he saw through her to the darkness in her soul. He had seen her rage, and he knew how destructive her mind could be."

"Destructive?"

A nod. "When she was young, she revealed her nature in bits and pieces—morsels she only told me about years later, during moments when she wanted me to fear her. She recounted to me once how she had burned a stable to the ground with the animals inside—because her father would not have a new velvet cloak fashioned for her."

My stomach surged with the thought of it.

"You have felt it," Kazimir said, looking into my eyes. "Haven't you? The power that pulses through her despite the ring of impediment. The rage that tries occasionally to escape, to unleash on her surroundings. More than once, you have been frightened in her presence."

There was no use in denying it.

"Yes," I said. "I know what you're talking about. I thought..."

"You thought the ring was hurting her, or that my cruel imprisonment had played too long with her mind. Because that's what she does, Lyrinn—she convinces the world that she is a victim. To this day, she arouses feelings of pity in me for which I curse myself. It's why..."

He ran a hand through his hair, letting out a hoarse laugh.

"Why what?" I asked.

"Why I brought you to Aetherion against your will, knowing you despised me. She had asked for it, you see. And I did it to appease her, to bring her some small joy. I left Leta behind deliberately—not because I didn't wish for her to be with us, but to protect her and you both—just in case the worst should..." At that, his voice cracked, but with a shake of his head, he forced himself to continue. "I have always been arrogant. My strength has made me so. But I have failed you in the simplest of ways—"

His voice fully broke then, his shoulders trembling with emotion, but he continued.

"I went against my instincts and lured you into the mouth of a lion when I should have wished you worlds away. I only hope that you can find it in your heart to forgive me."

He fell silent then, and I stared at him. At the beautiful, broken thing that had caused me so much pain over the weeks and months—the High King I never truly knew...because he had worked so hard to convince me he had no soul.

"If I should not find my way out of this cell," he said softly, "I want you to know one thing. One thing that may give you some small surge of strength when you need it most."

My voice was quivering when I asked, "Which is?"

"When you had your few days aboard Mithraan's ship on the sea—when I told you I had allowed his vessel to catch up as a kindness to you...I lied."

"Lied?" I asked. "But you caught us afterwards—easily. You brought me to Aetherion—"

"All of that is true, yes," he said, resuming his pacing. "Gods, why is this so difficult for me to admit?" He stopped and turned to face me. "It was all you, Lyrinn. It was you who slowed our ship to a crawl, though I suppose you were unaware of your powers, even then. You willed the wind to cease supplying our sails, so that there was no longer any hope of evading the Tírian ship. You even willed me to freeze in place—and the same for all my crew. It was not the Tírians who were responsible for my failure. It was you. Though admittedly, one of them did coil vines around me...the jackass."

He let out a snicker as if to confess he appreciated the touch.

"When it all happened," he continued, "I saw your mind...I knew exactly what you were doing, and it terrified me. In those moments, I saw your mother in you. I saw a strength that superseded my own, and one I knew could destroy worlds, if harnessed for that purpose. I was...frightened...of you turning into her. Every moment of defiance in you has been a jolt—a small terror of what may come to pass. But you are not like her, as it turns out."

"I wanted to be. I thought..."

Instinct told me not to break down in front of Kazimir, but I could feel my lip trembling. He was being honest with me now, but it had taken far too long, our trust far too broken.

"You may wonder why I put that ring on her finger," he continued, "tearing at her power as it did. As I said, your mother was sweet, charming when she wished to be. But in her moments of rage—the moments when she was angry because I refused to go to war or to kill off every sprite living in my realm —she showed her power, and it was terrible. I had never seen such cruelty, such ruinous wrath, from anyone—not even my greatest enemies in the midst of battle. And here she was, my mate, the woman I loved—laying waste to the land I loved even more. Do you know, we had a second palace on an island south of here—a beautiful, expansive place, all green hills and valleys.

Deer roamed it in enormous herds, and sprites made their homes there. It was pure peace."

"What happened to it?" I asked, apprehensive.

"Simply put, she was angry with me one day and burned it all. They call it the Scald now. Nothing dwells there—not a single bird or plant. The palace is nothing but smoldering remnants of what was once stone."

The Scald. Riah had mentioned it once—had talked of the wanton destruction of so much of Aetherion. I wondered if Riah had known—if *every* Lightblood in Aetherion knew who had flayed the flesh off their beloved land.

"Every living thing in that region died," Kazimir said. "All because I would not give your mother a ship she desired—a ship that belonged to a mortal lord and was not for sale, mind you. It would have involved the beginnings of a war, but she did not care for a moment. I suspect she craved war, in fact."

I leaned back against the stone wall, grateful to feel its coolness through my garments. "How did she come to be Chosen Elar?" I asked. "How could that come to pass without you knowing?"

He sighed.

"She studied with the Priestesses many centuries ago, in the North—trained and learned from them, and even earned her wings. It was a dream of hers to meet the Elar face to face, and I gave her what she wished for. I didn't see the harm in it—after all, the Elar had many years left in this world, and there was no real risk in your mother rising to the rank of High Priestess, so long as she did not abuse the power. I suppose part of me hoped it would teach her discipline, even kindness."

"So, you knew she was a High Priestess."

Kazimir grimaced.

"Oh yes," he said. "I knew. And Cassia made me a promise —after years spent wining and dining her, taking her traveling

and making love to her wherever and whenever she desired."
He shot me a quick glance and said, "I am sorry if that's more
than you wish to know, but it's the truth. She promised me she
loved me—though I did not love her. I have long been
disgusted by the very notion of love, as you know. In return for
my devotion, Cassia promised me that Alessia would never be
Elar. I had already refused to let Alessia practice, to conduct the
services in our temple. I didn't want her indoctrinating
followers—using their powers to follow through on her
destructive wishes. I wanted her silenced, submissive. And she
did submit—she told me she had long since given up on her
former ambitions. That and the ring were the only reasons I
agreed to take you from the Blood Trials and bring you to our
home."

His hands fisted, and he looked like he wanted to ram them
through the thick stone wall. I almost called out to warn him
against it...but he relaxed, dropped them to his sides.

"As for Cassia," he said, "I trusted her with my life. But
worse, I trusted her with yours." He looked genuinely contrite
when he added, "I am not good at...affection. At expressing
delight or pride. I take no credit for you—all of that belongs to
Martel, your *proper* father. The man who was good enough to
raise you as his own. But I want you to know that I am proud to
call you my daughter."

It was impossible now to look at Kazimir—such a terrifying,
intimidating figure—and not feel a swell of affection for him in
spite of everything.

None of us is wholly good, just as none of us is truly evil.

"You should probably be aware," he said, "that it was your
mother who told me Mithraan was with you in Aethos. She was
the reason I knew he was in your bed that night."

The words were a shock.

Even after everything he'd told me.

I stepped back, then doubled over with a sudden need to release my dinner.

After a few deep breaths, I regained control and pulled myself up again.

"I'm sorry," Kazimir said. "I was surprised, I'll admit, that she betrayed you in that way. But now, I understand that it was to keep you from trying to leave."

Another swell of nausea churned inside me as my mind formulated one last, awful question.

"I need to know something."

"Anything."

"Did you stab her?"

Kazimir laughed. "What?"

"Several nights ago—did you stab my mother while she was in bed?"

I knew the answer already, but I needed to hear it from him.

"Of course not. I would have killed her centuries ago had I wished her dead. Perhaps I should have."

I winced with untold pain as I let out a breath I was holding prisoner. "Then why did she need my blood? Why did Erildir—"

Kazimir's eyes shot to mine. He leapt over to me and grabbed hold of my shoulders. "Did he conjure Blood Magic?"

When I said nothing, he shook me gently.

"Yes!" I replied. "Why?"

Kazimir's teeth gnashed in a terrible growl. "Listen to me very carefully, Lyrinn. Do not go through that portal, whatever Cassia or your mother may tell you."

"Why not?"

The answer didn't matter.

Nothing would stop me walking into the Broken Lands to find Mithraan. Nothing Kazimir could say—no warning he could issue—would keep me from him.

Not even a threat of death.

"There is only one way into the Broken Lands, my Daughter. There is only one reason the High Priestesses should want you to walk through that portal. You are not safe." He released me and said, "I should never have allowed you to come north—I was blinded, taken in by Cassia's charm, and I am so deeply sorry. But you cannot go through the portal."

Tears were stinging my eyes now.

"But...I have to."

"Cassia promised me," he said, his eyes fixed on some distant thing—some memory that I could not access. "She promised so many years ago that she would not do this thing..." He stopped talking, his fists tight by his sides. "The rite of Blood Magic is not used for healing purposes, but to create a bond—one that is unbreakable, except by death. The shattering of the bond unleashes a power greater than almost any spell imaginable."

I didn't understand. "But...I saw my mother heal. I watched the poison leave her body..."

"Erildir is a talented healer," Kazimir said. "He did not need your blood for the purposes of extracting poison."

"What, then?" I asked, my voice as tight as a wire about to snap. "Why did she need to strengthen our bond? We're mother and daughter, for the gods' sake!"

"Princess!"

The word came sharp as a blade. It was Erildir's voice, coming from just beyond the cell's door.

"It's time," he barked. "We must go now."

In defiance, Kazimir grabbed my hands.

And for once, I didn't recoil.

"Listen to me, Lyrinn," he said.

The cell door flew open, and Erildir stepped inside. His eyes were glowing brightly—unnatural, terrifying yellow. I glanced down at his hands, shocked to feel the power pulsing in the air around him.

He was no longer wearing a ring of impediment.

"I do not want to strike you down, your Grace," he said, fixing Kazimir in his sights. "But I will do it if I must. You know what is at stake, and I cannot let you destroy it."

Kazimir narrowed his eyes, then locked them on mine. He spoke quickly. "The Broken Lands are not some pleasant retreat where Mithraan is being concealed, Daughter. They're his prison—and they will be your tomb. Do not go through the portal, whatever occurs. Mithraan is as good as dead already."

With a cry of rage, Erildir cast a spell, hurling a brutal projectile of ice that dug deep into Kazimir's side. I gasped in horror as his clothing turned deep crimson and he sank to his knees. Grasping at the weapon, his eyes filled with tears as he looked up at me. "Do not go through the portal," he said again. "Not if you want to live."

"Good-bye, your Grace," Erildir said, his chin in the air as he grabbed my arm to drag me out of the cell. I tried to yank myself free but failed. Thanks to the ring, I was little more now than my former, mortal self. A girl lost, with no understanding of what was coming for her.

As I stumbled away, I turned to see Kazimir—my father—pull his eyes to mine one last time.

And I wondered with more anguish than I ever would have expected if I would ever see him again.

CHAPTER FIFTY

With my feet feeling like lead weights, I followed Erildir through the dank corridor and up the stairs toward the street outside.

"The Ceremony will begin soon," he told me solemnly as he pushed the door open. He began to pick up his pace, making for the temple's entrance. "When the new Elar is named, she will proceed through the portal. You must follow if you wish to see Mithraan."

"Will you come to the Broken Lands as well?" I asked, struggling to keep up his walking pace.

"No," he replied. He said nothing more, and some quiet, growing dread inside me told me I didn't want to know why.

After a few minutes, we arrived at the temple's doors, which sat open. A sweet, slowly lilting melody was making its way to us, a sea of harmonious voices echoing through the air in the same manner I'd heard Varyn speak in Aethos.

Inside the temple, I could see a series of long, winged shadows standing around in a broad semi-circle. Instead of white, the Priestesses now each wore a different colored dress and veil, their hair and features obscured as always. Their heads were bowed, and as they sang, another Priestess flew down into the temple through the oculus, gracefully landing in the round chamber's center.

It was my mother, dressed in gold, her veil drawn over her face, silver and red wings spread behind her.

Behind the Priestesses along the temple's walls stood a sea of Fae spectators, all of them dressed in white. They watched in silent reverence as the ceremony began...and it was all I could do not to scream out a warning to each and every one of them.

As I watched, a small Priestess dressed in silvery-gray stepped toward my mother, bowing down onto one knee. She pulled her veil up to reveal her face, and I could see now that it was Lady Cassia, smiling reverently.

"Chosen Elar," she said. "It is time for you to pass through the portal and meet your fate. With your final sacrifice will come the power you seek, and the Elar's essence will pass to you. Long may you reign."

With that, Cassia rose to her feet. The Priestesses—including my mother—backed away, and Cassia gestured toward the temple's center, twisting her hand in slow, small circles. As she did so, a structure began to take shape before her —a large vertical ring of white stone tall enough for a full-grown man to pass through.

At the ring's center, a burst of white light exploded, then expanded until its brightness swirled through the entirety of the structure, terrifying and beautiful at once.

The portal to the Broken Lands had opened.

~Princess.

Lark's voice, inside my mind.

~You cannot pass through the portal.

Mithraan is on the other side. I have no choice.

~If you insist on going, then I will cut the ring from your finger.

What? You can't—

~*The ring of impediment is a living entity, forged by silver-casters and imbued with magical properties. The only way to remove it is to kill it—and I have recently learned how to do so. But you must not let them see that it has lost its power. Do you understand me? Conceal your strength and keep it on your hand until the time is right.*

I inhaled a deep breath and said, *All right. But Lark...*

~*I will follow you through the portal,* he said, reading my every thought. *When we find Mithraan, I will sever his ring, too. You have my word.*

Just be careful.

A moment later, I felt it—a tightening of the ring, as if it was suddenly trying to hold onto my hand for dear life...

And then a release as its tendrils weakened, lost their strength, and finally surrendered entirely. Lark had sliced through the silver with his small, impossibly sharp sword, leaving the ring just barely clinging to my finger.

An instant surge of power overwhelmed me, my body and mind suddenly imbued with all the strength I had lost. I forced a veil of glamour over myself—an illusion of weakness, of exhaustion, my cheeks sunken, my skin sallow.

I could only hope it would be enough to convince Cassia and my mother that I was still at their mercy.

"It is time," Cassia said, first looking at my mother, then at me. "The chosen Elar must now pass through the portal—and her daughter must follow."

As I watched my mother make her way toward the swirling circle of light, part of me wanted to take her down then and there.

But if I did anything so foolish, so impulsive, Cassia would seal the portal...and Mithraan would be lost forever.

Cassia gestured to the Golden Priestess—the Fae I had

come to know and love—to proceed through the ring of light and into the Broken Lands.

I watched, helpless, as she glided slowly toward the swirling brightness, her menacing wings pulling tightly together behind her.

"It's your turn now, Lyrinn," Cassia said. "Time for you—and me—to follow."

Lowering my chin pitifully, I nodded and, dragging my feet, stepped through the portal to meet a fate I had been warned about a thousand times over, yet had somehow never seen coming.

As the light consumed me, Kazimir's words echoed through my mind, a warning I could not heed.

It will be your tomb.

CHAPTER FIFTY-ONE

The Broken Lands had earned their name.

The landscape was stark, gray and grim, a thick mist swirling about the ground which stretched in every direction as far as the eye could see. Here and there, a scraggly, dead tree appeared then vanished behind the mist—mere specters of what had once been.

The vapor swirling about my feet reminded me all too much of the Breath of the Fae—the poisonous fog that had threatened Dúnbar's mortal population for so many years.

But it was another sight entirely that consumed me as I twisted around, trying desperately to understand what I was seeing—how this place could even exist.

All around me, shards of stone, crystal, and earth rotated in mid-air, weightless, uncertain where they belonged. There was something deeply disturbing about the sight—disorienting enough to make me wonder whether my own feet were even planted firmly on the ground.

Some distance away, the Golden Priestess hovered in mid-air, her wings beating in a slow rhythm, their red veins pulsing with power.

I saw no sign of the Elar, who was soon to fade from this world to be replaced by the terrifying, cold being that I called Mother.

No sign of Mithraan.

Cassia spoke softly. "He is coming—don't worry."

"Why did you bring him to this place?" I asked as I fingered the ring that still clung uselessly and deceptively to my hand. "What part does he have to play in any of this madness?"

The High Priestess replied as if her explanation was the simplest imaginable.

"We brought him here because you love him, of course. He and your sister are the only two beings in the world that you love enough to give your life for them. And since Leta has disappeared...well..."

I recalled with horrifying clarity how angry my mother had looked when I told her Thalanir was searching for Leta—that he had been sent to help her get away from Domignon. Now, I understood why. They wanted her in Domignon in case they needed her as a lure—as a sickening trap to set, to drag me to the Broken Lands if something happened to Mithraan.

"Your father told you a good deal in the dungeons," Cassia said. "But clearly, he did not tell you everything. Come—do you wish to see your Mithraan?"

"More than anything."

"Then you shall have this one wish."

She turned and let out a long, low call in a language I didn't understand, and in the distance, a figure appeared as if from nowhere, lurching his way forward through the mist. Flanked by creatures of shadow, I could see now that they were supporting him, holding his arms as if he would crumble without their aid.

The sound of grinding iron met my ears, a sickening,

torturous racket, and I realized with horror that he was dragging heavy chains with him as he moved.

Breaking away from Cassia, I ran toward him, not caring whether I was allowed to or not. I could see how wounded he looked, how pale, as if all the blood had been drained from him. His cheeks were sunken, his hair coarse, shoulders slumped. Pulling his eyes to mine, he fell to his knees before me, the mist swirling around him as if taking possession of his soul. The shadows that had held him melted into the air and I knelt down, taking him in my arms and pulling him close.

I didn't need to look at his hand to know the ring was still on his finger—that it was tearing at his flesh, stealing away his strength. Those who had promised him freedom once he was off the ship had lied. Because he was not being sent to the North to be free. He was a hostage—a bargaining chip, imprisoned in this terrible place to ensure my compliance.

"I'm so sorry," I whispered into his shoulder as I held him. "This is all my fault." Pulling back, I took his face in my hands and kissed him gently. "Are you all right?"

He nodded. "I'm weak," he said. "But unhurt. This damned ring..."

"It's all right. It's going to be all right," I told him, though I wasn't remotely sure I meant it. *Where are you, Lark?*

I kissed him once more before rising to my feet and turning to face Cassia. In the distance, I could see my mother, her feet now planted on the ground beneath the mist, the silver and red wings tucked behind her like two enormous spearheads.

As I watched, something rose up out of the mist before her. At first, it looked like an enormous table of stone. But I realized with a shock of horror that it was no table, but an altar—the sort used for a sacrificial ceremony.

"There is a rite involved in the Succession," Cassia said in that velvet-smooth voice of hers. "A final test for the chosen

Elar, before she may take up the mantle of her predecessor and receive her essence."

Though I suspected I knew what they had planned, my voice trembled when I said, "What rite?"

"The Successor must prove her loyalty—her willingness to surrender all worldly bonds—to demonstrate that she has offered herself, body and soul, to the ascension. The Elar has no ties. No family. No love. She is pure power—pure dominance."

"I see," I said. "And so, I am here to prove my mother's loyalty. To prove that she is devoid of feeling—of love."

"You misunderstand, Child. She is here to prove that she is willing to give what she loves *most* to save our realm," Cassia said.

I rounded on my mother, my fear replaced with rage as I recalled the look on Kazimir's face when he had learned of the Blood Magic Erildir had conjured.

"It's why you wanted my blood mingling with yours, isn't it? To create a bond the Elar would recognize as unbreakable. Because you need her to believe you love me more than all else in this world...but the truth is, you're incapable of love."

I could feel the power pulsing through my veins as I spoke. My heart was quickly freezing over, steeling me against the knowledge that the mother I had long dreamed of had never been anything more than a figment of a young girl's desperate imagination.

"I am capable of love." My mother's voice was the ironic sound of jagged ice.

"Indeed you are," I said. "In fact, I would say you love yourself entirely too much."

As I spoke, I moved away from Mithraan. I wanted them to forget he was here, to forget he existed. I needed to give Lark a chance to free him of the cruel ring. "Tell me, where is she?" I asked. "The Elar—this great and powerful being who has spent so many centuries stealing power from Fae? I would like to see her before I die."

The right side of my mother's lip curled up. "Yes, I suppose you must be curious," she said, gesturing toward a dark shape in the distance. "Come then, Lyrinn. It's time to meet her."

CHAPTER FIFTY-TWO

I ADVANCED SLOWLY, pulling myself as far away from Mithraan as I could get, deliberately drawing Cassia's and my mother's eyes along with me.

As I moved, the shadow in the distance began to take form. I could now see a figure seated on a large throne, her face just barely visible as it flickered in and out of focus.

I knew then with absolute certainty that the Elar's life hung by a thread—and her only hope of continued existence was to pass her essence, her very soul, to my mother.

Without her Successor, she would fall.

And just like that, a voice began to sing inside my head— the voice of the yellow-eyed Fae who had tried to kill me not so many nights ago.

"Only with the Calloc's death...
Shall the Elar rise again.
But if she should live,
The Elar falls..."

I stepped toward the Elar, trying and failing to focus on any one of her fleeting features.

If she should live...

"You stole from the High Fae long ago," I said, addressing the fleeting being before me. "You took their wings from them. Or was that an*other* Elar?"

"We are all one," a gasping voice responded. "But we...did not...steal. The High Fae did not deserve their Gifts. They were corrupted by greed...by lust for status. They were arrogant and proud...and flight should be granted only to the faithful...those who understand what it is to *sacrifice*."

She spoke the last word like a curse, and I shuddered against it.

I fought to control my voice when I asked, "What else have you stolen from our kind, Elar?"

"Lyrinn! Enough!"

My mother's voice was sharp as a razor, but I ignored her, staring into the Elar's flickering eyes as she pulled her chin up weakly.

"I take only what we need," she said. "What my Priestesses desire. The Elar grants Gifts to those who are deserving."

"Deserving," I said. "You mean those who kill their children?"

This time, the awful creature didn't respond.

It was my mother who did.

"Years ago," she said, her voice quivering, "I left you and your sister with a mortal man in a town I despised. You could have been raised inside a palace of silver and white—in a land so beautiful that it broke my heart. But I handed you to Martel. All because..."

I glared at her, the hurt inside me growing, flaring to life like a fast-spreading disease. "Because you wanted to protect us from Kazimir," I said. "That's what you told me. Because you were afraid of what he would do to us."

But I knew as I spoke that my words were a lie—one constructed to twist Alessia into something she wasn't. A caring, protective parent who wanted only the best for her children.

She shook her head. "Because I wanted to prove to the Order that I understood sacrifice. That I would surrender my children—give them away to lesser beings—just to prove my faith."

I could hear the pain in her words, and for a moment—one blessed, tiny gift of a moment—I thought that maybe, just maybe, she was hurting because she had missed Leta and me so very much for all those years.

But the moment passed, and the truth unfurled cruelly in my mind.

"The Order told you it wasn't enough," I said. "Didn't they? That handing your children off to a virtual stranger wasn't sufficient proof of your devotion. You gave all those years away —years you could have spent with us—and still, it wasn't enough."

"No!" she snapped. "It wasn't! They wanted more...they wanted me to sever a blood bond—one that is unbreakable. A blood bond with my eldest child."

"And so, when the time came for the Blood Trials, you sent Kazimir to get me, to bring me to Aetherion. He was convinced you wanted me by your side because it would have brought you joy to be reunited with your child. He stole me from my home because he loved you, in spite of every atrocity that you've committed. And you kept the truth from him, even then."

"Of course I did. The truth would have killed him."

"An ironic statement, coming from you."

Her silver wings fluttered, her eyes narrowing, and I could tell I'd struck a nerve.

"Cassia," she snarled after a moment. "There is no need for this conversation to continue. It's time."

With that, Cassia gestured toward the altar. "Come now,

Lyrinn. You understand your fate, don't you? With the breaking of your bond comes the new dawn—new life for all the realms. You are a savior. Your mother's sacrifice is your own, as well—and I know you will go willingly into the next world to save the one you love."

I gazed at the altar, my mind reeling with conflict. I should have been afraid, yet I wasn't. Instead, I was filled with quiet rage, with pain, with sorrow.

I would die for Mithraan—I loved him enough to give my life for his.

But I was not willing to die for the Elar's resurrection. For my mother's glory.

"Once you kill me," I said, my voice trembling more with ire than trepidation, "you'll set Mithraan free, yes?"

"You have my word that I will," Cassia said.

I moved toward the altar, my steps slow and measured. In the distance, I could see that Mithraan was still on his knees, still held down by the brutal chains. His chin pulled up slightly to watch me, his lips moving slowly, though no sound emerged.

Come on, Lark. You know what you need to do.

Cassia's wings emerged from her shoulder blades as we advanced—ash-colored and dull, their veins black.

I understood now why she was called the Gray Lady.

The wings had the appearance of decay, of age...but I could feel their immense power as they beat slowly at the air, lifting her just enough that she glided above the mist, a glinting silver blade appearing in her hand as she moved.

The blade that was meant to end me.

Lark, I called inside my mind. *Where the hell are you?*

But there was no response.

Had he failed to make it through the portal? Or worse—had something happened to him in this grim landscape?

"Mithraan?" I called out when I saw his hunched form

sagging further down, the chains' weight seeming to increase with each passing moment.

I spun around to Cassia, who was now hovering above the altar, waiting for me to give myself to her. "You must set him free!" I shouted. "You're killing him!"

"That's not the bargain," she said. "Not while you live. Now, come, child. Lie down. It will end soon."

I had gone this long with my glamour intact—without revealing that my ring had lost its grip on my powers. I had convinced Cassia and my mother, by pure force of will, that I was as weak as Mithraan.

But if I was to survive—if *he* was to survive—the illusion would have to come to an end.

Now.

I dragged myself closer to the altar, my head hanging low as I plotted my next move.

"Is there anything you'd like to say, Lyrinn?" Cassia asked.

"Yes," I said, pulling my chin up to narrow my eyes at her. "Is that the same blade you used to stab my mother? Or did she do it herself?"

"Insolent girl!" Cassia shouted, her wings flapping furiously as she lunged at me and thrust the blade deep into my shoulder.

I cried out in pain as she pulled back, readying herself to strike again. I could see the fury in her eyes, the savagery, as she came at me a second time.

But this time, I was ready for her. I thrust a hand forward, summoning a weapon of light—an enormous sword that lashed its way through the air, aiming itself squarely at her chest.

But before it could reach her, she went soaring skyward as if some immense force had shoved her brutally...

Or pulled her backwards.

The piercing cry of a bird of prey bit through the air. Cassia spun and twisted, her gray wings flapping madly as she tried to gain control.

I could just make out the shape of Mithraan's silver eagle, its talons tearing into the Priestess's flesh even as her silver blade fell to earth, disappearing into the mist.

In the air above us agonized cries rang out, echoing their torment off the sea of floating detritus. The high-pitched scream of an enraged Fae, then Mithraan's eagle screeching in pain as Cassia shot a cruel acid-fire spell at his chest, which sizzled and flared, burning into his flesh.

I watched in terror as Mithraan shifted in mid-air into his Fae form, then lost control.

He fell, tumbling horrifically toward the ground far below. Faster, faster he spiraled—until silver wings sprang from his back once again, and he shot upwards to collide at full speed with Cassia, tearing at her with his talons as she shrieked in pain, then freed herself from his grasp.

Once she was far enough away, she shot a bolt of ice at him —but he dodged adeptly, assaulting her with a barrage of flame-arrows.

We will craft our own destinies, I thought as I watched the brutal fight unfold, all too aware of Cassia's strength. *The question is—what will they look like?*

Seeing that her fellow Priestess might not win the fight as easily as she'd hoped, my mother let out a scream of frustration. Turning to face me, she pressed her hands forward, palms out.

"There is no rule that says Cassia must do it," she snarled.

"Mother." My chest heaved as I fixed my eyes on hers, my shoulder pulsing with pain where Cassia had stabbed me. "I came through the portal for one reason only. The promise you and Erildir made that I would find Mithraan again."

"And you *did* find him—did you not?"

I could feel the fire burning in my eyes when I growled, "You should never have brought me to this place. You should never have lied to me. Don't make me kill you—please. For Leta's sake, as well as your own. Do not force that destiny on us all."

"Who are you to command me?" she cried, her expression as feral as that of a cornered wildcat. "I am a High Priestess of the Order of the Elar—I am the chosen Successor." Her voice was ice when she added, "Your value, Lyrinn, lies only in your death. It has always been so. I only ever agreed to give birth to you and your sister because I knew this day would one day come—that one of you would be the key to my ascension."

The confession tore at me like Cassia's knife in my flesh all over again—but this time, it pierced me again and again, plunging deep into my very soul.

The words were poison—a cruelty beyond anything even Kazimir had ever inflicted.

For the first time, I was glad I had not been raised by this... the *creature*. This heartless, wretched being, driven only by her own lust for destruction.

It was in that moment that I knew everything Kazimir had told me was true. Every single awful morsel of information about my mother—everything I had hoped with all my heart was a lie.

And yet some part of him had still loved her enough to bring me across the sea...as a gift to her.

"My powers are stronger than you know," I breathed, remembering what the High King had told me—how I had slowed the Lightblood ship and frozen his crew with nothing more than a thought. "But I don't want to use them. Not against you."

As I spoke, her eyes moved down to my hand, to the ineffectual ring that hung limply from my finger. I tore it off and threw it into the mist-covered distance, then watched as her eyes widened in fear.

In the sky above us, flashes of light burst out like explosions, spells and counter-spells flung from one High Fae to the other.

My mother didn't have Erildir by her side now, or Cassia, or an entire order of Priestesses. All she had was her own power—and she could only hope it would be enough to fight me off.

"I know what you will do with the power granted to you by the Elar's essence," I said. "I know the destruction you will inflict upon the realms. And I will gladly die, if that's what it takes to prevent your ascension."

"You know nothing about it," she hissed, her eyes flaring a warning as she raised her arms from her sides, her hands glowing with ominous power. "You know nothing of the good I can do. You will never know—because you won't be around to see it, Daughter."

As her arms lifted into the air, creatures began to appear around her, each stalking slowly through the mist. They were small, at first—a fox, a wild boar, an asp slithering with its head held high...but as she raised her arms higher, they multiplied and grew. Massive lions. Enormous wolves, their teeth jagged and glistening with power and light. Bears as large as horses.

They moved slowly as if to torture me with their potential —and as they advanced, my mother cupped one hand in the air, summoning a ball of flame. It rotated menacingly above her palm as she fixed her eyes on me, a grim smile on her lips.

"It was the sprite, wasn't it?" she snarled. "He cut you and that vile lover of yours free."

"You thought Mithraan and I would be easy to kill," I retorted. "All this time, you've counted on it. It's why you told Erildir to teach me nothing—why you looked so horrified when you discovered I was a Thariel."

"On the contrary. I knew my daughter would be a challenge.

You would hardly be an adequate sacrifice if you were a weakling."

With that, she hurled the fireball at me.

I shot my hands out, reflecting the spell. The orbs of flame exploded in mid-air between us, falling harmlessly into the mist.

"I won't let you destroy the realms," I said, my voice quivering. "I know what you did to the Barren Lands, to the Scald. I've seen you delight in destruction, all to fill yourself with cruel pleasure. I have seen you in so many nightmares—I only wish I'd understood that I was looking at my own mother."

"Not nightmares, child. You have merely witnessed the earliest stages of the world's rebirth. We *must* start over. We must renew our realms—for the good of all."

She glanced over at the Elar, slumped in her throne, her chin against her chest, her body barely visible as it waned and threatened to fade to nothingness.

My mother's small army of beasts was still advancing slowly, and in the sky above us, cries and explosions still tore through the air, the battle raging as fiercely as ever.

I moved backward, the Elar's rasping breath growing louder as I drew nearer to her. I could *feel* her imminent death, smell it on the air.

"Mother," I said as a summoned bear opened its ghastly mouth and let out a roar of threat. "You don't have to do this. You know what I'm capable of. Please—don't force my hand."

High above us, a sharp cry sounded, and I looked up to see Mithraan's eagle once again tearing at Cassia with brutal talons, even as she cast spell after spell, each one flung uselessly into the ether, her body weakening with every wound he inflicted in his wild, protective rage.

I pulled my eyes to my mother's again.

"He will win the fight," I said. "He will kill her, and then there will be no chance for you. Call back your beasts and go back through the portal. Let the Elar die. Live out your life in Aetherion. You are still queen, after all."

She scoffed. "A queen by marriage is nothing but the shadow cast by her king. I wish to cast my *own* shadows upon the world, Daughter. *Why can't you see that?"*

Sharp screeches rang out above us, fear clenching at my heart. I pleaded with the battle to end—for Mithraan to emerge triumphant.

I need this to stop.

I spoke smoothly, evenly, though my voice threatened at every turn to fracture. "I was told long ago that I would be forced to make a brutal choice—that my fate dictated it. But I would never choose myself over Mithraan, and you know that. I came willingly through the portal. So the choice is now yours. Your reign as Elar...or my life. Which will it be?"

I stared into her eyes, watching as the angry flames faded to nothing and the bright blue of her irises returned. She blinked away tears, the beasts under her command halting in place, frozen.

A smile formed on her lips, in her eyes. And for a moment— a quiet, peaceful few seconds—I was certain she would choose me.

But then, like a tidal wave, her hands shot forward and the beasts surged toward me with feral snarls, their gleaming teeth bared.

CHAPTER FIFTY-THREE

IT WAS Kazimir's voice that came to me as I watched the conjured Light-Beasts stalk forward. Kazimir, who for all I knew was lying dead in the cold cell where I'd left him.

It was not the Tírians who were responsible for my failure.

It was you.

"Stop!" I commanded to the Light-Beasts.

And they did, freezing like statues. A lion in mid-roar, his giant mouth agape. An immense wolf in the midst of leaping, his front paws tucked under his chest.

They would not remain frozen forever—this, I knew.

But I didn't need forever. I only needed *long enough*.

Knowing what I had to do—that it was only a matter of time before my mother lashed out with every bit of power she had—I pulled my arms up from my sides and called forth a weapon that had been hiding in the depths of my mind since the day I had learned I was a Fae.

A weapon forged by two bloodlines in convergence.

The cry that sliced through the sky above us now was not Mithraan's eagle or Cassia's shrieking voice...but a deafening, drawn-out roar that shook the earth beneath my feet and shattered every piece of floating detritus that spun through the air. The formless objects burst and exploded into dust-sized fragments, as if the world itself were ending.

When the roar came again, I drew my eyes up to witness my conjured creation—an extraordinary, immense silver dragon, larger than any creature I had ever laid eyes on.

The very dragon that was etched on the pendant I wore around my neck.

Forged of pure light, the creature barreled down to earth impossibly fast, blasting a sharp, brutal bolt of blue flame as it came.

Horrible cries rang out then—the sound of torment, of suffering, as my mother's army of Light-Beasts was decimated.

I watched, my breath imprisoned in my chest, as the dragon banked and aimed itself next at the altar of stone. As if attuned to my thoughts and rage, its mouth opened, hurtling a spike of flame through space.

The altar exploded into a thousand fragments before the beast banked once again.

This time, its sights were set on the shadowy figure seated on her throne, her flickering eyes pulling to the dragon just as it unleashed one final, enormous fireball.

My mother screamed, but far too late. Searing flame tore into the Elar's nebulous form, and I watched as the fire engulfed her, her frail body collapsing in on herself.

A pair of emaciated violet wings, tucked pitifully behind her back, sparked, flamed, then vanished.

"She's gone," I said, turning to my mother. "The Elar is gone."

The dragon, too, vanished in a burst of light, its purpose fulfilled.

My hand reached for the fine chain around my neck, pulling at the pendant that I had worn since the Blood Trials. The silver dragon, the sigil of my grandfather's court. It was a part of me, of who I was.

It was in my blood.

In the sky above us, a harrowing wail rang out—and then Cassia's limp, blood-soaked body was falling, falling...and crashing to earth, the mist engulfing her like a great, starving creature of pure malice.

The Gray Lady was no more.

The silver eagle let out a final cry then swooped down to land nearby, shifting into Mithraan's Fae form, a look of pure rage in his eyes. He took a step toward me, but I raised a hand, shaking my head once to tell him to stay back.

"Mother?" I said.

She was staring at me, her eyes glassy. For a moment, I thought perhaps she'd entered some sort of distant dream-state, overwhelmed by the shock of what had just occurred.

~Lyrinn!

It was Lark's voice, crying out as my mother let out a scream of rage and shot out a blast of lightning—blinding and vicious, it was the very weapon I had seen in my nightmares—a weapon that had destroyed entire landscapes.

Moving faster than I thought possible, I mirrored her spell, meeting her blast in the air between us. The bolts of pure light —pure power—met with a brutal explosion that sent me reeling backwards to crash hard into the ground.

I lay still, catching my breath, my eyes filling with tears.

She will never be Elar now, and she knows it. No one will ever take up that mantle again.

And still...she wants me dead.

A rage unlike any I had ever known flourished inside me—a deep anger fueled by hurt for all that she had stolen from me, from Leta. For all the lies, the cruelty. For using me for her own ends—and for valuing my existence so little.

I thought of Martel then—of the father who raised us, and how much I had loved him. The best man I'd ever known had died...because of *her* selfishness.

With the memory of his face and of Leta's floating through my mind, I pushed myself to my feet and raised my hands into the air, my flesh glowing white with all the power of my father's Lightblood lineage.

I have no choice. Please, Leta, know that I have no choice...

"Lyrinn!"

Mithraan's cry was desperate. He was still standing some distance away, his silver wings spread—but he wasn't looking at me.

"Don't try to stop me!" I shouted through a sea of tears. "I have no choice..."

"It's true," he said, but the warning had left his voice now. He was striding toward me, his chin down. "You *don't* have a choice. Not anymore."

I stared into the distance, searching for the figure in gold—the wretched Fae I had grown to love.

It was then that I understood what Mithraan meant.

My mother...she was *gone.*

I turned to face the distant portal, which still spun with swirling white light. Could she have escaped? Passed through it into Aetherion...

Had she made the right choice at last?

"Vaelan." Mithraan was close enough now to take me by the hand. His voice was gentle—*too* gentle.

I looked into his eyes, confused. What did he know that I did not?

In a daze, I stepped forward, one foot after the other, and he moved with me...until I was nearly at the place where my mother had stood a moment ago.

It was then that I saw her.

She was lying on the ground, the mist swirling around her beautiful face, her throat red with blood. Her clouded blue eyes were staring at the sky.

One paper-thin line had been sliced across her neck...by a weapon so fine that only the smallest of hands could possibly have wielded it.

Numb, I fell to my knees beside her.

"Princess."

The sprite's voice was filled with sorrow and pain, and I wanted to weep at the sound of it.

"This was your doing, Lark."

"Yes, Highness."

Mithraan was next to me, and for the first time, I became aware that he was clutching the deep wound on his chest. I could see it through his tunic—and I could see that it was healing already.

He moved his hand to lay it on my back—a sympathetic touch, conveying wordlessly how sorry he was for what I had lost.

But I knew, looking down at my mother's body, that I had lost her before I was ever born. I had dared to convince myself, ever since arriving in Aetherion, that there really was someone in our world who would love me unconditionally. But she had never existed, not really. She had been a dream and a nightmare at once—a pretty invention of a hopeful mind.

And now, she was gone.

"Why did you do it, Lark?" I asked, my voice barely a whisper.

The sprite hovered before me, his kind eyes staring into mine when he said, "Because one day soon, you will find your sister. And I could not bear the thought that you would have to tell her you were the one who ended Alessia's life."

With that, he bowed his head and disappeared, and I wondered if I would ever see him again.

I wanted to thank him—to tell him what he had done for me. But it felt so, so wrong.

"The portal," Mithraan said, nodding to the twisting ring of light as he pressed a hand to my wound to heal me. "We need to go back through before it disappears. The Gray Lady's spell may not hold much longer. Lark—be sure to come with us. We wouldn't want to leave you in this hellish place."

I took in a deep breath as I looked up at him, tears clouding my vision.

Then I froze, wiping my eyes to see him more clearly.

"Mithraan," I said. "Your wings..."

"They're all right," he insisted, nodding over his shoulder. "Just a little battered from the fight."

I shook my head. "No—it's not that they're damaged. They..."

They've never looked more powerful or more beautiful.

The wings that jutted out from Mithraan's back now were not those of an eagle, or of any other bird.

They were the glowing, amber-colored wings of a High Fae.

NEXT IN SERIES: OF FLAME AND FURY

Coming soon: *Of Flame and Fury*

A Brief Teaser:

Leta

I had always associated hooded cloaks with my sister, Lyrinn, with her propensity for hiding away from every single person she encountered on Dúnbar's streets (or elsewhere, for that matter).

Ironic that it was I who now sat in the corner of a dark pub, my hood up, my face cast deliberately in shadow. The last thing I wanted was to be recognized by one of Corym's men and dragged back to that awful palace to be subjected to more of his "charms."

Prince Corym, who was utterly certain that I was devoted, heart and soul, to him.

And yes, admittedly, for a time I found him irresistible— particularly since the Blood Trials. No one could deny the scars on his cheeks suited him.

But it didn't take many days in his presence for me to learn to see through him as clearly as if I were staring through glass. Still, Corym was of little importance now. What mattered was finding my sister. I had to seek Lyrinn and warn her about the coming war—a war that would be waged against Fae and mortal alike.

As I sat, chin low, nursing my pint, a man strolled into the pub, his shadow moving with irritating determination in my direction. Out of the corner of my eye, I could see that his legs were long, his shoulders broad.

Gods. Tell me he's not one of them, I thought, surreptitiously eyeing his tunic to check for the sigil of Domignon.

But there was no mark on his chest—no indication that he worked for the prince or his allies.

It was only when I dared pull my eyes to his face that I realized what he was. His sky-blue irises shone with the light of a dozen torches. His ears were tipped with delicate points.

He was beautiful beyond compare...

Yet he frightened me more than Corym's entire army ever could.

AVAILABLE NOW: AN APOCALYPTIC DARK COMEDY

What happens when the first day of school is the last day of the world?

For sixteen-year-old Virtue, navigating 11th grade is hard enough. Throw in the mass carnage of the Purple War, the brain-mangling Lemming Plague, and the overnight, post-apocalyptic breakdown of civilization, and suddenly, arguing with her parents, being picked on by bullies, and tyrannized by her teachers doesn't seem quite so devastating.

Instead, her new priorities are saving her best friend (and potential boyfriend?), fending off Clique Baiters and Serial Daters, and rescuing Beynac—her golden retriever service dog. Oh, and surviving.

It took sixteen years of torment and insecurity to make Virtue a wallflower. It took a single day of classes (and an academy full of brainwashed killers) to turn her into the school's most feared and deadly badass.

Available now on Amazon: *Apocalypchix*

ALSO BY K. A. RILEY

If you're enjoying K. A. Riley's books, please consider leaving a review on Amazon or Goodreads to let your fellow book-lovers know about it.

Fantasy Books

Seeker's Series:

Seeker's World

Seeker's Quest

Seeker's Fate

Seeker's Promise

Seeker's Hunt

Seeker's Prophecy

Dystopian Books:

Viral High:

Apocalypchix

Lockdown

Final Exam

The Cure Chronicles:

The Cure

Awaken

Ascend

Fallen

Reign

Resistance Trilogy:

Recruitment

Render

Rebellion

Emergents Trilogy:

Survival

Sacrifice

Synthesis

Transcendent Trilogy:

Travelers

Transfigured

Terminus

Academy of the Apocalypse Series:

Emergents Academy

Cult of the Devoted

Army of the Unsettled

The Ravenmaster Chronicles:

Arise

Banished (Coming in January 2022)

Crusade (Coming in April 2022)

To be informed of future releases, and for occasional chances to win free swag, books, and other goodies, please sign up here:

https://karileywrites.org/#subscribe

Follow K. A. Riley on TikTok: @karileywrites

K.A. Riley's Bookbub Author Page

K.A. Riley on Amazon.com

K.A. Riley on Goodreads.com

Printed in Great Britain
by Amazon

26845726R00234